Franklin W. Dixon

# The Hardy Boys™ Mysteries

## The Hooded Hawk Mystery

## The Secret Agent on Flight 101

Armada
*An Imprint of* HarperCollins*Publishers*

*The Hooded Hawk Mystery* and *The Secret Agent on Flight 101*
were first published in the UK in 1973 by
William Collins Sons & Co. Ltd.
First published together in this edition by
HarperCollins Children's Books in 1995

1 3 5 7 9 10 8 6 4 2

HarperCollins Children's Books is a division of
HarperCollins Publishers Ltd,
77-85 Fulham Palace Road,
Hammersmith, London W6 8JB

*The Hooded Hawk Mystery*
© MCMLIV Grosset & Dunlap Inc.
*The Secret Agent on Flight 101*
Copyright © 1960 Grosset & Dunlap Inc.

Printed and bound in Great Britain by
HarperCollins Manufacturing, Glasgow

ISBN 0 00 694511 2

# The Hooded
# Hawk Mystery

# CONTENTS

*Joe sent the man flying over his shoulder.*

# ·1·

## Sender Unknown

"FRANK, come here!" Joe Hardy called excitedly to his brother from the front porch of their home.

It was early afternoon on a hot August day, but tall, eighteen-year-old Frank ran down the stairs at top speed. He knew from the tone of Joe's voice that something unusual was happening.

When he reached the porch, Frank stopped short and stared in amazement. A man from the express delivery, who stood there, grinning, had just delivered a burlap-covered crate and a package. Joe, blond and a year younger than Frank, had already removed the burlap. In the crate was a fine, proud-looking hawk.

"What a beauty!" Frank remarked. "Is it for us?"

"It says 'Frank and Joe Hardy, Elm Street, Bayport,'" the man answered, holding out a receipt for the boy's signature. As Frank wrote his name, the man added, "This is a peregrine falcon and you'd better take good care of the young lady. She's valued at five hundred dollars."

"Wow!" Joe exclaimed. "That's an expensive bird!"

"Who sent her?" Frank asked. He looked at the package and read the name and address aloud,

" 'Rahmud Ghapur, Washington, D.C.' Never heard of the man."

"Nor I," said Joe. "We'll ask Dad when he gets home."

As the man left, Frank opened the package. It contains several items which the boys knew were falconry equipment.

"Looks as though Mr Ghapur expects us to become falconers," Frank declared. "But why?"

They searched for a note in the wrappings but found none. "We'll probably get a call or a letter of explanation," said Joe.

Frank agreed. "In the meantime, let's learn something about falcons. Dad has some books on the subject in his study."

All this time the blackish-blue hawk, with a black-barred creamy breast, had been sitting quietly in the crate, eyeing her new masters. Now she raised up, fluttered her wings, and cried *keer, keer*, as if she wanted to be released.

The boys carried the bird and her trappings through the hall and upstairs to Mr Hardy's study. Here the famous detective had several file cabinets of criminal cases and photographs of underworld characters. Frank and Joe, endowed with natural sleuthing ability, had had many opportunities to work with their father. Frank was serious and an excellent student at Bayport High, while Joe was rather impulsive but always dependable. Though they had different temperaments, the boys made an excellent team.

Joe found two volumes on falconry in his father's bookcase.

He handed one to Frank and began to flip through the pages of the other book. When he came to a series of pictures of the articles that the man had delivered, he said:

"Look, Frank, this is the leather hood. It's put over the hawk's head, so she'll sit quietly when she's being carried. And one of these bells is fastened to each of her legs so the owner can keep track of her movements."

Frank nodded and looked at an illustration in his book. "Here are those two leather straps. They're called *jesses*. One end of each jess is looped and tied around each of the hawk's legs. The free ends of the straps are fastened to a swivel, which consists of two rings connected by a bolt that allows each ring to turn separately. Both straps are tied to one of the rings and this long leather leash to the other ring. Pretty clever, Joe, because in that way the leash never gets tangled or twisted with the jesses."

Joe's eyes darted towards the crate. "Think we should try these trappings on Miss Peregrine?"

Frank laughed. "Maybe. But first, let's find out some more about falcons."

Joe, reading on, remarked, "She prefers pigeons to all other foods. But she can be brought back from a flight with any kind of meat or even the lure, if she's well trained." He picked up the lure, a short stick on the end of which was a thick bunch of feathers.

Frank, meanwhile, was studying the falconer's glove which had come in the package. "Joe," he said, "this glove must belong to someone from India or the Far East."

"How do you know?"

"My book said that in those countries falconers use right-handed gloves, while Europeans and Americans wear left-handed ones."

"Come to think of it," said Joe, "the name Rahmud Ghapur sounds Indian—or Far Eastern."

Frank agreed. "But the whole thing's still a mystery. Well, let's put the hawk's gear on."

As Frank held the equipment ready, Joe carefully opened the crate door. Although not sure how to handle the falcon, he quickly grabbed both legs so that the bird could not use her talons. She struggled while Frank fastened the jesses, then tied the straps and leash to the swivel. The boys kept a wary eye on the hawk, in case she should suddenly slash at them with her beak. But the bird made no such attempt.

"I guess the book was right when it said a falcon seldom uses its beak for defence," Joe remarked.

After Joe attached the little bells to the hawk's legs, Frank pulled on the glove, grasped both jesses, and lifted the falcon to his wrist. She sat there proud and defiant—a truly noble bird.

"So far, so good, Frank," Joe said. "Now what?"

"We'll take her outside and let her fly around a bit," his brother replied. "And let's get that old block perch Aunt Gertrude once used for her parrot. It's in the cellar."

"Good idea," replied Joe. "Miss Peregrine can rest on it when she's not flying. By the way, the book said that hawks should get plenty of exercise."

As they started downstairs, Joe suggested they show the bird to their Aunt Gertrude, who was in the kitchen.

The boys and their pet got only as far as the ground-floor hall when suddenly the falcon yanked free and made a beeline for the living-room. Just then the doorbell and the telephone rang. Frank sprang towards the door and Joe headed for the phone.

At that instant the kitchen door at the end of the hall opened and a tall, angular woman rushed forward. She was Mr Hardy's sister, who lived with the family.

"Aunt Gertrude, watch the hawk in the living-room, will, you?" Joe requested, picking up the phone.

"Watch *what?*" his aunt exclaimed. But the bewildered woman received no further explanation. Joe was already speaking on the phone.

"Hello, Chet. Say, someone sent us a peregrine falcon."

"Great! What's that?" was the reply.

When Joe told him it was a hunting hawk, Chet said excitedly, "Bring it out on the farm, will you? I've never seen one."

"We will. Got to hang up because the bird's loose. See you later."

When Joe went into the living-room, Aunt Gertrude was standing motionless staring at the hawk, which was now alternately rising and diving from windows to furniture.

"Joe!" Miss Hardy finally managed to exclaim. "Get that bird out of here at once!"

Frank stepped to the doorway of the living-room and reported to Joe that the mail had come. There was a registered letter for Mr Hardy, but nothing about the mysterious bird.

"What's going on here?" Aunt Gertrude demanded. "Where did you get that monstrous creature?"

"Well, we don't know the person who sent her—" Frank began. As he told Aunt Gertrude how the bird had arrived, the hawk suddenly lunged at her and grasped at her hands.

"Help! Take it away!" she cried frantically.

Joe yelled, "It's that piece of meat you're holding, Aunty! She thinks it's a lure!"

Aunt Gertrude looked at the raw meat she had absentmindedly brought from the kitchen. Frank took it from her hand and immediately the falcon returned to his glove to eat the meat.

Joe put his arm around Aunt Gertrude. "The falcon was only doing what she has been taught to do. Pieces of raw meat are used as lures for training these birds. The falcon didn't intend to harm you."

"Well, maybe you're right," Aunt Gertrude conceded grudgingly. "But falconers don't train their birds in a living-room! Take her out of here."

With this ultimatum, Aunt Gertrude turned on her heel and stalked back to the kitchen.

Joe looked at Frank, grinned, and told him of Chet's invitation. "Let's take Miss Peregrine out to the farm," he said.

Chet Morton, a school chum, lived on a farm outside Bayport. A chubby, good-natured boy, he had frequently shared in the Hardys' adventures.

Frank took the hood from his pocket and attempted to put it over the head of the peregrine. The bird flew off his gloved hand, but the jesses and leash held her. She soon stopped flapping and perched on the glove.

"Boy, this is harder than I thought," said Frank.

Joe, recalling what he had read in the falconry book

on how to "break" a falcon to the hood, said, "We ought to lay a small piece of meat inside the hood before putting it on her."

Frank nodded. He said that the falcon is also fed a choice morsel of food after the hood is put on. Thus she connects a pleasant experience with hooding and does not struggle or fear the temporary blindness that the cover imposes.

After Joe had coaxed several scraps of raw meat from Aunt Gertrude, Frank managed to hood the hawk. He was awkward at it and resolved to practise until he could do it deftly.

As he carried the bird to the back yard, Joe ran to the cellar for the block perch. When he reappeared, Frank took the perch and said:

"I'll get the convertible and meet you in the driveway. You bring the hawk."

"Okay," Joe agreed, taking the glove and bird.

He paused to call goodbye to Aunt Gertrude, then started towards the driveway.

A man, masked by a red-and-white bandanna and wearing a battered felt hat pulled low on his forehead, darted round a corner of the house and crashed into him!

The boy whirled and swung his free fist. But the short, heavy-set stranger dodged and gave Joe a shove that sent him sprawling on the ground. At the same instant the man grabbed the leash, snatched the falcon, and sped down the driveway.

Quickly Joe got to his feet. Yelling to Frank to follow, he dashed off in pursuit of the thief!

# ·2·

## Peregrine's Prize

By the time Joe had reached the foot of the Hardy driveway, the thief was half a block down Elm Street. The man forced the bird into a cloth sack as he ran. Then, seeing Joe in pursuit, he leaped over a hedge and sprinted up a driveway between two houses.

As Joe reached it, a woman, leaning out a side window, gave a startled shriek. The masked man, evidently frightened, looked back to check Joe's progress. The side of his neck struck a clothesline, throwing him off balance, and Joe closed some of the gap between them.

"Drop that bird, you thief!" he shouted furiously.

The man staggered a few paces, then regained his balance. He jumped a low fence to the adjoining property and sped down its driveway, back to the street, still holding the bagged falcon!

Joe's shout and the woman's scream had attracted the attention of a policeman on Elm Street. As the thief reached the sidewalk, he slammed into the portly figure of Patrolman Smith and dropped the sack.

"Grab him!" Joe yelled to the officer.

But the masked man, recovering himself quickly, side-stepped Smith. Forgetting the bird, he cut across the street and disappeared into the dense, flower-covered foliage behind a house. Just then Frank swung the convertible alongside the kerb. Joe picked up the sack and thrust it in beside his brother.

Patrolman Smith had taken up the chase, and now Joe joined him. They searched the area thoroughly for two square blocks but were unable to find the fugitive or anyone who had seen him. As they retraced their steps to the convertible, Smith asked:

"What's this all about, anyway?"

"That fellow tried to steal our bird."

"What kind of bird is it—a parrot?"

"No," Joe replied. "A peregrine falcon—a hawk."

"One of those hunting birds? I didn't know they had them around this part of the country."

"This one was sent to us. It's valuable."

The patrolman nodded. "Valuable, eh? Did you notice anything special about that thief?"

"Well," Joe replied, "his face was masked. But this might help. When he grabbed the falcon, I got a good look at his hands. They were deeply tanned, so I guess he spends a lot of time outdoors. And he was wearing a carved ring with a ruby in it."

Patrolman Smith jotted down this information. When they reached the convertible, he said goodbye to the boys and hurried off.

As Joe climbed into the car, Frank gently lifted the falcon from the sack. Apparently, because the hood had prevented the bird from seeing, she had not become frightened by the experience.

"Since Miss Peregrine seems to feel okay," Frank said, "let's go on to Chet's as we planned."

With the falcon perched on Joe's wrist, the boys rode out of town. A short time later they arrived at the Morton farm. They saw Chet near a corner of the barn, making repairs on a door. The stout boy was alternately munching on an apple and hammering.

"Wow!" Joe grinned. "Chet's working!"

Although the Hardys needled their easygoing pal a great deal, they were close friends. Chet had been helping them ever since the days of their first mystery, *The Mystery of the Aztec Warrior*. Just recently, in the boys' latest case, *The Yellow Feather Mystery*, his skill with machinery and the operation of his motor sled had been instrumental in rescuing the Hardys from death in a sealed-up ice fort.

As Chet hurried over to see his friends, he called cheerfully, "Hi, fellows! Did you bring the hawk?"

The Hardys slid out of the car, and the falcon was transferred to Frank's wrist.

"Pretty neat!" Chet remarked. "Let's see her without her hat." He reached out to remove it.

"Wait a minute," said Frank. "She's been through a rugged experience this afternoon," and he told Chet what had happened.

Chet's eyebrows lifted. "Sounds like the beginning of another mystery for you fellows."

"Sure does," said Joe.

Chet looked at the hawk. "She seems really tame," he commented.

"She is," Joe replied as Frank removed the hood from the falcon.

Chet studied the notched beak and the long, tapered wings, which Frank said were characteristic of all falcons. "She's streamlined, all right," he declared.

"Yes, and she's a powerful flier," Joe added. "According to one of Dad's books, she's very courageous—but gentle, too. Notice her dark eyes and the way she holds her head up. The ancient falconers called the peregrines noble and gentle birds. This breed was the prize of medieval kings."

Chet was visibly impressed. "How about a trial flight?"

At that moment his sister Iola appeared on the back porch of the farmhouse and called, "Hi, boys! Would you like some lemonade?"

Frank waved and said that he would have some later. But Joe immediately hurried towards the house. The slender, pretty girl, with dark hair and eyes, was his date on many occasions as well as a capable sleuthing assistant.

Meanwhile, as they walked towards an open field, Chet asked Frank to let him fly the falcon.

"Better let me try it first," said Frank. "I'm not sure how successful I'll be, since all I know about falconry is what I read in the book."

He stopped, unfastened each jess from the swivel, and then, with a somewhat awkward movement of the glove, he threw the hawk into the air. With long, powerful wing beats the falcon circled, rising higher and higher until she was merely a dot above them in the sky.

"Now what?" Chet asked.

"See this," said Frank, holding out the feathered lure.

"What on earth is that?"

"According to the book, the falconer waves this lure in the air and the falcon immediately drops earthward and strikes it."

"You mean she'll come back to that thing?" Chet asked incredulously.

Frank nodded, watching the hawk intently. "See how she keeps circling us!" he exclaimed. "That's called 'waiting on.' She'll maintain her pitch there until I call her back, either by waving the lure or flushing a bird."

Frank swung the lure several times, then let it drop to the ground. Immediately the falcon turned and plummeted towards them at terrific speed.

"She's stooping!" yelled Frank. "Listen to the wind whistle through her feathers!"

The falcon came within a foot of striking the lure, then swung upward and mounted almost to her previous height in the sky.

"That was sensational!" breathed Chet.

The falcon made a wide circle and then headed off with deep, powerful wing beats.

"Hey! She's flying away!" Chet cried out.

"No," said Frank. "Look! She's after something!"

"It's a pigeon!" Chet gripped his friend's arm.

"I'll call the falcon to the lure," Frank said tersely.

But it was already too late. With unbelievable speed the falcon closed the distance and then streaked earthward, striking the pigeon in mid-air.

The boys saw a tuft of feathers fly and heard the sharp report of the impact. The pigeon dropped to the ground, and the falcon, after mounting from her stoop, dropped down again to claim her prize.

Frank and Chet went towards the two birds, hoping to rescue the pigeon. Slowly, in order not to frighten the hawk, Frank reached for the jesses. With wings and tail spread, the bird looked defiantly at him but made no attempt to fly off. The boy secured the jesses and put on the leash.

"Too bad," said Frank, "but the pigeon's dead."

He stroked the hawk, and then slowly lifted both the pigeon and falcon. As he did, he saw a small red capsule on one of the pigeon's legs.

"Gosh, it's a carrier pigeon!" exclaimed Chet.

Frank, concerned that the falcon had killed someone's prized bird, asked Chet to twist the cap off the small container. Chet did so and shook it gingerly over the palm of his hand. To the boys' amazement, instead of a message, out fell two glittering red stones.

"That's strange," Frank remarked.

Joe, who had been watching the falcon's performance, joined his brother and Chet. The trio bent over the stones in Chet's hands. Frank asked Joe to check the pigeon's other leg for an identification band.

"Nothing here," he reported.

Frank rubbed his fingers over the stones and recognized an oily feel to them.

"I believe that these are rubies—valuable rubies!"

## ·3·

## Smugglers

"RUBIES!" Chet exclaimed in amazement. Then he laughed. "You're fooling, Frank. In fact, if those stones are anything but coloured glass, I'll treat you both to a dinner."

Joe grinned. "We couldn't refuse an offer like that!"

"Let's get a jeweller's opinion!" Frank urged.

Wrapping the stones in a handkerchief, he put them into a pocket of his sports jacket. The boys buried the pigeon, then drove to the centre of Bayport and parked close to Bickford's Jewellery Store. While Joe stayed with the falcon, Frank and Chet went into the shop. The owner, Arthur Bickford, knew them well. He looked up and smiled.

"Well, what brings you here?"

Frank opened the handkerchief and revealed the two red stones. "We found these," he said, "and we'd like you to tell us whether or not they're genuine."

Bickford studied the gems for a moment, ran them through his fingers, then picked up his eyepiece. He peered at the stones one at a time, then marvelled, "I've never seen more flawless rubies. They're quite valuable. Where'd you get them?"

Frank evaded the question but remarked, "If they're so valuable, we'd better turn them over to the police."

The two boys thanked the jeweller and returned to the convertible. As Frank and Joe were discussing their great find, Chet reminded them that the rubies had been found on his farm.

"That's right," Joe admitted, "so it means you'll have to help solve the mystery."

Chet winced at the thought of the work involved, but said, "Sure, and then I'll get my share of the reward for the rubies."

Frank chuckled. "And you can use the money to treat us to dinner."

"Okay, okay," Chet said with a grin. "Any time you say."

"Let's make it right after we turn these gems over to Chief Collig," Joe said. "Chet, will you stay here to mind the falcon?"

The Hardys crossed the street to police headquarters, and five minutes later were seated in Chief Ezra Collig's office.

"What mystery have you boys turned up now?" the officer asked with a smile.

Frank handed over the rubies. "Mr Bickford told us these are valuable stones. Have you had a report of any robbery involving gems like these?"

Chief Collig said he could not recall any, but would ask one of his detectives, and buzzed for him.

"Nothing like that has been reported missing," the detective replied to Frank's inquiry. "And we'd sure hear about such a theft from other departments."

The chief thanked him and the man withdrew. They

talked about the stones and the carrier pigeon for some time but could come to no conclusions.

The boys left the rubies with Chief Collig for safekeeping. When they rejoined Chet, they decided to forego his dinner treat for the time being and return home, since it was time to feed the hawk. Chet suggested that they let him off at his father's real-estate office. Mr Morton would drive him back to the farm.

When Frank and Joe reached home their mother was setting the table for dinner. Mrs Hardy was a small, slim woman with blonde hair and sparkling blue eyes.

"What a noble-looking bird!" she remarked. "Your aunt told me all about her."

Aunt Gertrude appeared from the kitchen just as Frank noticed there was a plate at his father's place.

"Dad's home from Washington!" he cried out.

"He's in town all right," Aunt Gertrude replied, adding with a frown, "And when he hears about that vicious hawk you boys have, he's not going to like it."

"Perhaps he won't mind when we tell him about the rubies our bird got for us," Frank said, grinning.

When the boys related the story, the women gasped in amazement.

At Aunt Gertrude's insistence, Frank and Joe took the falcon to the garage. They set up the block perch and put the falcon on it. The boys fed her some parrot seed, set the burglar alarm, and locked the door.

Fenton Hardy arrived a few minutes later. He was a tall, dark, distinguished-looking man. His sons loved his keen sense of humour and admired his brilliant mind. Mr Hardy's preoccupied manner as the family sat down to dinner could mean only one thing. He was busy on an important case.

Sensing his sons' curiosity, he said, "I've been asked to help on an interesting problem which has the authorities baffled. Immigration officials have learned of the large-scale smuggling of aliens from India into the United States somewhere along the Atlantic coast. One suspected spot is Bayport."

"Bayport!" Frank repeated in astonishment, adding, "Any other clues?"

"None. But maybe you boys can find some," Mr Hardy replied with a twinkle in his eye. "I'm working on another case right now that I'll have to finish before I can concentrate on this smuggling racket."

"In other words, Dad, you're asking Joe and me to start from scratch. No leads or anything?"

"You know I wouldn't do that, son," Fenton Hardy replied, smiling. "I have two possible leads.

"While I was in Washington, I called on an old friend—an Indian importer. I talked with him about the illegal entry of aliens from his country and told him I was going to ask you boys to work on the case. He naturally frowns on anything that will detract from his country's good reputation, and has offered to assist in every way he can."

"Did he give you any leads?" Frank asked.

"No, but I mentioned to him that there must be some means of communication between the smugglers and their confederates on shore. We eliminated radio and telegraph because they could be monitored. But it occurred to me that secret messages, instructing the contact here to pick up the smuggled men, might be sent by carrier pigeons from the ships offshore to the racketeers' hideout on land. Ghapur agreed.''

"Ghapur!" Joe burst out. "Dad, is your Indian friend's name Rahmud Ghapur?"

"Why, yes, son," Mr Hardy answered.

The boys told their father about the falcon they had received from Ghapur, the attempted theft of the bird, and the ruby-bearing carrier pigeon which the peregrine had downed.

"That's very interesting," Mr Hardy said. "I'll phone Ghapur at once."

Fortunately the importer was at home. The detective talked with him for some time, then returned to the table.

"Mr Ghapur says he sent the falcon to aid you boys in bringing down pigeons you might be suspicious of. He mailed a letter of explanation. Didn't it arrive?"

"No," Frank replied, adding thoughtfully, "The letter could have been intercepted by the smugglers if they suspected what the falcon was to be used for."

"True," Mr Hardy declared. "Ghapur asked you boys to get in touch with a fellow countryman of his who lives here in Bayport. He's Ahmed, the rug dealer. You know him. He'll teach you how to handle the falcon properly."

This statement caused Aunt Gertrude to speak up sharply, deploring the fact that the boys were getting involved in such a cruel sport.

"Aunty," said Frank, "it's in the line of duty. And anyway, wild hawks eat ten times as many pigeons and other birds in a year than we'd let a trained falcon like Miss Peregrine go after."

"Humph!" Aunt Gertrude was unconvinced, and was about to continue her tirade when Mrs Hardy arose and started clearing the table. Her husband and sons got up too and went to the garage to see the falcon. After examining her trappings, Mr Hardy said with a smile:

"It will be rather unique to solve a mystery with a hooded hawk."

"Yes," agreed Frank. "Dad, do you think there might be a tie-in between the smugglers of aliens and the rubies?"

"Yes, I do," Mr Hardy replied. "And I have a hunch we'll find that carrier pigeons are the link between our two mysteries."

They talked for a while longer, then Fenton Hardy concluded with, "Well, boys, it will have to be your job for the time being to solve these mysteries. I must get back on my other case. From time to time I'll be in touch with you, though."

"You're leaving?" Joe asked.

"Yes. I'm flying back to Washington. Will you drive me to the airport?"

"Certainly, Dad."

After the boys had dropped Mr Hardy at the airport, Joe suggested, "Let's phone Ahmed. It's not too late, and I'd like to get to work."

"Good idea," replied Frank. "We should know more about training and flying the bird. We were just lucky this afternoon."

He put through a call to the elderly rug merchant. After identifying himself, Frank told him about the message from Rahmud Ghapur.

Though surprised, Ahmed gladly consented to teach

the Hardys how to handle the falcon. He said that they must first obtain permission from the State Fish and Game Department to fly the hawk. It was agreed that the boys would do this the next morning, then the three would drive out to the country.

"The Morton farm is a good place," Frank suggested.

At the Bayport office of the Fish and Game Department the next day, the clerk looked quizzical when the boys made their request. But when they explained it was in connection with one of their father's cases, he gave them each special hunting permits.

With their falcon and a bag containing its equipment, the Hardys drove to Ahmed's place of business. The rug dealer was standing in the doorway, waiting for them. He was close to sixty years old, but straight as a spear and lithe in his movements.

When the elderly man was seated in the car, he turned his attention to the hawk. Putting on the gauntlet, Ahmed wristed the bird. As he stroked it, he remarked:

"This hawk is well trained. As a fledgling she was probably lured into a net, then hooded, and carried constantly on the glove until she lost her fear of man and became tame. This is called 'manning.'

"The trainer strokes her, talks gently to her, and feeds her. The falcon becomes completely dependent on her master and learns that he intends no harm. Gradually she is made hungry or 'keen' and thus learns to respond to the falconer. At first she jumps a short distance to the glove for food. Gradually the distance is increased until she is flying several hundred yards on a string. Finally she can be flown free."

"Then she's actually trained through her appetite?" Frank asked.

"Yes," Ahmed replied. "And a young bird's instincts are channelled so that she performs in a natural way for her trainer. She is never taught to do anything that she would not normally do in the wild."

"Will she bring her quarry back to her master?" Joe queried.

"No," Ahmed replied. "She goes to the ground with her kill, then the falconer hurries to his bird. The hawk does not come to him. However, if the bird misses her quarry, she will return to the lure to be fed."

"It's a complicated sport," Frank remarked. "And I can see why it requires lots of time and patience."

"Well, one thing we do know," Joe spoke up. "Pigeons are a hawk's favourite food." He grinned. "But we didn't have a squab in our refrigerator, so I gave her raw oatmeal and parrot seed for breakfast."

Ahmed smiled. "You'll have to feed her starlings, sparrows, mice, and lean beef. It's obvious that she is used to people and normal sounds, since neither of these bother her."

When they arrived at the Morton farm Iola informed them that Chet had gone to market with a load of sweet corn. She promised to tell him where the Hardys were as soon as he came in.

The visitors strolled to one of the large open fields and Ahmed began his instruction. He suggested that Frank undertake flying the hawk first. Compared to Ahmed's dexterity, the boy felt very clumsy in putting on and taking off the jesses and the hood. He also felt that due to his inexperience the hawk must be tiring from the procedure.

"Let's give the poor bird a rest," he suggested. "In the meantime, I'd like to learn more about the history of falconry."

Ahmed agreed, and holding the falcon, he walked round the field with the Hardys. As they strolled along, the rug dealer told them about the short-winged hawks that are flown from the fist at such quarry as game birds and rabbits.

"These birds," Ahmed said, "such as the goshawk, the sharp-shinned hawk, and the Cooper's hawk are the best ones for a beginner to practise with.

"In my country, and in yours too, the peregrine falcon is considered the prize bird and only experienced falconers capture and train them. It is an unwritten law that novice falconers start on the less noble birds, and as they gain experience, they earn the right to train the peregrines."

"We're fortunate to start off with a trained one," said Joe.

"Indeed you are," replied Ahmed.

As the three walked back across the field, Ahmed gave the boys additional pointers on the care of their falcon, advising them to keep the bird with them at all times, so that she would recognize them as her masters.

"Remember," he said, "to put water out for her bath, to keep her in the shade, and to place her perch where she can't get tangled up. Above all," he cautioned, "be kind and gentle to her and she will reciprocate. Always bear in mind that she puts great trust in you; don't fail her."

Frank and Joe were assuring him that they would certainly do their best when they heard a loud yell.

"Hey, fellows!" It was Chet, standing at the edge of the field and waving at them. "Quick! I've got news!"

"Good or bad?" Joe shouted back as he and Frank started running towards their friend.

"Don't know. But you'll find out at police headquarters!"

# · 4 ·

## A Suspicious Sailor

FRANK and Joe sprinted across the field to where Chet was waiting for them.

"What's this news from police headquarters about?" Joe demanded excitedly.

"All I know," said the stout boy, "is the department called and said you should report there pronto!"

The same thoughts flashed through the brothers' minds: Was it news of the rubies or of Joe's masked assailant?

"We're on our way," said Joe as Ahmed caught up to them, the falcon still on his wrist.

They hurried to the convertible and drove to Bayport. After leaving Ahmed at his shop, the boys headed for police headquarters. Frank remained in the car with the falcon while Joe went inside. Officer Smith was waiting for him.

"You have news for us?" Joe asked.

Smith nodded. "I saw a man lurking around your house. Swarthy complexion, red-and-white bandanna round his neck, and wearing a battered felt hat."

"You mean you've caught our hawk thief?"

"I don't know if he's the one, Joe. You'll have to identify him. But he certainly fitted your description!"

Smith led the boy into a small room. A suntanned figure slouched on a bench. When the man saw Joe, he jumped up.

"Am I glad you're here," he said with a slight Italian accent. "I went to your house and looked for the lawn mower, and this cop took me down here for I don't know what!"

Joe grinned. "Sorry, Nicolo. It's a case of mistaken identity!"

Nicolo looked at the policeman defiantly. "See? I told you!"

"Nicolo is our gardener," Joe explained to Smith. "He comes every week to cut the lawn."

Smith shrugged and apologized to the man.

"That's okay," Nicolo said when he heard about the hawk thief. "Now can I go back to work?"

Since it was nearly lunchtime, the boys drove Nicolo to the Hardy home. As Joe carried the falcon towards the back door, Mrs Hardy appeared and said:

"Please don't bring the hawk into the house. It will only upset your Aunt Gertrude."

Frank took the hawk to its perch in the garage, set the burglar alarm, and locked the door. He had just sat down at the table for lunch when Joe appeared, carrying a volume of the encyclopaedia with him.

"It says here, 'Most hawks, peregrines especially, require a bath,'" Joe read. "'The end of a cask, sawed off to give a depth of six inches, makes a good tub. Peregrines which are used to "waiting on" require a bath at least twice a week.'"

"'Waiting on'! You certainly do have to wait on them!" Aunt Gertrude retorted.

Frank and Joe exchanged grins, then told their aunt what the term meant. Frank read on from the book in his brother's hands. " 'If the bath is neglected, the falcon is inclined to soar when flown, and may even break away in search of water, and so be lost.' "

Miss Hardy cleared her throat with a loud *harrumph*, which ended further conversation about the hawk.

After lunch the boys made a cask tub for the falcon and let her bathe. Then they laid plans for beginning their work on the case Mr Hardy had outlined for them.

"My guess is," said Frank, "that anyone smuggling immigrants into the country would probably do it after dark. Let's take the *Sleuth* out in the bay this evening and scout around for a few hours."

"Good idea," Joe agreed. "But remember, Miss Peregrine has to go along."

About seven-thirty the boys changed to old trousers and sweaters, then hurried to the garage. Joe put on the gauntlet and signalled for the hawk to come to his wrist. When the bird was in place, he hooded it, and Frank drove to their boathouse.

After climbing aboard the sleek motorboat, Joe attached the bird's leash to the jesses on her legs and set her on a short horizontal pole in the wheel cabin, which was intended for raincoats and jackets. The bird accepted the roost readily.

Moments later Frank had the *Sleuth* under way. As the craft knifed smoothly through the water, the boys were pleased to see that the falcon remained quiet. Presently Joe asked:

"What kind of boat do you think we ought to look for out here?"

"I surmise that the smugglers would come close to the twelve-mile limit in a large boat," his brother replied. "Then they contact the shore and make arrangements to have the immigrants transported the rest of the way in a speedboat."

"Sounds logical," Joe agreed.

Feeling a drop of rain, Joe looked up at the sky. In the distance he spotted a pigeon flying towards land. Grabbing binoculars, he trained them on the bird. Frank, too, had seen the pigeon. Both boys wondered if it were a carrier.

"Suppose we let the hawk bring it down on the beach," Joe suggested.

"It might help us more to know where the bird is going, so we can locate the owner," Frank asserted. "Get the pigeon's direction, Joe."

He handed his brother a pocket compass. Joe balanced it on his hand, and compensating for the bobbing of the speedboat, studied the movements of the settling needle carefully.

Frank and Joe were well aware that carrier pigeons' actions are fairly predictable. When turned loose at their departure point, they fly straight up into the air, circle, pick up the beam to their home cote, and set off in a straight line.

By the speed and assurance with which the pigeon overhead was flying, the boys were convinced that it was making a beeline for home. When the bird was finally out of sight, Joe remarked:

"The pigeon was heading straight southwest. The question is, How far inland is it going?"

"We have a starting point for our search, anyway,"

Frank commented. "Hey, that pigeon at Chet's farm was headed in a southwest direction, too."

"Right. And now, with a possible clue to the smugglers' mainland hideout, let's do a bit of aerial sleuthing."

"First thing tomorrow."

Presently Frank turned the wheel over to Joe. He was just about to head into the ocean when Joe said:

"We have company."

A deep-sea fishing cruiser was coming towards them from the open sea. Frank picked up the glasses and read the name *Daisy K*. The Hardys recognized this as a weather-beaten sports fishing craft used for charter trips. It was frequently tied up in Bayport. But they knew nothing about its owner.

"Think she's suspicious?" Joe asked.

"Take a look at the sailor leaning over the rail on the starboard side," Frank urged excitedly.

As the *Daisy K* approached, Joe adjusted the glasses and peered at the heavy-set, dark-skinned man, who had piercing black eyes. Both of the man's hands were resting on the rail, and at first glance he appeared to be just a tired sailor relaxing after a long, wearing day's work.

"What do you think, Joe?"

"Same as you do."

For a reason they could not explain, the boys felt sure that this was the mysterious masked man who had tried to steal the falcon! But on neither of his hands was the telltale ruby ring. In a moment the *Daisy K* had passed the *Sleuth*.

"I don't suppose," said Joe, "that we ought to

suspect every sun-tanned stranger. I have a funny feeling, though, that he is our man. Shall we follow him?"

"We haven't a shred of evidence against the fellow, Joe—and anyway, we know where to find him if we want him. I'd rather keep looking out here for clues to the smugglers."

"Okay."

It was choppy on the open sea, and as darkness settled, the wind grew strong.

"I guess we'd better go back," Frank proposed. "The waves are getting pretty high and I don't think Miss Peregrine likes it!"

The hawk was finding it hard to retain her perch and finally Frank took the bird on his wrist. "Too bad we couldn't continue our sleuthing," he remarked. "But then, it would be impossible for us to get near another boat on a night like this."

About half an hour later the Hardys nosed the *Sleuth* into the slip of their boathouse. Frank set the falcon back on her pole perch, and had just closed the door behind them when there was a low rumble in one corner of the boathouse. The next instant there came a blinding flash, followed by a sharp explosion that rocked the building!

A sheet of flame roared up the walls and across the boathouse directly towards the *Sleuth!*

## · 5 ·

## *Indian Intrigue*

STUNNED, the Hardys could see no escape from the flash fire which had trapped them in their boathouse. As the initial shock wore off, Frank cried:

"Open the door, Joe!"

The youth swung it up as Frank revved the boat's engine. The *Sleuth* shot backward into open water a split second before the fire reached its prow.

"Whew!" said Joe. "Sabotage!"

His brother nodded as he docked nearby. Joe quickly fastened the hawk's leash to a rowboat painter while Frank grabbed a fire extinguisher from the *Sleuth*. Both boys raced back to their boathouse.

Behind them, the boys could hear a watchman shout, "What's wrong over there?"

"Fire!" Frank yelled. "Give us a hand!"

One glance around the boathouse told the Hardys that a single fire extinguisher would do little good. Nevertheless, Frank played it around until it was empty.

Joe ran outside and called the fire department from a public phone. Then he looked for some clue to the fire's origin. Near the side door he noticed a small wad of newspaper on the floor. He put it into his pocket.

At that moment the watchman ran up with a hand line from a nearby hydrant, and the blaze was soon extinguished. But the boathouse was badly damaged.

The Bayport fire engines turned into the waterfront street. When the chief discovered that things were under control, he sent his men back but remained himself to talk to the boys.

"How did the fire start?" he asked.

"There was an explosion," Joe replied and told what had happened. After a quick inspection, the chief agreed that an arsonist was responsible.

When the fire chief had left and the watchman had returned to his shack, Joe pulled the wad of paper from his pocket. "This might tell us something," he said to Frank. "But it's too dark to read here."

The boys went to their boat and got a flashlight. To their amazement they saw that the printing was in a strange, oriental-looking script.

"It might have been printed in India," Frank said, "and if so, one of the smugglers could have set the fire."

"There's one man who can tell us if you're right," Joe reflected. "Ahmed."

"Think he'll be up this late?"

They decided that it would be worth a try. As they were about to leave, Joe suddenly halted and exclaimed, "Wait! We almost forgot the hawk!"

While he went to retrieve the falcon, Frank made arrangements with the watchman to leave the *Sleuth* at another dock. Then they drove to the small bungalow where Ahmed lived. The house was brightly lighted. They rang the bell, and the rug dealer admitted the boys and their falcon. He led them into an attractive living-room, furnished in oriental style.

Frank and Joe took turns supplying Ahmed with the details of their exploits. Frowning in concern, he spread the sheet of newspaper on a bronze table. He scanned the lines closely, then turned to his callers.

"It is part of a story which reports that Tava, the son of Satish Nayyar, a well-known industrialist from the Province of Hatavab where I come from, will visit the United States. The boy is eighteen and is to finish his education in this country. Satish Nayyar is one of the richest men in India and has a reputation of being a great humanitarian as well. Incidentally, the dateline on this paper is Delhi, two months past."

Ahmed glanced over the rest of the newspaper but found nothing in any of the other items that could be interpreted as a clue to the identity of the arsonist.

Frank asked, "How many persons around Bayport would be likely to read a newspaper from India?"

"A dozen, perhaps. I have six men from Delhi working for me, and there must be an equal number employed on the fishing boats in the vicinity."

"Thank you very much, Ahmed," Frank said, rising. "This information may shed some light on our case."

The Hardys said goodnight, returned to their car, and headed for home.

They were up early the next morning. After breakfast Frank telephoned a builder, who agreed to start repairing the boathouse at once. Then Frank called the local airport and found that they would have to postpone their aerial search for the smugglers' hideout, since the helicopter pilot was busy for the rest of that day.

Later that morning, Frank and Joe had a conference with Chief Collig about the fire and left the sheet from the Delhi newspaper with him. The chief promised to look into the matter.

"Joe," Frank said as they left police headquarters, "if we're going to use our hawk to help solve the mystery, we'd better do some more practising."

"Right. Let's go out to Chet's after lunch."

The Hardys decided to walk and carry the bird, since this would give the falcon an opportunity to become accustomed to them. Frank hooded Miss Peregrine as Joe picked up the falconer's bag, and they started out.

The boys talked all the way, knowing that it was important for the falcon to become familiar with their voices and thus obey them more promptly. By now, she came readily to either boy's fist for food, as well as to the lure.

When they arrived at the Morton farm, Mrs Morton told them that Chet had gone to town but was expected back soon. They left a message for Chet to join them, and immediately set off for the isolated spot where they would release the falcon. There, Joe unhooded the bird and removed the leash. He then directed her attention to several crows which were flying over a clump of trees and threw her off.

Instinct seemed to warn the crows, however, for almost as soon as the falcon had left Joe's glove, they flew into a thicket. The hawk circled for a while, then climbed upward into the sky until she appeared no larger than a swallow.

"Maybe we're going to lose her," Joe said, worried.

"I don't believe so," Frank reassured him. "She's 'waiting on,' expecting us to flush more suitable quarry for her to strike."

"Well, we'll give her some," said Joe, taking the lure from the falconer's bag and waving it.

"She's coming back!" Frank cried.

Both boys watched a tiny speck hurtling towards them, growing larger by the second. In a long, graceful swoop the falcon came in and struck the lure with a smack. Joe held it firmly and the hawk came to rest. He offered her some raw meat, then hooded her and set the bird on his wrist.

Just then Frank spotted Iola Morton running towards them. When she reached the Hardys, she paused for breath, then blurted out:

"Your father's home! He's been trying to reach you. Something important has come up about your new case!"

Surprised to learn that their father was back so soon from Washington, the boys dashed to the Morton house and called home.

"What's up, Dad?" Frank asked excitedly.

"I've just received a phone call from Mr Ghapur. He's coming here from Washington with a friend from India who has a strange story to tell us."

"What is it?"

"The matter was too confidential to discuss over the telephone, Frank. The men will arrive tonight. I thought you boys would want to be on hand."

"We'll be there," Frank promised.

As Frank put down the phone, Chet appeared with a huge container of ice cream. Frank told Chet of the meeting to be held at the Hardy home that evening.

"Maybe it's about our rubies," their stout friend suggested.

As dinnertime approached, Chet drove the Hardys and their falcon home in his jalopy.

"Let me know what happens, fellows," he called, waving goodbye.

Fenton Hardy was waiting. "Our callers will arrive about nine o'clock," he said.

Night had closed in and they were waiting for the front doorbell to ring, when a knock sounded on the back door. The boys and their father hurried to the kitchen and Fenton Hardy opened the door. Two men were standing there.

"Mr Ghapur!" the detective exclaimed.

"We thought we were being followed," the importer explained, stepping in. "Please pardon this strange way of entering your home."

Rahmud Ghapur was a dark-complexioned man, about fifty years old, with lines at his temples that indicated a normally jovial disposition. Right now, however, his expression was tempered by the seriousness of the situation. His companion, about ten years younger, was introduced as Mr Delhi, a trusted emissary and cousin of Satish Nayyar.

Ghapur added that the Indian, who retained a high government post, had assumed the name Delhi because he wished to remain incognito while in the United States.

"My real name is Bhagnav," Mr Delhi said.

Mr Hardy shook hands with him and introduced his sons. "We'll go up to my study," he said, "where we can be sure that our discussion will not be overheard by possible eavesdroppers at our doors or windows."

He led the way to the first floor. After everyone was seated, Frank offered to bring the falcon to Mr Ghapur, but the man advised against it.

"If the bird were to see me," he said, "the fine progress you have made with her might be undone."

Ghapur turned to his companion. "Please tell your story," he requested.

Mr Delhi began with a question. "Had you heard that Tava Nayyar was on his way to the United States in order to complete his education?"

"We learned it last night from a newspaper clipping," Frank replied, and told of their adventure in the boathouse.

"He arrived in New York all right," Mr Delhi went on. "Then he was kidnapped!"

"Kidnapped!" chorused the Hardys, and Joe added, "When?"

"About a month ago. Ransom was demanded in rubies. We received orders to leave the gems in a certain place in India. The orders were carried out and the rubies picked up. But Tava has not been released."

"You haven't heard anything?" Frank asked.

"Oh, yes. We have received a new ransom note which demands that more rubies be left at the designated spot. The note, like the first one, threatens Tava with death if payment is not made or if the story of his kidnapping is published."

Mr Delhi paused. "I—I am afraid Tava may not even now be alive," he said sombrely. "But his father has not given up hope."

Rahmud Ghapur picked up the story. "Satish Nayyar sent Mr Delhi to this country to see if he could track down the kidnappers. Since I am a native of the same province, he came to me for help. I suggested that we get in touch with you. Can you and your sons look into this matter for us?"

"We'll be glad to," Fenton Hardy assured them. "In fact, my boys may have picked up a clue already."

"Yes? How so?" both visitors asked in amazement.

Frank and Joe told them of the precious rubies from the carrier pigeon brought down by the hawk.

The Indians were astounded to hear this news and agreed that the rubies might very well be part of the ransom. They thought, too, that the missing youth might be held at the place from which the pigeon had been released or where it was heading.

"More likely it's the latter, since the pigeon came in from the sea," Mr Hardy said. "We'll do our best to find the spot."

Mr Ghapur leaned forward in his chair. "Nothing must happen to Tava. He is like one of my own family. When he was just a small child, I was the guest of Satish Nayyar." Turning to Mr Delhi, he asked, "Do you remember the cheetah hunt?"

"I certainly do," Mr Delhi recalled, "and my cousin will never forget how you saved Tava's life, at peril of your own, when the boy was attacked by the cheetah."

"It was a great honour," Ghapur said quietly. He turned back to Fenton Hardy and concluded, "I think we've finished our mission here. Mr Delhi will return with me to my home in Washington. His enemies must not know where he is, so we will leave the way we came. We are deeply grateful to you all."

"We'll try to justify your gratitude," Fenton Hardy promised.

Mr Delhi asked that they spare no expense in tracing down every possible clue. "Incidentally," he added, "Tava brought along his favourite goshawk on this trip. This might help you locate him."

When he and Rahmud Ghapur had left, Mr Hardy said to his sons, "I believe there's a connection between Tava's kidnappers, the rubies on the pigeon, and the smugglers of aliens from India. You boys made a start checking the coastline for clues. You might follow up on that, as well as try to locate the carrier pigeons' cote while I'm away. I'm due back in Washington tomorrow."

"We'll keep after the waterfront angle," Frank assured him. "We're going to do some sleuthing from the air, too, to track down the pigeon's owner."

The family was up early the next morning so that Fenton Hardy could catch the first plane to Washington. While the boys were feeding and watering the falcon, their mother brought them two hundred dollars cash and asked that they deposit it in the bank before three o'clock. They drove their father to the airport, then looked for their friend George Simons, who owned a helicopter.

"No passengers ahead of us today, I hope," said Frank.

"You're the first. Climb in. What are you fellows chasing this time?" the pilot asked with a smile.

"Carrier pigeons and their home cotes," Frank told him.

First they flew to the end of the bay and from there headed in the southwesterly direction which the two carrier pigeons had followed. The pilot kept the helicopter at low speed while Frank scanned the land below.

Meanwhile, Joe was watching the horizon behind them for any slow-moving boat that might be plying between some ship and the shore. He saw none but suddenly cried out:

"Here comes a pigeon northeast of us!"

Simons held the helicopter stationary until the bird had come alongside and moved ahead of his craft. Then he trailed it. For about eight miles the pilot kept the pigeon in sight while Frank plotted its course on a map he had brought. Then, suddenly, the bird made a dive for a sparsely wooded area.

Simons stopped his forward flight and lowered the helicopter to get a better look. The boys carefully scrutinized the area, but there was no sign of a house or barn with a cote. Frank and Joe were puzzled, but finally concluded it must have been a wild bird that had just happened to take the southwesterly route.

Although the Hardys spent most of the morning scouting the Bayport environs, they saw no other pigeons.

At the airport, as the boys climbed into their convertible, Joe asked, "Where do we go from here?"

"We ought to go to the bank," his brother replied, starting the motor. "But let's scout around the waterfront first for the heavy-set, sun-tanned man wearing a ruby ring."

Joe nodded. "How about looking for that suspicious sailor on the *Daisy K?* If he's the fellow, he may be wearing the ring now."

They parked their car a block from the shoreline, then walked briskly to the dock area, where fishing boats, excursion steamers, deep-sea charter cruisers, and pleasure craft tied up. As the two headed for the *Daisy K*, Joe gripped Frank's arm and pointed towards an outdoor lunch stand.

"Look at the ring on that fellow on the second stool!" he said excitedly.

A stocky, dark-skinned sailor sat there eating. As he lifted a hamburger to his mouth, the sun sparkled on a ruby ring—the same unusual ring the falcon snatcher had been wearing!

The boys passed quickly and ducked behind a building.

"What'll we do now?" Joe asked.

"Let's confront him and see how he reacts," Frank urged. "We'll move in on either side."

"Okay."

They took seats next to the man and Frank looked him straight in the eye. "What did you want with our falcon?" he asked.

The man looked up, startled. "Falcon? You've mistaken me for someone else," he mumbled and backed off the stool.

Joe gripped him by the shoulder. "If you won't tell us, you can explain it to the police!"

"The police? Say, what's going on? I don't know

anything about a falcon, I swear!" The sailor's voice grew loud and he shook off Joe's hand.

"Where did you get that ruby ring?" Frank broke in, stepping in front of the suspect.

This question brought a curious reaction. Apparently the man thought the boys intended to steal it, for he yelled, "Oh, no, you don't!" and plunged headlong at Frank, trying to move past him.

Frank thrust out a leg in front of the sailor, who tripped over it and fell. Instantly Joe came down on his back, pinning him to the ground.

"Now maybe we'll get an answer!" he said.

## · 6 ·

## A Big Boner

BYSTANDERS had gathered round the Hardy boys and the sailor.

"All right, talk!" Frank ordered, dragging the man to his feet.

The heavy-set, dark-skinned sailor straightened up. Glaring at the Hardys, he asked, "What do you want to know about my ruby ring?"

"Where did you get it?" Joe asked.

"Well, I didn't steal it, if that's what you think," the man said sullenly. "I bought it from another sailor just last night."

"What did this man look like?" Frank pressed.

The sailor suddenly reddened. "Why—er—I don't know, but he also was Indian. Say, I can prove everything I told you!"

Turning, he yelled to the counterman to verify his story. To the Hardys' chagrin the counterman did so, saying he had seen the transaction.

"We're sure sorry," Frank apologized. "We—we made a mistake. We'd like to make up for it."

The sailor grinned. "Well, all right, you can pay for my lunch," he said. "I'm broke."

"Maybe we can do even better," Joe said. "Want to sell the ring?" he asked, recalling that Mr Delhi had said to spare no expense in following up clues.

The sailor hesitated, then took off the ring, named the price he had paid for it, and said he would sell for a small profit. Frank paid him, as well as for the lunch, from his mother's two hundred dollars. The sailor saluted crisply and hurried away.

Shaking their heads ruefully, the Hardys resolved to be less hasty in jumping to conclusions. They went to the bank to deposit Mrs Hardy's remaining bills, then continued on towards the dock where the *Daisy K* tied up. She was not in port.

"As long as we're here," said Joe, "we may as well make some inquiries about the crew."

They quizzed supply men and ships' captains. Finally one of the captains declared:

"That sounds like a fellow named Ragu, first mate on the *Daisy K*. Heavy-set. Piercing black eyes. Came from India. I've seen a ruby ring on him."

Frank and Joe could hardly believe their good fortune. That sailor they had seen leaning on the boat's rail must have been the original owner of the ring! The captain said he had just seen him in the Sea Foam Restaurant. The boys hurried there and spotted Ragu at a table in the far corner.

As the Hardys approached, Ragu glanced up and half rose from his chair, then slowly settled back.

"You're Ragu, aren't you?" Joe asked.

"Of what importance is that to you?"

"We'd like to know something about a ruby ring you've been wearing," Frank told him.

"I own no ring," the sailor said belligerently.

Frank displayed the ring he had just bought. "You don't own this ring now," he said evenly, "but you did. Where did you get it?"

Ragu snatched the ring and hurled it away.

"You are evil boys!" he almost screamed.

Instinctively Frank and Joe turned to recover the ring. Frank picked it up. When the boys whirled back, Ragu was dashing out a side door.

The Hardys started after him, but suddenly Frank stopped and said, "Joe, let him go. I'm sure that Ragu's the fellow who grabbed the falcon from you. If he doesn't think we're after him, and if he's connected with the senders of those rubies, maybe he'll lead us to them."

"Guess you're right, Frank."

They went back to their convertible. As Frank was about to pull away from the kerb, a vivacious voice said:

"What a beautiful ring you're wearing, Frank."

Frank and Joe looked up into the smiling face of Callie Shaw, a close friend of Iola's. Blonde, quick-witted, and carefree, she appealed particularly to Frank. Although interested, and frequently very helpful in the boys' sleuthing, the pretty, brown-eyed girl loved to tease the Hardys.

"Is the ring a gift?" Callie asked.

"No," Frank replied with a smile. "It's a clue in a new case we've taken on."

Iola Morton had joined the group now and was talking to Joe. She said gaily, "Don't forget the fish fry at the farm this afternoon."

"Wouldn't miss it for all the mysteries in Bayport," Joe replied.

"The whole gang will be there," Iola said. "Why not bring along your hawk and give us a demonstration?"

"Sure thing!" Frank agreed.

"Be there about three," Callie said. "Games first and we'll eat at five."

The girls waved goodbye and headed for a waterfront fish shop.

"If we're going to exhibit Miss Peregrine," said Joe, "we'd better go home and groom her!"

When they reached the house, the boys showed their mother the ring and told her how they had paid for it. "Mr Delhi will reimburse us," Frank explained. "I'll put the ring in Dad's safe."

After lunch he and Joe fixed a bath for the falcon. Then they changed their clothes, picked up the bird, perch, bells and lure, and set off for the Morton farm. They found a lively gathering of a dozen couples playing spirited games of softball and badminton.

But the moment the young people saw the falcon, they focused all their attention on the bird. Joe set the perch on the ground and said they would let her fly later. The hawk remained quiet as he and Frank joined in the games.

Finally Chet, who was wearing a flashy dark-green shirt splotched with brown and white, said, "Show them what Miss Peregrine can do, fellows."

Frank looked around for a quarry. Suddenly a jay flew across the field at the edge of a woods. Frank picked up the hawk, yanked off the hood and flung the hawk in its direction. As the guests excitedly watched her fly towards the jay, a shortwinged goshawk came rifling in from the woods and dived towards the jay.

"That's a trained bird!" Frank exclaimed.

Instantly the two hawks began to fight over the jay. Joe started forward, calling excitedly to the falcon. Frank held him back, saying:

"It's too late now. They'll fight to the death."

But the falcon abruptly shifted to avoid the vicious talons of the goshawk and then climbed up where she would have the advantage. While the hawks were manoeuvring for position, the jay disappeared in the brush.

Frank and Joe whistled and shouted to Miss Peregrine hoping to stop the fight. Suddenly the goshawk took flight and disappeared into the shelter of the woods. The falcon oriented herself, located the boys by the sound of their voices, and came down obediently to the feathered lure.

"Hey! You're pretty good!" Chet exclaimed admiringly, and the other young people applauded.

The Hardys smiled, relieved that their falcon was safe, then looked inquiringly towards the woods into which the goshawk had vanished.

"Come on, Joe and Chet!" Frank urged. "Let's find the owner of the hawk! It could be Tava."

Frank hooded the peregrine and placed her on her perch. Then the three boys hurried into the woods.

Joe spotted a trail of recently trampled grass. Eagerly the trio followed it. They had gone only about a hundred yards when they were confronted by a large red sign with white lettering:

### DANGEROUS AREA! KEEP OUT!

The boys were puzzled, especially Chet, who was well acquainted with the woods. "Gosh, I never saw that before," he said. "What's going on here?"

The land looked undisturbed. There were no signs of digging, tree-felling, or other hazardous operations.

Farther ahead the boys came across similar warning signs.

Frank turned to Chet. "What could make this a dangerous area?" he asked.

"I don't know," his puzzled friend replied. "Old Mr Smith who owns these woods used to encourage the public to picnic here."

"If any big project were under way, everybody in Bayport would have heard about it," Frank remarked.

"Let's split up and see if we can find out what's going on," Joe suggested.

He and Chet searched a wide sweep on either side of the trail, while Frank followed the trampled path. The boys lost sight of each other as the foliage became more dense. But Frank could check the others' positions from the sounds of their passage through the under-growth. Soon these sounds were muffled, and the woods became a silent, twilight world.

Suddenly from Chet's direction came a cry for help. "Chet's in trouble!" Frank yelled.

Instantly he and Joe were crashing through the underbrush to their friend's aid.

# ·7·

## Dangerous Explorations

FOR several anxious moments Frank and Joe could not locate Chet. But finally they came upon him huddled in a clump of brush near a brook.

"He's unconscious!" gasped Joe.

They knelt beside Chet, then carefully carried their friend out of the thicket to a clearing. As the boys gently placed him on the ground, they noticed blood oozing from a wound near the back of his head.

"This was no accident," Frank declared.

"Someone gave him a heavy blow!"

Both boys glanced around cautiously to make sure none of them was in immediate danger, then they gave Chet first aid. As Joe chafed the boy's wrists, Frank started for the brook to soak a handkerchief to bathe Chet's wound and brow.

He had gone only a few feet when he heard a slight rustling sound. Looking around quickly, Frank spotted a movement in some bushes about fifty feet away. Without turning, he whispered:

"Joe, take care of Chet. I see someone. I'll be back as soon as I can."

Frank headed for the bushes, but almost at the same moment, someone went crashing through the underbrush. The young detective increased his own pace, following the fugitive by the sounds of flight.

Several hundred yards farther on, Frank spotted the back of a tall, thin man for a fleeting second.

Frank put on a burst of speed which brought him closer to the man. They were both making considerable noise now, as twigs and leaves crackled under their feet. For this reason Frank was not immediately aware of footsteps behind him. When he heard them, the boy started to turn, but the next second a heavy blow caught him on the side of his head. Knees buckling, Frank pitched forward and blacked out!

Back at the clearing, Joe had heard the sounds of the chase, but he was confident that his brother would be more than a match for any adversary. Then he went to the brook, soaked his handkerchief in the cool water, and bathed Chet's wound. The boy's eyes flickered open and he looked up dazedly.

"Take it easy," Joe advised. "Someone knocked you out. But Frank's after him now."

"I remember. Someone rushed up behind me and I yelled for help. He conked me." Chet relaxed and closed his eyes.

Joe sat down on a log to wait for Frank's return. Glimpsing the sky through the trees, he could see that the afternoon was waning. It struck him that their friends at the fish fry probably were wondering about the boys' long absence. Should he try to get Chet back and not wait for Frank? But Joe decided against this.

"Chet should take it easy," he thought.

As time passed and his brother still did not return, Joe grew worried. "Chet, I'd better look for Frank," he said. "Do you think you can make it back to the farm alone?"

"Guess so."

Joe helped him to his feet. The stout boy took a few steps, then stopped, admitting that he felt dizzy.

"You better rest a while longer," Joe said.

He rummaged in the undergrowth and found a strong, heavy stick. Handing it to Chet, he said, "You ought to be able to defend yourself with this. I'm going to hunt for Frank."

"Okay. I'll wait here."

Joe moved off into the woods, trying to follow the general direction Frank had taken. Several times he gave the Hardys' secret birdcall whistle, and listened eagerly for his brother's response. But it never came.

Joe trudged on, following the trail of trampled grass he had found. As he reached a dense section, he heard someone moving just ahead of him. Joe stopped and gave the whistle again. There was no reply, but the rustling grew louder. He looked about for a weapon, found a heavy stick, picked it up, and went forward.

As Joe crept around the bole of a large tree, he saw Frank staggering along!

"Frank, you've been hurt!" Joe cried. He gripped his brother around the shoulders and gently lowered him to the ground. As Frank looked up at him, Joe noticed that his brother was clutching a small pouch.

"Where did you get this?" Joe asked.

Frank blinked, looked down at the pouch as if seeing it for the first time, and muttered, "Don't know. Maybe the fellow who attacked me dropped it. Guess I picked it up." He sank back, exhausted.

Joe opened the small pouch and saw that it contained several reddish-brown nuts. He had never seen any like them and concluded they might be a good clue to the identity of the boys' assailant.

Right now, Joe faced a dilemma. Should he go for help and leave Frank and Chet? But he discarded the idea at once. Their enemy might return. He had to get both boys away as soon as possible!

"Suppose you rest for a few minutes, Frank," he suggested. "Then we'll get out of here."

Frank closed his eyes. He opened them ten minutes later, declaring he felt much better. Joe was seated beside him, gazing at the pouch.

"It's possible that we're close to the smugglers' hideout, Frank," he remarked.

A few minutes later Frank said that he felt strong enough to start back. Joe helped him up, and they moved off slowly in the lengthening shadows towards the spot where Chet waited. Because of the dusk and the condition of the two boys, further sleuthing was out of the question for the time being.

"But we'll pick up the trail first thing in the morning," Frank said with determination.

As they walked on, they discussed their experiences of the afternoon. When they reached the spot where Joe had left Chet, the Hardys did not see him.

"I hope he wasn't attacked again," Joe cried out.

"No such thing," came a voice so close to them that the Hardys jumped.

The next instant, Chet's perspiring head emerged from his splotched dark-green shirt, which blended well with the underbrush. The stout boy got up from his hiding place, grinning.

Frank and Joe roared with laughter. As their mirth subsided, Chet explained that he had felt too weak to fight anyone, even with the clublike stick Joe had given him. When he thought someone was coming, he had ducked into the bushes and put the shirt over his head as camouflage.

"But I guess it was my imagination," he said. "Haven't heard a thing since. Let's go!"

The boys made their way back to the trail and headed for the Morton farm. All the young guests had left except Callie. She and Iola were seated with Mr and Mrs Morton near the falcon's perch, keeping a close watch on the valuable bird.

At sight of Chet and Frank, the whole group ran forward. Mr Morton asked, "What happened?"

"Got banged up a bit," Chet replied. "But there's nothing wrong with us that some food and a night's sleep won't cure."

"You bet," Frank spoke up, also trying to make light of their ordeal. "Anything left from the fish fry?"

"Come and get it!" Iola said.

While they were eating, the boys told the others of their strange experiences in the woods. Chet's father said that he would try to find out if Mr Smith had posted the warning signs and why.

"Tomorrow we'll go back and investigate the place, anyway," Joe declared.

The Mortons and Callie begged the boys to be on their guard.

The following day was a cold and dreary one for

August, but after breakfast Frank declared he felt well
enough to further invesitgate the woods near the
Morton farm. He proposed that they take Ahmed
along on their exploration.

"If we do run into a group of Indians, his knowledge
will come in mighty handy."

Joe agreed. "I'll phone him. You get the car."

Ahmed, amazed to hear about the incident with the
goshawk and the attacks on the boys, was eager to go.
The boys asked Mrs Hardy to keep an eye on the falcon,
then set off in the convertible to pick up Ahmed at his
bungalow. The rug dealer was hardly seated when he
said tensely:

"If you have really found the hideout of these
despicable smugglers and can bring them to justice,
India will never be able to repay you."

Remembering the small pouch he had found in the
woods, Frank pulled it out of his pocket and handed it
to Ahmed. "I picked this up in the woods yesterday.
Do you think it might be a clue?"

Ahmed's eyes narrowed as he scrutinized the bag
and its contents. Then he said cryptically, "I believe
this is indeed a clue in your search. These are betel nuts.
Only lower-caste Indians chew them." Ahmed turned
to Frank. "The person who attacked you and your
friend may be one of the smuggled men or a servant to
an Indian of wealth."

The Hardys looked at each other. The kidnapped
Tava, perhaps? He was indeed one of great wealth.
They wondered whether to tell Ahmed of Tava's
disappearance, but decided not to do so unless it

became necessary. "At least we should ask Mr Delhi's permission first," they reflected.

A short time later Frank turned the car into the Morton driveway and Chet joined them at the barn. The foursome set out for the woods, taking a different route from the trail they had followed the previous day which Frank thought was closer. But a new obstacle presented itself—a long, impenetrable wall of vines and branches.

Ahmed paused and studied the barrier carefully. "These vines and branches," he said, "have been woven together by master craftsmen. Whoever had this constructed is indeed anxious to keep out strangers."

"I've never seen anything like it," said Frank. "Have you, Ahmed?"

"You have heard tales of the beaters who go out to stir up the tiger and the wild boar? They often use this weaving technique to make sure the animals will not escape while the hunter is moving in with his elephant, or the pig-sticker with his lance."

"What we need is a machete!" Joe remarked.

Ahmed and the three boys picked up stout pieces of fallen tree limbs and started to beat their way through. Now and then they stopped to listen for sounds that might indicate trouble. But apparently they were alone in the woods.

Presently a disturbing thought came to Frank. "It looks," he said, "as though we may have frightened our attackers away from the woods permanently."

Joe nodded but made no comment. Finally the searchers broke through the thick mesh of vines, spotted a fairly well-marked trail, and went ahead.

They walked for some time, searching carefully for clues, but saw nothing suspicious. Presently the foliage began to thin out. Frank held up a hand for silence. Then, dropping to his knees, he crawled forward.

"There's a hunting lodge ahead," he whispered. "And smoke is coming from the chimney."

Chet explained that Mr Smith had built the lodge to entertain his friends during the hunting season, but that he never used it in the summer.

For several minutes Ahmed and the boys observed the lodge. Then Frank said:

"It looks deserted, though someone must have built a fire recently. Let's see what we can find out. But be careful!"

Did the lodge conceal dangerous smugglers—or the kidnappers? the Hardys wondered.

## ·8·

## *A Strange Lead*

THE searchers warily circled the hunting lodge, but they came upon no one, nor was there any sign of activity inside. Still cautious, however, Frank whispered:

"Keep an eye on me, will you, while I get close enough to look through the windows?"

Frank hurried forward, zigzagging so that he would be an elusive target. At last he reached a corner of the low, wide veranda which ran around three sides of the building. Crossing to a large window, he looked into a handsomely furnished living-room with a log fire burning. The room was unoccupied.

Frank moved stealthily from window to window. There were several rooms in the lodge, all well furnished. The bedrooms and kitchen showed evidence of a hasty exit of several people. Dirty dishes were piled high in the sink, and bureau drawers were open.

Frank signalled to the others and they came forward. Moments later all were inside the lodge, looking for clues to the vanished occupants.

Joe, who was more interested in where the occupants had gone, went through the kitchen and out to the back yard. At the edge of the woods he discovered a spring which flowed into a small creek. In the muddy earth around it were a number of footprints.

"Hey, come here!" he called. Ahmed, Frank, and Chet joined him. "Let's see where these tracks go."

"And look!" cried Chet, pointing in turn to several bright-red splotches on the ground.

"Looks like blood!" Joe exclaimed.

"Dried blood would be dark," Frank said. "That is brilliant red."

"This is a real clue," said Ahmed. "A user of betel nuts spits a bright-red fluid."

Their hopes raised by these latest discoveries, the searchers dashed into the woods, following the footprints Joe had discovered. When that trail ended, the boys spotted crushed leaves and broken twigs that marked the recent flight of several people. Red splotches made by the betel-nut user were here and there.

The foursome followed the trail to the edge of a rock-filled brook. There it was lost. Frank and Joe knelt at various points along the opposite bank, looking for some sign to indicate where the fleeing group had come out. But they found nothing and concluded that the fugitives had gone far downstream.

Convinced that there was no way of picking up the trail beyond the stream, Frank suggested that they all return to the lodge and try to find some clues to the occupants' identities.

In the rambling log structure each of the quartet took one of the bedrooms. There were visible fingerprints everywhere but not one clear set.

Suddenly Ahmed called out, "In here, boys! Look what I've found."

The others ran to a bedroom which was furnished more luxuriously than the others. Ahmed was holding a dark-brown object the size of a robin's egg. It looked like a salt shaker, was delicately carved, and had a number of coloured bands for decoration. The initials T.N. were engraved on the bottom.

"What is it?" Frank asked, puzzled.

"A sandalwood scent box," Ahmed replied slowly.

"And the initials could stand for Tava Nayyar!" Frank cried.

"This must have been his 'prison'!" Joe said.

Frank nodded, then said, "I guess now we'd better tell the others about Tava."

Completely astounded, Ahmed and Chet listened to the story of the kidnapped Indian and the Hardys' suspicion that he had been held here.

"But where have they taken him?" Chet asked.

"Wherever Tava's been taken," said Frank, "you can be sure the place won't be so easy to find as this one was. His captors will see to that and will make it dangerous for anyone trying to find him."

"Then what's next?" Chet asked.

"I guess we'd better follow up the pigeon angle for further clues," Frank replied as all of them sat down to rest before starting back through the forest. "I haven't seen any signs of cotes around here. I thought for a while that maybe pigeons were kept here, both as food for the goshawk and as carriers for the smugglers. But I guess that the pet goshawk was given other food."

Chet sighed, "Let's go home. I'm hungry." He went into the kitchen, helped himself to a box of biscuits, and passed them around.

Both Frank and Joe felt that the lodge and grounds should be guarded, in case Tava's kidnappers returned. As soon as they reached Chet's home they would phone Mr Hardy's operative, Sam Radley, to take on this job.

Radley and the boys worked closely together. He admired Frank and Joe's sleuthing abilities, and encouraged them in every way he could.

Feeling rested, Ahmed and the boys started back through the forest. Several hundred paces later Frank spied a movement in the bushes and halted his companions.

"Who's there?" Frank called out.

No response. When he repeated his call, a boy about twelve years old stepped into the open.

"It's me, Gene Moran," the youngster said.

Relieved, the three sleuths pushed forward to meet the boy, who lived near the Hardys. Joe asked what he was doing in the woods.

"Looking for tree toads for my Boy Scout merit badge," Gene replied.

Chet grinned. "Find any?"

"Sure, a whole pocketful," the boy said, laughing.

"By the way," Frank put in, "did you see anyone else in these woods today besides us?"

"Yes, a bunch of dark-skinned people. They looked sort of like your friend." Gene bobbed his head at Ahmed.

"Where?"

Gene pointed in a southwesterly direction. "They were in a big hurry. Say, one fellow—about the same age as you, Frank—had a pet bird on his right wrist. And it had a funny cap pulled over its head."

"Were any of the people wearing foreign clothing?" Joe queried.

"No. They all had on American suits."

"Did they have a leader?"

Gene thought for a moment. "Guess you'd call the lightest one the leader. He was tall and cruel-looking. Wore a cap like a ship's captain and a dark-blue coat. Bet he is a captain, because I heard one of the other men ask him, 'Cap, got the stones?'"

Stones! Frank's and Joe's eyes flashed. Elated, they thanked Gene for his information. The boy looked at them curiously. "You working on a case?"

"That's right." Joe winked at Frank. "We're after a couple of toads ourselves. Big ones."

Gene grinned. "Hope you catch 'em."

"And good luck on your merit badge," said Frank.

Once more the Hardys, Chet, and Ahmed headed for the Morton farm.

"One thing I don't understand," said Chet. "Why didn't Tava escape yesterday when he was evidently within sight of us?" Chet asked.

Joe suggested that perhaps the youth was not being held against his will.

"It could be," said Frank, "that he has been given some phony story, believes it, and isn't even trying to get away!"

When they arrived at Chet's house, Frank telephoned Sam Radley. He related all the happenings in the woods and described the location of the hunting lodge. Mr Hardy's operative assured him that he would start guarding the place at once.

"But I doubt that those people will return," he said.

Iola insisted that the Hardys and Ahmed stay for lunch.

"We don't need a second invitation," Joe said with a grin.

When the meal was over, the Hardys drove Ahmed home. They thanked the rug dealer for his help. He bowed politely and replied:

"It is you who are helping my friend Gaphur and my people. I shall be forever grateful to you."

Frank and Joe waved goodbye, and the convertible moved away. As Frank turned into the Hardy driveway, Joe declared, "Boy, am I tired and hot! A shower will feel good!"

"That goes for me, too," Frank admitted. "About the liveliest thing I'm going to do the rest of today is make up a list of pigeon fanciers nearby and try to find out if one of them has lost any carrier pigeons recently."

Before locking the garage, they stopped to talk to the falcon. She was bobbing back and forth on her perch as though in welcome. Joe brushed his fingers along the bird's back between the shoulders and on the feathers of her wings.

"We sure deserted you today," he remarked.

After they had showered and put on clean clothes, Frank and Joe went to their father's study and started to check the classified telephone directory for pet shops.

"The owners ought to know something about pigeon fanciers," Joe declared.

They made a series of telephone calls which netted no information. There were only four listings left when

Frank and Joe heard a noisy car coming down Elm Street.

"Sounds like Chet's jalopy," Joe said, getting up to look out a window. "And it is!" he added.

Usually the stout boy nursed along his prized possession as though it were made of solid gold. But today he was evidently in a hurry. He slammed on the brakes and rushed into the house and up the stairs so fast that he was out of breath for several moments.

"Hey, Chet, somebody chasing you?" Joe quipped.

Without replying, Chet held out his hand in which lay a capsule, similar to the one containing the rubies.

"Where did you get this?" Frank asked quickly.

Chet finally calmed down enough to speak. "I was standing outside the barn when I heard a plane. At the same time I spotted a pigeon overhead. Suddenly the pigeon flew directly towards the craft and crashed into its windshield."

"Wow!" Joe said. "That must have been the end of the poor bird."

"It was," Chet went on. "It plummeted right down into the middle of a field!"

"And you found it?" Frank queried.

Chet nodded. "This capsule was on its leg. Wait till you see what's in it!"

# · 9 ·

## A Harsh Skipper

ALTHOUGH Chet had opened the capsule when he had removed it from the pigeon, he would not reveal the contents to the Hardys. Instead, he waited as Frank removed the top.

Inside was a tightly rolled bit of paper.

Frank smoothed out the note. A message, printed in block letters, read:

CAUGHT L ABOUT TO SQUEAL. HOLDING HERE. NO DELIVERIES UNTIL REPLACEMENT ARRIVES.

Frank slapped Chet on the back. "Good work, pal. This may help to speed up our case."

As Chet beamed with pride, Frank turned to Joe. "I guess we'd better forget those pigeon fanciers for the time being and concentrate on this new clue."

"You bet!"

They examined the paper to see if it held any further clues. Holding it to the light, Frank studied the watermark. It looked like a fouled anchor insignia with several other figures that might be porpoises or sea horses.

"Look at this, fellows," he said. "The next step is to see if we can trace the origin of the paper."

From a list in Mr Hardy's files, they selected the best-known paper manufacturers and called them asking if it belonged to a special customer.

They were told in each case that the company would check and let them know.

"Now all we can do is wait," Frank said.

The next day the boys stayed at home all morning, but no telephone calls came from the paper manufacturers. At lunchtime Joe said, "While we're waiting, let's invesitage that man Gene Moran told us about yesterday—the one who might be a ship's captain."

"Okay. How about trying the Bayport waterfront again? Maybe the owner of that restaurant where we saw Ragu can give us a clue."

The Hardys drove to the docks and headed for the eating place. When they questioned the proprietor about a tall, cruel-looking sea captain, he grinned and shouted to two men who were busily eating steaks at a table in a far corner of the room.

"These boys are looking for a tall, cruel-looking captain, men. Either one of you like to take the job?"

"What's it for?" asked one. Then laughing loudly, he said, "A high school play?"

Chagrined, the Hardys headed for the door. To their amazement they heard the restaurant man remark, "The Hardy boys. Their pop's a big-time detective."

"Hey, Zeke! We'll have to watch our step!"

Raucous laughter followed as the boys left. They visited other spots along the waterfront but saw no likely suspect. Finally they paused near a small fishing craft. A jovial-looking man called down to them from the upper deck:

"Are you the lads who are huntin' for a cruel-lookin' skipper?"

"How'd you hear about it?" asked Joe.

"Joke's all up and down the waterfront," the man told them. "Just the same, if I was lookin' for a fellow of that stripe, I'd check with Captain Flont of the *Daisy K*."

The *Daisy K* again, the Hardys thought excitedly.

"Was Captain Flont's boat out at sea yesterday?" Frank queried.

"No. She was tied to her bollards all day. I can swear to that, since I didn't leave port either."

"Was the captain aboard the *Daisy K?*" Joe asked.

"Not until late in the evening."

The Hardys thanked the man and hurried to the anchorage of the *Daisy K*. As they drew closer, they spotted Captain Flont in the deckhouse. Ragu was lounging on the rear deck.

Frank and Joe halted at the gangway, and with nautical courtesy, Frank called, "Ahoy, the *Daisy K*. May we come aboard?"

Captain Flont leaned out the window and said harshly, "If you've got business with us, come aboard. But make it snappy!"

When the boys stepped onto the deck, Ragu looked up with an insolent stare. They peered at him intently in return, but the mate did not flinch.

As Captain Flont approached the Hardys, Frank decided that the best way to obtain information was through a ruse. Choosing his words carefully, he said, "We're trying to locate a couple of our friends who were going fishing with you yesterday."

"We didn't go fishing yesterday," Captain Flont replied quickly.

"Oh, then maybe you were the captain who was in Smith's woods yesterday," Joe broke in.

Flont scowled. "I wasn't in any woods. Now get off this ship!"

The Hardys held their ground. "How about your man Ragu?" Frank asked. "Was he there?"

At this, Ragu stalked up behind them. "I was with Captain Flont yesterday," he growled. "We were on ship's business."

"Now you have your answers," the skipper shouted. "Get off my ship!"

Frank and Joe did not move quickly enough to suit the captain. His shout had aroused the other two crew members, who came up from below. They gripped the unwanted callers by the elbows and rushed them off the vessel. The boys were thrown forcibly onto the dock.

As the sailors returned to the gangplank, Frank and Joe heard one of them mutter, "It's lucky they didn't show up for the moonlight ride!"

The Hardys brushed themselves off and walked back to their car. As Frank drove off he said wryly, "We found out one thing—those men sure don't want *us* around."

Joe nodded. "It's strange that it takes a captain, a mate, and two crew members to run a fifty-foot fishing cruiser. What do you think that fellow meant about a moonlight ride?"

"I don't know, but we ought to find out if he meant tonight. There'll be a full moon. Let's take the *Sleuth* out and keep an eye on the *Daisy K.*"

At home the boys found a telegram from one of the paper mills. Frank read it and said:

"Joe, did you ever hear of the Mediterranean Steamship Line? The records of this paper company show that the fouled anchor stationery was made for them and is used on all their ships. It was sold through the London office."

Joe said he had never heard of the line, but went to one of his father's bookcases and brought back a book containing ships' registries. He thumbed through it, then stopped at one page.

"Here it is," he announced. "Some of their ships ply between New York and the Middle East. I'll check recent arrivals and departures."

"Good idea."

As Joe scanned the shipping news in the *Bayport Times*, he said, "Here's an item on one—the *Continental*. She arrived in New York early this week. Her normal course would have taken her close to the coast at Bayport. Say, do you think the *Continental* might be the ship that's bringing aliens to the United States?"

"Could be," Frank said. "But it might just be a ship on which one of the gang was travelling."

Determined to track down every possible clue, Frank called the Mediterranean Line's New York office. He explained that the Hardys were detectives, working on a government case, and asked for a list of Indian passengers on recent voyages to New York. The passenger agent assured him that it would be mailed at once, together with any other helpful information the line could give.

"With that co-operation, it sounds as if the company's on the up and up," Frank remarked.

Just as the moon was rising that evening, Frank and Joe headed for the *Sleuth*, which was still moored at the dock they had left it the night of the fire. They paused to note the progress of repairs on their boathouse.

"It'll be at least two weeks before we can take the *Sleuth* back," Frank commented.

"Yes, and the firebug hasn't been caught yet." Joe said as Frank took the wheel.

Soon they were speeding out of Bayport harbour. There were a number of islands near the inlet where they could wait for their quarry. Frank chose one that lay in shadows, cut the motor, and turned off their running lights.

"I feel like one of those falcons 'waiting on' until its prey comes along," Joe said, grinning.

In the moonlight the boys could see boats moving up and down the harbour, but all of them were pleasure craft. Finally, however, Frank whispered:

"There's a boat with the *Daisy K*'s lines."

Both boys positively identified Captain Flont's craft as it chugged past them. They gave it a reasonable lead, then started after it. The chase continued for about five miles, then the *Daisy K* slowed down. Frank cut his engine.

A few minutes later a large motor dory appeared beyond the fishing boat and pulled alongside. A rope ladder clattered over the rail of Flont's ship and two men scrambled down the rungs into the dory.

As the smaller boat pulled away towards the open

sea, the *Daisy K* started up again, turned in a wide arc, and headed back towards Bayport.

"We've *got* to find out where that dory's going!" Joe said.

The *Sleuth* took up the case!

# · 10 ·

## *Hunting a Hawk*

THE Hardys had been following the mysterious dory for some time when the *Sleuth*'s motor began to sputter and the craft lost way.

Joe, seated on the forward deck as lookout, whirled around and asked, "What's the matter?"

"Sounds as if we're out of fuel," Frank replied.

"Impossible," Joe said. "The gauge read full when I checked at the dock."

Frank unscrewed the tank cap and beamed his flashlight inside. "I have news for you, Joe," he said. "It still reads full, but there isn't a drop of fuel in the tank!"

The Hardys examined the gauge and discovered that it was jammed.

"This didn't jam by itself," Frank declared. "Someone tampered with it!"

"Someone from the *Daisy K!*" Joe guessed.

By this time the motor dory was out of sight. In disgust the boys brought out the emergency fuel can and emptied its contents into the tank. Since there was little hope now of locating the dory with their limited fuel supply, the Hardys headed for home. While Frank fixed the gauge, they speculated about where the dory

had come from. Perhaps from a ship waiting at sea?
The boys could see no lights to indicate any vessel,
however, and concluded that the dory might be planning to meet a passing ship later.

"I wonder who those two men were who climbed off
the *Daisy K*," Frank said thoughtfully.

Joe shrugged. "I guess our only hope of solving that
is to keep the *Daisy K*'s crew under close observation,"
he commented. "When we get back to town, let's ask
one of Dad's operatives to watch them."

"Jeff Kane's in town," Frank suggested.

When the boys reached Bayport, Frank telephoned
the detective. Kane readily agreed to take over the
assignment.

Early the next morning, after feeding the falcon, the
boys took turns phoning the pet shops which they had
not had time to call the day before. This time they were
more successful. Two of the owners supplied them with
the names of carrier pigeon fanciers. Some of these were
in Bayport, while the others were a distance away.

With Frank at the wheel of the convertible, the
Hardys started on their quest. The first place was only
a half mile from their home. The pigeon keeper, a
young man about twenty-five, proved to be a squab
breeder who kept a few carrier pigeons as a hobby. He
showed them to Frank and Joe.

"I enter these in cross-country races," he said. "My
birds have brought me several cups and ribbons," he
added, stroking one of the racers fondly.

In reply to a question from Frank, the young man
said he had never taken his birds out on the water and
released them.

"In fact, I don't know anyone around here who would have reason to," he said, "because the contests are always from inland cities to the coast."

The Hardys thanked him for the information and went on their way. Both of the other local men proved to be above suspicion as well.

The next name on their list was Reed Newton, who lived five miles away. When Frank and Joe reached his home, they found him to be a retired carpenter in late middle age, who had flown pigeons as a hobby for many years. He had a large cote and several breeding cages.

"You raise more pigeons than you train and fly, don't you, Mr Newton?" Frank asked.

"Oh, yes," the fancier replied. "I sell them." He smiled boyishly. "I may sound a bit vain, but my pigeons are becoming known all over the world."

"Has anyone purchased a large number of birds from you recently?"

Reed Newton wrinkled his brow for some moments, then replied, "Not recently. But about two years ago I had a big order. A young man from India, named Bhagnav, bought a whole flock of pigeons."

"Bhagnav!" Joe exclaimed, but recovered quickly and added, "That's an unusual name."

"Can you describe this man?" Frank asked.

"Well, as I remember, he was a tall, slender, rather handsome fellow of about twenty-five. One thing I particularly remember was a scar at the base of his chin. It stood out clearly because it was a slightly lighter shade than the rest of his face."

Frank and Joe could hardly believe their good fortune in picking up this clue. Was the Bhagnav who had purchased the pigeons related to the Indian government official who was now using the name of Delhi?

After the Hardys had left Mr Newton, they speculated about the man named Bhagnav who had bought the pigeons.

"It's possible," said Frank, "that he was an impostor who had planned this smuggling racket as far back as two years ago."

"Right. Figuring that if anyone uncovered the plot, the real Bhagnav would be blamed. We must phone Mr Delhi about this as soon as we get home."

The drive to the farm of John Fenwick, the last pigeon fancier on the boys' list, was long. On the way they stopped at a roadside restaurant to have lunch.

When Joe spotted a sign with the name FENWICK at the foot of a lane, he exclaimed:

"What a weird set-up for a pigeon fancier!"

On the lawn inside the cyclone fence that lined the property were several perches. Each of them held a hooded hawk!

"Fenwick must be breeding fighter pigeons!" Frank grinned as he turned into the drive.

A pleasant-looking man in his middle thirties strode briskly from the back yard. He was dressed in rough clothing, had on a tight-fitting cap, and held two coils of nylon rope over his arm.

"We're looking for John Fenwick," Frank announced.

"That's me," the man said with a smile.

"We're interested in your pigeons," Joe said.

Mr Fenwick laughed and remarked, "You're about two years too late for that. As you can see from the perches on the lawn, I've switched my interest to falconry."

"We have a peregrine falcon," Joe replied. "That's the reason we came to talk to you. Our falcon brought down a pigeon and we were trying to find the owner so we could settle accounts."

"Fine attitude, son," Mr Fenwick declared. "Since you're interested in the birds yourself, you might like to come along with me today. I'm going to Cliff Mountain to get a young hawk from an eyrie—that's a nest—I've been observing."

Frank and Joe were thrilled at this idea. Frank suggested that Mr Fenwick put his gear in their car and let them drive him to Cliff Mountain. He accepted, and as they drove along he explained that he was particularly interested in peregrines.

"I spotted one of their nests out on the moutain, and have been watching the tercel and the falcon. The eggs have been hatched now. There are four of them. I'll take only one young hawk out of the eyrie and leave the rest to fly away and raise broods of their own. The parent birds will return next year to nest again."

When he and the boys arrived at Cliff Mountain, Frank parked the car and Mr Fenwick led the way up the trail to the precipice that had given the mountain its name. The going was rugged, but the boys' enthusiasm for hawking and adventure spurred them on.

When they reached the edge of the shaly cliff, Mr Fenwick tied a heavy rope around a sturdy oak which seemed to be growing out of the rocks. The loose end was dropped over the side of the cliff, its entire one hundred and twenty-five feet hanging down.

"Usually," Mr Fenwick explained, "it's a good idea to have a rope that will reach all the way to the bottom of the cliff. Then, if you can't climb back to the top safely, you can at least get to the ground without injury. But this cliff is too high for that. No alternative but to come back up."

Mr Fenwick went over the edge of the cliff. He lowered himself about sixty feet, then called to the boys:

"There are three fledglings. One egg didn't hatch."

The mother hawk was not in sight. But Mr Fenwick wasn't taking any chances and called up again, "Keep your eyes open for the mother. She's likely to resist an invasion of her nest. I don't want any trouble, if I can help it. I've been attacked before and it's no fun."

In a few minutes Mr Fenwick announced that he had one of the young birds in his pack and was coming up. He signalled to be lifted to the rim. As he came over the edge and the rest of the line was pulled up, Mr Fenwick said:

"Funny, I haven't seen any sign of the tercel, either. Usually he'll do the hunting for food for the young. Then the falcon will take the quarry from him in mid-air, pluck it, and feed the fledglings."

"Do you think someone might have shot the tercel and the falcon is getting the food?" Frank asked.

"That's possible," Mr Fenwick replied. "And she will have to do all the work herself until the young ones can fly."

Then the hawk hunter displayed the fledgling. The falcon's tail and wing feathers were short because the bird was so young. Small tufts of down clung to them. The bird's feet were a light greenish grey instead of brilliant orange like the adults'.

Both Frank and Joe noticed how large the feet were. They were already fully grown, even though its feathers were still developing.

The thing that amazed them most was that the young falcon was brownish black instead of blackish blue like their own hawk. Mr Fenwick explained that the young birds never have the same plumage colour and markings as the adults.

"Next spring this bird will begin to moult—that is, drop her old feathers and grow new ones. Those will be adult plumage like your peregrine's."

"Is that true for all hawks?" Joe asked.

"Yes," Mr Fenwick replied as he put the fledgling back in the pack to begin the return journey.

When they reached Mr Fenwick's home, the falconer extended a cordial invitation to return soon.

Back at their own house, they found Sam Radley waiting. He was seated in the garden with Mrs Hardy and Aunt Gertrude. The falcon sat on the perch beside them.

As Radley began his report, the two women stood up and went into the house.

"No one returned to the hunting lodge and I doubt that anyone will, since they'll figure it's being watched. But as I was leaving Smith's woods, I met Mr Morton. He told me that Mr Smith's lawyer informed him that the property was leased for the summer to a dark-skinned man by the name of Sutter. I have a feeling he's one of our Indian boys."

Frank first phoned Chet, who said, "Count me in. I sure would like to go along."

Then Frank called George Simons, who agreed to meet them at the farm in half an hour. Joe got the hawk's equipment, hooded and wristed her, and the boys drove off. When they reached the farm, the helicopter was already settling in an open area behind the barn. The boys headed for it to tell Simons their plan.

Chet, seeing them from the kitchen window, came outside and followed them. As he ambled past a corner of the barn, a masked figure moved up behind him. Chet's arms were pinned behind his back and a hand was clamped over his mouth!

In a low, fierce whisper, the masked man ordered, "Bring that falcon to your barn and leave it there. If you don't, you and the Hardys will be in serious trouble! And don't tell anyone why you're doing it!"

Desperately Chet squirmed and twisted in the grasp of his assailant but could not free himself!

## · 11 ·

## *A Ruse*

THE masked man tightened his grip.

"*Listen, fat boy! Get that hawk if you value your life and the Hardys'!*"

"All right," Chet finally said. "I'll do it."

The masked man pushed Chet along until they were close to a small door in the barn. Then he turned him loose and darted into the darkness of the barn, closing the door behind him.

Chet walked towards the Hardys with trembling legs. As Frank and Joe explained their plans to Simons, Chet interrupted, saying:

"Sounds swell. M-mind if I hold the f-falcon on the trip?"

"But the bird isn't accustomed to you," Frank said. "She wouldn't respond to your commands."

"Well, can't I at least h-hold her until you s-spot the pigeon?" Chet pleaded.

Frank and Joe exchanged puzzled glances. They both sensed something was wrong with Chet, for he was not usually so nervous.

"That wouldn't work too well, either," Frank told him.

Chet cast an anxious glance over his shoulder in the direction of the barn, then stared at the hooded falcon.

She was standing quietly on Joe's gauntlet. He was checking the jesses to make certain that they were firmly fastened to the bird's legs. Then he unsnapped the swivel hook, so that he could release the falcon quickly.

Suddenly Chet dived at Joe and grabbed for the bird! With a startled cry Joe stepped back and the falcon flapped her wings to hold her balance.

Frank clutched the stout boy's arm. "What's wrong with you, Chet? You act as though you're crazy! This bird can be ruined if she's disturbed. You mustn't make a move at her like that! Move gently and slowly or she will bate off the hand."

Finally Chet decided the Hardys must be told about the threat. He glanced again at the barn, then said in a hoarse whisper:

"L-listen, fellows. A masked man stopped me at the barn a couple of minutes ago and ordered me to get the falcon from you. He told me to leave it inside the barn. If I don't, your lives and mine won't be worth a nickel!"

Simons, who had heard Chet's explanation, leaned out of the cockpit in amazement and said:

"Trouble! Can I help?"

Frank and Joe were grim, realizing that the only way out was through a ruse.

"You sure can," Frank told the pilot. "We'll give the hawk to Chet. He can take his time about getting it to the barn. In the meantime, Joe and I will pretend we've gone off with you in the 'copter, but we'll sneak out the other side, double back, and try to nab this guy and anyone who might be with him."

Joe helped Chet put the gauntlet on. Then he switched the falcon to the youth's wrist and handed him the end of the leash. In a loud voice he called "good luck!" as though Chet had asked to borrow the hawk for an afternoon's hunting.

Simons jumped to the ground and the Hardys entered the passenger compartment. Then, while Chet and the pilot stood close together beside the helicopter to cut off any view from underneath the craft, Frank and Joe quickly slipped out the far side and took cover behind some bushes. From there they made their way towards the barn as the 'copter rose and headed towards the woods.

Chet, who had started for the barn, was having trouble with the falcon. She bobbed up and down on his wrist, turned towards the throbbing sound of the rotors on the helicopter, and flew out to the end of the leash several times.

Chet, however, however, managed to get her to the barn. He rolled open the big door and placed the bird inside.

"Pretty rough on the hawk," Frank whispered to Joe. "But I guess Chet is scared plenty, too."

The frightened boy turned and hurried to the house. After he had climbed the rear steps and quickly slammed the kitchen door behind him, the masked man slipped furtively out of the barn with the hawk under one arm.

Instantly the Hardys were upon him, and at a shrill whistle from Joe, Chet dashed back on the double. As Joe took the hawk, Frank pinned the prisoner to the ground and ripped off his mask.

*Ragu!* The first mate from the *Daisy K* stared insolently at the boys.

"Well," said Frank grimly as he let the sailor up but kept hold of him, "suppose you talk."

"You threatened me and the Hardys," Chet growled.

"That was just to make you get the hawk," Ragu answered. He watched Joe sullenly as he took the gauntlet from Chet and wristed the falcon.

"I know someone who will pay me well for a trained bird," Ragu went on.

"You'll have to give a better reason than that," Frank told him. "How did you know we would have the falcon out here?"

"I—I was hiding in your back yard this afternoon and overheard you making plans to bring the hawk here."

"Keep talking," said Joe.

"I've told you all I know," the sailor insisted.

"It will go easier with you if you tell the truth," Frank said. "What do you know about the smuggling and kidnapping rackets around here?"

Ragu winced but remained silent. Joe burst out, "I'm sure you can tell plenty about Captain Flont and the *Daisy K.*"

The sailor's muscles twitched nervously. "Let me go!" he shouted. "I don't know anything."

The boys marched the man to the kitchen porch. Frank and Joe kept a close watch on him while Chet went to phone Chief Collig.

"Tell him," Frank said, "that we have a prisoner for him. He can book Ragu for assault on you today and Joe the other day, and attempts to steal the falcon."

The group waited until they saw the Bayport patrol car turning into the Morton driveway. Then, with Frank and Chet holding the sailor firmly by the arms, they started towards the police car.

Chief Collig and Patrolman Smith climbed out. As they eyed the hawk, Frank explained the circumstances of the capture, and told Smith that Ragu was the thief they had been looking for.

Before Smith or the chief had a chance to comment, Frank suddenly cried out:

"Joe, there's a pigeon! It's winging from the same direction as the other ones we've spotted. Let the hawk loose!"

Hearing this, Ragu began to cry out oaths in his native language. The Hardys were sure he must know that the pigeon was carrying a message or more rubies!

Joe unhooded the falcon. She spotted the pigeon, took off into the air, and climbed towards it.

"Chief, I'm sure Ragu is guilty of a lot more than he's admitting," Joe said.

"It seems that way," the officer said.

"We'll be in to prefer charges against him sometime tonight," Frank said.

"Good enough," Chief Collig agreed.

Smith hustled Ragu into the patrol car and the three rode away.

The boys, shading their eyes, were following the flight of the bird. The peregrine and its prey had moved off over the wooded area and a moment later the pigeon was lost to view.

The Hardys' hearts sank. Had the bird escaped?

# · 12 ·

## Intercepted Ransom

"THE hawk mustn't lose that pigeon!" Joe cried.

As the boys watched tensely, the peregrine poised for a second, then dived like a miniature rocket. Frank, Joe, and Chet ran across the fields, their eyes still following the hawk.

Suddenly, through a rift in the trees, they could see both birds.

"The hawk's got it!" Frank exclaimed a moment later as the two birds dropped into the woods.

"Come on!" Joe shouted, starting to run.

When the boys did not immediately find the spot where the pigeon and the hawk had fallen, they spread out and searched the bushes for some time, but without success.

"Your falcon's got to be here some place," Chet said.

Just then they heard the whirring of the helicopter and hurried to a clearing, where they could spot the aircraft. They saw Simons beckon them to follow him.

The boys nodded and moved along the edge of the woods, guided by their friend in the sky. Presently he turned the craft and flew directly over the trees. Now Simons whirled up, then lowered quickly.

Frank interpreted the manoeuvre. "He's trying to tell us the birds are right around here."

Joe held out his gloved hand and whistled sharply. There was a movement in the brush a few yards ahead of the boys. Then they spotted the peregrine falcon and her quarry.

The younger Hardy moved in slowly and picked up the falcon and the mangled pigeon.

"This time she earned a meal," Joe said, spotting a telltale red container fastened to one of the pigeon's legs.

Frank removed the capsule and opened it. As he shook it gently, two rubies fell out.

"More of the ransom gems!" he declared.

Excitedly the trio ran towards the Morton farm. The helicopter was still hovering overhead when they came out into the clearing. Joe waved their thanks. Then the pilot headed for the airport to keep another appointment.

When Frank and Joe reached their car they said goodbye to Chet and drove home. After putting the falcon in the garage and setting the burglar alarm, the boys went into the house. A message was waiting for them to phone Jeff Kane. He had shadowed the captain and crew members of the *Daisy K*, and had investigated their reputations, but could find nothing suspicious in their activities. He learned that Captain Flont ruled them with an iron hand and they seemed to fear him.

"If anything crooked is going on," Frank said to Joe, "it's well concealed, that's for sure."

Joe put through another call to Rahmud Ghapur, who answered at once. When he told Mr Ghapur that the Hardys had two important pieces of information for Mr Delhi, the importer asked that Joe not reveal them on the phone.

"I'll pass along your message to Mr Delhi," Ghapur promised. "He'll probably want to fly up to Bayport sometime tonight."

"We'll be waiting for him."

The Indian arrived about eight o'clock, and he and the boys went to Mr Hardy's study.

As Mr Delhi settled himself in a chair, Frank unwrapped the two rubies and the ring, and explained how the Hardys had obtained them. Mr Delhi examined them, then finally said:

"I could almost swear that these are some of the ransom rubies. This poses a serious problem."

He looked from one boy to the other and they felt that something had displeased him. "I do not want to seem ungrateful," Delhi said, "but if these are part of the ransom, and are not received by the fiends who are holding Tava, he may come to harm."

Frank and Joe were thunderstruck.

"I'm afraid we didn't realize that," Frank replied. "But we may be close enough to these kidnappers to catch them before they attempt anything drastic."

The Hardys told Delhi about the goshawk and the hunting lodge in the woods and the possible flight of Tava with his captors.

Then Frank showed him the sandalwood scent box that Ahmed had found at the lodge. Tenderly Delhi cupped the box in his hands.

"My friends," he said with emotion, "this box was

given to Tava by his father at a ceremony I myself witnessed. May I keep it until Tava is found?"

"Of course," Frank replied.

Delhi asked, "You have someone watching this hunting lodge at all times?"

The Hardys reassured him on this point. Then they concluded with the story of the man who had purchased carrier pigeons from Mr Newton under the name Bhagnav.

"My real name!" Delhi exclaimed. "But not one of my relatives has ever been in this country."

"We thought he was an impostor," Frank said.

"What does this man look like?" Delhi asked.

"We were told he is tall, slender, handsome—about twenty-five years old. He has a prominent scar on his chin."

As the Indian weighed this information, his brow furrowed. Then he said, "The description sounds vaguely familiar. I shall speak to Rahmud Ghapur about this. Perhaps he will recognize the man. In any case, I'm sure the impostor is an enemy."

Joe changed the subject. "Does the name Ragu mean anything to you?" he asked.

Mr Delhi thought this over, then said, "No. Can you describe him?"

But the description of a swarthy, short, heavy-set man did not help.

Frank said, "Ragu works here on a fishing boat called the *Daisy K*. Right now, though, he is in jail. We promised to go there tonight and prefer charges. Will you come with us and see if you know Ragu?"

"I shall be glad to go," he said. "But I suggest, in

case we should be followed, that we try to throw off any pursuers."

Driving to police headquarters, Frank took every precaution to be sure that no one trailed them.

They learned, when they arrived, that Chief Collig was at home for a late dinner, but would return in a few minutes. The sergeant on duty assisted them in filing charges against Ragu. When the boys explained the reason for Mr Delhi's presence, he took the callers to the cell where Ragu was being held. On the way the sergeant said that the prisoner had been informed of his rights, had refused a lawyer, and had admitted nothing.

When Ragu saw the Hardys he stared at them balefully. He was about to say something, but suddenly his glance rested upon Mr Delhi. A look of awe and fright spread over his face and he staggered backward.

"Mr Bhagnav!" he cried.

Mr Delhi gazed at the prisoner, then said to the boys, "I do not know this man, but apparently he recognizes me from newspaper photographs or public functions."

Following up the advantage of the prisoner's discomfiture, Frank asked him whether he was ready to talk. Ragu did not answer.

Just then Collig arrived. After the police chief was introduced to Mr Bhagnav, the boys turned the ransom rubies over to the officer for safe-keeping.

When Ragu saw the gems he gasped but made no comment. The police chief ordered the jailer to unlock the cell door. They all went inside. Forming an arc about the prisoner, they began to question him.

Ragu remained defiant and unco-operative, but the Hardys felt he was almost frightened enough to make a full confession.

Chief Collig asked him to explain the reasons for the attempted thefts of the falcon and the threats to Chet and the Hardys, then added, "And tell us all you know about the operations of the *Daisy K.*"

Again the mention of Flont's ship had a visible effect on the first mate. Eyes wide, he stared at Chief Collig for a long moment. Then, abruptly, his shoulders sagged and he looked at the floor.

All further questions about Captain Flont or the *Daisy K* aroused no response.

Finally Mr Delhi asked Ragu probing questions about the smuggling of aliens from India into the United States, and more particularly about the kidnapping of Tava Nayyar.

Ragu looked up, eyes flashing, and uttered one brief phrase in his native language. Mr Delhi nodded, then turned to the others.

"Ragu wishes to talk to me alone," he said.

The boys and the police chief left the cell and waited at the end of the corridor.

Ten minutes later Mr Delhi called, "It is settled."

When the others returned to the cell, Mr Delhi said, "Ragu has convinced me that he knows little. But he is willing to tell us that much."

# ·13·

## Attack in the Night

CHIEF Collig called in a police stenographer to take down Ragu's statement. As Mr Delhi nodded to Ragu, the *Daisy K*'s first mate began his story.

"First, I know nothing about any smuggling of my countrymen into the United States. I—I did join the group that was planning a kidnapping. But you must believe me—I did not know until too late who the victim was going to be."

"But you know that kidnapping is a criminal act!" the police chief said severely. "Just what was your part in it?"

"A very small one," Ragu insisted. "I ran errands. Once a man that came to our ship gave me a letter. He told me to deliver it to the Bayport Hotel."

"What was the name of the man who came to the *Daisy K?*" Chief Collig broke in. "And what did he look like?"

"I do not know his name," Ragu said emphatically. "He was short, and had brown hair. The man at the hotel was called Mr Louis."

Frank and Joe exchanged knowing glances. Mr Louis probably was the "L" mentioned in the note Chet had found attached to the downed carrier pigeon.

"How did you expect to get paid for the job, if you didn't know the name of the man who hired you?" Frank asked Ragu.

"He promised to pay me with a ruby ring. It was left in a secret place," Ragu replied. "The only time I wore it was when I came to your house to take the falcon. After that, I was afraid and sold the ring. You know about that."

Frank confirmed this, then Joe asked, "Who hired you to steal our falcon?"

"I don't know that, either," Ragu replied. "I got a phone call at my boarding house. An unfamiliar voice said if I could steal the falcon, I would receive another ruby in payment."

"What part do the pigeons play in this racket?" Frank asked the prisoner.

"They carry messages, but I don't know where they go. And I don't know what the notes say."

Chief Collig turned to Mr Delhi and asked him if he had any further questions. He had none.

Frank spoke up. "Ragu, tell us about Captain Flont and his activities. He's more than a fishing boat captain, isn't he?"

Ragu bit his lip. He looked at Mr Delhi, then settled back on his bed.

"I don't know much about Captain Flont," he said. "I've only worked for him a short time."

No amount of persuasion could elicit any further information from the first mate. It was evident, as Kane had learned, that the crew of the *Daisy K* was afraid of their captain.

"I guess we've found out all we can tonight," said Chief Collig when the visitors left the cell.

On the way back to the Hardy home, Mr Delhi was silent, but just before they turned into the driveway, he asked, "How will you boys proceed now? When Captain Flont hears of Ragu's arrest he may make trouble."

"We'll have to take that chance," Joe replied. Then he snapped his fingers. "Frank, how about you and I disguising ourselves and joining a fishing party on the *Daisy K* for a day?"

"To do some detecting?"

"Right."

Joe decided to take the falcon indoors for the night. Ragu's arrest might mean trouble, as Mr Delhi had said. At any rate, the smugglers would be doubly determined to get the hawk.

Mr Delhi followed the boys through the kitchen door and into the living-room where Mrs Hardy and Aunt Gertrude were reading.

While Joe took the hawk to the boys' room, Frank introduced their visitor to the women. Mrs Hardy said, "Mr Delhi, it's much too late for you to start back for Washington. We should like to have you spend the night with us."

"I'm grateful for your thoughtfulness," the man declared. "Thank you. I will accept."

By eleven o'clock the boys and their guest found it impossible to keep from yawning, despite the interesting conversation about the differences in customs between India and the United States. Mrs Hardy suggested that they retire to bed.

"I shall wait for my husband," she said. "He'll be back about midnight."

The boys were pleased to hear that their father was coming and would have liked to talk to him as soon as he arrived. But they were very sleepy, and also they had to rise early for the fishing trip.

They kissed their mother and aunt goodnight, then escorted their visitor to the guest room. The boys provided him with pyjamas, gown, and slippers.

The three said goodnight and within half an hour Frank and Joe were sound asleep. But some time later Frank awoke with a start. He glanced at the luminous dial of their alarm clock. It was almost two o'clock.

Joe awoke a moment later and called from his bed, "What's the matter? Is it time to get up?"

"No, it's only two o'clock. But do you hear someone moving around downstairs?" Frank asked.

"No."

"An intruder couldn't be in the house," Frank mused. "Mother and Dad would have set the burglar alarm before going to bed."

Joe got up and tiptoed across to the door. He opened it and listened for several seconds.

"Not a sound," he reported.

"That's good," Frank replied, stretching and relaxing again. "Now let's go back to sleep."

Joe closed the bedroom door, then walked over to the side window and opened it wider. As he did, he saw something move on the lawn.

"*Psst*—Frank! Come here quick!" His brother was at his side in a second.

"What's up?" Frank asked.

"Someone's down at the edge of the lawn," Joe said. "Over by the hedge."

"Let's throw the spotlights on him," Frank suggested.

The Hardy home had a bright spotlight under the eaves on each side of the house—a precaution occasioned by too many prowlers interested in the detectives' work. The lights were controlled from switches in the upper and lower halls.

"Okay," Joe agreed.

Frank dashed from the room to snap on the first-floor switch. Instantly the front lawn was flooded with light. Outlined against the hedge was a hooded figure with one arm raised above his head. In that position, he froze for a moment, evidently blinded by the glare.

Frank had rejoined his brother at the window. "Looks as if he was going to throw something!" he whispered.

Before Joe could make a reply, the hooded figure hurled a large, round object straight towards them.

Both boys jumped back. The man missed his mark and the object crashed into a side window of the living-room directly below them.

Instantly the burglar alarm clanged, then was drowned out in a deafening roar! The spotlights went out and the Hardy home shuddered on its foundation!

Frank and Joe were flung violently to the floor!

# ·14·

## *Doubting a Friend*

DAZED by the explosion, Joe Hardy picked himself up in the pitch-dark bedroom and groped about.

"Frank, you okay?" he asked.

There was no reply. Fearful, Joe felt around the floor for his brother but could not find him. Bumping into the bureau which had been shifted out of place by the impact of the blast, Joe opened the top drawer and found a flashlight.

Its beam revealed Frank's unconscious form between the beds.

"His head must have hit the bedpost," Joe decided as he knelt beside his brother.

Frank stirred and opened his eyes.

"Our house was bombed," Joe told him. "Are you all right?"

"Y-yes," Frank replied weakly. With Joe's assistance he stood up.

They opened the door to the hall. A wave of acrid smoke rolled towards them. Through it, they could see their father with a flashlight coming from his room. "I just called the fire department," he said.

"Is everybody all right?" Joe called.

"Your mother is. I don't know about the others."

Behind him, they could now see Mrs Hardy. A moment later Aunt Gertrude's door flew open. She began to sneeze and cough.

A police siren shrilled and minutes later two fire trucks arrived. Mr Delhi appeared and everyone went downstairs to survey the damage.

There was no sign of a blaze, but part of one wall in the living-room gaped open and the room was a shambles. The boys told the fire chief what they had seen and he checked the house thoroughly for safety.

Since there was no blaze, the trucks left, and the fire chief followed after taking down all the details. By now a crowd of neighbours had gathered and all offered their sympathy and the accommodations of their homes.

"Thank you," Mr Hardy said to each, "but since the damage is so extensive, I think we'd better move to the Bayport Hotel. It looks as though it will be quite a while before our home will be habitable."

When the neighbours had dispersed, Mr Delhi addressed the family. "I'm no doubt responsible for what has happened," he began. "Apparently my identity is known to my enemies, regardless of our precautions last evening. I feel I cannot subject you to further damage and wish to relieve you from the case at once. You have already suffered enough in trying to help me and my country."

Mr Hardy looked first at his sons, then at their guest. "Mr Delhi," he replied, "we will see this thing through with you. We can't bow out of a case, especially one that's so near a solution!"

"And I don't believe," Joe put in, "that the bomb was thrown into our house because of you, Mr Delhi. I saw the fellow aim it directly at Frank and me as we were looking out of our bedroom window."

Frank suggested that he and Joe stay at the house to guard it from looters while the others took rooms in the hotel.

Mr Hardy grinned. "You'll be needed for sleuthing elsewhere. I'll put Jeff Kane here."

After everyone had dressed, and the Hardys had packed a few clothes, they gathered outdoors.

Chief Collig was at the scene now, having been summoned from his home. He had ordered searchlights to be set up and had stationed men round the Hardy house.

The chief reported that the hard ground had yielded no footprints and that his men had found no clue to the person who had thrown the bomb. However, in the living-room they had found parts of the bomb. The remnants had been collected for the police laboratory to examine.

Satisfied that the situation was under control, Mr Hardy and the others went to the hotel. It was dawn when they were finally settled in their suite.

By that time all desire for sleep had vanished for everyone except Mr Hardy. The detective said he had worked late the previous two nights and needed a few hours' rest before tackling several important problems. Not the least of these was the attempt on the lives of himself, his family, and their visitor.

After he had gone to bed, his sons talked with Mr Delhi about the mystery bombing incident. One thing was certain. The hooded man certainly was not Ragu, since he was still in the Bayport jail.

When the hotel coffee shop opened at six o'clock, the three went in to have breakfast. Half-way through the meal, Mr Delhi excused himself to make a phone call. He returned, much disturbed.

"Forgive me," he began nervously. "I have just learned that I must fly to New York at once. Should you want to reach me, call Mr Ghapur. He will know of my whereabouts. And please make my apologies to your family."

"Let us drive you to the airport," Frank offered.

The Indian said quickly, "Thank you, no. You have been most kind to me. I shall take a taxi. Goodbye."

With that, he strode out the door of the coffee shop. The boys followed him to the hotel entrance. As he climbed into a brown-and-white taxi, they waved farewell.

"What do you suppose upset him so?" Joe said as they returned to the coffee shop.

"He sure acted strange," Frank agreed.

When the boys finished eating, Frank suggested that they drive to their house to search for a clue to the person who had thrown the bomb. Perhaps the police had overlooked something.

It was shortly after seven o'clock when they turned into Elm Street. The story of the explosion had spread all over Bayport, and scores of people had gathered outside the police barricades. One of the officers on guard approached the Hardys and said:

"There's a young fellow over there by the barrier who says you boys would want to see him."

Turning, Frank saw Chet waving at them excitedly and urging a police officer to let him through. Chet hurried to the Hardys, his eyes popping as he studied the damage to their home.

"Gosh, fellows, I'm sorry this happened," he said. "Is everybody all right?" At a nod from Joe, he went on, "How'd Miss Peregrine take it?"

Frank's and Joe's mouths dropped open. In the excitement they had completely forgotten the prize bird!

They dashed up the porch steps two at a time and ran pell-mell up the stairway. There was only a slim chance that the falcon would still be alive. The door to their room stood ajar and one glance inside revealed the bird's perch lying in a corner.

*But the falcon was gone!*

After the initial shock was over, Joe said, "She couldn't have flown away, Frank. Her leash was fastened to the ring at the base of the perch stand. It would have to be twisted or broken to free her. Someone took her!"

Frank nodded. "With all the police and bystanders around here, someone must have seen who it was. Let's ask them."

By this time Chet had caught up to the boys and was saying, "I asked you about Miss Peregrine and you acted as if you'd been shot." When the Hardys explained, Chet said, "Maybe the house was bombed so those smugglers could get your bird."

"That might have been part of the plan," Frank conceded, but he was convinced there was much more behind it than that.

The three boys headed back downstairs. They checked with Jeff Kane and the policemen guarding the house, but none of them had seen the hawk, nor had any one of them entered the house since the second shift of men had come on duty at seven o'clock.

"Let's ask some of the people in the crowd if they saw anyone carry off the bird," Joe suggested.

The boys separated and began questioning the bystanders. Finally a woman neighbour approached Frank and said:

"I saw your falcon. About six-thirty this morning, when I was walking my dog, a man in a taxi came up and spoke to the policeman on duty at the front door. He went upstairs with him and they came down a few minutes later with the falcon. The man drove off in the taxi with it."

"Which policeman was it?" Frank asked.

"I don't see him around just now, so I guess he's gone off duty."

"Can you tell us the kind of taxicab the man who took the bird came in?" the boy asked.

"It was a brown-and-white one belonging to the Bayport Taxi Company, I think."

Frank thanked the woman for her information and relayed it to Joe and Chet. Then they got into Chet's jalopy and drove to police headquarters.

They traced the officer and learned that he was at his home. Frank reached him by phone. The man said that the stranger had told him the Hardys wanted him to get the falcon, and he knew just which room the bird was in.

"No, he didn't give his name," the policeman said.

"He was dark-skinned and seemed to be in an awful hurry."

The Hardys were astonished. Dark-skinned man. Brown-and-white taxi. Taking the falcon during the time they were finishing breakfast. It all seemed to piece together—unfortunately. Could Mr Delhi have taken the hawk? Had his phone call to New York prompted this? He certainly had been very much disturbed.

As Frank started to ask the policeman for a fuller description of the thief, the connection was broken. He was about to call the officer again when Joe suggested that they get it from the taxi driver, as well as information on his passenger's destination.

The boys headed for the office of the Bayport Taxi Company, a modern outfit with a fleet of radio-equipped taxis. Convinced of the importance of the Hardys' request, the dispatcher willingly contacted his various drivers.

The one they sought appeared at the office about ten minutes later. Frank explained about the missing falcon and their desire to apprehend the thief. The taxi driver's eyebrows went up.

"I remember the guy all right," he said. "I picked him up in front of the Bayport Hotel at six-thirty this morning.

"After the man collected the falcon from a house on Elm Street," the driver went on, "he ordered me to drive him down to a wharf on the waterfront. I was curious about why he wanted to go there at that early hour. The guy said that someone was going to pick him up in a boat."

"Could you give us a description of this man?" Frank asked excitedly.

The taxi driver furrowed his brow for a moment, then replied, "Well, he was young and good-looking and dark-skinned, like one of them Indian rug makers down at Ahmed's place. And he had a scar on his chin. I mean a scar that really stood out—looked lighter than the rest of his skin."

Frank exchanged glances with Joe. They both heaved a sigh of relief. The falcon thief was not Mr Delhi after all! It must have been the Indian who had bought pigeons from Mr Newton two years before—the impostor who had used Mr Delhi's real name of Bhagnav!

The driver noticed the boys' amazed expressions and asked, "Does that description help you?"

"It sure does," Frank said. "Thanks a lot. Now will you drive us to the wharf where you took this passenger? He may still be there."

The three boys climbed into the taxi. Moments later the driver let them out on one of the wharves and promised to wait. They hurried down the length of the dock, but the dark-skinned man was not in sight. No one they questioned on the small boats at the dock had seen anyone carrying a hooded hawk.

"Looks like a dead end," Joe declared in disappointment.

Frank agreed, but Chet tried to cheer them up, saying:

"Listen, fellows, you're due for a real break. Wait and see!"

The Hardys smiled at Chet's words of encouragement and Frank said, "We'd better go to the hotel and brief Dad on this latest development. He ought to be awake by now."

The taxi driver took them back to Chet's jalopy, and Chet in turn drove the Hardys to pick up their car at their home. Then Joe and Frank headed for the hotel.

Mr and Mrs Hardy and Aunt Gertrude listened in amazement to the boys' story. When it was finished, their father leaned forward intently in his chair and reached for the telephone.

"I think we have our man," he said as he lifted the phone and waited for the operator. "The light-coloured scar on the chin is the giveaway. The description fits an Indian by the name of Nanab. He is Rahmud Ghapur's personal servant."

# ·15·

## A Nautical Clue

TEN minutes later Mr Hardy placed the phone in its cradle and turned to his sons. "Well, boys, the pieces are beginning to fall into place. Ghapur says that his servant Nanab quit his job very suddenly the day before yesterday and has disappeared."

"Wow!" cried Joe, adding, "Why didn't Mr Delhi identify him from our description? He must have seen Nanab at Ghapur's home."

"Nanab apparently kept out of his sight on purpose," Mr Hardy replied. "He may have feared he might be recognized. The only relative in India that Nanab wrote to while he was in Washington was a brother whose name is Bangalore. So far as Ghapur knows, Bangalore is still in India."

Frank said excitedly, "No, he isn't, Dad. You were away when we learned that Bangalore was the name of an Indian who jumped ship on the *Continental* while the vessel was docked in New York. That happened two years ago."

As he finished speaking, Radley came in, holding an envelope. He said he had been to the house and was amazed to learn of the bombing and was relieved to see that the Hardys were safe. He handed over the envelope, saying:

"I got this in the mail. When I opened it, I knew you boys would want to see it." He held up a photograph. "It's a picture of that fellow Bangalore. The steamship line sent it."

"Bangalore!" Mr Hardy exclaimed. "He's Nanab's brother all right. Looks just like him, except that he has no chin scar. Good work, fellows. It certainly seems as if Banglore is one of the ringleaders in this smuggling and kidnapping business. Nanab has probably been working with him part of the time and is now spending full time on the rackets."

"Dad, do you think he could have been the one who intercepted Mr Ghapur's letter to us?" Joe asked.

"No doubt of it. Unfortunately, Ghapur trusted Nanab implicitly and always confided in him. Nanab destroyed the letter, but why do you suppose he let the falcon get through to you?"

"That does seem strange," Frank agreed. "Anyway, we know he learned all the plans and developments in the case by eavesdropping on Ghapur and Mr Delhi."

"There's one bright side to this whole thing," said his father. "You boys must be much nearer a solution than you think, or I doubt that Nanab would have left his job at Ghapur's. He probably knew the net was closing around him."

Frank and Joe, certain that part of the solution was to be found on the *Daisy K*, determined to carry through with their fishing plan. Since it was too late for the trip scheduled for that day, Frank phoned the booking office for Bayport's charter boats to find out if the *Daisy K* was going out the following morning. He was told there would be a trip.

Mr Hardy said he would make the necessary arrangements for repairs to their home, then he must return to Washington on urgent business.

The phone rang and Joe answered. The caller was Chet, who said, "How about you fellows coming out here to live until your house is repaired? The folks say it's fine with them."

"Sounds good, Chet. Wait till I ask Dad and Mother."

The family agreed that the boys would find it far more enjoyable staying with Chet than living in the hotel, so Joe promptly accepted. Then, at their parents' request, Frank and Joe worked nearly all day at the bombed house storing away pictures, lamps, and other small furnishings, and moving clothes to the hotel. It was late afternoon when they arrived at the Morton farm.

"Before it gets dark today," Frank proposed, "let's go over to the deserted hunting lodge and see if Radley has anything new to report."

After the Hardys had deposited their luggage in the Mortons' guest room, the three boys set off for the lodge. Radley said there was no evidence that anyone had returned to the lodge and felt further watch of it was useless. He remarked that he would like to tackle the mystery from another angle.

"I've had a lot of time to think out here," he said, "and I came up with an idea. Maybe these smugglers don't send their pigeons from a boat at all. They may be working from an island."

"An island! Could be!" Joe replied enthusiastically. "When we get back to Chet's, let's take a look at a map to see what's northeast of here."

"And," said Radley, "why not let me take a plane and see if I can spot something out there."

"Okay," Frank agreed. "Joe and I are planning a fishing trip on the *Daisy K* early tomorrow morning. Among the three of us we may uncover something either on the sea or from the air."

Radley and the boys walked back to the Morton home where they pored over a map.

"Hm!" said Radley. "Islands galore northeast of here. The closest ones are Shoals, Pine Haven, and Venus, but that doesn't mean they're the ones. The smugglers may be taking no chances and using an island quite a distance away. I'll look over as many as I can from the plane, though."

That evening, after Radley had left, Frank and Joe got their fishing gear ready and tried out their disguises. Their father, an expert in that field, had taught his sons many of the techniques, and they kept all the prerequisites on hand. Hair dye, cheek pads and sideburns changed the countenance of the boys. Dyed eyebrows and a small beard for Frank completed their outfits.

Iola and Chet laughed when they saw Frank and Joe. "You look rather cute as a redhead," Iola told Joe, who had tinted his hair a reddish brown.

Before dawn the next morning, the Hardys set out through a drizzle for the wharf where the *Daisy K* was tied up. Four other sports fishermen already were there, waiting to go aboard. Frank and Joe kept a wary eye on Captain Flont, who did not give any indication that he recognized them. In fact, he paid little attention to his passengers.

The day's fishing went along with reasonable success. All of the *Daisy K*'s passengers managed to net a fair-sized catch of tuna and mackerel. Under various pretexts during the trip, both Frank and Joe wandered around the ship, but the falcon was not aboard. The boys had also made a point of trying to pick up conversations between the captain, his crew of two, and any passengers that might be in league with him, but learned nothing.

In the late afternoon, when the *Daisy K* started back for Bayport, Frank and Joe were seated inside the deckhouse as close as they dared to Captain Flont, who was at the wheel.

Suddenly, above the throbbing of the motors, they heard him say to one of his crew, "It beats me where Ragu went."

"I'm afraid he's in trouble," the man replied.

"It's going to be hard to take care of things at windward without him," the captain said, then shifted the conversation to another subject.

The Hardys got up and walked out to the stern of the boat. When they were alone, Frank whispered, "Did you have the same thought I did? That it was strange for a nautical man to say '*at* windward'?"

"I sure did," Joe replied. "If he had meant a direction, the captain would have said 'to windward'."

"*Right. Windward must be a place!*"

The *Daisy K* reached port just before dinner. As Frank and Joe walked along the waterfront with their day's catch of fish, they questioned sailors from other boats about Windward. No one had heard of it. Finally they headed for the hotel, deciding to have supper with the family before going to Chet's.

The young detectives, still in their disguises, turned their mackerel over to a startled bellhop and asked him to deliver them to the hotel chef. Then, learning from the desk clerk that Radley was waiting for them, they went at once to their room. The detective grinned at their disguise. While they were removing the make-up, he said:

"I flew all over the coast for about five hours, but I couldn't spot any activity that would indicate smuggling operations. I did see several deserted sections along the shores of some of the islands that would make good hideaways. Guess we'll have to investigate all of them."

"Ever hear of a place called Windward?" Frank inquired.

"No," Radley replied. "What about it?"

Frank repeated the conversation that he and Joe had overheard on the *Daisy K*. Radley nodded thoughtfully, then remarked:

"Let's go down to the Skippers Club. I know some of the seafaring men who stay there. Maybe one of them will be able to help us out."

After dinner with Mrs Hardy and Aunt Gertrude, the three went to the old building near the water-front, where many of the old-timers played cribbage, chess, and billiards in between spinning sea yarns about the good old days. Sam Radley was hailed by several of the captains. He quizzed some of them about Windward. The name meant nothing to the first half dozen he spoke to, but finally a grizzled man of the sea looked up from a game of solitaire.

"Sure, I know the place. Windward was our old-

timers' name for the windside o' Venus Island," he
said. "The lee side's green an' right pretty. Folks live
there. But Windward's rocky an' barren. Broken up by
stretches o' pine woods here an' there."

Radley thanked the old salt and the three left the
club. Outside, Frank remarked, "That sounds like an
ideal spot for smuggling operations!"

"Let's check on it right away," Joe proposed.
"Maybe we can round up some of the fellows to help
us."

"As a matter of fact," said Frank, "Biff Hooper and
Tony Prito were planning to go out to Chet's tonight.
Let's put all three of them to work on the case."

Radley was eager to go along. They stopped at a
drugstore with a couple of phone booths. Joe called
Chet to explain their plan to take the *Sleuth* out to
Venus Island for a reconnoitring expedition.

"Sounds like a dangerous job," said Chet, "but I'll
come and bring Tony and Biff. I expect them here any
minute."

"Meet us at our boathouse," Joe said. "And make
it as soon as you can."

Frank, meanwhile, had called the hotel from the
other booth to inform his mother of their plans. Next
he put in a call to Chief Collig to tell him of their new
lead and to ask if Ragu had had any visitors.

"No, and it doesn't look as if he's going to have any,
either," Collig replied. "He refuses to see anyone, even
an attorney! And he's made no attempt to raise the bail
money. Frank, that fellow is plenty scared of somebody!"

"My guess," Frank said, "is that it's Captain
Flont!" He said goodbye and hung up. Then he drove

to the boathouse with Radley and Joe. A quick look around showed that repairs were well under way and that the *Sleuth* could be returned to its berth before long.

Presently Chet's jalopy rattled up the street and pulled to a stop. Lanky, good-natured Biff Hooper swung his long legs over the side, and Tony Prito followed. Chet squeezed himself out of the driver's seat and joined the group. They all walked to the *Sleuth* and went aboard. Frank took them across Barmet Bay, out through the inlet, and into the swells of the ocean beyond. It was just past midnight when Frank outlined the Hardys' plans.

"When we get to Windward, we'll cruise around and find out what we can," he said. "If we don't learn anything, then Joe and Radley and I will go ashore to investigate."

Tony, who owned a boat of his own, would be left in charge of the *Sleuth*.

Two hours later the forbidding rocky slopes of Windward were etched in black against the moonlit sky. The motor of the *Sleuth* was throttled down and a search of the waters began. They found no boats anchored and none were visible in any of the many inlets among the rocks.

At three-fifteen Radley and the Hardys decided to go ashore. They donned their swimming trunks and slid over the side without a sound.

Treading water beside the boat, Frank said in a low voice to the boys in the *Sleuth*, "You fellows cruise back and forth, keeping your eyes open for anything that

might be stirring. We'll swim out again just at daybreak
and meet you."

Chet, Tony, and Biff wished them luck, then started
off. They cruised around for some time without seeing
another boat or sighting anything suspicious. Finally,
as the first streak of dawn appeared in the east, Tony
moved the *Sleuth* to the spot where they had left the
swimmers.

After what seemed like a long wait, Tony said,
"Fellows, I'm worried. Frank, Joe, and Radley are
overdue."

The three in the boat could not see anyone along the
shore or in the water that lay between the *Sleuth* and
the rocky beach. Tony moved the boat a little closer
and got out the binoculars. There was not a sign of
anyone on the rocks.

"I'll—I'll bet the smugglers got them!" Chet said
nervously. "What'll we do now?"

"Give them fifteen minutes," Tony advised, "and
then storm that island!"

# · 16 ·

## *Forbidding Island*

FRANK, Joe, and Radley had swum easily to the narrow, rocky beach on the windward side of Venus Island. The water was chilly, but their brisk strokes had kept them from feeling the cold.

A jagged cliff that rose abruptly about twenty feet back from the shore was clearly outlined in the moonlight. Before emerging from the surf, the swimmers had made sure that no guard was on duty on the beach. They gazed around the desolate shore but could see no evidence of anyone having been there recently.

Frank mused, "Footprints or signs of beaching a boat could have been washed out by the waves."

They climbed a trail that wound up the face of the cliff and turned their attention to a wood of windswept pines, which came to within a hundred feet of the cliff's edge. The three sleuths peered ahead.

Frank spied a light among the trees "I wonder if that light is coming from a house. I thought this area of the island was uninhabited."

"Let's find out," Joe urged.

They found a path among the trees and followed it until Joe held up his hand in warning.

"I think I hear voices!"

He and the others paused to listen. Not far from them several men were talking, part of the time in English, part in a foreign tongue the trio had come to recognize as a dialect of India.

The Hardys and Radley crouched behind a clump of bushes, trying to fathom the conversation. The voices carried clearly on the night air, and the listeners were provoked at not being able to translate the foreign words. Presently the watchers were electrified upon hearing:

"Cap's late. I hope he didn't run into trouble. A motorboat was cruising around here a while ago. Better go take a look."

There was no verbal response to the command, but a blond man began to walk towards the watchers' hiding place. After he had gone a short distance, they followed silently, hoping the *Sleuth* was now far enough from the island not to be noticed.

"If that fellow has a boat hidden nearby and decides to set out for the *Sleuth*," Joe whispered tensely, "we'll jump him!"

"Right!" Frank replied.

The man paused briefly at the edge of the cliff, then gingerly made his way down the trail to the beach. Radley and the Hardys crept to the brink and peered below. They did not see the *Sleuth*, but a surprise awaited them. A large motor dory, its engine off, was being propelled by oars towards the beach. As they watched, it glided to a stop just beyond the rocky shore. The watchers could see two men in the dory, but the figures were not close enough to be identified.

"Say, Frank," Joe whispered, "that sure looks like

the same dory that met the *Daisy K* on the night of the moonlight sail."

The blond man on the stony shore gave a low whistle. Almost instantly Radley and the boys became aware of tramping feet and a few moments later a dozen dark-skinned men, carrying trousers and shoes, came down the trail, passing just a few feet from the three in hiding. They were followed by a light-haired man. When they reached the beach, he pointed to the dory and immediately the men splashed through the waves towards it.

"Smuggled Indians!" Joe said in a hoarse whisper. "Let's try to stop them!"

Radley gripped Joe's arm. "That would only mean our capture. They outnumber us almost six to one!"

Joe calmed down as the aliens climbed aboard and the oars dipped into the surf. The dory was some distance from shore before its engine was started.

As the two islanders came up the path and moved off among the trees, Frank whispered to Joe:

"Those men obviously are guards here," he said. "Do you suppose they're the two we watched being transferred from the *Daisy K* to the dory?"

"Come on!" Joe urged. "Let's collar them!"

He sprang into action. Without a backward glance to see if the others were following, he set off on a run among the trees after the blond men.

Frank and Radley tried to stop Joe. They hurried after him, but within a few seconds, they heard sounds of a struggle.

"Joe ran into trouble," Frank said in a tense whisper. Minutes later they spotted the two guards prodding

Joe towards a group of small buildings set deep in a grove and almost hidden from view. One of the men kicked open the door of the nearest building and Joe was thrust into a lighted room.

"We've got to free him!" Frank said. "This gang will stop at nothing!"

Radley restrained him. "Hold it, Frank," he said sternly. "Look what happened to Joe. The thing to do is to outwit these men."

"You're right," Frank replied. "Tell you what," he said, noticing that the sky was lightening. "Tony, Chet, and Biff will be waiting offshore. Suppose you swim out to the *Sleuth* and try to follow the dory with the aliens in it. See where it goes. Then bring help back here. In the meantime, I'll try to think up a way to free Joe and maybe pick up more evidence."

His companion nodded and left at once. Frank waited until he heard the familiar roar of the *Sleuth*'s engine as it took off at high speed, before he started his own work. Moving swiftly and cautiously, he edged in close to the building where Joe was imprisoned.

Through a closed window he saw that his brother had been bound to a chair. A coil of rope and a knife lay on a nearby table.

As he watched helplessly, the two middle-aged guards began cuffing Joe's face. Quickly Frank moved to another window which was open. He heard one of the guards say:

"This kid just won't talk. Put the gag back in."

"I don't buy his story," the other man said as he replaced the gag, "that he came to Windward to swim all by himself in the middle of the night. He's a spy. We ought to check the area to see if there are any pals of his lurking around."

Frank ducked round the corner just in time. For an instant later, the door of the cabin burst open and the two men rushed out. Frank, desperately realizing he must conceal himself, dodged behind a tree.

One of the guards announced he would circle the cabin. Frank held his breath, as the man passed without noticing him. The other zig-zagged through the woods between the house and the beach, looking for trespassers, but shortly returned to report there was no evidence of other intruders.

The two men re-entered the house. Frank returned to the open window. There was no possible way he could move in on Joe's captors without being seen.

A few minutes later one of the guards said, "Keep an eye on our prisoner while I go to eat breakfast. I'll relieve you later, after I've talked to Cap. I've got a hunch about this kid!"

Frank wondered what he meant by the last statement, then smiled triumphantly. This was his chance to free Joe!

He ducked into hiding again as the guard came out, closed the door behind him, and walked towards one of the other buildings. Frank waited until the man had entered the cabin, which stood about a hundred yards away, then quietly moved to the door of Joe's prison and slowly turned the knob. The door was unlocked!

Picking up a piece of shale from the path, Frank threw it at a windowpane. When the piece of rock crashed through, Joe's guard whirled away from the boy's side and dashed to the window. At the same time,

Frank flattened himself against the door, his hand on the knob. As the guard gingerly leaned out of the shattered window, Frank eased open the door and entered the room, his bare feet making no sound.

With lightning speed Frank whipped the gag from Joe's mouth with one hand, and with the other grabbed a knife from the table and slashed at the rope which bound Joe's hands.

This was barely accomplished when the man at the window pulled his head in. Before he could turn, Frank gripped him round the throat, stuffed the gag in his mouth, and caught one of his arms in a judo hold. Then he threw him to the floor. Joe quickly bound the guard with the rope that had seconds before secured him.

The prisoner glared at the Hardys as they consulted in low tones. "I sure messed this deal up," Joe remarked ruefully. "Thanks for turning the tables."

Frank grinned understandingly. "I'll keep a lookout in this room while you investigate the rest of the cabin," he said. "If that other guard heard the glass breaking, he'll come to see what happened."

Joe picked up a flashlight from the table in order to explore the dark rooms beyond. Frank posted himself at the door. In a few seconds Joe was back at his brother's side.

"There are two more rooms in this building," Joe reported. "One's locked and—what do you know?—in the other there are five carrier pigeons in cages!"

Frank was excited at this news. "That clinches it. We've come to the right place. Let's go see if we can find out if Cap is who I think he is."

The boys checked the bonds on their prisoner, then

rolled him under one of the bunks which lined two walls, and left the cabin. As they approached the building which the other guard had entered, Frank pointed out a high radio aerial that rose from the roof. "They have a powerful set," he said.

Both boys peered cautiously in a window, and noted that it must be the building where the guards and the aliens ate their meals. At one end was an old-fashioned cooking stove. Two long dining tables, capable of seating a large number of people, stood at the other side of the big room.

Seated at a smaller table which stood against the far wall was the guard. In front of him was a short-wave sending-and-receiving radio. Over it, he was sending the startling message:

"We've captured a spy. From your description, I think he's one of those Hardy boys!"

Frank and Joe gulped. The news was out! But no more must be sent!

Joe sprang through the doorway and threw himself at the man, knocking him away from the instrument and clipping him soundly on the jaw. The man sprawled on the floor, unconscious.

With the mike switch released, the transmitter was cut off. Frank, who had followed his brother into the room, instantly turned on the receiver. The cold, hard voice of Captain Flont was saying:

"We're being followed! I'm going to open fire!"

Terror in their eyes, Frank's and Joe's hearts sank.

"The *Sleuth!*" both boys thought. "It must be the *Sleuth* that Captain Flont has spotted!"

## · 17 ·

## *An Escaped Prisoner*

A FEELING of hopelessness swept over Frank and Joe. There was no way to warn their friends that Captain Flont intended to fire on them!

Frank paced up and down the cabin, clenching his fists. Then, suddenly, he thought of a way in which Captain Flont might be tricked.

Grabbing a paper napkin from one of the dining tables, Frank wrapped it round the mouthpiece of the short-wave microphone. Perhaps the napkin would muffle his voice enough to prevent its being recognized. He pressed the mike switch.

"Flont! Don't shoot! Orders from the boss!"

Frank clicked on the receiver but there was no answer. He kept repeating "Come in, Flont." Still no reply. As Joe looked on tensely, Frank continued this call intermittently for ten minutes. Finally, receiving no response from the captain, he gave up.

"Maybe Flont had turned off his set before I started sending the order," Frank said, worried. "Or he may have recognized my voice."

"You tried the only thing possible," Joe said. "Besides, even though there wasn't any answer, Flont might have heard it and been fooled. All we can do is hope."

Joe suggested that he hurry across to the other side of the island and contact the local police. "In the meantime, you stand by the radio, just in case Flont should call in again."

"Okay," Frank agreed. "But let's tie this fellow up first."

They bound the captive's ankles and arms, and put a gag in his mouth. Joe found a pair of shoes and a sweater, put them on, and started off.

He located a rocky trail and followed it a couple of miles, until he came out of the woods. Finally, nearly an hour after leaving the smugglers' cabin, Joe spotted a farmhouse and dashed up to it.

Fortunately the residents were awake. They listened with some scepticism to the boy's story. But they permitted Joe to use their phone and offered to drive him to the Chief of Police in Venus Village.

But Joe could not get through to either Chief Collig or his mother at the Bayport Hotel, due to the inadequate service between the island and Bayport. After several attempts, however, he finally contacted the Coast Guard. The young detective was told that men would be sent out at once to apprehend Captain Flont and learn what had happened to the *Sleuth*.

On the drive to town the farmer remarked, "This is the first time I remember anything happening around here which needed the police. Chief Barton's appointment was kind of an honorary one."

When the farmer stopped at the police chief's home in Venus Village, Joe thanked him for the lift, then rang the bell.

Chief Barton was a man past middle age, with a paunch and a good-natured smile.

"Well, what brings you around here so early in the morning, stranger?" the man asked.

"I'm Joe Hardy from Bayport. My brother and I have located the hideout of a ring of smugglers here on Venus Island. We've got two of them tied up. We'd like you to come and make the arrests."

"Smugglers on Venus Island!" The chief roared with laughter. "Who you trying to kid, son?"

"It's true," Joe insisted, trying not to show annoyance. "The Coast Guard and the immigration authorities have been trying to track them down for months. The State Department's interested, too!"

"How does the State Department figure in this?" the officer asked curiously.

"These smugglers are also kidnappers," Joe said. "They're holding a young Indian captive."

The man finally seemed to realize the seriousness of the situation and said, "Well, no one can say that Chief Barton doesn't tend to business. I'll phone my deputy and we'll be right with you. Just sit down in the parlour."

It seemed an eternity to Joe while Barton made the contact with his deputy and dressed. But at last the chief brought in a tall, lanky man whom he introduced as Al Richards. The deputy studied Joe for a moment, then commented:

"So you're one of the Hardy boys, eh? I've heard about you fellows down around Bayport. What's this wild-goose chase we're going on?"

"Smugglers!" Joe said tersely. "And let's get going before it's too late."

They drove part of the way back to the smugglers' hideout in a jeep. They stopped about a mile from the cabins, and Joe led the men the rest of the way on foot. A fork in the path brought them to the first cabin.

Frank, who had found shoes and a shirt, heard them coming and went to meet the group. He said he certainly was glad to see the police, and reported that no radio messages had been received.

"One of the smugglers is in here," he told the men as they paused at the cabin door.

"Well," drawled Deputy Richards, "we're ready for him. Let's see what a smuggler looks like."

They opened the door and Joe walked across to the bunk. He knelt down to pull out the trussed-up man.

*The prisoner was not there!*

"He's gone!" Joe cried.

"Gone!" echoed Frank. "But how?"

Deputy Richards remarked laconically, "Told you this would be a wild-goose chase!"

The chief shook his head slowly and shrugged, eyeing the Hardys dubiously. Frank and Joe were staring at each other, blaming themselves for the prisoner's getaway. Apparently they had not tied him securely enough.

But perhaps he had not had time to go far, the boys thought. In fact, he might still be in the building! They dashed into the adjoining room. The escaped man was not there and only three of the pigeons were left in the cages.

Frank tried the door to the next room—the one Joe had reported locked. It was unlocked now.

As the door swung open a wholly unexpected scene met their eyes. Joe cried out, "Here he is!" and Frank yelled, "Stop!"

The police chief and his deputy rushed in. At an open window stood the man who had been the Hardys' prisoner. He was releasing two carrier pigeons.

Joe, noticing there were capsules on the birds' legs, leaped forward to stop their flight. But he was too late!

"Where are those messages going?" he demanded, but the man made no reply.

Frank spotted a large perch in a corner. On it rested a hooded hawk. Certain that the falcon was their own, he picked up a heavy leather gauntlet from a window sill. Quickly donning the glove, Frank took the bird on his wrist. As he removed the hood, Frank spoke softly to her. The hawk recognized him instantly and uttered a joyful *keer, keer*.

Frank turned to the police officers and said, "Here is support for our story. This is a prize hunting hawk, and it was stolen from our home in Bayport."

"Arrest this man!" Joe said. "He's in cahoots with the thief and he's one of the smugglers."

Chief Barton made no move to take the man into custody. Instead, he stared at the smuggler. "Why, John Cullen, what's going on?" he asked.

Frank was puzzled by the chief's friendliness, but he did not take time to ask questions. He was afraid that the pigeons might be carrying messages which would alert the men holding Tava Nayyar. If so, harm might come to the youth. Frank hurried outside with the falcon and unhooded her.

Looking up, he saw that the carrier pigeons were circling above the cabin, picking up their directional beam preparatory to making a beeline flight to their destination.

Frank turned the falcon loose. To his dismay she responded sluggishly. Her reactions were considerably slowed down as a result of being imprisoned for so long. There was nothing the impatient young detective could do to hasten matters. He must wait until she regained her keenness.

At that moment Chief Barton and Deputy Richards came out of the cabin with John Cullen and Joe. In an angry tone the Chief of Police said to the Hardys:

"If your whole story's as phony as this part of it, I'm afraid we can't help you."

"What do you mean?" Joe demanded.

"This so-called smuggler, Mr Cullen, is one of the leading citizens on the island, though he has only lived here a couple of years. He's a pigeon fancier and has been racing birds for a year or more. His cote's on the mainland."

The Hardys were not impressed. Turning to Cullen, Joe asked suspiciously:

"How do you account for our stolen falcon being in your cabin?"

"My assistant got furiously angry about the whole deal, I'm afraid," the man replied suavely.

"What deal?" Joe probed.

"He knew that a number of my best pigeons had

been killed by a hunting hawk. Someone told him that your falcon was responsible."

Frank's and Joe's minds were racing. Suddenly a thought came to them. *Nanab!* He had doubtless brought the falcon to the island!

"Go on!" Frank said icily to Cullen.

"My assistant brought the bird here, so that I could use it as evidence in my damage suit against you," the man concluded triumphantly.

It was obvious that both Chief Barton and Deputy Richards believed the story and were about to reproach the boys when Joe challenged Cullen with:

"That sounds smooth enough. Now try to explain why the other man we captured was talking by short-wave to a boat with smuggled aliens on it."

"You're crazy," Cullen retorted. "Chief Barton, these boys are the ones who ought to be arrested!"

All this time Frank had not taken his eyes off the falcon. She had finally roused from her lethargy and was now winging after the two pigeons. The hawk was still some distance from the birds, who were lining out for the mainland. Completely confident of the falcon's skill, Frank remarked:

"Chief Barton, maybe our hunting hawk will prove to you that Mr Cullen is not merely racing pigeons. *She* may prove he is aiding smugglers and kidnappers!"

All eyes turned towards the three birds in the morning sky.

# · 18 ·

## The Falcon's Victory

THE falcon was only a tiny speck in the sky. The pigeons were out over the water but well below the climbing hawk. Frank turned to Joe and said:

"I guess this is what those old-time falconers called a 'ringing flight.' I'm going to the beach to watch it." The others followed him.

At the height of her pitch, the falcon plunged towards the pigeons in a long, angling stoop. Faster and faster she dropped—until the onlookers saw only a blur of moving wings. At a speed approaching a hundred and eighty miles an hour the hawk struck one of the pigeons. It plummeted into the water.

The peregrine mounted from her stoop and gave chase to the remaining pigeon.

Frank shouted, "Joe, take this and watch Cullen!" He thrust the hawk's hood into Joe's hand, kicked off his shoes, and ran into the surf. He set off at a strong, fast crawl towards the floating pigeon and soon reached it.

As Frank swam towards the beach with it, he glanced up. The second pigeon had reversed its course and was heading towards the brushy cover of the island. With awe and admiration he and Joe watched their falcon overtake her prey in a tail chase and bind to it in mid-air. In a long glide Miss Peregrine came to rest with her quarry in her talons.

"Good girl!" Joe cried. He ran forward and picked up the pigeon.

At that moment Frank came out of the surf and joined Joe. John Cullen cried angrily, "Leave those birds alone! They're my property!" With a vicious lunge he grabbed for both of them.

To the boys' dismay Chief Barton said, "I guess he's right, fellows. Let him have the birds."

Frank and Joe were nonplussed. "I'll give them to you, Chief, but not to this man," Frank said firmly.

Frank quickly flipped the capsule off the leg of the pigeon he was holding, while Joe removed the one on the other bird. Cullen tried to snatch the capsules, screaming in a hysterical voice that this was thievery and against the law. He demanded that the policemen do something.

But the chief and his deputy were stunned by the swift-moving events. Before the men could collect their wits, the Hardys had twisted open the tops of the capsules.

*Two rubies dropped into Frank's hand!*

Joe's capsule contained a tightly-folded note, which he opened and read aloud:

" '*Twelve a's gone. Spies here. We're leaving island. Advise you move at once.*' "

Chief Barton stared in amazement. Turning to Cullen, he demanded, "What does this mean?"

But Cullen was already fleeing pell-mell over the rocks.

"I guess that proves he's guilty!" Joe exclaimed. "Twelve a's must mean those aliens who left here in the dory!"

Stuffing the note into his pocket, he dashed after Cullen, with the police at his heels. The chase was soon over. As the fugitive attempted to get away in a motorboat hidden in a cove, he was caught and marched back.

"I guess you're not innocent after all," said Chief Barton. "But you sure had me fooled."

Cullen looked with hatred at the Hardys. "You idiots!" he snarled. "I'll get you for this!"

Frank suggested to the officers that they pick up the other smuggler at once. Silently he and Joe hoped the man had not been able to loosen his bonds and send a radio message!

Joe hooded the falcon and led the way to the second cabin. They found the man on the floor, still bound and gagged. Chief Barton stared at him, then exclaimed in amazement:

"Arthur Daly! You're mixed up with the smugglers, too!" He turned to the boys and remarked, "Mr Daly owns one of the most successful lobster businesses in this area."

The Hardys did not comment, but Frank said, "I suggest you handcuff these men."

At a gesture from Barton, Deputy Richards took care of this detail. Then the chief advised his prisoners of their rights. Both sullenly declared they did not want a lawyer.

"How about telling us the truth now about this whole thing!" Barton said. "We'll find it out anyhow."

The men refused to talk, but the Hardys explained what they knew of the illicit entries of the Indians, the kidnapping of Tava Nayyar, and the ransom demanded in rubies.

"The pigeons carried the stones and notes from here to their home cote," said Joe. "And that's the next place we'll have to locate."

Barton shook his head in amazement. "And we had no idea that something like this was going on at Windward!"

His deputy nodded. "You two have done quite a job!"

"We'll take these men to jail and notify the Federal authorities," Barton said. He suggested that they all proceed to town at once. Carrying the falcon and the three remaining pigeons, the group headed for the jeep.

Barton promised to station men at Windward to arrest any smugglers who might show up.

Back at Venus Village, the once respected islanders were put in cells, then Barton dispatched special deputies to the Windward area. Next, he talked by phone to the immigration authorities. Ten minutes later, a broad smile on his face, he leaned back in his chair and said:

"Things are moving along fine. Federal men will be out soon to take over."

"Good," said Joe. "And now may I phone the Coast Guard? I want to find out what happened to the friends who came out here with us."

"Go ahead," the chief replied.

At the first words of Lieutenant Commander Wilson,

who answered, Joe looked relieved. He put his hand over the mouthpiece and said to Frank, "They caught Flont and his two crewmen as well as those twelve smuggled aliens! They're at the Coast Guard station now."

As Joe listened intently to the lieutenant commander, he sobered. When he hung up the phone, he reported that there was no news of their friends. Flont would not say whether he had fired on them before his capture. A Coast Guard helicopter was out now searching for the *Sleuth*.

The Hardys were worried. Frank asked, "Chief, could someone take us back to the mainland right away?"

"Sure thing," Barton agreed. "I'll run you to Bayport myself in my own motorboat. And, say, will you fellows take these pigeons? I don't know what to do with 'em and you might find the birds useful."

"Okay. We will," said Frank.

Barton kept his boat in good shape, and a little over an hour later, the chief, Frank and Joe, the hooded hawk and the three pigeons were speeding across Barmet Bay towards Bayport.

Joe, who had been scanning the water through binoculars, suddenly called, "There's the *Sleuth* now, Frank!"

About a quarter of a mile ahead was the Hardys' boat. Barton sounded his siren and minutes later he drew alongside the *Sleuth*.

"You all right?" Frank and Joe asked.

Upon being assured that Chet, Tony, Biff, and

Radley were unharmed, Frank introduced the police chief.

Chet, his eyes bulging, exclaimed, "You got the falcon back! And are those the smugglers' pigeons?"

"They sure are," Barton replied. "And we got the ringleaders behind bars, too!"

Frank and Joe let the last statement go unchallenged, even though they knew the hardest part of the case—catching the real ringleaders—still faced them. They told their friends that Captain Flont had been captured, then asked what had happened to the group in the *Sleuth*.

"We g-got fired on," Chet answered promptly. "The captain missed, thank goodness, and he didn't try again. I don't know why."

"Because Frank short-waved him not to," Joe said, and explained about the radio message. "Then what happened?"

Tony, Chet, and Biff tried to tell the story at the same time. Quickly Radley summarized the situation.

"We picked up the trail of the *Daisy K* shortly after I swam back to the *Sleuth*. Flont had already taken aboard the smuggled Indians from the dory. He had a long-range rifle and we were his target! I think Flont fired the first shot to scare us, because I don't see how he could have missed!

"Before he could follow it up with another, Frank's message must have reached him. Anyway, he stopped firing and started off, full speed ahead. When we followed, he kept the rifle trained on us. We finally gave up the chase, deciding to make a wide sweep round him, then race to shore and send the Coast Guard out for the *Daisy K.*"

Radley went on to say that as they headed for a cove, the *Sleuth* ran out of fuel. "And to make matters worse," he continued with a wry smile, "the emergency fuel can was empty."

The operative said that another boat had finally come by. As it was transferring fuel, the Coast Guard helicopter flew over, hovered above them, and dropped a note instructing them to proceed to Bayport.

When Frank and Joe finished comparing notes with their friends on the night's adventures, the Hardys climbed into their own boat, taking the birds with them. The police chief promised to keep them informed of developments on the island.

As soon as they reached Bayport, Radley and the Hardys headed for the Coast Guard station. There Lieutenant Commander Wilson was questioning the prisoners, who had been properly advised of their rights. He had been in touch with Washington, and was impressed with the importance of the capture. He looked up as Frank, Joe, and Radley entered and motioned them towards empty chairs alongside his desk.

Captain Flont glared at the Hardys as he was asked to repeat his statement.

"I've told you a dozen times I'm innocent," he declared. "I didn't know those Indians were aliens. Someone radioed to me that a party of picknickers had been stranded on Venus Island. They offered to pay me my usual fishing fee to bring them back to Bayport."

Radley asked, "Why did you fire on the *Sleuth?*"

Flont was ready with an answer. "You were following us, and it made my passengers nervous. I just fired in the air to scare you."

Frank walked over to the group of aliens and asked if any of them spoke English. One young man came forward.

Before he could say anything, Flont's face turned purple with anger and he shouted, "You men keep your mouths shut!"

The Indian looked frightened, turned, and talked with the other aliens for some time. Then he faced Frank with determination. "We pay these men lot or money for bring us to this country. Now bad trouble. We want to go home!"

Frank said to the lieutenant commander, "I guess you've got your evidence."

"One more question," said Joe, looking at the young Indian. "While you were with these men who were trying to smuggle you in, did you ever hear anything about the kidnapping of Tava Nayyar?"

The spokesman shook his head. "Know nothing. What bad men do this?"

Joe did not answer the question. The Coast Guard officer thanked the Hardys and Sam Radley for their help, then the three departed. The operative decided to return to Windward. He would wait for the Federal authorities and give them all available information on the case.

The boys went to the Bayport Hotel and immediately got in touch with their father in Washington. He was delighted with the turn the case had taken, and promised to fly home at once. He would ask Mr Delhi, who had arrived from New York the day before, to accompany him. Working together, the detective said, they ought to be able to locate Tava and wind up the case.

When the call was completed, Frank said, "Joe, I have a hunch we can find the mainland hideout by the time Dad and Mr Delhi get here."

"How?"

Frank indicated the three cages with the pigeons in them. "We'll turn these birds loose from three different parts of the surrounding countryside and keep an eye on them with our glasses. If we map their lines of flight, they'll serve as bases for a triangulation fix."

"That's a swell idea," Joe agreed, "but first let's have lunch. I'm starved."

Immediately after a hearty meal, the boys began their work. Joe found a piece of paper, similar to those on which the other messages had been written, and printed:

SIT TIGHT. EVERYTHING OKAY THIS END.

He folded the message and inserted it in one of the capsules they had collected.

Meanwhile, Frank had hurried to see their jeweller friend. Mr Bickford supplied him with four imitation rubies that would lull the suspicions of the kidnappers until the showdown.

When Frank returned, he and Joe went to the roof of the hotel. From there they released the first pigeon with the message capsule. The boys watched the bird circle, then they lined up its course with a compass and marked the exact direction.

They divided the rubies between the two remaining

pigeons. Joe took one bird five miles north of Bayport while Frank went five miles south with the other. When the boys returned to the hotel they compared notes and marked the chart again. Both grinned in satisfaction as they looked at the spot where the three lines crossed.

"I guess we've pinpointed the hideout," said Frank. "It's at the top of Lion Mountain."

The almost inaccessible spot was about twenty-five miles from Bayport, and it was reputed that mountain lions once had inhabited it. A few years ago the boys had climbed to the top and knew that it was a rugged hike.

"Frank," Joe said, "I think you and I should investigate Lion Mountain at once."

"You mean not wait for Dad?"

"We can't wait, Frank. If Bangalore and Nanab learn that Flont has been captured, and realize their whole plot is falling apart, I'm afraid they'll take revenge on Tava!"

"You mean kill him?"

"Yes."

Frank nodded. "We'll go at once."

# ·19·

## Confessions

THE boys told their mother of the proposed plan and gave her the pinpointed map for Mr Hardy. She said she would agree to their going only on one condition. They were to do nothing more than try to get word to Tava and help him to escape.

"Leave the capture of those smugglers and kidnappers to your father and the police," she said.

Frank and Joe promised they would. As they were about to depart, a telephone call came from Radley, who reported that the two men who ran the dory had been captured while docking it at Daly's lobster pound.

"Well, that settles everything at this end," the operative said. "I'll be back shortly."

The boys told him their plan, and he wished them luck. When they arrived at the near side of Lion Mountain, Frank parked the convertible where it would not be spotted and they started off on foot.

"I wonder how near the top the hideout is," Frank remarked. "Think we'd better circle the mountain to see if we can pick up a clue?"

"Yes. But I'll bet it's near the summit," said Joe.

"On the other hand," Frank said, "they might be nearer the bottom so that they could get away in a hurry if necessary."

The boys had nearly completed the circle before they found a clue. It was an indistinct trail and led upwards.

Frank and Joe proceeded cautiously, constantly on the lookout for any traps. Half a mile up the trail, Frank spotted a suspicious-looking pile of leaves and twigs in the path. Picking up a long stick, he gently poked at the leaves and uncovered a bear trap.

"Wow!" Joe said softly as Frank threw a stone at it, springing the trap. "Did the smugglers or some trapper set that?"

Frank thought that probably the smugglers had. Farther on, they came across an uprooted tree cleverly braced into position, with its roots and a taut rope stretched across the trail, covered with earth and leaves. But it was ready to fall on anyone who might happen to trip over the rope.

About a half mile from the top in an open section, the boys came to a barbed-wire fence. It was about eight feet high and the upper strands were tilted outwards, making it almost impossible to scale.

"Look!" whispered Joe from the shelter of the trees. "That fence is electrified!"

"It probably has a charge heavy enough to knock a fellow out," Frank remarked. "I'll bet it sets off an alarm, too."

"What a way to be stymied," said Joe.

Frank looked through the fence, his eyes probing the trees beyond. No one was in sight.

"What do you say we pole-vault over, Joe? Eight feet isn't too high."

"We'll do it," Joe said with determination. "About

a hundred yards back I saw some saplings that had blown down. We can use them."

He located two stout saplings which suited their purpose. One he tossed over the fence to use when coming back. Meanwhile, Frank had dug a heel hole just short of the fence and braced it with flat stones.

"I'll go first," said Joe.

"Be careful," Frank warned. "Don't hit that fence!"

Joe ran forward lightly, hit the heel hole with a slight thud, and whipped up and over the fence. Frank grabbed the pole to keep it from striking the barrier.

Frank's jump was a bit trickier than Joe's, because he had to thrust back on the pole to keep it from hitting the fence and sounding the alarm.

The boys knew the hardest part of their job lay ahead. Through the scrubby bushes and trees they could see several crudely-constructed huts. Near one of them stood a handsome, pensive-looking youth about eighteen years old. He was holding a hooded goshawk. From the colour of his skin and his characteristic features the Hardys were sure he was an Indian.

*The boy must be Tava!*

Some distance from the youth were several dark-skinned men. They were no doubt some of the smuggled Indians.

In the shelter of the trees, the Hardys crawled towards Tava. When they were close enough to talk to him without revealing themselves to the others, Frank called in a whisper:

"Tava!"

As the young man turned and stared, Frank smiled and went on quickly, "We are Frank and Joe Hardy,

American friends sent here by your cousin Bhagnav."

The youth moved slowly towards the boys and asked in a low voice, "Why does Bhagnav send you here?"

"To rescue you from your kidnappers."

"But I was not kidnapped," Tava explained. "Evil men are after me, and my friends are protecting me."

"That's not true," Frank insisted. "Your father has already paid a fabulous ransom in rubies for your return, but these people continue to hold you and demand more payment."

Tava still did not seem to be convinced. Finally Frank said:

"Your cousin and your friend Rahmud Ghapur are very much worried. Mr Bhagnav has engaged my father and brother and me to search for you. Mr Ghapur told us of the time when he saved you in the cheetah hunt. He's afraid that you're in much greater danger now."

The boy's eyes widened in surprise. He whispered the name Ghapur several times. Then he replied:

"If Rahmud Ghapur and my cousin sent you, then I will go with you."

"Act as if you were just strolling around and follow us," Frank directed.

The Hardys crawled away. The Indian followed slowly, laughing and talking to the goshawk all the while. When the three were well out of sight of the buildings, and close to the fence, Joe said:

"I'm afraid you'll have to leave the goshawk here for now. When your abductors learn of your disappearance, they'll start a search. We may become separated. If this happens, take our car and meet us at the Bayport Hotel. My mother and aunt are staying there. Ask for Mrs Hardy." He added detailed directions about the location of their hidden car and directions for reaching the hotel.

Tava regretfully fastened his goshawk's leash to a tree, picked up the pole, and gracefully vaulted the fence. He moved off quickly into the shadows of the trees beyond. Joe, pole in hand, was getting set to make his jump when Frank heard someone running.

"Jump, Joe!" Frank whispered tensely. The next second, a lariat slapped over his shoulders and he was pulled back.

As he hit the ground, Frank caught a glimpse of his brother halfway up in his leap. But suddenly Joe was snatched violently in mid-air. Frank, his heart sinking, knew Joe had been lassoed, too.

A half-dozen fiery-eyed men gripped both boys roughly and dragged them towards one of the buildings. They were thrust through the doorway into a well-furnished room, and confronted by two young Indians who resembled each other strongly. One, however, had a scar on his chin.

*Bangalore and Nanab!*

"The Hardy boys!" Nanab gloated. "A fine catch indeed."

"What were you trying to accomplish here?" Bangalore demanded.

Joe tried to act casual as he replied, "We came to get details of your smuggling and kidnapping plot. But I don't suppose we'll find that out now."

Nanab smiled and said, "Why not? We're proud of what we've done. We've fooled your authorities for a long time. Except for you two young snoops, everything has run smoothly. But since you are our prisoners, we can tell you the full story, then arrange a convenient accident for you."

Bangalore nodded agreement and Nanab began his revelation. "Captain Flont and his crew used the *Daisy K* to smuggle aliens into Bayport."

So Ragu had been lying all the time!

"Captain Flont," Bangalore went on, "is a clever man and will not betray us."

Despite the gravity of the situation, the Hardys could hardly keep from smiling. It was plain that the two ringleaders were not aware of any of the arrests that had been made. Frank's message sent by the pigeon must have arrived. Now, if the boys could only keep the men talking long enough, their father and the police would have time to get there.

"We started making plans two years ago when my brother Bangalore came to America," Nanab went on. "We spread word to dissatisfied citizens of our country that legal entry into the United States was impossible. However, by paying us a large fee they could be brought in surreptitiously and protected by us."

"How could you protect them?" Frank asked.

"We got them jobs and arranged for their social activities," Nanab explained.

"The kidnapping was my idea," Bangalore declared. "Both rackets were worked with Windward as the relay station. The property was bought cheap by our American friends John Cullen and Arthur Daly. They fed and housed the aliens who came in on a special American-Far East freighter, the *Red Delta*. It made an unscheduled stop outside a port in India to pick up the men, and another a few miles from Windward to discharge them onto a dory."

"And who is the Mr L who was going to squeal?" Frank asked.

Bangalore and Nanab bristled at this. Then Nanab remarked, "Mr Louis is a friend of Captain Flont's. He owns the dory."

"How did you get the ransom to this country?" Frank asked. "Not by the *Red Delta*, too?"

"Oh, no," Nanab answered. "The ransom rubies were picked up in India, flown by private plane to Europe, and brought to America on an ocean liner which passed in the vicinity of Windward. To avoid customs, small pouches containing the stone were thrown off into Louis's dory by a ship's officer who is one of our group.

"Unfortunately, Louis kept too many of the second shipment for himself. When we exposed him, he threatened to squeal. That is why we are holding him a prisoner here."

"You leased Mr Smith's hunting lodge under the name of Sutter," Frank accused Bangalore.

Bangalore nodded. "I wanted to impress young Nayyar and make him comfortable. When you boys discovered the place, we left it, telling him that this was to avoid the evil men who were after him. He readily agreed to the move."

"You were staying at the lodge, too?" Joe asked.

"Oh, yes," Bangalore leered. "I was the one who knocked out your fat friend. One of the guards did the same to you," he said, looking at Frank. "When you found out too much, Nanab quit his job in Washington and came up here."

"And you, Nanab, destroyed the letter Mr Ghapur sent us, but why did you let the falcon be shipped to us?" Frank queried.

Nanab smiled with self-satisfaction. "I was in charge of sending it. I could have destroyed the bird, too, but Ghapur would have realized I was responsible if you never received it. So I let it go through, then commissioned Ragu to steal it. He failed! He is a fool!"

"You also threw the bomb into our house and stole the falcon," said Joe. "But who set our boathouse on fire and jammed the *Sleuth*'s feul gauge?"

"I did," Bangalore admitted. "And now that you know the whole story, we will carry out our original plan."

He clapped his hands and several men stepped into the room. In their hands were sturdy rawhide whips!

"You're going to flog us first?" Frank shouted.

An evil smirk on his face, Bangalore said, "We usually plan a quick death with a sleeping potion for our enemies. But because you boys have caused us a great deal of trouble, Nanab and I have decided we will not make it so painless. Before you are put to sleep, we will use these whips and watch you squirm!"

"You're a bunch of sadists!" Joe cried out in protest.

"You won't get away with this!" Frank added.

Bangalore raised his hand, looked at the boys with a sinister smile, and said, "Flog them!"

# · 20 ·

## A Touch-and-Go Triumph

FRANK and Joe were seized by four guards, while two others raised their whips. But the boys did not flinch.

Instead, Frank leaned towards Joe. "Here we go again!" he whispered.

A knowing smile crossed Joe's face. Frank's statement was their secret signal for action. Before the whips could descend, the Hardys, using a jujitsu twist, flung their would-be floggers to the floor and tore the whips from the men's hands. The guards shrank back as the boys raised the whips.

Bangalore's jaw dropped. "How did you do that?" he asked, amazed, then added, "I like your courage. My men are skilled in wrestling, but you took them by surprise. It will entertain me to have you demonstrate your skill. Perhaps it can save you a flogging—or maybe even your lives."

Frank and Joe knew that Indians are great lovers of the sport of wrestling. If they could prolong a match, their father might arrive in time to rescue them.

"We accept," Frank said. "But let's not decide our fate on a single fall. That's not sporting. We'll make it two out of three."

Bangalore laughed raucously. "You are prisoners, yet you make the terms!"

Nanab spoke up. "Let our men punish them in the manner they suggest," he said. "We'll teach them that Indians are the greatest wrestlers."

"Two out of three falls it is!" Bangalore conceded. "We will go outside," he said, leading the way.

As Frank and Joe laid aside the whips, the smugglers selected two lithe, smooth-muscled guards. In a crouched position they moved forward quickly, hands outstretched. But Frank and Joe were ready. Playing for time, they moved carefully, darting in, and then leaping back in an effort to catch their adversaries off balance.

Joe was first to find an opening. Seizing his opponent's left wrist, he spun him round, and pulling with all his strength, sent the man flying over his shoulder. The guard landed on his back, groaning as Joe leaped on him and applied a pinning hold that in a moment gave Joe his first fall.

Frank's foe cast his eyes on his defeated partner for a fraction of a second. With the speed of a stooping falcon, Frank charged, catching his adversary in a leg trip. The man hit the ground hard but jumped up quickly. Before he recovered, Frank caught him in a headlock that sent both sprawling in the dirt. There was a flurry of dust as the two fought savagely for the advantage.

Suddenly the guard's powerful legs closed about Frank's stomach in a crushing scissors grip. Frank tried in vain to break the tightening hold. As the guard pressed Frank's shoulders nearer and nearer the ground, it appeared that the boy would lose his first fall.

Then the guard shifted his hold slightly to make the pin. Frank, in spite of his weakened condition, saw his advantage and using all his strength he twisted free. Before his surprised opponent could recover, he spun round and seized the guard in a powerful cradle hold and drove him into the ground for a fall.

"Ready for the second fall?" Frank asked, breathing deeply.

The beaten man looked towards Bangalore and jabbered imploringly. The ringleader scowled and replied in their native tongue. Then, while the boys were resting, the Indian leader called forward two more guards.

The Hardys were to have new opponents for each fall! They realized it would be senseless to object.

When time was called, they approached their new rivals, and from the start it was apparent that the Hardys had the upper hand through their knowledge of the ancient Japanese art of jujitsu. In the midst of the second fall, a guard ran up, shouting:

"Tava! He is gone! I cannot find him anywhere!"

For a moment everyone froze. Then Bangalore screamed, "This is a trick! And you Hardys are responsible. You must die at once. Nanab, the potion!"

Guards swarmed around Frank and Joe, pinning the boys' arms back, so that they would be unable to resist. Nanab passed one of the poison pellets to his brother. He and Bangalore took up positions before the Hardys, forced their heads back, and pried open their jaws.

With all eyes on the scene, it came as a shock when a voice commanded, "Hands up!"

Fenton Hardy stood at the edge of the clearing. With him were Mr Delhi, Ghapur, and Radley and several police officers. As everyone turned, a State Police captain announced:

"You're all under arrest!"

The ringleaders and their guards were quickly seized and handcuffed. Then the officers went to round up the smuggled Indians.

Mr Hardy ran up to his sons. "Are you all right?"

"Yes," Frank assured him. "And we rescued Tava. He's on his way to the hotel."

"Wonderful!" cried Mr Delhi and Ghapur.

A search of the premises was instituted at once. Under the floorboards in Bangalore's bedroom they found the cache of rubies.

"Amazing!" Ghapur commented.

"Enough evidence for a conviction on the kidnapping charge!" Mr Hardy declared.

After the police left with the prisoners, the Hardys picked up Tava's goshawk and with their friends hurried to Bayport. When they reached the hotel, Tava was in the Hardy suite with Mrs Hardy and Aunt Gertrude. Hugs, handshakes, and bowing followed with fervour and profusion. During the happy celebration Mr Delhi and Rahmud Ghapur expressed their relief at finding Tava healthy and unharmed.

After the Indian youth had recounted his adventures, he motioned his countrymen aside and conversed in their native tongue. Rejoining the others, he explained that they were trying to decide on some fitting reward for the Hardys other than the usual fee for services, plus expenses which Mr Hardy would be paid.

The entire family protested, but Tava turned to Mrs Hardy and bowed. Then he took off his handsome ruby ring and presented it to her.

"Please accept this token of my deep gratitude," he said with a gentle smile. "I give it to the mother of the two bravest boys I have ever known."

Mrs Hardy accepted the gift graciously. Later the whole group went to dinner in the hotel dining room. Even precise Aunt Gertrude enjoyed the victory celebration.

Early the next morning Chet Morton burst into his friends' room, demanding to hear the whole story. As they finished it, a telegram was delivered to Frank and Joe.

"Listen to this," Frank cried excitedly. "It's from Satish Nayyar!" He read aloud:

" 'Cannot thank you enough for aid to my son. Tava is to continue his schooling. When he returns home next summer, will you accompany him and bring the boy who helped you?' "

"That's me!" cried Chet. "Wow, some reward!"

The three boys beamed. "We'll go!" Joe declared. "What a whale of an invitation!"

When the group gathered for breakfast, Frank and Joe told their parents about the telegram. Mr and Mrs Hardy heartily approved of their sons accepting the invitation. Silently the boys wondered if the next mystery they would solve would be in India. But long before the following summer arrived, they became involved in the mystery of *The Secret Agent on Flight 101*.

After the excitement died down, Mr Bhagnav said, "I must explain something to Frank and Joe. I understand my leaving in such a hurry after the bombing gave you cause to wonder about my motives." He laughed. "My trip to New York was to meet another cousin of mine before he could be kidnapped!"

Frank and Joe smiled broadly. After a pause, Mr Ghapur said:

"I have a gift of my own to offer—the falcon. I want you boys to keep the noble, courageous bird."

Frank and Joe accepted with alacrity, and added, "It would have been pretty hard to part with our hooded hawk."

Chet grinned. "Well," he said, "I guess the least I can do is treat you fellows to that dinner I promised. How about all of you coming out to the farm for a big celebration?"

Everyone accepted.

"And bring the falcon with you," Chet urged.

Joe grinned. "We will, if you'll have a pound of raw beef ready for Miss Peregrine as the reward."

Chet readily agreed. "But for all she did, the falcon deserves the best steak money can buy!"

"You're right," Frank said. "Without her, we couldn't have solved the mystery."

"Bravo, Miss Peregrine!" Joe said.

And Tava echoed, "*Shabash!* Bravo!"

# The Secret Agent
## on Flight 101

# CONTENTS

*With a splintering crash the staircase gave way!*

# ·1·

## A Vanishing Act

"How can the hand be quicker than the eye?" asked Chet Morton. "That's hard to believe!" He climbed into the back seat of the Hardy boys' convertible next to Joe.

"Perhaps the Incredible Hexton will convince you," remarked Frank, who was at the wheel. "All set, Dad?" he asked the handsome man beside him.

"Take off!" Mr Hardy said, smiling.

It was Friday evening. Bayport High had closed for summer vacation the day before. To celebrate, the Hardy boys and their stout friend Chet were being treated to a magician's show in the nearby city of Claymore.

"I read in a newspaper," Chet went on, "how pickpockets use sleight-of-hand methods. In fact, I have the clipping here in my—" Suddenly he sat bolt upright. "My wallet!" he cried. "It's gone!"

Frank brought the car to a stop. "Are you sure?" he asked.

Chet searched his pockets frantically. "It's gone all right!"

"Probably dropped out when you got into the car," Frank suggested.

"Then we'd better go back," Mr Hardy said.

Joe tried to hide a grin. But Chet noticed it. "Wait a minute!" He eyed Joe suspiciously. "Okay, mastermind. Hand it over!"

Joe burst out laughing and gave his chum a brown leather wallet. "Just wanted to prove to you the hand really is quicker than the eye."

"You caught me off guard," Chet replied good-naturedly.

Joe Hardy, blond and seventeen, enjoyed joking and was more impulsive than his dark-haired, eighteen-year-old brother. Both boys were trim all-around athletes. Chet, their schoolmate, had a chunky build and played on the Bayport High football team.

"Let's go, boys!" said Fenton Hardy, grinning. "Any more pocket-picking and I'll pull you in!"

Frank and Joe's father was a nationally known detective who had earned his fame as a member of the New York City Police Department. After his retirement from the force, he had set up his own sleuthing organization. Both sons were following in his footsteps and already had solved many challenging mysteries on their own. Chet often joined in their adventures. Although the stout boy preferred safer pursuits, no danger could make him desert his friends.

"What do you know about Hexton the magician?" Frank asked his father.

Mr Hardy said the man was a performer of some renown throughout the world, and was much acclaimed for his demonstrations of sleight-of-hand.

Joe asked, "Dad, do you by any chance have a professional interest in him?"

The detective laughed but did not reply and Joe decided not to press his query further. But he sensed that he had hit upon the truth.

They drove into Claymore, parked in the car park behind the theatre, and took their seats just as the houselights dimmed. A tall, dark figure slipped through the curtains and the spotlight blazed upon the Incredible Hexton.

The gaunt magician wore a top hat, flowing black cape, and carried a silver-handled cane. His face sent a chill through Chet.

Hexton had heavy brows, a sharply pointed chin, and the piercing eyes of a medieval sorcerer. He moved into his performance with a cat-like grace which indicated a disciplined and powerful body.

The boys watched eagerly as the magician caused coins, cards, and other small objects to disappear, then reappear at his fingertips.

The finale of the show was billed as the "Vanishing Man Act". Hexton led a short, muscular aide to a boxlike compartment, walled in on three sides by curtains and on the front by draperies. He opened and closed these a couple of times. Inside the curtained area was what looked like an oversized picture frame, supported at each end by posts.

Hexton's aide was strapped to a plank, which the magician and a tall, thin assistant set horizontally into the frame. This was tilted towards the audience at a forty-five-degree angle.

Hexton closed the small curtain and gestured with his cane. In seconds the curtain was reopened. The audience gasped in amazement! The magician's aide, and the plank to which he had been strapped, had vanished!

Hexton bowed low, and his aide strolled on to the stage from the wings, to thunderous applause from the audience. Hexton bowed several times more, and stepped behind the curtain.

"Great performance!" Frank said as he rose from his seat and stretched.

"Do you know how he did it, Dad?" Joe asked.

"I have an idea. Let's go backstage. I think it would be interesting to talk to Hexton."

The detective and his companions made their way over to a door at the side of the stage. They went through it and up a short flight of steps to the wing, where they found Hexton.

Mr Hardy introduced himself and his party. "You had us baffled," he said. "Good show!"

"Especially the last trick," said Joe. "That was great!"

The performer smiled cordially. "Perhaps you would like to see how it is done."

Frank looked surprised. "I thought magicians never gave away their secrets."

"Customarily they don't," Hexton replied smoothly, "but, you see, I have recognized your name. I know Fenton Hardy is a star performer in his own field. We both deal in secrets. Mr Hardy, my job is to mystify, yours just the opposite. I will show you the trick as a professional courtesy."

"That's very gracious of you," the detective replied.

"Not at all," Hexton said quickly. "I have a feeling we ought to become better acquainted."

Mr Hardy smiled. "An excellent idea."

"One moment," said Hexton. "I must alert my assistant. In the meantime, will you boys please take seats down in the auditorium." Hexton strode off but returned in a couple of minutes. "Follow me, Mr Hardy."

He led the detective onstage in the now-empty theatre. "Would you do me the honour of being my subject?" he asked with a sweeping bow.

The short assistant strapped Fenton Hardy to the plank. With the three boys watching intently, the magician closed the curtain and waved his cane. When he opened the compartment, the subject had vanished.

"That's neat!" Chet said.

The boys watched for Mr Hardy to reappear. When some time went by and he did not come out of the wings, Frank and Joe became worried.

"What's happened?" Frank asked anxiously. He and Joe ran on to the stage to examine the compartment, but Hexton blocked them.

"I can't permit you to inspect my device," he said, dropping his pleasant manner.

"Then tell us where our father is!" Joe demanded.

"I don't know," Hexton said slyly. "He must be playing some kind of joke on you."

Joe moved towards the magician. "Step aside. We're going to take a look at that gadget of yours."

Hexton called quickly, "Vordo! Stony!"

Two men emerged from the wings. The first one appeared to be nearly seven feet tall. His massive shoulders, muscular arms, and hard features made him a formidable sight. The other was the thin fellow who had helped with the vanishing act.

"See to it that these boys leave immediately," the magician ordered.

Joe was ready to fight, but Frank caught his brother's upraised arm. Perhaps Hexton was telling the truth.

Joe acceded. "All right, have it your way!" he said. "But we'll be back!"

The trio hurried out of the theatre. Joe insisted upon going to nearby Claymore Police Headquarters to request that a couple of officers go back to investigate.

"All right," said Frank.

When the group returned to the theatre, Hexton became enraged. "If you try to look at my equipment without a warrant, I'll sue you!" he stormed.

The officer told the boys that since there was no evidence of a crime, the only thing they could do was to file a missing-persons report.

"But we can't just sit and wait!" Joe declared hotly.

"On the other hand, it's possible Dad is staying away on purpose," Frank reasoned in a low tone. "Let's wait a while before we report him missing."

Joe was not satisfied. "At least let's search the theatre."

The police agreed to this and the manager was summoned. He gave permission, but stressed the point that he had no jurisdiction over Hexton's equipment.

The magician and his assistants glared at the Hardys and Chet as they inspected the stage thoroughly. Then they searched other sections of the theatre. There was no sign of Fenton Hardy. Frank suggested that they return home, in the hope that his father would try to reach them there.

Deeply worried, the three boys hurried across the dark car park and got into the Hardy car. As they sped along a straight stretch of road leading from the city. Chet looked out of the rear window. He noticed the headlights of a pickup truck drawing swiftly closer.

"Some character is following us," Chet said. "Doesn't he know that's dangerous?"

"Best thing is to let him go by," Frank replied, and pulled closer to the shoulder of the road.

The small truck roared past the Hardys' car.

"A speed demon!" Joe said sarcastically as the truck disappeared from sight.

The route Frank had chosen led them along a narrow, winding mountain road, bordered on one side by a guard rail. Below it was a sheer drop of several hundred feet.

As the car rounded a sharp curve, the boys were horror-stricken to see the headlights of a car directly in front of them. They had only the fraction of a second to brace themselves for a collision!

# ·2·

## The Hexton File

CRASH! There was a loud, piercing sound of shattering glass as the oncoming headlights made contact. Yet there was no collision! Like an apparition, the other vehicle had vanished completely.

Frank struggled to manoeuvre the car away from the guard rail. He jammed on the brakes and skidded to a stop. They all looked startled.

"Wh-what happened?" Chet asked.

"I don't know," Frank said. "This is weird—"

Joe pulled out a flashlight. "Let's go back up the road and investigate!"

The boys walked to where they had encountered the headlights. As Joe played the beam along the road, they noticed broken glass scattered about. Frank picked up a fragment.

"Look at this!" he said.

"It's a piece of mirror!" exclaimed Chet.

"So that's it!" Frank exploded. "Someone set a mirror on the road. What we saw was the reflection of our own headlights!"

Joe's eyes widened in anger. "We might have swerved over the embankment!"

"Exactly!" Frank answered. "Whoever planted the glass put it too close to the bend in the road. We came upon it so quickly I didn't have time to swerve!"

The young sleuths wondered if Hexton or his assistants had set the trap for them. Or had it been intended for another unsuspecting victim?

"This mystery is getting too dangerous," Chet said gravely. "A guy could get hurt."

"Don't worry. We'll get to the bottom of it," Frank vowed.

The Hardys searched the area more closely. Joe picked up a sliver of wood. He noticed several similar pieces scattered along the road.

"What do you make of this?" he asked.

Frank examined it. "Undoubtedly this is part of a wooden easel that was used to support the mirror."

"Magicians often use them in their acts," remarked Joe. "Hexton could have had a big mirror brought here in a pickup truck."

Frank agreed. "The one that passed us was certainly travelling fast enough to reach this spot well ahead of us."

"If Hexton did plant the mirror, how could he know we'd take this road?" Chet inquired.

"It's the fastest way back to Bayport," Frank replied. "He may have had us followed."

After scuffing the glass and wood off the road, the boys drove on. At the Morton farm on the outskirts of Bayport, Chet got out.

"S'long, fellows," he said. "Keep me posted about your dad."

Frank and Joe drove home in silence. Their mother

and Aunt Gertrude were waiting for them in the living room. Reluctantly the boys told what had happened.

"Oh dear!" their aunt shrilled. "Quick! Call the police. Fenton's been kidnapped!"

Gertrude Hardy, tall and angular, was the sister of Fenton Hardy. Although she admired the sleuthing abilities of her brother and nephews, she constantly worried about the dangers involved.

Mrs Hardy, an attractive and gracious woman, was too stunned by the shock of her husband's disappearance to talk. Frank put a comforting arm about her.

"In case Dad disappeared on purpose, let's not notify the police. Joe and I will find him. He may not be far away."

The boys excused themselves, then went to their father's study.

"I think Aunty's right about the kidnapping," said Joe. "Dad must have had something pretty big on Hexton."

"In that case," Frank said, "we ought to find it in his files."

But there was no record of Hexton under the letter H.

"Try M for magician," Joe suggested.

Frank looked. "Not there."

They checked several other headings, but did not find any mention of the man. Then Joe noticed a folder marked "School".

"That's funny," he said. "I don't remember Dad having a case to do with a school."

He took out the file and opened it. "Frank! Look here! This is it!"

Fascinated, the boys read the notes. Mr Hardy

described the magician as a diabolical man who for years had headed a gang of thieves. Working as the crew for his show, they moved about the country with him, pulling the robberies he planned. The detective had discovered the set-up recently. "So far no real evidence," he had noted. Written at the bottom of the page was: "Last two years—agent UGLI."

"UGLI!" Joe exclaimed. "Undercover Global League of Informants!"

Frank gave a low whistle. "This is really big! UGLI is the most powerful espionage ring in the world."

"And hostile to democratic countries," added Joe.

The boys exchanged grim looks. If their father had been kidnapped, he was in ruthless hands!

"I think I know now why this is filed under school," said Frank.

Joe nodded. "That's probably a camouflage word for SKOOL. Dad must be working for them."

Both boys had heard of the famous supranational counterespionage ring which worked on behalf of democratic powers. The letters stood for Secret Knowledge Of Organized Lawbreakers.

"If only we could contact them," said Frank, "they might be able to give us a lead. But the organization is so secret, there's no way to reach them."

"Unless they've called you first," said Joe. "Maybe Dad left a note on how to get in touch."

But a thorough search turned up no information. The boys perused the report again and learned that for the past two years State Department secrets had been leaking out of Washington to enemy countries at an increasing rate. The detective had written, "Offices, cars, and homes of diplomatic corps must be very cleverly bugged. Agents probably transmit microtape to couriers who take it abroad."

On the margin at the left were the words, "See Dell."

Frank and Joe searched the file and all the other drawers in the room, but could find no further reference to Dell. Who was he?

Before they put the Hexton report away, Frank read aloud the note at the end of it: " 'Do not think Hexton is aware of investigation. Perhaps should discuss with Frank and Joe when more substantial evidence is found.' "

"It's dated yesterday!" Joe exclaimed.

"Somehow Hexton must have learned that Dad was on to his game," Frank observed.

"And our showing up at the theatre," Joe said, "probably made him nervous. So he pulled a kidnapping."

Frank reminded Joe of the magician's suggestion that the two men get better acquainted. "I'll bet Dad thought if he went along with the idea he might be able to get the goods on Hexton. The first step was taking part in the trick."

"But what a risk!" said Joe.

"You know Dad," Frank said quietly. "If he figured it was worthwhile, he'd take it."

The night wore on with no word. Finally Aunt Gertrude insisted upon phoning a missing-persons report to the Bayport police. The next morning there was still no word from the detective, and the police had found nothing.

Frank and Joe decided to drive back to Claymore.

They arrived at the theatre to find the front door locked. Walking round to the back, they were confronted by a guard. He told them that Hexton had given his last performance the night before and had already departed. The magician had left two of his assistants behind to supervise the packing of the show's equipment.

"Our father disappeared here last evening," Frank said. "We'd like to have a look inside."

"Sorry," the guard answered, "I can't permit anyone to the theatre. Manager's orders."

"Then we'd like to see him," Joe said.

"He's not here. I'd advise you to go."

"Okay," Frank signalled Joe with his eyes and the two walked off briskly round the side of the building. There they stopped abruptly and Frank peered back.

After a few minutes the guard left his post and disappeared round the far corner.

"Let's go!" Frank commanded.

Quietly the boys edged their way towards the stage door. They pulled it open and darted inside, stopping to let their eyes adjust to the dim light. Then, cautiously, they made their way to the stage. Nobody was there.

"Where are Hexton's men?" Joe whispered.

"Out for a coffee break," Frank guessed.

The stage was cluttered with packing cases containing the magician's equipment. At the rear the boys spotted the vanishing-man device. It had already been partially dismantled.

"Look! The plank's missing," Joe said. "Maybe packed in one of these cases."

Further examination of the device revealed that it

had a false bottom, beneath which was a secret compartment.

A soft rustling noise had sounded overhead. "What's that?" Frank said. He glanced up in time to see a ballast sandbag hurtling down towards them from the flies.

"Look out!" Frank shouted. He leaped aside, pulling Joe with him. The sandbag crashed to the stage and burst open. The boys looked up and saw a man running along a catwalk.

"After him!" Joe yelled.

"Hold it!" commanded a harsh voice. "Stay right where you are!"

## ·3·

## The SKOOL Man

THE Hardys whirled to see the theatre guard approaching. "So it's you two!" he shouted angrily. "Didn't I tell you to shove off?"

"Yes, but—" Joe began.

"That crash—" the guard cut in. "What happened?" He looked at the sand scattered about the stage.

"Someone tried to drop a sandbag on us," Frank explained.

"A likely story." The guard eyed the boys suspiciously. "You're probably up to something. I'm calling the police!"

Keeping an eye on the boys, the guard walked to a wall telephone and dialled. Within minutes an officer arrived.

"Oh, the Hardy brothers," he said, and turned to the guard. "I heard about these kids. They're trying to find their father."

"I thought that was a gag," the man replied.

"No. It's on the up and up."

The guard apologized and helped the young sleuths examine the sandbag. They discovered that the ropes which held it had been cut.

At that moment the magician's thin assistant walked

onstage. When the policeman questioned him, he gave his name as Stony Bleeker. The man said he had been out for a walk and insisted he had had nothing to do with dropping the sandbag.

"Where's the other man who was helping you pack?" Frank asked.

"How should I know?"

"I suppose you're going to tell us that you don't know what happened to our father, either!" Joe said.

"You're nuts!" Bleeker growled.

The Hardys climbed up to examine the flies, but there was no trace of their attacker. "He must have sneaked down the ladder and out the side door while we were arguing with the guard," said Joe.

Back on the stage, the boys found further questioning fruitless. The policeman said he would request that the detective squad investigate the matter.

Stony Bleeker quickly set about packing the rest of Hexton's equipment, telling the policeman that a truck would call for it shortly.

"Well, that's that!" Frank said glumly. "Come on, Joe. Let's go home."

On the way back to Bayport, the boys decided to search their father's study again.

"Maybe we can find out who or what Dell is," Frank said. "That might give us a lead."

But their efforts were of no avail until Frank examined the books on his father's desk. A torn envelope flap was sticking to the back cover of one. On it was the notation, "Kenneth Dell, Great Circle Airways, Westboro, 789-1010."

"You found it!" Joe exclaimed.

The boys surmised that their father had put the book down on the gummed paper and failed to notice later that it had stuck to the cover.

Quickly Frank dialled the Westboro number. A man with a deep, commanding voice answered and identified himself as Kenneth Dell. Frank explained why he had called, and Dell revealed that he was chief of security for Great Circle Airways.

Amazed to hear about the disappearance of Mr Hardy, Dell said it was imperative that he talk to the young detectives and he would fly to Bayport the following day.

"Meet me outside the airport restaurant at twelve-thirty," Dell said. "I don't want to come to your home for fear we're being watched by Hexton's men. I'll explain everything when I see you."

After church the next day, Frank and Joe drove through the heavy Sunday traffic to the airport and anxiously awaited the security chief's arrival at the restaurant. Soon they were approached by a tall, stocky man, with distinguished features and slightly grizzled hair. Accompanying him was a thin, grey-haired man in a dark suit.

"You're the Hardy boys, I take it," said the stocky one. "I'm Dell. This is Mr Smith."

Both men shook hands and Dell added, "Your father has told me a lot about you two. He's very proud—says his sons are great detectives."

The four entered the restaurant and seated themselves at a table by a front window. Mr Smith kept looking down at his hands.

"Who is he?" Frank wondered.

Both boys noticed that Mr Smith was twisting a crested gold ring on his finger.

"Looks like a school emblem," Frank thought, then suddenly realized what the man was telling him. "*He's from SKOOL!*"

Joe got the message at the same time and threw a quick glance at his brother.

Dell smiled. "I felt sure you would understand. It is safer if some things are not said aloud. Mr Smith and I work together." So Dell was also a member of SKOOL, working under the guise of security officer for Great Circle Airways!

He went on to say that Mr Hardy had come to him some weeks before and asked for dossiers on all employees and the passenger lists for the past two years. "I supplied the information."

Dell was interrupted for a minute while a waitress took their orders. Smith gave none. Then the security chief leaned closer.

"Your father found out that Hexton owns a castle in the north of Scotland. It's a retreat, the magician claims, where he rests and devises new tricks for his show. He goes there several times a month on our planes."

"Sounds like a great set-up for smuggling secrets out of this country," Frank said softly.

"That's just what your father concluded," Smith said. "But he disappeared before he had a chance to give me a detailed report. So far nothing has been proved."

In turn, Frank and Joe quickly told about the information they had gleaned from Mr Hardy's file on Hexton.

"Where is Dad?" Frank asked urgently. "Have you any idea?"

"I had a reliable tip that Hexton has taken him to South Africa," Smith replied. "My organization will move in on the situation there." He glanced at his watch and abruptly stood up. "If you need me, contact Mr Dell. Good luck." He walked off quietly.

A few moments later the food came. As they were eating, Joe suddenly exclaimed, "Look!" He clutched his brother's arm and pointed towards the large front window of the restaurant.

"What is it?"

"A man just peered in here! I'm sure he's Stony Bleeker!"

The boys darted outside, followed by Dell. But Bleeker was not among the passers-by.

"Maybe he ran to the back!" Joe suggested.

"Quick!" Frank ordered. "Let's split up and check the building on all sides! Joe, you stay here in front! Mr Dell, I'll take the east side, if you'll take the west!"

"Let's go!" the security chief agreed.

Frank raced along the east side of the building. Carefully he rounded the corner, but did not spot Bleeker. Just then he heard sounds of a scuffle coming from the far side.

"*Uhff!*" someone groaned.

Frank ran to the spot to find Dell lying on the ground. He bent over the prostrate man.

"Are you all right?" Frank asked worriedly. He helped the security chief to his feet.

"I almost had him," Dell said, breathing heavily.

"But he got in a fast punch." Dell pointed. "There he goes now!"

Frank turned and saw Bleeker dashing into the airport car park. The boy bolted after him. The man had too big a lead, though. Before Frank could reach him, Bleeker scrambled into a car and sped away. Disappointed, Frank returned to the restaurant. Dell was already there.

"Any luck?" Joe asked his brother.

"No. Didn't even get the licence plate number."

"Bleeker's thin," Dell commented as he rubbed his chin, "but he packs a lot of power."

"What'll we do now?" Joe asked.

Frank thought for a moment. "We'll check the list of cities scheduled on Hexton's tour. If we can trail him without his knowing it, we might trap him into revealing where he took Dad."

"I still have a copy of the programme from his last show," Joe recalled. "I believe his tour schedule is listed in it."

"Good thinking," Dell remarked. He instructed the boys to call him if they wanted help. Then he boarded a plane to return to the Great Circle Airways base at Westboro near New York City.

"Let's go home and check that programme right away," Frank said.

"Hexton knows that we're on to him and his gang," Joe remarked. "Do you think he'll continue with his tour?"

"Probably not," Frank answered. "But right now it's our only chance to find him."

When they returned to their car, the Hardys were

surprised to see a pencil-printed note attached to the steering wheel. Frank removed it and read the contents aloud:

" '*Mind your own business! Or you'll never see your father again!*' "

# · 4 ·

## *Cryptic Message*

"BLEEKER must have left the warning here!" Joe exclaimed.

"That's for sure," Frank agreed. "And it's no idle threat. Besides, I have a hunch Dad wasn't taken to South Africa. Otherwise, Hexton wouldn't be so determined to keep us off the trail."

The Hardys were more eager than ever to get their investigation under way. Upon arriving home, they examined the programme which listed the cities on the magician's tour.

"According to this list," Frank observed, "Hexton is scheduled to appear at the Tivoli Theatre in Darville tomorrow."

Joe paged through the atlas and pinpointed the location of the city. "Here's Darville. It's about four hundred miles from here."

The boys telephoned Jack Wayne, pilot of Mr Hardy's twin-engine plane, and arranged to fly to Darville the following day. Frank and Joe had private pilot licences, but thought it wise to have Jack along. "He's a tough man in a fight," Joe said.

When they invited Chet, he eagerly accepted. "I'll meet you at the field."

The next morning Mrs Hardy and Aunt Gertrude nervously prepared breakfast for the young detectives.

"Now don't do anything foolish," their mother cautioned. "This Hexton fellow sounds terribly dangerous to me."

"I fear the worst!" Aunt Gertrude said, shaking her head. "Detective work involves taking too many chances. No good will come of this. I can feel it in my bones."

"Don't worry about us," Joe assured them. "Hexton might be a clever magician, but we have a few tricks of our own."

After receiving more admonitions at the doorway, the boys drove to the airport. Jack Wayne, the tanned, lean-faced pilot, was waiting for them at the plane. Chet came puffing up a few moments later. Soon they were airborne and streaking towards Darville. Two hours later they circled it and touched down.

Frank rented a car and they drove directly to the theatre where Hexton was scheduled to appear. As they approached the Tivoli, the boys were amazed to see a man standing on a tall ladder against the marquee, removing the big black letters which spelled out the magician's name.

Frank pulled up in front of the theatre, and Joe called out, "What's going on? Hexton's first show is scheduled for tonight!"

The man on the ladder shrugged. "I only follow orders. Sorry."

He pointed to the box-office window. A cancellation notice was spread across a large poster advertising the show.

"Let's have a talk with the theatre manager," Frank suggested. He parked and they hastened to a door marked "Manager L. Sardella". Joe rapped loudly.

"Come in!"

When the four entered, a small, thin man with a waxed moustache removed his feet from a desk and glowered. "Yes?"

"Mr Sardella, where is Hexton?" Joe asked tensely.

The man rose and eyed them sharply. "You want refunds?"

"No. We're private detectives," Chet said importantly. "Where is he?"

"Hexton? That's what I'd like to know. The skunk! I'll spend the rest of the day giving refunds on my advance ticket sale, and still have no show tonight."

"Why didn't he come?" Frank asked.

"Search me. He phoned long-distance. Gave no reasons. I'll sue him!"

Sardella said that the magician had mentioned he was cancelling the remainder of his tour with the exception of one last performance.

"Where?" Frank asked.

"Some little place called Granton. Don't ask me what state, because I don't know. Said they pushed up the date to tonight to accommodate him. Accommodation—bah!"

The Hardys and their friends thanked the manager and hurried back to the car. They returned to the airport and hastened to the operations room to consult a large aeronautical chart mounted on the wall.

"Here's Granton," the pilot said, pointing. He

quickly plotted a course. "It's a little bit more than a thousand miles from here."

"Good grief!" Chet exclaimed. "We'll never get there in time."

Frank glanced at his watch. "We ought to be able to make the trip in under seven hours, wouldn't you say, Jack?"

The pilot manipulated a small flight computer, which he had taken from a jacket pocket. "With the present winds, I'd say we could do it in seven hours easily."

"If we take off right now," Frank said, "we can be in Granton before Hexton's show ends."

"I'm game, fellows," Chet piped up, "if you'll let me get some chow for the trip." He trotted towards the airport cafeteria and returned a few minutes later with a bag of sandwiches and milk.

Soon the four companions were in the air, speeding towards Granton. They touched down late that evening at an airport thirty miles from the town, rented a car, and started off. Fortunately, the speed limit was generous. Also, Granton had only one theatre, which Frank found easily.

It was nearly time for the show to end. Frank parked the car across the street from the lighted marquee.

Joe walked down an alley to the rear and reported that there was only one other exit besides the front. "It's on the side."

"Keep a sharp lookout for Hexton and his men after the performance," Frank instructed the others. "Also, remember that they mustn't spot *us* or our chance to follow them might fail."

Twenty minutes later the show ended and people

spilled out through the doors. Presently a green saloon car drove up in front of the theatre.

"Look!" Joe said in a loud whisper. "The driver is Stony Bleeker!"

Four men appeared from the alley exit. "There's Hexton!" Chet whispered.

"And Vordo with two short men!" Frank observed.

"They look like twins!" Joe exclaimed.

"I'll bet that's how Hexton works the vanishing bit," said Chet. "One twin disappears in the box and the other appears from the wings! From the audience, who could tell they weren't the same man?"

The magician and his assistants got into the car and sped off. Frank and his companions followed at a safe distance. Several blocks farther on, the green car passed a high wall surrounding a garden behind a hotel, then pulled round the corner and stopped in front of the Granton Inn. The men got out and entered, while a doorman drove the car into the hotel's underground garage.

Frank parked a short distance from the entrance. "Let's stay out here and see what happens," he said. "We'll take turns keeping watch. Good thing there are no exits except to this street or the garden." The foursome settled down for a long vigil.

As they waited, Joe noticed that Chet seemed preoccupied. His stout friend was staring at something high on the side of the hotel.

"What are you looking at?" Joe asked.

"That window up there near the top. The room light is going on and off."

The young sleuths watched the light for a time before

noticing that it was following a definite pattern.

"Dit-dit-dit dah-dah-dah dit-dit-dit," mumbled Frank in tempo with the light.

"An SOS!" Joe cried. "In Morse code!"

"No doubt about it!" Frank exclaimed. "Maybe it's from Dad! He could be a prisoner in Hexton's room!"

Throwing caution to the winds, the Hardys dashed into the hotel. Chet and Jack Wayne remained in the car to watch the exit. The clerk at the reception desk was startled when the boys rushed in.

"Which is the Incredible Hexton's room?" Frank asked.

The man automatically answered, "He's in Suite 924. What are your names? I'll announce you."

"Never mind," Joe said.

"But I have to announce all visitors," the clerk insisted. "It's a hotel rule."

As he scooped up the house phone, Frank and Joe darted into an elevator. They burned with impatience while the car rose slowly. When it reached the ninth floor, the boys hopped out and rushed to Hexton's suite. To their surprise, the door was partly open. On it hung a sign: DO NOT DISTURB.

"Careful!" Frank warned. "It might be a trap."

Cautiously they entered and hurriedly glanced into each of the rooms of the suite.

"Nobody here!" Joe declared.

"They were warned by the call from reception," Frank said. "Let's go after them! They must have escaped by a stairway."

The boys ran along the corridor towards an exit sign and bounded down the staircase. Reaching the foyer, they asked the clerk if he had seen Hexton or his assistants pass through.

"I've seen no one," was the response. "What's this all about?"

"No time to tell you now," Frank said. "How do we get to the underground garage?"

"By the elevator or the back stairs," the clerk answered.

"Quick! Outside!" Frank shouted to Joe. "Maybe we can cut them off!"

They raced from the hotel and headed for the driveway leading to the underground garage. Just then the green saloon roared out.

"Watch it!" Joe yelled. They fell backwards as the speeding car grazed their jackets. Scrambling to their feet, the boys ran for their own car. It was gone!

"Chet and Jack must have recognized Hexton," Frank surmised, "and followed him."

He and Joe hurried back to the hotel to search the magician's rooms for clues.

"Come here!" Frank called softly to Joe as he opened the door to an adjoining bedroom. "This is where the SOS was sent from!" The electrical plug to a lamp was only part way in the wall outlet.

"The signal must have been sent by manipulating the plug," Frank said.

"What's that?" Joe exclaimed, pointing to something written near the base of the wall. The pair bent down to examine the faint scribbling. It read:

441810682300 *Am all right—*

"That's Dad's writing!" Joe exclaimed. "He was trying to tell us something!"

"The 'Am all right' is clear enough," Frank remarked as he carefully studied the writing. "But the numerals—what do you make of them?"

Joe rubbed his chin thoughtfully. "Nothing—yet. But I'll bet they're mighty important."

Frank took a notebook from his pocket and jotted down the cryptic message. The boys then went downstairs and walked out of the hotel just as Chet and Jack Wayne drove up.

"We chased 'em!" Chet said.

"Any luck?" Frank asked.

"No! Only their licence number. Lost 'em in traffic," Jack answered.

"But," Chet continued eagerly, "we did get close enough to see that there were six men in the car."

Frank nodded. "I'm sure the sixth was Dad!"

After phoning a description and the licence number of the green car to the police, Jack and the boys decided to return to the theatre.

"Hexton must have left his stage equipment behind," Frank said. "Perhaps he gave instructions where he wanted it sent."

At the theatre a local truck was parked near the side entrance.

"Maybe it's waiting to pick up the gear," Joe said.

"Let's ask some questions," Frank suggested.

Chet and Jack Wayne were instructed to keep an eye on the truck while the Hardys went inside. They confronted the theatre manager just as he was locking his office, and asked him where Hexton's equipment was to be taken.

"As far as I know," the man replied, "Hexton made

arrangements to have it stored in a local warehouse."

"Did he leave anyone behind to dismantle and pack the stuff?" Frank inquired.

"Yes—a man I never saw before. Said he had just arrived in town this morning," the manager replied. "Hexton took his four regular assistants with him."

A shout came from the street and the boys rushed outside.

Chet's face was flushed with excitement. "A man forced Jack into the truck and drove off! He had a gun!" Chet pointed down the street. "There they go!"

Frank and Joe caught a glimpse of the vehicle as it rounded a corner several blocks away. They grabbed Chet's arms and dashed for their car!

# · 5 ·

## *Mysterious Rendezvous*

FRANK jumped behind the wheel, the doors were slammed shut, and the car roared off in pursuit of Jack Wayne's kidnapper! Seconds later, the headlights picked the truck out of the darkness on a road leading from the city.

"The driver must know we're after him," Frank observed as the vehicle speeded up. "I'll try to head him off." He bore down on the accelerator until the needle touched the speed limit.

"We're gaining!" Chet yelled. Gradually the car moved alongside the truck. Then, with a burst of power, it pulled ahead and in front.

"Be careful!" Joe pleaded. "That truck could plough right through us!"

The two vehicles reeled back and forth across the road as Frank tried frantically to prevent the truck from pulling ahead of them.

"If someone comes towards us from the opposite direction, we've had it," Chet mumbled as he wiped his forehead.

He relaxed a bit when the speedometer indicated less than forty miles per hour. Frank had noticed that the truck had suddenly slowed and begun to wobble violently.

"What's happening?" Joe asked.

"Leaping mackerel!" Chet yelled. "Jack and the driver are fighting! Oh, I hope that man doesn't shoot!"

He had hardly finished speaking when the truck skidded off the road. *Crash!* With a thud the heavy vehicle tumbled on its side into a shallow ditch, its wheels spinning.

Frank squealed to a stop. The boys leaped out and ran to the wreck, just as Jack Wayne pushed his door open.

"Jack! You all right?" Frank panted.

"A little shaky, but this guy's been kayoed."

Jack climbed out and the others dragged the driver through the door. He regained consciousness a few moments later and weakly shook his head.

"Who are you?" Frank demanded.

"None of your business," the man muttered. He was tall and husky, with bulging muscles. He looked for his revolver, which now lay on the road.

"The police will be interested to know you kidnapped Jack Wayne," Joe said, pointing to the pilot.

"All right!" the driver bellowed. "My name is Burly Wilkes!"

"How long have you been working for Hexton?" Frank asked.

"Just today. And I didn't try to kidnap anybody!"

"I suppose you just felt like taking our friend for a ride at pistol point," Chet remarked scornfully.

"Hexton hired me to take care of his equipment," Wilkes said. "He told me there were some guys trying to steal his stuff. When I saw your friend snooping around the truck, I thought he was one of 'em. I just wanted to give him a scare."

At that moment a police car arrived on the scene. An officer jumped out and walked towards them. "What's going on here?"

When the boys explained, the officer took Wilkes into custody and requested that Jack Wayne follow him to police headquarters to file a complaint.

Further questioning of Wilkes by the police revealed nothing more than what he had already told the young detectives. Apparently, Frank reasoned, he was more afraid of Hexton than of being thrown into jail.

The Hardys and their companions checked in at a motel to get a little sleep. Early the next morning they flew back to Bayport. Chet said goodbye and headed for the farm in his jalopy.

Mrs Hardy and Aunt Gertrude were overjoyed to see Frank and Joe, and instantly asked about Mr Hardy. They received a detailed report.

"I'm still fearful," said the boys' mother, "but the news is somewhat encouraging. You say he wrote, 'Am all right—'?"

"Yes," Frank assured her.

Aunt Gertrude said in her forceful way, "That's enough for me. I'm sure Fenton is a better magician than Hexton when it comes to escaping from traps. He'll get out of those villains' clutches!"

"You're right," Joe agreed. "Just the same, I think he needs our help."

Directly after supper Frank and Joe went to their

father's study and tried to decipher the message scribbled on the hotel wall.

Joe read aloud, " '441810682300.' "

"I'm stymied," Frank admitted. "The numbers don't fit into any code Dad's used with us before."

"Maybe it isn't a code at all," Joe suggested. "The numbers might represent something else."

Just then Chet arrived. He strolled into the study with a large silver bowl tucked under one arm. In his other hand he held a big square of blue silk.

"Okay, you masterminds! Give me your attention!" he demanded. "You see standing before you the dean of sorcerers! The master of legerdemain! The world's most outstanding thauma—thauma—thaumaturgist!"

"Wow!" Joe exclaimed. "Listen to him! You'd better get the dictionary, Frank!"

Chet placed the bowl on the desk as the Hardys watched in amusement. "You are most fortunate," he said, "since you will see a private performance by the great—the incredible—the fantastic Morton!"

Chet paused, a faint smile curling his lips and added, "Perhaps you hadn't heard that I've been taking a mail-order course in magic!"

The Hardys looked unimpressed and said nothing. Chet eyed them with a smug expression. "Will you please bring me an egg, some relish, mustard, ketchup, and perhaps some vinegar and water."

"Yes, master!" Joe left the study and returned shortly with the items. "Here you are." He grinned. "And whatever you plan to do with them it had better be good. Aunt Gertrude almost took the broom to me for bringing this stuff."

Ignoring Joe's remark, the chubby youth continued with his spiel. "All right! Prepare yourselves for the impossible!" he declared. "Listen now to my weird and strange incantations! Utterances that will mystify the ages!"

The boys watched as Chet cracked the egg and dropped it into the bowl, shell and all. He added the vinegar, water, and other ingredients.

"What a crazy concoction!" Joe said as his chum stirred the mixture.

Chet covered the bowl with the silk cloth. "Brace yourselves for the most amazing feat of all time!" He began to pass his hands slowly over the bowl. "*Ezard, Kazard Mokim, Whumpf!*"

"Now what?" Frank asked.

"Ah!" Chet announced. "You have just witnessed an astounding display of my mystical powers! The ingredients in this bowl have vanished. *Puhff!* Just like that!"

"Okay, Merlin," Joe said, laughing. "Prove it. Uncover the bowl."

"You doubt my magical skills?" Chet said. "I won't just uncover the bowl—I'll go a step further to prove my powers." He placed the bowl on his head upside down.

"There! You see, I—" He stopped short as its contents flowed over his head and face. Some spattered on the floor. "Oh, ugh!"

The Hardys howled with laughter. "You'd better clean up that mess fast," Frank warned. "If Aunt Gertrude sees it she'll cause *you* to vanish. *Puhff!* Just like that!"

Joe rushed out of the study and returned with an armful of paper towels. It took considerable rubbing before Chet became recognizable again and the carpet clean.

"I can't understand," he murmured. "The book said it would work!"

Joe chuckled. "Maybe you got your incantations mixed."

"Anyway, I was just trying to cheer you fellows up," Chet mumbled.

"We appreciate that," Frank said. "But how about less spectacular tricks for a while?"

At a loss for words, Chet sat down in an armchair and examined his silver bowl.

The ringing of the telephone broke the silence in the study. Frank took the call. "Frank Hardy speaking."

"If you and your brother want to see your father," said a muffled voice, "come to the old Landon Mansion in an hour. And come alone!"

"Who is this?" Frank demanded. There was a sharp clicking sound. The mysterious caller had hung up!

The message startled the boys. "Did you recognize the voice?" Joe asked.

"I'm not sure," Frank said, "but it sounded like Hexton's giant helper, Vordo!"

"The Landon Mansion, eh?" Joe queried. "That old dilapidated house hasn't been lived in for years. I understand it'll be torn down soon."

"If I remember correctly, it's just off Highway 18," Frank recalled. "It'll take us about thirty minutes to drive there."

"But it may be a trap!" Joe declared.

"We must take the risk," Frank insisted. "Dad really might be there."

They asked Chet to post himself at the telephone. "If we're not back in two hours, notify the police," Frank requested.

He and Joe stopped to tell Mrs Hardy their plans. Though worried, she conceded they should go. Ten minutes later the Hardys' car was humming down the highway on the outskirts of town. The night was clear and a strong breeze lent a chill to the air. A full moon bathed the trees and fields in an eerie, silvery light.

Before long, the Hardys came to a narrow dirt road and turned on to it. Neglected for many years, it was pitted with holes and covered in spots with clumps of grass and weeds. There were signs, however, that some kind of vehicle had travelled on the road recently. Much of the grass had been flattened and there were tyre tracks.

At the end of the rutted road, the two sleuths discovered iron gateposts. The gates had long since fallen from their rusted hinges. In the distance stood the Landon Mansion, ghostly in the moonlight. Frank and Joe got out of the car and walked towards it. The only light came from a window on the first floor.

Reaching the house, they stopped and listened for a moment. All was quiet.

The Hardys furtively made their way to the door and eased it open. Silently they slipped in, but froze like statues when Vordo's voice boomed from upstairs.

"Your father's waiting here!"

Frank and Joe broke into a cold sweat. "That guy

must have radar eyes," Frank whispered. "Come on, Joe! We can't turn back now."

The boys climbed the creaky staircase, which groaned under their feet. Just before they reached the top, a grinding sound echoed through the old building. With a splintering crash the staircase parted just where they were standing. The lower section fell away and the boys plunged towards the darkness below!

## ·6·

## Aerial Chase

FALLING, Frank made a grab for the step ahead of him and hung on as Joe gripped his waist. Though his arms ached from the strain, Frank pulled desperately, hoisting himself up inch by inch.

Finally Joe reached out and grasped the step. After much effort, both boys worked themselves safely on to the next tread.

"These guys don't play around," Frank murmured, rubbing his swollen hands. "Well, up we go."

They climbed the few remaining steps and entered the room straight ahead. It was empty, except for a small table, on which a single candle burned.

At the end of the room was a window. The boys rushed to it and looked down into the yard in time to see Vordo and Stony Bleeker leap into a car and speed off.

"Neat getaway," Joe muttered.

"No use trying to chase them," Frank said. "They'll be out of sight by the time we get to our car."

"Dad wasn't with them," Joe commented.

"Of course not. Calling us over here *was* just a trap," Frank replied. He pulled angrily on the rope which

Vordo and Bleeker had used to get from the window to the ground.

The boys went to examine the remaining section of the staircase. It had been sawed more than halfway through! In a sober mood Frank and Joe returned to the window, slid down the rope, then drove home. Chet was greatly relieved to see his friends.

"What about your dad?" he asked excitedly, and was quickly told what had happened.

"Wow! Well, I'm glad you're safe," Chet said. "While you were gone two important phone calls came in. The first was from the police chief in Granton. He said Burly Wilkes has escaped!"

"What!" Joe exclaimed. "How did that happen?"

"A detective had handcuffed Wilkes to a table in the interrogation room while he went out for a few minutes," Chet said. "When he returned, Wilkes was gone. Somehow, he had slipped out of the handcuffs."

"A trick he could have learned from Hexton," Frank mused.

"And another thing," Chet went on, "the green car was Hexton's and it has not been picked up."

"What about the second call?"

"It was from Kenneth Dell," Chet answered. "He wants to talk to you as soon as possible."

Frank picked up the phone and dialled the private number of the Great Circle Airways' security chief.

Dell sounded excited. "I've had a report that one of our flight stewards, named Timken, has been acting suspicious lately. He used to be friendly and stay around for a while after landing. Now shortly after he gets in from Scotland on Flight 101, he leaves in a waiting

STOL. He never says where he's going."

"That is strange," Frank remarked. "An STOL! The kind that can take off and land in short distances?"

"Right! It can also fly at very low speeds."

"Have you any idea where the steward goes?" Frank asked.

"No flight plan was filed," Dell said.

"Who owns the plane?" Joe inquired.

"I don't know, but now I mean to find out," Dell replied. "Whenever the pilot has asked for landing instructions, he has identified himself as 'STOL 345'. Of course those are only the last three figures in his whole number."

Joe asked, "What about Timken as a steward?"

"He was hired by our firm only a couple of months ago. Seems efficient and so far we haven't found anything incriminating in his record. Flight 101 is part of his regular schedule, and I'm watching it for anything the least bit suspicious. With Hexton's headquarters probably in a Scottish castle, we can't be too careful about our Scotland flights."

"I have an idea," said Frank. "The next time Timken takes the STOL, Joe and I will follow him."

"Follow him?" Dell said. "How?"

"In Dad's plane."

"But if you were to take off immediately behind the STOL and trail it on the same course," Dell countered "wouldn't that arouse the pilot's suspicions?"

"We would take off from a different airport," Frank said. "Hold on just a minute, will you?"

He beckoned Joe, who handed him an aeronautical

chart. Spreading it out, Frank examined the area in the vicinity of Great Circle's base. Then he picked up the phone again.

"There's a small general airfield at Burnsbie near your base," he told Dell. "We'll land there and wait. When you see the steward boarding the STOL, let us know."

"It might just work at that," the SKOOL agent agreed.

"What is Timken's first name and when is he scheduled to return from his next flight?" Frank asked.

"Stand by. I'll check the crew schedule." There was a brief pause, then Dell came on again. "His first name is Guy, and he's scheduled for an outgoing flight tonight. He'll be back here at ten o'clock Thursday morning, our time."

"Good!" Frank said. "Barring bad weather, we'll plan to be at the field at least an hour before Timken is due back."

Frank said goodbye, then called Jack Wayne and informed him of the plan. The pilot said he would have the plane fueled and ready to fly on Thursday morning at the crack of dawn.

As the first rays of sunlight appeared in the east that day, the Hardys got up and dressed. They were surprised to find their mother and Aunt Gertrude already in the kitchen preparing breakfast for them.

"Um! Sausage and cakes!" Joe said with a grin.

Immediately after breakfast, the boys drove to Bayport Airport. There they made a final check on the weather. The forecaster told them it would be CAVU—

Ceiling And Visibility Unlimited—for at least another forty-eight hours.

"The ship's all set to fly!" Jack Wayne called as they walked across the ramp.

He and the Hardys got into the plane and fastened their seat belts. A sudden roar echoed across the field as Jack started engines. He made a quick but thorough check of the instruments. Minutes later, they were airborne and climbing rapidly above Bayport.

"We should get to Burnsbie with plenty of time to spare," Frank said as he glanced at his watch.

Upon arriving at their destination, Jack attended to the refueling of the plane, while Frank and Joe waited in the operations room for a call from Kenneth Dell.

It was a few minutes after ten o'clock when the telephone rang. The airport manager scooped up the receiver, then announced that the call was for the boys.

"This is Kenneth Dell, Frank! Timken just got into the STOL They're taxiing out now for take-off."

"Roger!" declared the young detective. "We're on our way."

In a matter of minutes, Jack Wayne and the Hardys were approaching Great Circle's base at several thousand feet.

"There's the STOL!" Joe exclaimed. "It's at the three-o'clock position."

The craft veered slightly to a northeast course. Jack followed at a safe distance.

A short time later the STOL made two complete turns, then reverted to course. Jack did the same. Moments later, their quarry repeated the manoeuvre.

"Why all those turns?" Joe asked.

"He's probably checking to see if he's being followed," Jack replied.

"Do you suppose he spotted us?" Joe asked.

Frank replied, "No doubt. But we've nothing to lose by continuing the chase."

The gap between the two crafts, however, decreased more and more as the STOL reduced speed.

"That plane up ahead can fly much slower than we can." Jack's voice showed concern.

He attempted to keep his distance, but another glance at the airspeed indicator told him that their plane was dangerously near to a stall. The Hardys tightened their seat belts when the craft began to buffet.

"Sorry, boys," the pilot said. "I can't make it." He was about to increase power when suddenly the STOL executed a sharp turn and headed directly for them. Jack quickly manoeuvred out of the way, but the sharp movement of the controls caused the aircraft to stall.

The plane rolled into an almost inverted position and dived vertically towards the ground!

# Suspect on the Run

FRANK and Joe were thrown against their seat belts as
the plane dropped earthward, and the wind whistled an
eerie dirge against the wings.

"Hang on!" Jack shouted as he pulled the throttle
closed and applied aileron and rudder control.

He managed to level the wings, then concentrated on
recovering from the steep dive. As he eased back slowly
on the wheel, the boys were pressed down into their
seats by the increasing G force.

Finally Jack had the aircraft back to straight and
level—but with not much altitude to spare. He
increased power and the plane climbed higher. For a
moment nobody spoke.

"Whew!" Joe finally exclaimed as he wiped perspiration from his face. "I can't say I'm too keen on this kind
of manoeuvre."

"Whoever is flying that STOL," Jack Wayne
remarked, "is a pretty good pilot."

"Keep a sharp lookout," Frank urged as he searched
the sky above them.

They continued to gain altitude and the boys scanned
the area on all sides. Ahead, puffy white cumulus
clouds built up over the hilly terrain.

"I'm afraid we've lost our quarry," the pilot said. "And I'll bet they're members of UGLI!"

"Yes, worse luck," Frank answered. "The clouds offer excellent cover. Trying to find those agents in it would be like trying to find a flea in a fog."

The Hardys decided to discontinue the chase and return to Great Circle's base. Upon landing, an announcement came over the public-address system.

"Frank and Joe Hardy, please report to the operations room."

The young sleuths sprinted to the administration building. In the operations room Kenneth Dell was clutching a telephone to his ear.

"What's up?" Frank asked.

"Flight Service has just given me the STOL's full registration number. I told them to let me know if they heard anything from the pilot," Dell said. "Looks as if we're in luck! He ran into bad weather north of here, and had to file an instrument flight plan."

"What's his destination?" Joe asked.

"Logan International Airport, Boston," the security chief replied.

"Jeepers!" Joe exclaimed. "Do you think that's where he was headed all the time?"

"I doubt it," Frank replied. "Timken wouldn't want anyone to know where he's going. I think they're just planning to land and wait for the weather to clear. Then they can continue the trip without a flight plan."

Dell signalled for silence as he pressed the receiver closer to his ear. He jotted down a few notes and then hung up.

"Here's something else," he announced. "The pilot's

name given on the flight plan is Mazer. And the owner of the STOL is the Coastal Courier Service."

"Say," Joe spoke up, "why don't we have Jack fly us to Boston right away? Logan is a busy airport. Timken might not notice our arrival."

"Good idea," Dell said. "In the meantime, I'm going to check out this information."

An hour and a half later Jack Wayne and the boys were cleared for landing at Logan International Airport.

"Looks as if the weather's beginning to improve," Jack remarked as they taxied to the parking ramp.

"I don't see the STOL anywhere," Joe observed.

"We'll check with operations," Frank said.

The boys hurried into the administration building. They located the operations manager and inquired about the STOL

"Why, yes," he said. "I remember the craft distinctly. It caught my eye, since that kind of thing is a rarity around here."

"Where is it now?" Joe asked.

"I think it took off about thirty minutes ago," the operations manager replied. "But why don't you check with the control tower?" He pointed to a wall telephone. "That's a direct line."

Frank picked up the phone.

"Logan Tower! Stigand speaking!" crackled from the receiver.

Frank said, "An STOL departed from here about half an hour ago. Can you tell me its destination?"

"Stand by!"

There were a few seconds of silence, then Stigand

reported, "The pilot filed an instrument flight plan for Concord Airport, New Hampshire. However, he broke into clear weather at Manchester and cancelled his flight plan."

"Thank you," Frank replied, dejected.

"So we've lost them again," Joe remarked.

"Timken and his pilot played it smart," Frank said. "They knew they'd fly into clear weather. I'll bet they never had any intention of landing at Concord."

Just then two men approached the youths.

"What's your interest in the STOL?" one of them demanded.

"Who are you?" Joe retorted.

"We're detectives! Boston Police Department!" They flashed their badges.

"My name is Amory," one said. He pointed to his partner. "And this is Detective Sergeant Doran."

Frank introduced himself and his companions.

"Hardy!" Amory exclaimed. "Any relation to Fenton Hardy the private detective?"

"We're his sons," Joe answered.

"Why did you ask us about our interest in the STOL?" Frank inquired.

"A couple of hours ago a local jeweller was approached by a fellow who tried to sell him a diamond. When the jeweller began to question him as to where he got it, the guy walked out. The jeweller became suspicious and called us."

"What started you looking for this man at the airport?" Joe asked.

Amory replied, "The jeweller said he was wearing a Great Circle Airways uniform. So the airport seemed a logical place to begin a search, although Great Circle doesn't come in here. We want to ask that fellow a few questions."

"He's gone," Frank said. "The man you're looking for is the same one we've been following. He took off in the STOL about half an hour ago."

"That adds up," Doran commented. "The operations manager told us a fellow answering the jeweller's description had already left."

"We approached you boys," Amory added, "because we heard you inquiring on the phone about the STOL"

There was little more the young sleuths could do, so they took off. During the return flight to Bayport, they mulled over the latest event.

"What do you make of Timken trying to peddle a diamond?" Joe asked.

"It sounds to me like an attempt to get rid of stolen goods," Frank concluded.

"Could be," Joe said thoughtfully. "You remember Dad's report said that Hexton's gang were robbers. If Timken is one of them, he may be smuggling in jewels stolen overseas and disposing of them here."

Frank agreed. "But UGLI's business is espionage. I doubt if they would become involved in jewel robberies. On the other hand, Hexton and his gang might be playing the two games at once."

When the boys arrived home, Frank at once telephoned their suspicions to Kenneth Dell.

"You have a good theory there," Great Circle's security chief said. "I'm going to call the police authorities in Scotland and inquire about recent jewel robberies." He promised to get in touch later.

After Frank hung up the phone, he stood silent for a moment. "Next we *must* figure out that message Dad left on the hotel wall," he told Joe.

Again they examined the row of numerals: 441810-682300. But after more than an hour of attempting to decipher them, Joe gave a sigh of frustration. "It doesn't make any more sense to me now than when we first started," he admitted.

"If this is a code, it's a real puzzler," Frank agreed. "But we've *got* to crack it!"

When Mrs Hardy announced that dinner was ready, the boys reluctantly interrupted their task. They ate quickly, then went right back to the message.

Frank stared at it. "Neither the substitution nor transposition ciphers work."

The young detectives worked late into the night. Exhausted, they finally went to bed.

Early the next day Frank and Joe continued to study the message, but all their efforts to decipher it ended in failure.

Shortly after ten o'clock Chet arrived at the Hardys' home. He plodded up the stairs to the detective's study.

"You're too late for breakfast, chum," Frank said with a grin.

"Aw, cut it out," Chet mumbled. "Anyway, I stopped at Biff Hooper's house before I came here. His mother was baking the most delicious pancakes I ever saw, with sausages and all the trimmings."

"Glad to hear that," Joe said jokingly. "We wouldn't want to see you fade away."

"How is Biff?" Frank inquired as he glanced at his friend. Biff Hooper was a schoolmate of the boys at Bayport High.

"He's just fine. I wanted to show him a couple of my magic tricks."

"Don't tell us you took that silver bowl of yours along?" Joe asked.

"No, that's old stuff," Chet retorted. "My new tricks are more sophisticated."

"Oh yeah!" said Joe, chuckling.

"Go ahead and laugh if you want to," Chet continued indignantly. "At least Biff appreciated the great latitude of my genius."

At Chet's remark, Frank sat bolt upright in his chair.

"What's the matter?" Chet asked, startled.

"Would you repeat what you just said?" Frank asked excitedly.

"You mean about Biff's appreciating the latitude of my genius?"

Frank sprang up. "The key! You've given me the key!"

# ·8·

## Sailing Sleuths

CHET looked confused. "What key? I don't see any key," he said, glancing around.

"You mentioned latitude! That must be it—latitude and longitude!" Frank pointed to the numerals in the mystery message.

"I still don't get it," said Chet.

Frank explained. "Notice that there are a total of twelve digits. The first six—441810—must mean 44 degrees, 18 minutes, 10 seconds of latitude. The remaining figures—682300—would then stand for 68 degrees, 23 minutes, 00 seconds of longitude."

"You're right!" Joe exclaimed.

Frank riffled through a stack of maps and selected one showing the Atlantic seaboard. "Those co-ordinates would locate a position in the area covered by this map."

"Hold on!" Joe said as he glanced at a chart of the world that he had just unfolded. "The message doesn't specify whether the latitude is east or west, or the longitude north or south. Therefore, these co-ordinates might designate a location in Asia, the southern tip of South America, or the middle of the Indian Ocean."

"True," Frank agreed. "But since Dad didn't make

that clear in the message, I'm certain he means the position is in our own hemisphere."

He marked the spot on his map indicated by the co-ordinates. It was about eighteen miles off the northeast coast of the United States.

"But that's a spot in the Atlantic Ocean!" Joe exclaimed.

Frank pulled out a nautical chart. It was on a smaller scale and showed more detail. Replotting the position, he discovered several small islets in the vicinity—so small they did not have names. The latitude and longitude co-ordinates lay directly over one.

"Gosh!" Joe exclaimed. "It looks as if we're on to something! My guess is one of two possibilities—either the place is UGLI's headquarters for the U.S., or else it's where Dad was taken."

"Maybe it's both," Joe added. "We'd better make a trip to that island!"

"What about me?" Chet demanded. "Can I come, too? After all, I found the key!"

Frank bowed towards his chum. "It'll be a pleasure to have you along, genius," he said. "We might need your help." Then he walked to the telephone. "I'll call Jack and tell him to have the plane ready tomorrow morning."

When Frank told the pilot their destination, Jack assured him there were several aviation radio facilities in the vicinity that would permit them to pinpoint the islet from the air.

Early the following day the Hardys, Chet, and Jack were winging their way towards the mystery spot. Soon they paralleled the Atlantic coast.

"How long do you estimate it'll take us to reach the place?" Frank asked Jack.

The pilot checked the bearings indicated by the radio compass and omni-navigation receiver, then thumbed his small computer. "I'd say about thirty minutes from our present position."

The boys gazed below. Ocean waves broke against the craggy coastline, tracing it with a ribbon of white foam that stretched as far as the eye could see.

As they passed over a small sailboat, Joe took out binoculars and scanned the area below. "Little islands ahead," he announced, and soon the others made out small sprinkles of land dotting the surface of the water.

"According to the cross bearings I calculated," Jack announced, "we should be over the place you want within one minute."

"And what exactly are we looking for?" Chet queried.

"I don't know," Frank answered. "But if—"

"Hey!" Joe interrupted. "I see a lighthouse on that islet just below us."

Frank took the binoculars. "You're right. It appears to be abandoned, but there are several cylindrical-shaped objects just to the left of the lighthouse."

Jack took the plane to a lower altitude and Frank readjusted the glasses. "They look like drums of oil, or petrol," he said.

"But for what?" Joe questioned. "A boat? Certainly couldn't be for an aeroplane."

The pilot asked for the binoculars and studied the islet. "The surface is level enough for a plane," he observed, "but it's much too short to be used as a runway—that is, except for a helicopter, or perhaps an STOL!"

Frank and Joe glanced at each other. Could there be a connection between the islet and the STOL in which Timken had eluded them?

Frank suggested they fly back to the coast and land at the nearest airport. "I want to find out about the islet," he said.

Jack found a small field not far inland and set the plane down. The Hardys hopped out and hastened to the operations shack. There they met a solid, middle-aged man with a shock of grey hair, who introduced himself as Ty Carter, the owner of the airport.

"I don't know much about that islet with the abandoned lighthouse," Carter told them, "except that it is private property. It was sold by auction recently."

"Have you any idea who bought it?" Joe asked.

"Fellow named Bodkins. He's not from around here so I can't tell you anything about him."

"Bodkins?" Frank thought. A possibility struck him. "Could this be an alias of Hexton's?" Aloud he questioned, "Have you ever seen an STOL in the vicinity of the islet?"

"Funny you should mention that," Carter replied. "During the past couple of weeks I saw one headed in that direction several times. But whether it was going to the islet or not, I wouldn't know."

The boys thanked the man for his co-operation, then returned to the plane.

"Fellows," Frank said suddenly, "I have an idea. Why don't we rent a boat and look at the place?"

"What if Hexton and his men *are* on the islet?" Chet asked.

"That's a chance we'll have to take."

After lunch Jack remained with the plane, while Chet and the Hardys hiked to the nearby coastal town. They found a boat-rental place, but unfortunately all the power craft were in use. Frank finally selected a small jib-headed racer.

He manned the helm while Joe and Chet hauled the sails to the top of the mast. A strong breeze carried them quickly away from the dock. Nearly three hours passed before the islet appeared off the port bow of their craft.

"Seems deserted," Joe said.

Frank manipulated the helm to direct the boat in a wide circle round the tiny point of land. From the other side of the islet a fast powerboat appeared.

When it drew closer, Joe exclaimed, "That's Stony Bleeker at the wheel! And Vordo's with him. They must have spotted us!"

"The boat's going to ram ours!" Chet shouted as the craft headed directly for the yacht.

Frank applied hard helm and changed course quickly. The powerboat missed the stern by a few inches and threw a heavy spray of water over the boys. Its wake rocked the yacht violently.

"Hold fast!" Frank cried out. "Stay in the centre, fellows, or we'll capsize!"

"Look!" Joe yelled. "They've turned and they're coming at us again!"

As the powerboat sped perilously close, more water foamed over the gunwales.

"We can't stay upright much longer!" Joe shouted.

The next pass by the powerboat was so close that the two craft touched each other. The boys hung on, but plunged into the sea an instant later as the yacht went over on its side.

Vordo burst into wild laughter. Stony was so preoccupied watching the boys come to the surface he failed to notice that he was steering directly towards the islet.

"Watch out!" Vordo bellowed at him.

Bleeker made a desperate, last-minute effort to turn away. Too late!

*Crash!*

The powerboat's momentum carried it on to the craggy shore, and a sharp rock ripped through its hull.

The men leaped out. Furious, they shook their fists. "We'll get you for this!" Vordo thundered at the three boys, who now lay across the half-overturned hull of the yacht.

"Now what?" Chet asked.

Frank and Joe were glumly silent. They knew that trying to right their boat with its water-soaked sails would be next to impossible and the only haven within swimming distance was the islet!

# ·9·

## The Lighthouse Prison

In a split second Frank had made up his mind. "Quick!" he shouted. "Help me haul in the mainsail! It's our best bet."

Joe unfastened the lanyard while the other two, with great effort, pulled the top of the partially submerged sail down the mast. When they had it tightly lashed round the boom, the boys secured the working jib.

"Jumping catfish!" Chet yelled in alarm. "We're drifting closer to the islet!"

While he and Joe watched the movements of Vordo and Bleeker, Frank swam to the other side of the boat. He put his weight against the bottom of the keel and tried to force it downwards into the water.

"Push up hard on the mast!" he shouted to Joe and Chet.

The power of their combined efforts started to rotate the yacht.

"Harder!" Frank yelled. "Push up harder!"

Suddenly the boat rolled to an upright position. Frank reached for a hand bail-out pump clamped against the inside of the hull. Working frantically, he pumped the water out of the boat. Then he flung himself over the gunwales, followed by Joe and Chet.

"They're taking off!" Vordo bellowed to Bleeker. "After 'em!"

The two men plunged into the water and swam towards the three boys.

"Up with the sails!" Frank commanded. "I'll take the helm."

Joe and Chet hoisted the sails into place. A strong breeze caught them and began pushing the boat ahead. Frank turned the craft sharply away from the islet.

Vordo screamed at them furiously, "Stop!"

"He seems to be the excitable type," Chet said, weak with relief, as they went speeding back towards the mainland.

"We certainly didn't win that battle," Joe observed wryly. "We're retreating."

Frank nodded. "We'll have to find another way to get here, and fast," he declared. "If Dad's a prisoner in the lighthouse, they'll probably move him out as quickly as they can."

The boat had covered nearly half the distance to the mainland when the sails became almost limp.

"The wind is dying down," Joe said, alarmed. "We're barely moving."

Gradually the breeze subsided to a complete calm. The yacht ceased to move ahead and rocked gently with the waves. Frank grabbed a paddle that was clamped under the gunwale. "Guess we'll have to get back the hard way."

"It'll take us all night at this rate!" Chet exclaimed. "There can't be much more than another hour or so of daylight."

"We have no choice," Frank said. "Let's take turns paddling."

Chet's prediction proved to be right. It was well into the night before they could see the vague outline of docks strung along the coast.

Presently they heard the put-put of an outboard motor and a bright beam of light swept the surface of water ahead. As the boat drew closer, they recognized the pilot as the man who had rented them the sailboat.

"Hey!" he shouted. "You said you wanted the boat for the day, not for the night!"

"Right." Frank grinned. "We were becalmed. How about giving us a tow to your dock?"

The man threw them a line and went on, "I've been searching for you guys since dark. In an hour I was going to notify the Coast Guard."

"I'm sorry," Frank said.

When they reached land, the boatman saw that the youths were totally exhausted. "I have extra bunks in my shack," he said. "It'll be daylight in another couple of hours. Why don't you lads eat a bite, then get some sleep?" The boys accepted his offer gratefully.

Before turning in, Frank called the airport and asked to speak to Jack.

"I was worried about you fellows," the pilot said with deep concern. "I've been waiting here in the operations shack, wondering what happened. I almost notified the police."

Frank told him of the day's adventure, then suggested that they meet in the morning for breakfast.

It was five o'clock when Frank was awakened by the sound of a motor. He climbed from his bunk and peered out of the window. What he saw caused him to snap wide awake. Vordo and Bleeker in their powerboat! "They must have made temporary repairs," he thought.

Frank awakened his companions. "Wh-what's the matter?" Chet mumbled, rubbing his eyes.

"Look!" Frank said, pointing to the boat. It was just docking at a pier where a sign read: CLARK'S BOAT REPAIRS.

"That's it!" Joe declared. "They're having the hull fixed." An idea flashed through his mind. "Now would be a good time to return to the islet!"

"Don't tell me we're going to paddle ourselves all the way," Chet complained.

"We'll rent a motorboat," Frank said. He made arrangements for the craft, then telephoned the airport and explained his plan to Jack. "Vordo and Stony Bleeker just arrived with their damaged powerboat. It's docked at Clark's Boat Repair place. Could you rent a car, drive down here, and keep an eye on those two? If they should start back to the islet before we return, fly out and warn us by making a low pass. If they start to leave town, notify the authorities."

"Wilco!" the pilot replied. "I'll get going right away."

When the boys went to the dock, the owner said, "Fellows, I've just learned by radio there's some bad weather in store—a nor'easter." He pointed towards a darkening ridge of clouds far off on the horizon. "You can see it stirring up already."

"But this is important!" Frank insisted.

The boatman pondered for a moment. "Well, if you promise to keep a sharp eye to the weather and to pull into land if it starts blowing too much, I guess you can have a boat."

The boys thanked him and after a quick breakfast started out to the islet. The trip took less than half the time it had required in the sailboat. Nevertheless, when the lighthouse came into view, the sky had grown dark and the howling wind had developed into gale force.

"A hurricane!" Chet cried out.

Torrential rain burst upon the boys and the boat was tossed around like a cork in the heavy seas. But Frank skilfully kept it headed for the islet and finally manoeuvred close to shore.

Joe tied the mooring line round his waist and leaped into the water. He swam hard to the craggy shore and soon had the boat on solid ground.

"Whew!" Chet groaned. "It's going to take me a month to dry out."

The boys peered through the sweeping sheets of rain at the lighthouse. Frank signalled his companions to be silent as they crept towards a lighted window near the base of the structure. Peering inside, they saw a man seated at a table.

"Burly Wilkes!" Joe whispered.

"He's alone," Frank observed. "That's a break for us."

"But what about Dad?" Joe asked.

"If they're holding him prisoner here," Frank said, "he's in another room."

"Let me take a look," Chet suggested, and stretched higher for a glimpse inside. He slipped on a rock and banged his head against the glass. Burly Wilkes whirled round.

"Hide!" Frank ordered.

As Wilkes stomped to the window, the boys flattened themselves against the wall. Apparently satisfied nothing was wrong, he returned to his chair.

"That was close," Joe commented.

"Sorry," Chet mumbled sheepishly. "Now what?"

Frank whispered a plan. "We'll break in and take Wilkes by surprise. When I give the signal, hit the door with all you've got."

The boys positioned themselves. Frank raised his hand slowly, then dropped it. The three threw themselves against the door and it burst open. Wilkes jumped up from his chair, too startled to utter a cry.

"Stay where you are!" Frank commanded.

But Wilkes, recognizing the Hardys, bolted for a staircase which spiralled up to the top of the lighthouse. The boys raced after him.

Reaching the top, Wilkes rushed through a doorway and started to swing the metal door closed behind him. But Joe managed to prevent it from slamming shut by jumping into the narrow opening.

"There he goes!" Chet shouted as he spotted Wilkes running out on to a catwalk encircling the top of the structure.

Finally the fugitive could go no farther. He was trapped and turned to face his pursuers. He threw a punch but missed. Frank countered with a blow to the stomach that sent the man sprawling. In a flash, Joe and Chet were on him and Wilkes was pinned helplessly to the metal grating of the catwalk.

"Let go of me!" he screeched.

Frank motioned the other two off, then dragged the

man to his feet. "Hexton kidnapped our father, didn't he?"

"Yes. But I had nothing to do with it!"

"Where are they keeping him?"

"He *was* here."

"Was?"

"Well, he's gone!"

"Where?"

"I don't know. Mr Hardy escaped more than five days ago. Those SKOOL men are pretty smart!"

# · 10 ·

## Wing Signal

THE boys were dumbfounded. "What do you mean our dad escaped?" Joe asked. "How?"

"I don't know. I wasn't here."

Frank believed that Wilkes was telling the truth. But where could their father be? And why hadn't he been in touch with them?

The Hardys tied Wilkes securely to a chair. Then Frank, Joe, and Chet settled down to wait out the storm.

While the wind and rain beat against the lighthouse, Frank and Joe questioned Wilkes further. Their prisoner said he did not know the whereabouts of Hexton, nor just what sort of an operation he was running.

"I'm a new man in the outfit. The magician hasn't taken me into his confidence," he added.

"So you're just learning the UGLI business," Frank remarked. Wilkes nodded.

He admitted that the metal drums which the Hardys had spotted contained aeroplane fuel, but now were empty. This was confirmed by Joe's thorough search as soon as the rain subsided and the sun burst through the broken clouds.

"Okay, Wilkes," Frank said tersely when his brother returned. "You told the truth about the drums. What about the STOL?"

The man's jaw dropped. "Wh-what'd you mean—STOL?"

"You know all right!" Joe said. "So far, we've made things easy for you, Wilkes, but if you don't tell the whole story, we'll have you charged as an accomplice to a kidnapping!"

"No, no!" he whined, blanching a sickly white. "I saw the plane land here twice. Both times it stayed for a few minutes, then took off again."

"Were there any passengers aboard?"

"Just one guy wearing some kind of uniform." The man began to perspire freely. "Hexton will kill me if he finds out I told you."

"Don't worry about him," Chet said. "The Hardys will take care of that crooked magician."

Just then they heard an aeroplane and rushed outside. Looking up, they saw their own plane coming in from the west. It dived and made a low pass over the islet.

"The signal!" Frank exclaimed. "Vordo and Bleeker must be on their way back!"

"Let's wait and nab 'em," Joe suggested.

Frank was about to answer when Jack Wayne headed in towards the islet again. He made another low pass, but this time the boys saw a small object drop from the plane. It bounced along the rocky surface and rolled to a stop close by. It was a metal box with a message inside:

*Vordo and Bleeker on way back! Have two other men with*

*them. Believe they are armed. Suggest you leave immediately.
Head north before turning towards mainland to avoid their
boat.*

"Let's get out of here fast!" Chet said.

"I don't like the idea of running," Frank said, "but
the odds are against us. We'll go back to the mainland
and notify the police."

Pushing the reluctant Wilkes before them, the boys
hastened to their motorboat. Luckily it was undamaged
by the storm. A quick check of the fuel, however,
showed they could not take the northerly course Jack
had suggested.

"We have just enough fuel to make shore," Frank
announced.

"What about Vordo and his men?" Chet asked.

"Maybe we'll be able to slip by without their
noticing us," Frank answered.

Wilkes became arrogant at hearing that his accomplices were on their way back. "You'd better leave me
behind if you know what's good for you," he growled.

"Nothing doing," Joe retorted angrily. "And don't
try to attract the attention of your buddies. I'm sure
they'd reward you for having talked," he added
sarcastically.

This frightened Wilkes. He slumped down.

While Jack circled overhead, the boys made a beeline
for the coast. A little more than half an hour had
passed, when Jack throttled the engines on and off
several times.

"Is he having trouble?" Chet asked.

The pilot revved the engines again.

"No!" Joe exclaimed. "He's signalling us!" Joe

pointed to a small object in the distance, moving across the water. "That must be Vordo!"

Frank quickly turned the motorboat on to a different course as the approaching boat drew steadily closer. In it were four men. The pilot, a tall, massive fellow, was unmistakably Vordo. He was steering directly towards the boys' boat.

"They've seen us!" Joe cried.

Frank attempted some evasive manoeuvres, while still heading for the mainland. But the other boat was faster. Although Frank spun his wheel sharply in a series of turns to port and starboard, their pursuers continued to gain.

Finally Vordo bore down, but as he did, Frank pointed skyward and yelled, "Look up there!"

Jack roared down in a screaming dive and pulled out directly in front of the powerboat. Then, just as a collision seemed imminent, Jack pulled up, missing Vordo and his men by inches. Vordo veered out of the way but Jack repeated his manoeuvre.

The Hardys and Chet momentarily forgot their predicament as they admired Jack's flying skill. At times he came so close to the surface that little water spouts were generated by the whirling propellers.

"Wow!" chortled Chet. "Vordo's getting discouraged."

"I'd say he's scared to death—and who wouldn't be. Attaboy, Jack!" Joe grinned.

Again and again Jack Wayne made close passes at the powerboat, forcing Vordo and his associates farther away from the boys. By the time the three sleuths neared the mainland, their pursuers were lost from sight. Jack then flew high above the boys, waggling his wings in salute.

Upon reaching shore, the Hardys turned Burly Wilkes over to the authorities. A police helicopter was immediately dispatched to the islet. Soon a report was radioed in from the 'copter. The island was deserted, and a search of the surrounding area had revealed no clues to the suspects.

Frank asked an officer if he might make a phone call to Ty Carter's airfield. Moments later he had Jack Wayne on the wire.

"Thanks for getting us out of this one," Frank said. "That was great flying."

The pilot chuckled. "I don't mind a little exercise now and then."

"Did you notice where Vordo was headed?"

"They took a northerly course, but I couldn't trail them because my fuel ran low. Sorry. I did give the police the lead."

Frank asked Jack to meet them at the hotel. "We'll stay at least another day, in case something turns up. Better bring the car you rented."

Next morning the Hardys received a telephone call from Ty Carter. He said an STOL had just landed at his field.

"What's the registration number?" Frank asked excitedly.

When Carter told him, Frank noted that it was identical with that of the STOL they had chased.

"I don't think it'll be staying here long," the man

continued. "The pilot is sitting in the cockpit. Apparently he expects some passengers to show up at any minute."

"Can you delay their take-off for a while?" Frank asked.

"I don't know. The guy seems to be in a great hurry. But I'll try."

Jack Wayne and the boys drove to the airport immediately and ran to the operations shack.

"They're taxiing out for take-off right now," Carter told them. He pointed through the window at the STOL as it moved slowly towards the active runway. "I couldn't delay them any longer. The pilot asked that his plane be refuelled. I told my line boys to take their time about it. But the pilot's passengers arrived."

"Vordo and his gang!" Joe exploded.

"Let's head them off!" Frank urged.

The boys dashed to their car and drove out after the taxiing aircraft. Moments later the car came to an abrupt halt, bogged down in a stretch of marshy ground just off the airport taxiway.

"Oh, no!" Chet blurted.

"They're getting away!" Joe shouted.

Frank jumped out and chased after the STOL. His companions followed. He was the first to reach the craft, just as it lined up for take-off. He recognized three of the passengers—Vordo, Bleeker, and the steward Timken. Frank lunged at the plane, but stumbled, lost his balance, and fell across the tail. The aircraft was moving so fast he could not let go.

Joe, Chet and Jack, who had continued the chase,

now stopped in their tracks and watched in horror.

The plane continued its take-off run, with Frank clinging desperately to the tail!

# ·11·

## Important Assignment

FRANK fought back panic as the STOL lifted off the runway. With both hands he grabbed hold of one of the elevators and hoisted his body farther on to the tail.

He could feel the pilot tugging at the control wheel, but Frank's desperate hold on the elevator kept it from moving. The pilot was forced to reduce engine power and drop back down on to the ground.

He jammed the brakes on hard, then executed a partial ground-loop to avoid going off the end of the runway. The movement flung Frank from the tail on to the grass-covered shoulder.

Getting to his feet, dazed but unhurt, he watched helplessly as the plane headed down the runway. In a moment it had left the ground and was soaring upwards.

"Quick!" Frank shouted as he ran to meet Jack Wayne and the others. "Let's follow them!"

"You okay?" Joe asked.

When Frank said he was, the four pursuers leaped into the Hardy plane and took off. Ahead, Joe caught a glimpse of reflected sunlight flashing from the STOL's metal wings.

"There it is!" he yelled to the others.

Jack rammed the throttle ahead as far as it would go. He climbed rapidly above the altitude of the fugitives, then dived to get extra airspeed. The manoeuvre began to close the distance between the two craft.

"We're gaining on it!" Joe observed.

Chet pointed to the right wing of their own plane. "Look!" he yelled. "The fuel cap is loose!"

"On the left wing, too!" Joe shouted. By now both caps were vibrating furiously.

"That can't be," Jack Wayne insisted. "I checked them myself after I refuelled!"

"This must be Vordo's doing!" Frank surmised.

The next moment the two caps came loose and fluttered in the wind on the small chains which held them to the tanks. Instantly the slipstream began to drag fuel from the wings. As two gossamer-like columns sailed off into the distance behind them, Jack Wayne applied hard aileron and rudder and turned back to the airport.

"I'm landing!" he said. "We're losing every drop of petrol. I just hope a spark from the engine exhaust doesn't ignite that trail of fuel, or we're goners!"

Tensely the boys watched gallon after gallon of high octane spray from the open tanks.

"How long will she keep running?" Frank asked anxiously.

"I don't know!" Jack replied. "But by the look of our fuel gauges—not long!"

Finally the airport came into view. Jack entered the traffic pattern just as their tanks ran dry. Starved of fuel, the engines sputtered, then quit completely.

Fortunately, the plane was high enough to glide safely to the field.

"Whew!" Chet murmured as the wheels touched down lightly. "That's the closest I've ever come to being barbecued."

Jack grinned. "I was once told that flying involves long hours of boredom, interrupted by moments of extreme fright." He took a deep breath. "This was one of those moments."

"No use trying to go back up after the STOL," Frank said disconsolately.

He telephoned Kenneth Dell at Great Circle Airways and told him of Burly Wilkes' capture and their father's escape.

"I learned about it yesterday," Dell replied. "In fact, your father was in contact with me."

"What!" Frank said excitedly. "You talked to Dad?"

"Yes. I would have told you sooner, but I didn't know where to get in touch."

"But he escaped over five days ago," Frank said. "Why didn't he let us know? Is he okay?"

"He's fine," Dell assured him. "However I don't know where he is. He wants his whereabouts kept secret. Said he'd explain everything later and asked me to inform your mother, which I did."

Dell added that he had an important assignment for the boys, and would like to meet them at their home in Bayport the next day.

"Thanks," Frank said. "See you tomorrow."

Mrs Hardy and Aunt Gertrude were overjoyed to see Frank and Joe that evening. But they were worried that Mr Hardy was keeping his whereabouts a mystery.

"He's probably travelling incognito and in disguise," Aunt Gertrude said.

Thoroughly exhausted by their recent adventures, the boys went to bed shortly after dinner. The next morning they enjoyed a hearty breakfast of wheatcakes and sausages, then adjourned to their father's study. Kenneth Dell arrived shortly and joined the boys in the upstairs room.

"Well, I suppose you want to hear the assignment?" he asked, smiling.

"Yes," the boys replied, and Frank added, "What's your plan for us, Mr Dell?"

"How would you like to fly to Scotland?"

The query caught the young detectives by surprise. "Scotland?" Joe echoed incredulously.

"That's right." Dell rose from his chair and began to pace the floor slowly.

"Two days ago I called police authorities in Scotland. They told me there have been several remarkably clever jewel thefts lately in Scotland. Each of them occurred on a day when the steward Timken was over there. They checked and learned that he had visited Hexton's castle on those days."

"So we were right," said Frank. "He is one of the gang."

"Yes, but as usual there is no usable evidence."

"If only Frank and I could get inside that castle," said Joe, "we could get the goods on both the UGLI operation and the robbery ring."

"That's exactly the idea," said Dell. "My air-line is co-operating with the Scottish police and Detective-Inspector Clyde of C.I.D. I want you to go over as my operatives, if you would."

"We'd sure like to take a crack at it!" Frank declared.

"What about SKOOL?" Joe asked.

Dell shook his head. "No sale. They're going straight for Hexton himself and they're sure he's not at the castle just now."

"Have the authorities over there made any progress on the thefts?" Joe questioned.

"So far, they haven't turned up any evidence incriminating Hexton. One police official there will be working with you—Detective-Inspector Clyde. He's a member of the C.I.D.—that stands for Criminal Investigation Department, you know."

The boys nodded.

"Clyde is on a special assignment to see what he can dig up on our magician friend."

"When do you want us to leave?" Frank asked.

"One of our planes departs day after tomorrow."

"We'll be ready!" Frank promised.

"And by the way," the security chief added, "if you'd like to bring your friend Chet—"

"A herd of elephants couldn't stop him from coming!" Joe put in.

Dell said he would meet the boys at the Great Circle base for a final briefing on the day of the flight. He then wished them luck and left.

Brimming with excitement, Joe phoned the news to Chet. "A castle in Scotland!" their chum exclaimed. "Wow!"

"Maybe we can find another magic silver bowl for you," Joe said jokingly. "One that works."

"Aw, come on," Chet protested. Then he perked up.

"But wait till you see some of my new tricks!"

"We'll see them when we get back," Frank advised him. "Right now we'd better think about packing."

"You fellows just don't have any appreciation of my uncanny skill," Chet said and hung up.

Mrs Hardy's and Aunt Gertrude's reactions to the coming trip were quite different. "Scotland!" the boys' aunt exclaimed. "First your father decides to play hide-and-seek, now you two want to go traipsing into danger on the other side of the Atlantic!"

Mrs Hardy looked at her sons with a worried smile. "You know you have my permission. Just promise me you'll be careful."

"Of course we will," Frank and Joe assured her.

After supper they began preparations for their trip. Frank had just brought suitcases from the attic when the phone rang. He picked up the receiver.

"Are you Frank Hardy?" a man asked.

"That's right."

"I've got to see you." There was a note of urgency in the caller's voice. "It's important."

"First, suppose you tell me who you are," Frank said.

"I'm Stan Mazer, pilot of the STOL!" was the astounding answer.

## ·12·

## A Startling Welcome

AMAZED and perplexed by the call, the Hardys agreed to meet the STOL pilot the following day at their home.

"Why should he want to come here?" Joe asked. "If he's an UGLI agent, you'd think this is the last place he'd visit."

"It's sure strange," Frank agreed. "I can't wait to hear what he has to say. In any case, I think we should notify Dell to have him followed when he leaves here."

"Right." Joe telephoned the SKOOL man.

Late the following morning Stan Mazer arrived at the Hardy home. He was a middle-aged man, of medium height and slender build, and had a troubled expression.

"I'm Mazer," he announced.

The Hardys led him into the living room and they all sat down.

"You're the pilot of Hexton's STOL?" Frank asked.

"That's right," Mazer answered. "I was hired about two months ago." He shifted nervously in his chair.

"I needed a job so badly I snapped it up without question. But I didn't know it was connected with anything illegal."

"Weren't you ever suspicious?" Joe asked.

"Yes, from time to time, but I wasn't sure. Actually I closed my mind to the whole situation until you tried to stop my take-off."

"It was a pretty unnerving experience," Frank said dryly.

Mazer apologized. "I didn't know you were clinging to the tail until you were thrown clear," he explained. "I wanted to get out and help you, but Vordo forced me to take off."

"What about the day we chased you and Timken?" Joe said. "You turned right into us. We nearly collided!"

"I didn't know that was you," Mazer said, surprised. "I thought it was some hot-shot pilot wanting to play games. I pulled that manoeuvre hoping I'd throw a scare into him. Sorry."

When Frank asked Mazer where he had taken Vordo and his accomplices, the pilot replied, "To a large airport near New York City. When we landed, Vordo and his companions got out of the plane and disappeared—I had no idea where."

Mazer said that while he was parking the STOL, he was confronted by a Federal airport authority agent, who told him that all their offices had been alerted to be on the lookout for the aircraft. To his surprise, the registration papers turned out to have been obtained under a fictitious name and address.

"The agent immediately impounded the plane,"

Mazer said, "and my pilot's licence was revoked pending a hearing."

The Hardys asked him if he knew anything about their father being kidnapped.

"I know nothing about that," he insisted, "although I did suspect something strange was going on in the lighthouse."

"In what way?" Joe asked

"I was never allowed to enter," the pilot answered, "or even to remain long on the islet after delivering my passengers."

Frank pretended to be suspicious of the story. "Are you going to tell us you don't belong to the same secret criminal organization Hexton does? He wouldn't let you work for him if you didn't."

"What do you mean?" Mazer asked, and his amazement seemed genuine. "I never heard about any criminal organization and I'm certainly not a member!"

Joe asked him, "How did you learn who we are, and where to contact us?"

"Vordo mentioned your names during my last flight," Mazer replied. "He said that you were smart detectives."

Frank looked at the pilot searchingly. "What made you decide to come here and tell us all this?"

Mazer appeared harried. "After what happened at the airport, I knew I'd become involved in something that would get me into deep trouble," he confessed. "I thought if I told you fellows what I know, you'd help me."

Frank and Joe sensed that the pilot was being honest, and a slight nod between them said, "He's okay." They promised to do what they could and advised Mazer to repeat his story to Kenneth Dell.

"I'll do it at once," he said.

When the pilot left, the boys chuckled at the thought of the agent who had been assigned to follow Mazer. "I'd like to see his face when he tails him to Dell's office," said Joe.

The Hardys spent the rest of the day packing. Their flight to the Great Circle base was scheduled for the following morning.

Late that afternoon Chet's bright yellow jalopy screeched to a halt in front of the Hardy home and the chubby youth leaped out.

"I'm packed and champing at the bit!" he exclaimed as he greeted his friends.

"Good!" Frank said. "How about dinner? Aunt Gertrude's trying out a new recipe for beef stew."

"Well—okay, but I'll have to make it fast. I want to get home in time for supper!"

Chet then assumed a nonchalant air. Strolling slowly round the room, he began to whistle softly. The boys watched as he extended his arms in front of him, then clenched his left hand into a fist. From it, with his right hand, he drew out a vivid purple silk scarf, followed by a train of multi-coloured kerchiefs.

"Bravo!" Joe said, clapping loudly.

"Great trick, eh? I thought you'd like it."

When the last scarf refused to come out, however, Chet became aggravated. "What's the matter with this thing?" He tugged on it violently.

"Something go wrong?" Joe needled.

Suddenly the kerchief pulled free and dragged the

lining of Chet's jacket sleeve along with it. A small black container was revealed. From it popped a metal spring which shot through the air, then bounced around the floor like a grasshopper.

"So that's where all those scarfs came from," Frank said. He tried not to laugh.

Chet whipped off his jacket and frantically stuffed the lining back into the sleeve. As he chased the bouncing spring round the room, the Hardys burst into howls of laughter.

"You fellows are a jinx when it comes to my magic tricks," Chet said indignantly.

"Maybe Hexton will give you a few pointers when we get to his castle," Joe teased.

By the time Mrs Hardy and Aunt Gertrude announced dinner, Chet had regained his composure. He had a second helping of dessert, then decided he must leave.

"Thanks for the delicious meal," he said.

Chet slowly rose from the dinner table. He stuffed the string of silk kerchiefs into his pocket and lumbered out to his jalopy.

The next day Frank and Joe said goodbye to their mother and Aunt Gertrude, then drove off. They picked up Chet and went directly to the Bayport field. Jack Wayne was already warming up the engines when they arrived.

Tossing their luggage into the plane's baggage compartment, the boys climbed aboard and strapped themselves into their seats. Minutes later they were streaking down the runway on take-off.

Kenneth Dell was waiting for them at Great Circle's

base. He gave a long briefing, then at six p.m. led the boys to the plane that was to whisk them overnight to Scotland. Chet and the Hardys took their seats with the other passengers. Soon the sleek jetliner roared down the runway, lifted off, and headed over the Atlantic.

After a while Chet struck up a conversation with a pretty red-haired stewardess. She managed to keep him amply supplied with food, while he related stories of his long and daring hours in the air.

"I don't like to boast," Chet said as he munched on a plateful of cookies, "but I'm going to wake up some morning and find I've sprouted wings if I don't spend more time on the ground."

Frank and Joe, meanwhile, studied every passenger aboard, occasionally strolling up and down the aisle on the chance they might recognize some member of Hexton's gang. But nothing seemed to be amiss. Also, no one indicated to the Hardys that he was a SKOOL man.

Suddenly the loudspeaker crackled to life. "This is your captain speaking," announced a deep voice. "We expect to encounter a cold front in a few minutes. The weather forecast lists it as a weak system, so there should be only light to moderate turbulence. We should be through most of it in forty minutes. Please fasten your seat belts and relax."

The boys looked out of the window. Already the blue sky was beginning to be obscured by wisps of grey clouds. It grew so dark that the cabin lights had to be turned on. The jetliner began to toss jerkily. Chet fell quiet as the stewardess returned to her seat. He stared straight ahead with a blank expression.

"What's wrong with you?" Frank called across the aisle.

"I—I feel awful," Chet moaned. Seeing the stout boy's expression, the Hardys knew he had overeaten.

Chet remained tight-lipped for nearly fifty minutes until the plane came out of the churning clouds and into clear air. By this time he was asleep.

Several hours later the captain announced that the plane was commencing a gradual descent to Prestwick Airport. For a moment the jetliner was enveloped in a milky whiteness as it entered a blanket of stratus clouds that stretched for several miles north of the Irish Sea.

Frank looked down while the plane descended through the overcast. "That chain of islands over there must be the Hebrides," he said.

"And look!" Joe added, pointing off in the distance. "There's Ireland."

Suddenly Chet snapped alert. "Wh-where are we?" he asked.

"Just coming up on the Scottish coast," Joe told him. "How do you feel?"

Chet rubbed his eyes. "Oh—okay, I guess," he answered sleepily. "But never again so much food!"

"Oh no?" Joe grinned.

At seven o'clock Greenwich time, the jetliner's wheels touched down on the macadam surface of the runway and taxied to the parking ramp.

As the boys walked across the ramp towards the administration building, a car marked "Police" sped up to them. Seated behind the wheel was a man with a large sweeping moustache and a hat pulled low over

his eyes. He rolled down the window and called out,
"Are you the Hardys?"

"That's right," Frank answered. "And our friend
Chet Morton."

"Inspector Clyde sent me to fetch you. He wants
to see you right away. We'll send for your luggage
later."

"What about customs?" Frank inquired.

"We've already arranged special clearance," the
driver explained.

Frank, Joe, and Chet squeezed into the back seat.
On the floor in front a blanket covered a large package.
The car started off with a violent lurch. It sped across
the airport ramp, out through an exit, and on to a road
leading away from the field.

At that moment the driver yanked off the blanket.
A man crouched beneath it straightened up and settled
in his seat. The boys were flabbergasted at his sudden
appearance.

"Wh-what—?" Frank started to say, when the man
turned round and faced them. They gasped.

*Vordo!*

# · 13 ·

## Sky Spies

As the boys stared in dismay, the driver pulled off his false moustache and removed his hat. Stony Bleeker!

Vordo looked at the Hardys with contempt. "Insist on poking your noses into our business, hey?" he growled. "We'll fix you for good!"

Frank realized that the boys could not risk attacking their abductors. The driver would surely lose control of the car and all might be killed. Besides, the men undoubtedly were armed.

Frantically the Hardys searched for a way out of their dilemma. Frank noticed that Bleeker was beginning to drift to the right.

Vordo also saw what was happening. "Get over to the left!" he snapped. "You know they drive on the opposite side of the road here!"

Bleeker swerved the car sharply to correct his mistake. "Sorry," he said, mopping his forehead. "I keep forgetting we're not in the U.S."

"See that you don't forget again," Vordo growled, "or the Hardys and their fat friend won't be the only ones to regret this ride!"

Farther along, the road bent sharply in a hairpin

curve. As Bleeker rounded it, he again instinctively favoured the right side.

"Get over, you idiot!" Vordo bellowed, seeing a double-decker bus coming head-on.

Bleeker spun the wheel and the car rocked violently. Then, with a splintering crash, it tumbled over on its side! Vordo and Bleeker were thrown clear.

The three boys scrambled dazedly from the vehicle. The bus had stopped a short distance down the road. Its driver and several passengers were running towards them.

"Are you lads all right?" shouted the driver.

"Yes!" Frank called out. He then ran round to the front of the car. "Our men! Where are they?"

One of the passengers pointed off into the distance. "I saw two men disappear over that fence as we ran from the bus."

The boys gave chase but found no sign of Hexton's henchmen.

"We've let Vordo and Bleeker slip through our fingers again!" Joe said in disgust.

"But we're free," Frank reminded him.

"And still in one piece," Chet observed.

He and the Hardys walked back to the bus. Frank asked the driver to notify the police. Before long, three constables arrived to take the boys' story and examine the car. They said it was a stock model, rigged up to look like a police car.

"Clever job," a constable remarked. "I can see how it fooled the airport police."

He drove the boys back to Prestwick, where they checked through customs. One of the officials, recognizing their names on the passenger manifest, said that an Inspector Clyde had telephoned him shortly before they had landed.

"You're to meet him at Chief Superintendent Burns's office in Glasgow," he said. "A car has been sent to pick you up."

The boys thanked him and lugged their suitcases to the front of the terminal, where the car was waiting. This time the driver produced a card to identify himself and the boys got in.

The trip to Glasgow took little more than an hour. The visitors were intrigued by the pleasant rolling countryside.

At the chief superintendent's office they were greeted by a tall, distinguished-looking man who introduced himself as Inspector Clyde.

"Boys," he said crisply, "I am sorry you have had such a rough reception." He turned to a stocky man with bristly grey hair and moustache. "This is my superior, Chief Superintendent Burns."

"I've had a report on your kidnapping, of course," said the chief superintendent as he shook hands. "It was a daring trick. I think this gang has the wind up."

"They're scared," Frank agreed. "And that makes them more dangerous. But it doesn't matter. Through Hexton we might be able to identify the other members of UGLI and break the whole organization. But first we must get the goods on Hexton."

"That we must," Inspector Clyde said grimly. "UGLI has secret eyes and ears in almost every country of the world."

Burns nodded. "The jewel robberies are big—and

very cleverly done—but they are nothing compared to the international danger."

"Will you be in charge of the investigation?" Frank asked the inspector.

"Yes," Clyde replied. "My special assignment is to dig up information about your magician friend Hexton and to work with you to bring him to justice."

"There's something that has always puzzled me," Chet interrupted. "I don't know much about the police system in the British Isles. I've heard about Scotland Yard but how come Scotland Yard isn't in Scotland?"

"Many years ago—in 1829 to be exact," the inspector explained, "a police station and office were set up in a private house at Number 4 Whitehall Place in London. The rear of the house opened on to a court named Scotland Yard because it was part of the palace grounds where the kings and queens of Scotland lodged when they visited the English Court in medieval times."

Frank was eager to return to the case. "Inspector Clyde," he said, "Joe and Chet and I would like to try to get into Hexton's castle."

"Good boys," said Clyde. "Dell told me you suggested it."

"Where is the place?" Joe asked.

Chief Superintendent Burns unfolded a map on his desk and the boys leaned over to study it. "About one hundred miles north of Glasgow." He put his blunt finger down on a spot. "There it is. A huge stone fortress, set deep within a private park surrounded by miles of high iron fence."

Joe grinned. "Sounds like fun, getting in."

"Actually," said Clyde, "since the gang have impersonated officers and attempted kidnapping, we have a right to go there and demand entrance. But it would be defeating our purpose."

Frank nodded. "Yes. Vordo and Bleeker have sounded the alarm by now. Besides, by the time you got through the gates and up to the castle, every bit of evidence would be well hidden."

"It'll have to be an undercover job," Joe agreed.

"Maybe we could start by spying on it from the air," Frank suggested.

"Good idea!" the inspector said.

"I know exactly the man who can help you," said Burns. "Aaron McHugh. He's an excellent pilot."

The chief superintendent said McHugh flew in the vicinity of Hexton's castle on a charter to the Hebrides, so the sight of his plane in the area would not be likely to arouse the suspicion of the magician and his men.

After leaving the chief superintendent's office, the boys went to their hotel and registered, then had showers, food, and several hours of rest.

That afternoon they were introduced to Aaron McHugh, a middle-aged man with a jutting square jaw and a crop of wiry brown hair that sprang out from his head.

The pilot was unusual looking, but his plane, which he used to haul cargo, was even more so. The boys were surprised and amused to see a metal-covered, trimotored craft with unusually thick wings and a system of exposed control cables that stretched back to the tail. Although the craft appeared antiquated, McHugh assured them that it was as durable and reliable as the day it was built.

"My tin bird is no' verra fast, lads," he explained, "but it's a splendid workhorse."

Frank decided that they should waste no time in getting their first look at Hexton's castle.

"Chet, Joe," he said, "got your binoculars and cameras?"

"Righto," Chet replied.

Joe grinned and slapped the leather case slung over his shoulder. It also contained the Hardys' high-power photographic equipment.

The trio climbed aboard the plane and sat down on the floor. McHugh fired up the three engines. The craft lumbered along during the initial take-off run, then began to bounce lightly across the rough turf runway.

Soon it lifted off the ground and started to climb slowly, like a tired bird. When McHugh felt he had sufficient altitude, he tapped the various instruments on the panel with his finger to make sure none of the dials were sticking and giving false indications.

"We have a wee bit of a headwind," he announced, "so it will take about an hour to reach our destination."

The boys enjoyed the flight as they gazed down at the craggy landscape of the Scottish coast. As McHugh had estimated, nearly an hour elapsed before he pointed ahead.

"There it is!"

He adjusted his course, then rolled the plane into a shallow bank to give the boys a better look. Far below was the large stone castle. Its sturdy grey battlements were sharply defined from an altitude of three thousand feet.

"It must be centuries old," Joe observed.

"About the eleventh century," McHugh said.

Chet exclaimed, "It has a moat, too, just like in the history books, but there's no water!"

"Nowadays, with planes," said their pilot, "a moat of water isn't much protection."

Frank asked McHugh to circle the castle without getting too close. Using binoculars, they peered down. Frank observed that the castle was on high ground, without trees or shrubbery, and noted that it would be impossible to approach it on foot without being seen.

Joe extracted a camera, attached a telephoto lens, and clicked off one frame after another. Presently his viewer picked up two men on the castle wall.

"Oh—oh!" he exclaimed. "We'd better get out of here. I think we've been spotted."

McHugh turned the plane back towards Glasgow. When the craft landed, the Hardys hurried to the police darkroom to develop their photographs. To their disappointment, the glare of the sun on the plane's window had obscured a clear view of the castle.

"Rotten luck!" Joe exclaimed.

"We'll take another crack at it," Frank said.

He suggested that in order to avoid arousing suspicion, this should be done during one of McHugh's regular charter flights.

"Tomorrow morning I'm taking a load of feed to the sheep raisers near Stornoway in the Hebrides," the pilot told them. "Come along."

Shortly after dawn, McHugh and the boys again

boarded the plane. Its fuselage was crammed with feed bags, and the three passengers had to worm their way to separate spots near the windows. The pilot started the engines and taxied out for take-off.

Without warning, a man appeared from behind a stack of feed bags and darted for the passenger door. Frank grabbed him and uttered a cry of surprise when he recognized the intruder's face. Timken, the Great Circle's steward! UGLI spying again!

"Let me out!" Timken shouted frantically. "I want to get off! You hear me?"

"I'm not deaf," Frank said, pinioning the man against one of the sacks. "Why are you here?"

As he spoke, the plane lifted. "We're already airborne," Frank continued. "I wouldn't suggest your taking a walk just now!"

With a snarl, Timken thrust his feet against the cabin wall and broke Frank's grip. He grabbed a feed bag and threw it at the boy, knocking him to the floor. But Frank sprang up and leaped at his attacker. Timken threw a punch, which Frank ducked. He got off a hard counterblow, catching the man squarely on the chin. The steward fell, unconscious.

"Joe, Chet!" Frank called out over the roar of the engine. "Lookee here! We have company!"

The boys climbed over the sacks.

"Timken!" Joe cried as he gazed in amazement at the man on the floor.

"Right."

"What's he doing here?" Chet asked.

"I don't know," Frank answered. "But we'll sure find out when he comes to!"

They tied up their unexpected passenger, then tried to revive him. Several minutes elapsed before Timken regained consciousness. When he realized he was still in the plane, he became panic-stricken. "How long have we been in the air?" he screamed.

"Why do you want to know?" Frank retorted.

"Quick! Tell me!" The steward's face turned pale with fear.

Frank glanced at his watch. "Ten . . . maybe fifteen minutes."

"Let me out of here!" Timken screeched. "You've got to land this plane, or we'll all be killed! There's a bomb aboard!"

# ·14·

## Nerves of Steel

"A BOMB!" Frank shouted frantically.

"That's right!" the steward cried.

"Where is it?" Frank demanded, shaking Timken violently.

"In the nacelle of the left engine! You can't reach it!"

Frank dashed to the pilot's compartment to tell McHugh, who looked out of his window at the stretch of rocky coastline below. "I canna land in this area, lad!" he said grimly.

"But we have only minutes!" Frank looked out at the cowled engine, located beneath the left wing. "There's just one thing to do!"

"What's that?" the pilot asked.

"Climb out on the strut and try to reach that engine nacelle. I'll do it."

"But I dinna have any parachutes aboard," McHugh told him. "The slipstream might pull ye off the strut!"

"I must take that chance," Frank declared, "or we're goners!"

He went back to Timken. Seizing the steward by his collar, Frank pulled him to his feet. "Exactly where in the engine nacelle did you place the bomb?" he demanded.

"I ... I put it just inside the access door to the oil-filler cap!" Timken stammered. "But it's too late! There's nothing you can do!"

Frank grabbed a screwdriver from the pilot's tool kit and slipped it in a pocket. He asked Joe and Chet to help him kick out the window located directly above the strut leading to the left engine

As the boys kicked with all their might, the window cracked in several places, then shattered and disappeared below. The thunderous roar of the slipstream echoed through the interior of the fuselage.

Frank squeezed his body out the window. Hooking his legs round the strut, he pushed himself away. The force of the slipstream felt like the hand of some vengeful giant trying to hurl him off into space.

Frank, crouching low, locked his arms about the strut. He then proceeded to shimmy, at a painfully slow rate, towards the engine nacelle. Drawing closer, he moved into the area of the propeller blast and the engine exhausts. The sound was deafening, and the fumes and heat stifled him. However, they made him insensitive to the fact that he was hanging thousands of feet above the ground. Once Frank almost lost his grip.

McHugh reduced power on the right engine in an effort to ease Frank's ordeal. Joe and Chet watched anxiously, their nerves stretched almost to the breaking point.

Frank tightened his grip on the strut with one hand. With the other he took out the screwdriver and reached for the fasteners which secured the small aluminium access door on the nacelle.

The wind lashed against his outstretched arm, but he

continued to probe for the fasteners. Finally the door loosened. It popped open and flapped violently.

Frank reached in through the opening and desperately felt for the bomb. Nothing! He stretched his arm in farther, his efforts becoming more frantic as his strength began to ebb. Then his hand felt something cylindrical in shape and about the size of a flashlight. Frank locked his fingers round the object and slowly drew it out. There was a small timing device at one end, revealing that the bomb had only seconds to run!

*Now to get rid of it!*

Looking down, Frank saw that they were still flying over a desolate stretch of coast. He flung the bomb from him and watched it hurtle down and behind the plane. It was almost out of sight when a white-and-black puff of smoke appeared. Seconds later the faint, thudding sound of an explosion could be heard.

Frank slowly worked his way back to the window and with the help of Joe and Chet dragged himself inside. Exhausted, he slumped to the floor.

"Whew!" Joe exclaimed. "That was close!"

"You can say that again," Frank said shakily. "Another ten or twenty seconds and it would have taken searchers a year to pick up the pieces."

"That was a brave deed, lad!" McHugh shouted from the cockpit. "And I'm grateful to ye for saving my ship! Do you want to go back to Glasgow with your prisoner?"

"No," Frank replied. "Let's continue with the flight as planned. Timken isn't going to give us any trouble."

The boys returned to Timken. Joe asked, "Who put you up to this?"

"I didn't want to plant the bomb in your plane," Timken muttered, "but Vordo ..." The UGLI assistant stopped short. Obviously their prisoner was fearful of what might happen to him if he talked.

"And Vordo got his instructions from Hexton, didn't he?" Frank pressed.

Beads of perspiration oozed from the steward's forehead. "I don't know! Vordo threatened me. I had to do it!"

"When did you and the others arrive in Scotland?" Joe questioned.

"The day after you tried to stop our take-off in the STOL," Timken answered. "While we were at an airport near New York City, the plane was impounded by a Federal agent. When I told Vordo and Bleeker, they decided to get out of the country right away."

The steward's answer confirmed what Mazer, the pilot of the STOL, had told the Hardys.

"Besides the pilot, there were four men that day," Joe said. "Who was the fourth?"

"One of Hexton's cronies. A guy named Arnold."

"Is he a spy for UGLI?" Frank snapped.

Timken jumped. "You know about—" The steward caught himself. "I won't talk to you guys. I've said too much already!"

Joe spoke up. "Don't get so nasty, Timken. You forget that my brother saved your life. What kind of gratitude is this?"

Still no reply.

"Listen, buddy," Joe continued, "you know you're

going to prison for trying to kill the rest of us. You might get a lighter sentence if you answer a few questions. For instance, what was your racket on the Great Circle flights?"

"I won't squeal!" Timken shouted, and clamped his lips together.

Joe shrugged. "Have it your way." The boys left their prisoner.

The plane landed at Stornoway and was quickly unloaded. After a conference, McHugh and the boys decided to return the UGLI agent to Glasgow. On the return trip the pilot adjusted his course so the boys could take more aerial shots of Hexton's castle.

Back in Glasgow, the Hardys handed their prisoner over to the chief superintendent, who was thunderstruck at the bomb story. He then let them develop their latest photographs. Frank spread the prints out on a table and they all scrutinized them closely. But the pictures revealed no clues.

"The ground round the castle is as clean as a whistle," Joe observed. "We couldn't possibly sneak up on the place without being seen."

"What about climbing up the surrounding wall?" Chet suggested. "Robin Hood used to do it all the time."

"Not a bad idea." Joe grinned. "But it brings us back to the original problem. How do we get inside the fence and up to the wall without being seen?"

Frank's brow creased in contemplation. "I'm afraid this is a tough one." He sighed. "Whatever plan we come up with will have to be pretty far out."

At that moment Inspector Clyde arrived. He carried

a long, slim, black umbrella, which he hooked to the coat rack when he entered the room.

"Ah, there you are," the inspector said. "I have some interesting news for you. Mr Dell telephoned from the States while you were gone. He's leaving for Scotland immediately. Something very important and highly secret has come up!"

# · 15 ·

## A Furious Scot

DELL arrived in Glasgow that same night and met the boys at the inspector's office. There Inspector Clyde ushered them into the interrogation room and the young sleuths told about the capture of Timken.

"Great work!" the security chief exclaimed. "I'll want to question him myself before I go back to the States."

When Clyde left the room, Frank said, "I understand something important has come up on your end, too."

"Yes," Dell replied. "Our investigation has turned up a very interesting lead. Timken has been spending a lot of time with another Great Circle steward named Ross. We checked him out thoroughly and learned that he had a record for petty theft under another name. We suspect he's part of the Hexton–UGLI set up, but that he and Timken were working together."

"You mean they were double-crossing Hexton?" Joe asked.

"Yes. I doubt if Hexton would dispose of stolen goods in the clumsy way Timken has been doing."

"I see," said Frank. "These two manage to hold out a diamond here and there from the gang's robberies, then sell them."

"Right. We could pick Ross up on suspicion, of course. But I'd rather give him a little rope. Maybe we'll get a stronger case on him. Catching him first might make it easier to get Hexton."

"Where do we fit in?" Chet spoke up a bit fearfully.

Dell smiled. "Your assignment is to make a trip to the United States on our Flight 101. Ross will be a steward. Use assumed names and occupations on the plane. Watch Ross and see if you can pick up any leads for SKOOL."

Joe grinned. "I'll feel like a secret agent on Flight 101!"

When Clyde returned, the Hardys told Dell about their aerial reconnaissance of Hexton's castle and of their efforts to think of some way to get inside.

The security chief laughed. "Sounds tough! But I'm betting on you." Dell told them that the next Flight 101 trip from Prestwick to New York was scheduled to depart in forty-eight hours.

"We'll have time to make another flight to the castle before we leave," Frank said. "I wonder if McHugh—"

Just then the telephone rang and the inspector picked up the receiver. "Hello. Inspector Clyde here! . . . Oh, it's you McHugh. . . . What? . . . Good heavens! That's incredible, I must say. Yes! The boys and I will start for the airport straight off!"

"What is it?" Frank asked.

"Somebody has cut the external control cables on McHugh's plane," he answered. "He wants to see us right away."

While Dell stayed behind, the inspector and the boys leaped into a police car and drove to the field. McHugh, in a furious mood, stood glowering beside his plane.

"Can you no' find the brigand who did this?" he shouted. "I'd like to get my hands on him! Here! Look at these!"

The boys examined the severed control cables, which dangled loosely from their connections at the tail and at the point where they entered the cockpit.

"Gee," Chet remarked, "they're cut clean in half."

"When did this happen?" Frank asked.

"It couldn't have been more than twenty minutes ago," McHugh replied. "While I was at the plane, I was told there was a telephone call for me in the office, so I went there. But no one was on the other end of the line. When I came back here, I found the cables cut!"

"Obviously the call was a trick to lure you away from your plane," Frank observed.

Just then there were sounds of a loud commotion in the airport office. McHugh hurried towards the building, followed by the others.

When they entered, an aircraft mechanic was clutching a stocky man by the arm. Another man, who McHugh said was the airport manager, was questioning the stranger.

"What's going on here?" Inspector Clyde demanded. He showed the man his identification.

"I found this fellow going through my clothes locker," the mechanic said. "And look at what he was carrying!" He held up an oversized pair of scissors.

"Those are metal cutters," McHugh stormed. "So this is the brigand who cut my cables!"

"I didn't cut anything!" the man growled.

"Let me at him!" McHugh bellowed, and started to roll up his shirt sleeves.

"Calm yourself!" the inspector ordered. He turned to the man. "What were you doing at the locker?"

"It was open. I thought I'd look around. That's all!"

"What about these cutters?"

"I found 'em! Besides, is there any law against carrying metal cutters?"

The boys gazed at the man. There was something familiar about him, Frank thought, but he could not recall where he had seen him before.

Inspector Clyde demanded that the stranger show him some identification. The man hesitated. Then he pulled a wallet from his pocket and handed it to the inspector. It contained an international driver's licence in the name of Karl Arnold.

"Arnold!" Frank exchanged a quick glance with Joe. "The man Timken said was the fourth passenger in the STOL the day I tried to stop its take-off!" he said to himself. Aloud he exclaimed, "You're one of Hexton's men!"

"Hexton? Never heard of him," the man insisted.

"Don't lie to us!" Joe snapped. "We know who you are!"

"You've got me mixed up with somebody else," Arnold retorted with a smirk.

"Let me shake it out of him!" McHugh bellowed.

The boys urged the pilot to relax. Then they suggested that Arnold be taken back to the inspector's office to have Timken identify him. The inspector agreed to do this.

Arnold seemed unconcerned as they returned to

Glasgow. When they reached the office, they found Dell questioning Timken in the interrogation room. The steward was visibly startled when he saw Arnold.

"We ran across one of your friends at the airport," Frank announced.

Timken was obviously nervous. "Friend?" he said shakily. "What friend?"

"This man right here," Frank replied sharply, pointing to Arnold.

"Why—I—I never saw him before," the steward insisted. "I don't know him."

"Stop playing games!" Joe ordered angrily. "This man is Karl Arnold. You told us about him!"

Arnold's face flushed with anger, but he said nothing.

"That was somebody else," Timken said. "I've never seen this man before."

"Satisfied?" Arnold said indignantly. "Now, if that's all, I'll leave!" He turned and stormed out of the room.

"But we can't let him go!" Joe protested.

"I'm afraid we must." The inspector sighed. "We haven't any evidence to hold him on, but we'll keep track of him."

"The inspector's right," Frank assured his brother. "We have no witnesses who saw him cut the control cables. And there is no law against carrying wire cutters. If he'd resisted the temptation to ransack the employees' lockers, he'd have got away altogether."

Dell looked discouraged as he and the boys left the interrogation room. "I didn't have much luck, either," he remarked. "Timken wouldn't tell me anything more than he told you."

"I suppose it's a pledge the UGLI men take," Frank

said. "Besides, Timken is afraid of Hexton. That's why he wouldn't identify Arnold."

Minutes later, McHugh stalked into the inspector's office. "I hope you have that Arnold fellow in jail!" he declared.

"We had to let him go," Frank admitted.

"What!" the pilot exclaimed. "Why, he's as guilty as sin!"

"You don't have to tell us," Joe murmured.

"Can you repair the control cables?" Frank inquired.

"No," McHugh replied. "A new set will have to be made up specially. It'll take two or three days before my tin bird will be flying again."

"Well," Frank said, "that washes out our plan for another reconnaissance flight before our trip. We'll have to wait until we get back."

The next day Dell, wishing the boys luck, returned to New York. The following morning the Hardys and Chet were on their way to Prestwick Airport, enthusiastic about their new assignment and the opportunity to spend a couple of days at home before returning to Scotland. Soon they were winging their way westbound across the Atlantic on Flight 101.

Frank was using the name Bud Richmond and introduced himself to a few passengers as an announcer on station WHOX, meaning to him HOAX.

Joe had chosen to be Larry Walker, a student returning from a hike through Scotland. Throughout the flight, both Hardys kept an eye on the steward Ross. Chet, as a pro-football player named Chuck Brown, spent most of his time in the galley getting lemonade and asking Ross a hundred unimportant questions.

He was always being interrupted by a whiskered old man wearing dark glasses, who was seated near the galley. From time to time both the steward and stewardess had to assure him that the wings were not bending off, that the engines were not about to catch fire, and they were sorry that the tea they had served was weak.

The only incident out of the ordinary occurred after landing at Great Circle's base. The elderly man accidentally tripped Ross with his cane while disembarking from the plane. The steward fell flat in the doorway and the old man leaned down to help him up.

"So sorry," he said in a high, quavering voice.

The boys had arranged to have Jack Wayne meet them, and after clearing customs, were soon on their way to Bayport. They were sorry not to have picked up any clues for SKOOL, but assumed Ross would be shadowed by agents.

The Hardys dropped Chet off at his farm, then drove quickly to their home. "Hello!" Mrs Hardy cried out, and hugged her sons. "Did you see your dad?"

"No, Mother."

"He phoned a few minutes ago but didn't say where he's going. He's all right, though."

"Where did he phone from?" Joe asked.

"I don't know."

"You two boys look peaked," Aunt Gertrude spoke up, "but a few home-cooked meals will remedy that."

"It's good to be back," Frank declared.

The two women showed their disappointment when they heard that Frank and Joe would be returning to Scotland so soon.

"But we're sure eager for a shower and some American chow!" Joe said, grabbing the boys' two suitcases and bounding up the stairs. He set his bag on the bed and opened it to get a clean shirt.

"Hey! What's this?" he exclaimed, and picked up a carelessly hand-printed note from the top of his shirts. It read:

*YOUR FATHER WARNS BE CAREFUL. GAME IS VERY DANGEROUS.*

# ·16·

## Secret Compartment

"But who could have written this note and put it in your bag?" Frank exclaimed. "Didn't you lock it?"

"No, I never do." Joe looked at the message. "Maybe Hexton found out about our assignment, and had one of his UGLI men plant the note to throw us off the track."

Joe nodded. "And I bet I know when. At Prestwick the porter put our bags on his cart with a lot of other luggage, but then he went away for a while and the cart stood unattended."

Frank shrugged. "But what could Hexton possibly hope to gain? He knew it wouldn't stop us and we're aware it's dangerous."

Two days later Frank and Joe were again saying goodbye to their mother and aunt. They picked up Chet at the Morton farm and headed for the airport, where Jack was waiting to fly them to the Great Circle base.

On the return trip to Scotland, the plane encountered moderate turbulence, but all the passengers took it calmly. The steward proved to be Ross. When he saw them, the man at once became ill at ease.

After the boys took their seats, Joe whispered to

Frank, "I wonder if he suspects we're watching him."

During the first half of the flight a blond-haired man, wearing dark glasses, sideburns, a small moustache and a beard, made his way down the aisle several times.

"I have a feeling he's looking us over," Frank said. "We'd better watch him as well as Ross."

Nothing suspicious happened during the flight, however, and in the morning the jetliner landed at Prestwick Airport. Frank and Joe made a point of being the last passengers to leave. Chet was just ahead.

While disembarking, they all noticed that the steward seemed in a hurry to leave the plane. He ran down the steps after them and shot past. Instantly the man in the dark glasses hurried towards the steward. Ross, seeing him, broke into a run. The passenger sprinted ahead.

"Come on!" Frank exclaimed. "Let's see what's up! It could be that passenger is a SKOOL man! Maybe we can help him!"

The boys dashed after the two men, who disappeared round the corner of a hangar. Frank spotted the steward running into the building.

"Chet! Stay outside and cover the exits!" Frank cried. "Joe and I will go in after him!"

The building was filled with aircraft, which made it difficult for the Hardys to spot their quarry.

"Let's split up," Frank suggested. "I'll cover the left side, you take the right."

The boys separated. As Frank slowly wound his way among the aircraft, he heard a muffled noise and stopped to listen.

*Bummf.*

There it was again! The young sleuth's attention

focused on a twin-engine plane directly ahead. Cautiously he stalked towards the cabin door. Just as Frank reached it, the door burst open and slammed into the boy's head with a force that made him cry out and sent him crashing to the floor. Half dazed, Frank looked up to see Ross leap from the craft and dart towards a side exit of the hangar.

"What's going on?" Joe called as he ran past the closely packed planes to his brother's side. "Are you all right?"

"I'm okay," Frank replied, getting slowly to his feet. "Just a little dizzy. Quick! Outside! Maybe Chet spotted Ross leaving the hangar!"

As the Hardys dashed from the building, they saw Chet leaning against a low wire fence which enclosed a car park. He was breathing hard.

"G-golly, but that guy could run!" the stout youth gasped as the Hardys approached him. He gulped in more air. "He's faster than a gazelle."

"You mean the steward?" Joe asked.

"Yes."

"Where did he go?" Frank queried.

"He jumped the fence into the car park and roared off in one of those little foreign sports cars," Chet answered. He stared at the ground with a sheepish expression, then began to shuffle some pebbles with his foot. "Sorry I goofed, fellows. I was checking the rear of the hangar when Ross zipped from the side exit. He had too much of a head start."

"That's okay," Frank said. "It would take a dozen men to cover a building that size."

"Hey! And something else!" Chet exclaimed, glancing up. "Just after you two chased inside after the steward, I caught a glimpse of that guy in the dark glasses watching from around a corner of the next hangar."

"Did you let on that you saw him?" Frank asked.

"Yes," his chum admitted. "In fact, I started walking towards him and he ducked behind the hangar. I thought of chasing him, but I didn't want to leave the exits unguarded."

"It's funny," said Frank. "He was chasing the steward, but apparently didn't try to catch him."

"That's not the only mystery," Joe added. "Chet, we wonder if that passenger is a secret agent from SKOOL. Let's try to find him and give a sign we're sort of working second-hand for the organization."

"What kind of sign?" Chet asked.

"Oh, we could talk about school and school rings," Frank answered.

Chet was enthusiastic at once. "I'd feel a lot safer if I could hook up with a fully-fledged SKOOL man."

The three boys made a thorough search of the place but failed to find the man. At last they gave up, went through customs, hired a car and drove to Glasgow. When they arrived, they found Inspector Clyde and Chief Superintendent Burns anxiously awaiting them.

"One of the constables was rechecking Timken's personal effects and he discovered a secret compartment in his wallet," the inspector explained. "Look what he found there—most extraordinary."

He handed an envelope to the young sleuths. Inside were a one-way train ticket to Edinburgh and a newspaper clipping. The item was headed:

## Nairn Loch Manor to Be Opened to Public
## Newly Discovered Jewel Collection on Display

"Nairn Loch Manor? Jewel collection? What's this about?" Joe asked.

"The Manor is to be maintained by the National Trust as a historical shrine," Burns explained. "When they began to renovate it a few months ago, a worker discovered a magnificent collection of jewels hidden beneath the floor. It is said they were placed there about four hundred years ago."

"I remember reading about the discovery in a newspaper back home," Frank recalled. "The value of the collection is considered second only to the crown jewels in the Tower of London."

"Precisely," the inspector replied.

Joe looked at the clipping and train ticket again. "Do you think Hexton and his UGLI men might be planning to steal the collection?"

"I don't know," Inspector Clyde admitted. "We have to consider that possibility, of course. But the place will be so heavily guarded that any thieves will be caught."

"Why would Timken go to Edinburgh by train?" Joe asked. "I should think the thieves would use a car for a quick getaway."

"Most likely they will," Frank said. "Maybe Timken was only being sent there to case the place for Hexton."

"Exactly the conclusion I came to," Inspector Clyde declared. "Now they'll have to use someone else."

Joe snapped his fingers. "Perhaps that's where Ross was heading."

"We'll check," Clyde told him.

Frank was thoughtful for several seconds, then said, "Probably Hexton, with his sleight-of-hand ability, will do the actual stealing."

The conversation turned to the reason the boys had come to Scotland—to get into Hexton's castle.

Inspector Clyde paced the floor in thought. "The question remains, just how do you manage to do that?"

"Perhaps another reconnaissance flight will give us an idea," Frank suggested. "Let's alert McHugh."

"Oh!" Burns said quickly. "He isn't available at the moment. He's off ballooning."

"He's what?" Joe asked, with a puzzled expression.

"Ballooning," the chief superintendent repeated. "McHugh belongs to a club of enthusiasts who go darting about in bags filled with hot air. Jolly good fun, they think, unless they get caught in a tree, or on a church spire. They're having a race somewhere near Perth."

"What a ball!" Chet burst out. "I'd like to see that."

"Hold on!" Frank put in. "That solves our problem. We'll balloon into Hexton's castle!"

# · 17 ·

## Night Attack

INSPECTOR Clyde laughed. "See here, my dear fellow. You're not serious about ballooning into Hexton's stronghold, are you?"

"I realize it sounds fantastic," Frank admitted. "But at least it's worth discussing with McHugh."

Joe scratched his head dubiously. "Hexton's guards are bound to spot a balloon."

"Maybe not if we drop in at night," Frank replied.

Chet pointed a determined finger at his friends. "Don't think you two are going to get me to ride in one of those oversized basketballs!"

Joe grinned. "Okay. Anyway, I don't believe there's enough hot air in Scotland to lift *you* off the ground!"

A little later the boys rented a car and drove to the site of the race. On a grassy plain a few miles west of Perth, more than fifty balloons of all shapes and sizes were preparing for the competitions. Their bright colours and vivid designs gave the scene a touch of the pageantry of a medieval tournament.

"Look at that!" Chet yelled as they walked across the field. He pointed to a balloon displaying the French national colours from its car. "What a beauty!"

At the firing of the starting gun, the contestants

leaped on to bicycles, sped to their balloons, and jumped into the airships. Then the balloons were released from their moorings and sailed across the field. One of them never lifted off the ground; another, the French entry, rose into the air but became snagged in a tree branch.

"*Nom d'une pipe!*" screamed the flier. "*Il est fichu, mon beau ballon!*"

"Tough break," said Joe.

Frank asked one of the club members for McHugh. He learned that the pilot was not racing that day, but was helping another contestant a short distance down the field.

McHugh was surprised to see the boys. Frank told him about the plan for getting into Hexton's castle.

McHugh chuckled. "So ye want to be invaders?" he teased. " 'Tis a daring plan ye've come up with, lad. And it will no' be an easy thing to do."

"Can you get a balloon large enough to carry all of us?" Frank asked.

"Sure. We'll borrow one from the club."

"*I'm* not going," Chet insisted.

"But we need you for ballast," Joe said with a grin.

"If we get into Hexton's castle," Frank added, "you might see some of his magic equipment!"

"Well—" Chet muttered, weakening. "I guess you'll need somebody around to keep you two out of trouble."

After the races, McHugh and the boys returned to McHugh's house in Glasgow to plan their daring adventure. The pilot examined an aeronautical chart and carefully plotted the position of the castle. He pointed out that their success depended entirely upon the winds and the position from which the balloon was launched.

"I understand a balloon has no directional control," Joe said.

"That's not entirely true," McHugh replied. "Since the wind direction generally changes with altitude, we can get some control by ascending or descending."

"How do you do that?" Chet questioned.

"By varying the amount of ballast, or weight carried in the form of sandbags," the pilot explained. "The more ballast dumped overboard, the higher the balloon will go. To descend, we simply release some of the gas from the bag by means of a valve."

"Just one thing," Joe put in. "If we manage to reach Hexton's castle, how do we keep from floating right on past it?"

"By using a length of rope attached to a grapnel," Frank replied. "We'll lower it as we approach the castle—and hope it catches somewhere on the wall. This will act as a mooring. Then we can slide down the rope."

Chet took a deep gulp.

"Obviously," Frank continued, "we can't keep the balloon moored there. Hexton's men would spot it sooner or later. So, after we're down, we'll release the grapnel."

"Then I'll sail the balloon a short distance away and land," McHugh added. "With your approval, I'll ask one of the club members to help us. He can drive the lorry containing the launching equipment and assist in our take-off preparations. Later, he can rendezvous with me at the landing spot."

The boys thanked McHugh and drove back to Clyde's office.

"A report that will interest you chaps came in while you were gone," the inspector said. "A Glasgow resident said he was involved in a minor car accident several hours ago. It happened on a road north of here. According to the report, it was a near head-on collision. Luckily, both drivers jammed on their brakes and merely smashed bumpers.

"This fellow stated that the other driver seemed in a devil of a hurry. He simply backed away and sped off in his sports car."

"Sports car!" Frank exclaimed. "Did the other driver get its licence number?"

"Yes," the inspector replied. "I've checked it out. The car belongs to a chap named Ross."

"The steward we chased into the hangar!" Joe exclaimed.

"And another thing," Inspector Clyde said. "The accident occurred not far from Hexton's castle."

"I'm not surprised," Frank mused. "Ross could have been on his way there from Prestwick."

The boys were eager to get their balloon trip under way. Weather conditions the next night were unsuitable for the venture. But on the following night, McHugh telephoned the Hardys at their hotel room that, in his estimation, conditions were ideal.

"The way I calculate the winds, lads," he said, "we should take off from a point about five miles southeast of Hexton's castle. I'm familiar with the area, and know several open fields that will serve our purpose."

"Good!" Frank replied. "We'll meet you in a few minutes."

Frank relayed the message to the other boys and all checked the equipment they would take—miniature tools, two-way radios, and pencil flashlights.

McHugh had telephoned his fellow club member and soon the lorry containing the balloon and launching equipment was at the door. McHugh was in his own car and the young sleuths hopped in with him. About two hours later the pilot pointed to a clearing just off the road.

"There's a good spot," he announced.

The boys helped to unload the balloon and set up the equipment to inflate it. Makeshift moorings were established to prevent the craft from floating away. Soon a large, spherical, gas-filled bag was looming over their heads, tugging gently at the mooring lines. McHugh and the boys climbed into the airship and prepared to launch.

"Aye, the surface winds are very light," McHugh observed. "That'll make our attempt to moor at the castle much easier."

As they rose slowly into the air, Chet watched the ground slip away. "Hey!" he declared with a wide grin. "This isn't bad at all!"

A half moon in the night sky provided enough illumination for them to distinguish the terrain below. McHugh varied the altitude by dumping ballast and manipulating the gas-relief valve. The balloon altered its track slightly with changes in wind direction.

More than an hour passed, then Joe pointed directly ahead. "There it is!"

The medieval structure, turrets looming skyward, presented a ghostly image in the dim moonlight. As they drew near it, Chet called attention to a far corner of the courtyard.

"Look!" he said. "A light! Seems to be coming from one of the castle windows."

"No more loud talking," Frank ordered. "We're getting close. Help me lower the grapnel line over the side."

Slowly the balloon drifted towards the castle. The pilot released gas and eased down to a lower altitude. Just then a sharp, metallic sound pierced the night air.

*Ping!*

"The grapnel just made contact with the castle wall," Frank observed.

"What's that?" Chet whispered as he and the Hardys heard a faint scraping sound.

Frank peered over the side of the car. "The grapnel is being dragged up the side of the wall," he murmured. "It isn't catching hold."

They floated over the courtyard towards the opposite wall. With a lurch the balloon came to a halt.

"We've made it," Joe whispered excitedly. "The grapnel caught."

"So far so good," Frank said tensely. "Now, over the side and down the rope. I'll go first."

"Good luck, lad!" the pilot called.

The boys waited for a moment to make certain the coast was clear. Then Frank eased himself over the side of the airship and got a tight grip on the line. He hung precariously above the ground for an instant, then began to slide down.

Lowering himself gently on to the stone rampart, he peered through the darkness and listened. He then signalled for Joe and Chet to follow. When they were down, they freed the grapnel. The balloon drifted off into the darkness.

The three groped their way along, finally coming to a flight of stone steps. Frank cautiously led his companions down the stairs into the courtyard below.

"There's the light I spotted from the air," Chet whispered, pointing across the courtyard.

"And the door right next to it is partially open," Joe observed.

The boys crept forward slowly until they reached the door. Frank eased it open wider. Peering inside, they saw a long, dimly lighted corridor which extended deep into the castle. It was lined with suits of armour mounted on low, wheeled platforms.

"I don't see anybody around," Joe whispered. "Let's go in."

At intervals along the corridor were large wooden doors with massive iron hinges. As the young sleuths neared the end, they heard muffled voices coming from a room. Its door was slightly ajar. Slowly they stalked towards it and Frank looked inside.

*Clustered round a huge oak table were Hexton, Vordo, Bleeker, Arnold, Ross, and the short twins.*

Hexton's voice carried through the opening. "Now get this straight, Vordo. You all know the layout of Nairn Loch Manor?"

"Every detail," Vordo replied.

"No mistakes," Hexton said harshly. "You especially, Bert and Lou." The twins nodded.

"Then it's all set," Hexton said. "Day after tomorrow we'll have in our hands the most valuable collection of jewels in Scotland!"

Frank stiffened. So Hexton *did* plan to steal the Nairn Loch collection before it went on display!

The men stood up to leave, their chairs scraping on the stone floor. Instantly Frank motioned Joe and Chet to retreat down the corridor. Chet hesitated before a suit of armour.

"What are you doing?" Joe whispered.

"Getting myself a weapon." Chet began to tug at a mace.

A metal gauntlet pulled loose and crashed to the stone floor. The sound echoed through the corridor like a burst of thunder. The door creaked open and the men sprang from the room.

"W-why, it's those snoopers!" Vordo bellowed in surprise.

"Get them!" Hexton commanded.

When the men lunged at the trio, Joe caught Arnold with an uppercut that sent him spinning across the corridor. Frank pushed a suit of armour from its platform, directly into the path of the UGLI men.

"Watch out for Vordo!" he yelled at his brother.

Joe whirled to see Vordo picking up the gauntlet. He flung it at the young sleuth. The heavy object grazed Joe's head, stunning him.

Meanwhile, Chet was leaping behind one platform after another, pushing suits of armour into the paths of Bleeker and Ross, who were lunging at him. The stout youth grabbed a lance and charged the men.

"Look out!" Bleeker howled.

Chet continued his gallant charge, with Bleeker and Ross running just inches ahead of the point. But the lance proved too cumbersome. The tip lowered to the stone floor, throwing up sparks. Chet stumbled and the two men were quickly upon him.

Arnold, meanwhile, recovered from Joe's uppercut and ran to help Hexton and Vordo, who were grappling with Frank. Three adversaries proved too much and Frank was finally overpowered.

Joe gradually regained his senses and scrambled to his feet. Hexton glared at them.

"How did you get in here?"

"Figure that out for yourself!" Frank snapped defiantly.

"What now?" Vordo asked Hexton.

The magician's decision came quickly. "We've no time to waste," he said. "Let's take these sons of Fenton Hardy and their friend through the secret passageway to my storeroom. We'll keep them around as insurance —in case we run into any trouble."

"I'll go ahead and open the door," Bleeker volunteered.

The boys were searched and the tool kits were removed from the secret pockets of their jackets. Their miniature short-wave radios were also taken.

"Leave 'em their flashlights," Hexton said, and added with a sardonic chuckle, "It'll help 'em see what a lot of trouble they got themselves into."

The three prisoners were prodded along the corridor, then through a camouflaged opening in the wall. Single file, they walked down a long, stone staircase and through a secret passage beyond. The boys could see nothing of their surroundings other than what Vordo's flashlight picked out of the darkness, but they felt a clammy dampness in the air.

"Here we are," Hexton said finally.

Directly ahead was a huge iron door. The hinges squeaked as Vordo pulled it open.

"Get in there!" Bleeker growled.

The Hardys and Chet were shoved into a large dungeon-like room. Scattered about were various devices that Hexton had developed for his magic shows.

"We can't keep 'em here!" Vordo warned. "The lock on this door is so old it won't work!"

"I know," Hexton replied. "But I've something else in mind."

He pointed to an oversized trunk, standing on end. It was constructed entirely of heavy steel, and held together with large rivets. Near the base were several air holes.

Hexton removed the three massive padlocks that secured the trunk. "Put them in here," he ordered. "They'll never escape from this!"

"You can't do that!" Joe shouted. "There isn't enough room!"

"Shut up!" Vordo snarled.

The magician's henchmen pushed the boys towards the trunk and forced them to step inside.

"This will give you time to regret that you ever thought you could outsmart the Incredible Hexton!" the magician declared, uttering a spine-chilling laugh.

Seconds later the trunk was slammed shut, and the Hardys and Chet were locked in inky blackness!

# ·18·

## Chet's Big Assist

"We'll never break out of here!" Chet told the Hardys.

"It does look pretty hopeless," Joe admitted glumly.

"Think!" Frank commanded. "We have to come up with something!"

He and the others took the pencil flashlights from their pockets and played the beams round the small steel prison. They saw no chance of escape.

"Hexton was right," Frank conceded gloomily.

"Hey!" Chet burst out. "Turn your flashlights this way."

He began to explore the top and sides of their enclosure. Finally he said, "Hmm. There might be a way out of here—"

"No kidding," Joe declared. "In case you're thinking of a magic trick to make us fit through the keyhole, forget it."

"Nothing short of an acetylene torch can solve our problem," Frank put in. "These trunk walls must be an inch thick."

"I know," Chet said, "but look at those rivets."

"What about them?"

"The ones along the top," Chet explained, "are just a bit shinier than those along the sides."

The Hardys nodded in agreement.

"Do one of you have a pocketknife?" Chet asked. "Or did the UGLI's take it?"

"That's something they missed," Frank answered. "Here."

He and Joe looked on quizzically as Chet placed the point of the blade against the edge of a rivet at the top of the trunk. Clenching his fist, he hammered against the end of the knife. After several sharp blows, the rivet turned slightly.

"Eureka!" Chet shouted. "I was right!"

"How about letting us in on whatever you've found?" Joe pleaded impatiently.

"The top of this overgrown trunk," Chet explained, "is attached by false rivets."

"False rivets?" Frank queried.

"Yes," his chum replied. "Actually they're not solid rivets, but are cut through in the middle and threaded so the ends can be screwed together just like a regular nut and bolt."

The Hardys looked at Chet in amazement. "How did you happen to know about this?" Frank asked.

"When I began to study magic," Chet replied, "I read a book about famous magicians. A few, like Houdini, were also great escape artists. The book described false rivets as one of the tricks they used."

Chet continued to pound his fist against the knife. Soon the rivet head was loose enough to turn by hand. After several twists, it came apart.

"This is the hard way of doing it," Chet said. "The escape artist uses a special wrench which fits over the rivet head. That's why these are shinier than the others."

"Boy, your interest in magic really paid off," Frank remarked with a grin.

"But why would Hexton lock us up in something we could escape from?" Joe asked.

"He never expected any of us to figure it out," Frank surmised.

By this time Chet had loosened three of the rivet heads. Frank and Joe each took a turn working with the knife. The job was hard and tedious. Several hours passed before the last of the false rivets was unfastened.

Grinning in satisfaction, the boys pushed up against the metal top. It broke free and toppled to the floor with a loud bang. Elated, they quickly scrambled out of the trunk and stretched their aching bodies.

"Great going, Chet," murmured Joe.

Frank echoed this, then beckoned the others to the door. The lock was, indeed, defective and the boys had no difficulty in opening it. They stepped outside into a small vestibule. There they saw the entrances to several passageways.

"Leaping hyenas!" Joe exclaimed. "Which way do we go?"

"Golly!" Chet gasped. "Do you fellows remember which passage Hexton and his men brought us through?"

"I didn't realize there was more than one," Frank admitted. "It was too dark to see."

"This is like a maze." Joe shook his head in bewilderment.

Using his flashlight, Frank led the others through one

of the passageways, up flights of stone steps, through places where the ceiling was so low that they almost had to crawl, then along several sharp turns that completely confused them.

"We're not getting anywhere," Chet complained.

"This castle must be honeycombed with secret corridors," Frank said.

He swept his flashlight beam ahead and saw that the passage branched off in three different directions. They went down the middle one for what seemed like an hour, but could only have been a few minutes. It came to an abrupt end. They were facing a blank wall.

"Now what?" Joe sighed.

"What I wouldn't give for a road map of this place!" Chet mumbled.

The boys backtracked, then turned down the left passageway. More stone steps led them deeper and deeper inside the cellar of the castle.

Presently Frank stopped short. "Wait a minute," he ordered. "Do you fellows notice anything?"

"Not me," Chet said.

"I don't—Say!" Joe replied. "The air is getting real damp and clammy!"

"Right," his brother agreed. "Just like it was in the passage to Hexton's storeroom. Maybe we're on the right track."

The boys continued on and made several sharp turns. Frank pointed his flashlight ahead and uttered a cry of dismay. They stood before the iron door to the storeroom, the very same place from which they had started!

At that moment they heard muffled footsteps. Frank snapped off his flash. From a distance, beams of light played across the iron door. The trio flattened themselves against the wall where it angled away from a little alcove.

Frank leaned closer to Joe and Chet. "It must be a couple of UGLI's to check on us," he whispered. "Watch where they come from. It'll have to be the passageway that will lead us out of here."

The men drew near. Would they see the escaped prisoners? Fortunately the men failed to notice the Hardys and Chet in the darkness and entered the storeroom.

"Hey!" came a shout almost immediately. "They're gone!"

By this time the boys had dashed down the corridor, along which the men had come.

"There they go!" one of Hexton's pals yelled. "After 'em!"

Frank, Joe, and Chet had a good head start. They ran as fast as the narrow, winding passageway would permit. Behind them swept the beams from the flashlights of their pursuers.

Ahead, the tunnel forked out into two flights of steps. "Oh no!" Joe cried despairingly. "Which way?"

Frank searched the steps with his flashlight. The ones on the left were more worn. "This way," he said as the sound of the pounding feet behind them grew louder.

The three boys raced up the long flight of steps and down another corridor, but soon realized that their choice was wrong. The passage ended in a blank wooden wall!

"There *must* be a way out!" Frank declared. He picked up a loose stone and hammered against the wall.

"Listen!" he said. "This wall doesn't sound solid. It must have a secret panel. Quick! Help me get it open."

Joe and Chet pushed against the wall with all their strength.

"It won't budge!" Joe gasped.

The sounds of their pursuers' approach pounded in their ears. As the trio braced themselves for the oncoming struggle, there was a sudden grinding noise in the wall. They turned to see a panel slowly opening. A man, holding a flashlight, poked his head from behind the secret door. The boys' eyes widened in astonishment.

Kenneth Dell!

# ·19·

## "Prepare to Ditch!"

"FRANK! Joe! Chet!" Great Circle's security chief exclaimed.

Behind him in a hallway stood Inspector Clyde. "Good heavens!" he declared. "What are you boys doing in there?"

Before the three startled boys could reply, their pursuers rushed up. They almost collided as they came to an abrupt halt. Wide-eyed, Hexton's pals gazed at the lawmen, reinforced by other police. The UGLI's whirled about and ran back through the passageway.

"Come on!" Frank shouted. "After them!"

The boys rapidly gained on the men. Frank, in the lead, caught the nearest one with a flying tackle. He fell against the pair ahead, causing them to topple like a row of dominoes. There was a brief struggle while Inspector Clyde and several police officers rushed up to help the boys subdue their captives.

The UGLI men were handcuffed and led away by the police, while Frank, Joe, and Chet followed Dell and the inspector through the open panel into the main hall of the castle. They noticed it was already daylight, and Chet yawned sleepily as the group went to sit down in a huge library.

"We're amazed to see you, Mr Dell—and you, Inspector," Frank said. "How did you get in without being caught?"

"First, let me tell you why I came here," Dell said. "SKOOL's work is paying off at last. Frank and Joe, your father has almost single-handedly cracked UGLI's operations in all European countries except the British Isles, and in the United States."

"That's great!" Frank exclaimed.

"It sure is," Joe added. "And the mystery of the undercover work here is—well, half solved."

Clyde said that shortly after dawn McHugh had telephoned him, fearful something must have happened to the boys. "I gathered a few constables together and came straight here."

"Lucky break for us!" Joe remarked.

"At the castle gate," Clyde continued, "we met a most unsavoury-looking character. One of the constables recognized him as a thief wanted by the police in Glasgow. He resisted arrest and ran into the castle. We chased him."

Clyde told the boys that inside he and the constables had encountered four other men who also resisted arrest. They were Arnold, Ross, and the twins.

"I questioned them," he said, "but they refused to talk."

"What about Hexton, Vordo, and Bleeker?" Frank asked.

"Apparently all three got away," the inspector said. "Tell us, what happened to you?"

Joe briefed the men, then said, "I'll bet Hexton and the others are on their way to Edinburgh. Last night we overheard them discussing plans to steal the jewels at Nairn Loch Manor before it's opened to the pub—"

Joe stopped speaking at the sound of a faint hissing and turned abruptly. Then he burst out laughing and pointed to Chet, who had fallen asleep in an easy chair. His hands were folded on his stomach and he snored lightly.

"You all deserve a good sleep," Dell suggested, but the Hardys were too excited to accept the idea. There were still many questions to be asked.

"How did you find the entrance to the secret passageway?" Frank wanted to know.

Dell replied, "We were starting to search for you when a pounding sound came from the other side of the wall. All of us suspected it might be you signalling for help and hunted for a secret panel. I discovered that by moving the left gauntlet on one of the suits of armour in the main hall, a portion of the wall began to open!"

"And thank goodness," said Joe. "We thought that wall was the end of the line for us."

"Somewhere in this castle," Frank spoke up, "there must be evidence of Hexton's espionage set up. Have you found it?"

"No," Dell replied. "Haven't had time to look."

"Let's see if we can find it," Joe suggested.

No one had the heart to awaken Chet, so they left him. Inspector Clyde offered to investigate the library. Dell and the boys started down the adjoining hall to examine various other rooms.

The Hardys looked into several, but saw nothing to indicate espionage paraphernalia. At the end of the hall, they found themselves facing an enormous faded tapestry.

"Maybe this hides something," Frank said.

He and Joe slipped behind the hanging and found a large double door which opened inwards. As they entered, the Hardys were awed by the vastness of the room. The ceiling arched high above their heads, and lancet windows spilled bright sunlight on to the floor. At one end was a huge map of the world with coloured pins stuck in various cities.

"UGLI's centres of operation!" Frank exclaimed. "If Dad missed any, this will tell him where else to look!"

In the centre of the room stood two oak tables. There was an elaborate radio set up on one. Joe whistled. "Powerful baby!"

On the other table were several metal cases, sealed without any visible means of opening.

"Trick boxes," said Frank. "One of Hexton's specialties."

Dell walked in as the boys looked them over and tried pressure in several places. Nothing worked. Then Frank had an idea. He turned one box towards him and the side slowly opened.

Joe grinned. "Hardy, the magician!"

"No," said Frank. "Electric eye." He moved the other two cases and each opened in the same way, revealing rows of drawers.

In the first one the boys found packages of microfilm and microtape, each labelled with a code tag.

"Tells where they came from and where they're going," Frank guessed. "Hexton brings them here.

UGLI operators make the pick up and take them to countries hostile to the United States and other democratic powers."

Dell frowned. "These are probably films of secret plans and drawings of highly classified material."

"Here's the roster of UGLI operators!" Joe exclaimed, rifling through a notebook. "Probably these names are in code."

"Doesn't matter," said Frank. He held up a red leather volume. "Here's the codebook!"

"Well," said Inspector Clyde, entering the room, "that will come in handy when it's time to round up those UGLI blighters. I saw the tapestry hanging awry and guessed you might have found a hidden door."

He stood in amazement at the boys' discovery. "What a treasure for our counter-espionage people"

"And SKOOL," Joe spoke up. "UGLI, the biggest undercover subversive operation in the world, cracked wide open!"

Frank's enthusiasm was dampened by the fact that some of UGLI's top men were still at large. "Unless we catch them, they'll start a new operation somewhere else."

"That's true," Clyde said, and the others agreed.

"Then let's find them!" Joe cried.

At that moment a constable ushered in McHugh.

"I returned to Glasgow to get my plane," the pilot said, "and flew 'er back here. Thought I might be a wee bit o' help." He had landed on an open field close to the castle, he told them.

"That's great!" Frank replied eagerly. "Will you fly us to Edinburgh?"

"Certainly."

McHugh was introduced to Dell. The pilot grinned. "Man, ye got a couple o' fine detective lads here," he said. "Well, I'm ready to start."

Inspector Clyde decided to stay at the castle. "I'd better remain here in case something important pops up at this end."

Frank and Joe roused Chet, who rubbed his eyes and stubbornly demanded breakfast.

"Come on!" Joe urged. "We'll grab a bite when we land. Chet, wait till you hear what we found!"

This roused the stout boy and he followed the Hardys and Dell to the plane. All the boys catnapped during the flight, and later at Edinburgh Airport stoked up on bacon and eggs. Then, while McHugh stayed with the plane, the boys and Dell went to the nearest police office to reveal Hexton's daring scheme of robbery the next day.

The constable on duty, a plump man with reddish hair who introduced himself as Sergeant Watson, was highly indignant. "Impossible! Thieves could not get within five hundred feet of the Manor without being challenged!"

"Don't underestimate Hexton," Dell warned. "He's an extremely clever crook."

"Now that he knows we're after him," said Frank, "he might very well pull the robbery today."

"Is Nairn Loch Manor far from here?" Joe inquired.

"Oh, just a few minutes by car," Watson replied.

"Will you come with us?" Dell asked him.

"I'll have to get permission from my superior. But I tell you, this man Hexton hasn't got a chance!"

Ten minutes later they climbed into a police car and soon arrived at the large, fortress-like structure built of stone. The windows were heavily barred, and the thick oak doors were secured by large iron bolts.

Watson showed his credentials, then introduced his companions. He asked to see the custodian, Angus Hamilton. The custodian scoffed when he heard about Hexton's intentions. "Impossible! Utterly impossible!" he asserted. "The Manor is too well guarded."

"What about burglar alarms?" Frank asked.

"A complete system is now being installed," Hamilton answered. "In fact, the Manor will not be opened to the public until it's completed." He grinned. "No, I'm afraid your fears are unwarranted. This Hexton fellow would have to render himself invisible to get on to the premises."

"I'm not sure he couldn't do just that," Chet mumbled.

"May we see the jewel collection?" Frank requested.

"I'll be happy to show it to you," Hamilton said with pride.

He led them down a long hallway. At the far end was a heavy oak door, flanked on each side by a guard. With a large black key the custodian unlocked the door. He ushered the Hardys and their companions into the chamber.

"You gentlemen," Hamilton said, "are about to see one of the most splendid collections of—" His voice trailed off, and his face turned ashen. "The jewels!" he gasped. "The jewels! They're gone!"

The Hardys ran to the glass cases in which the treasure had been kept. Except for a gold crown and several sceptres, the cases were completely empty!

"B-but how?" the custodian cried, almost in a state of panic. "I checked the collection just a little while ago!"

The local constable took command of the situation and questioned the guards. None of them had seen any suspicious strangers in the area. A quick inventory revealed that all the smaller, but extremely valuable jewels were missing.

"Hexton left the crown and sceptres behind because they're too bulky," Frank surmised.

"What's your guess, Mr Dell," asked Joe, "as to the way the thieves got in here?"

Dell turned to the custodian. "Are there any architectural plans of the Manor available?"

"Indeed yes. I have them in my files. But if you're looking for a secret passageway, you won't have any luck. I've studied those plans thoroughly."

Watson, meanwhile, had radioed his office and orders were given to set up road-blocks on the main roads leading out of Edinburgh. Also, airports and ports throughout the country would be alerted at once.

"Do you think Hexton is headed back to his castle?" Joe asked.

"If so," Frank said, "he'll find quite a welcoming committee waiting for him. But now that he knows the police were there, I'd say he'll stay away from the place."

"We'd better phone Inspector Clyde about the robbery," said Chet. But when Joe tried to do this, he found there was no telephone at the castle.

"We'd better fly back there right away," Frank said.

Dell announced he must return to the United States.

"If Hexton comes there, I'll be on hand to pursue that part of my assignment." He said goodbye and went off in a taxi.

Watson drove the boys to the airport, then went back to his office. As the young detectives hurried towards the trimotored plane, they saw that the pilot was already seated in the cockpit. Frank signalled to him and McHugh responded with a not-too-enthusiastic wave of his hand.

"Something seems to be troubling him," Joe observed as they climbed into the cabin and slammed the door. The pilot started the engines and the plane began to taxi towards the runway for take-off.

Frank walked up to the cockpit. "What seems to be the mat—" He stopped abruptly and gasped. Crouched in the seat next to McHugh was Stony Bleeker! He held a gun pointed at the pilot.

"Get back into the cabin!" Bleeker commanded.

Frank turned to see two men emerge from beneath a tarpaulin at the rear. *Hexton and Vordo!*

"It's nice of you boys to accommodate us like this," the magician said with a smirk. "We happened to be in need of fast transportation."

"W-when did you get aboard?" Joe stammered. "We thought you'd be a long way from Edinburgh by this time!"

"Our car broke down on a back road near the airport," Hexton snapped. "Then Bleeker spotted this plane and we decided to hitch a ride."

"Where to?" Joe demanded.

"We're all going for a nice little flight to Ireland," the magician announced sarcastically.

"I told you I canna make it there!" McHugh shouted. "We've no' enough fuel!"

"Don't try to fool me!" Bleeker growled. "Your gauges show full tanks!"

"The gauges haven't worked for weeks!" the pilot insisted. "I calculate my fuel consumption by the amount of time I fly. And I tell ye, we've no' enough fuel to make Ireland!"

Hexton let out a spine-chilling laugh, and eyed the Hardys and Chet. "Your pilot will have to think up a cleverer trick than that, because I don't intend to go back to my castle and meet your Inspector Clyde!"

"How do you know about that?" Frank asked.

The magician's weird, piercing eyes focused on the boys with a fixed stare. "Bleeker stayed behind when Vordo and I left for Edinburgh," he replied. "He was there when the police arrived, and escaped without being seen. Of course he came straight to Edinburgh to warn us."

"Incidentally," Frank put in, "how did you manage to pull off the Manor robbery?"

"Shut up!" Vordo growled. "You're asking too many questions!"

"No, no, Vordo. I don't mind telling them," Hexton said boastfully. He reached into his jacket pocket and withdrew a folded piece of parchment. "This," he said, "is the architect's original plan of Nairn Loch Manor. There are copies, of course. But this is the only one showing the secret passageway."

"The passageway," Frank said, "that leads into the chamber where the jewel collection was kept."

"Yes, and very convenient for me," the magician

replied smugly, "especially since its entrance is located in a hill nearly a quarter of a mile away. As for this," he added, tapping the parchment, "it used to be on display in a small private museum, but a master key and a little sleight-of-hand put it in my pocket."

As the plane continued on course, the Hardys noticed that their captors' jackets bulged and a sealskin pouch jutted from one of Hexton's pockets. Undoubtedly it contained the stolen jewels!

A few minutes later McHugh shouted another warning. "We're leavin' the coast! We canna go any farther!"

Frank gazed below. They were passing over the west coast of Scotland and heading out over the Irish Sea. Just then the port engine sputtered. Seconds later the centre and starboard engines began to quit.

McHugh whirled the plane in a tight turn back towards the Scottish coast. Levelling the craft out on a reciprocal course, he tightened his grip on the control wheel.

Frank and Joe stared at the propellers as they windmilled noiselessly in the powerless glide. Below them was the choppy surface of the Irish Sea.

"I canna reach land!" McHugh shouted. "We're goin' down. Prepare to ditch!"

# ·20·

## Desperate Flight!

McHugh flicked his radio transmitter to 121.5 mega-cycles—the international distress frequency.

"Mayday! Mayday! Mayday!" he shouted into the microphone. "This is Trimotor—Victor—Victor—Fox! About twenty miles southwest o' Skipness radio! Lost all power! Have t' ditch!"

Hexton and his associates were pale with fright as they watched the plane sink closer to the water.

"Quick, lads! Jettison the cabin door!" McHugh ordered.

Near the door was a red handle. Joe dashed to it and gave a sharp pull. As the door shot off into space, there was a thunderous rush of air through the cabin.

"Sit with your backs against the forward bulkhead!" the pilot yelled. "Clasp your hands behind your heads and brace yourselves!"

Everyone took ditching positions. The wait was nerve-shattering. Finally the plane hit the water. It bounced off the surface on first contact, then nosed down into the choppy sea with a violent impact. Water gushed into the cabin. As the boys recovered from the shock, Frank turned to see Hexton pushing himself out through the cabin entrance.

"We're sinking fast!" Joe yelled.

"Look!" Chet shouted. "McHugh's unconscious!"

"So are Vordo and Bleeker!" Joe added.

"We must get them out of here!" Frank declared. "I'll take McHugh! You two grab the others!"

Clutching the unconscious men, the boys edged their way to the cabin entrance and pushed themselves clear of the sinking aircraft. They were not too far from land and began swimming.

Joe, who was dragging Vordo along with him, looked towards the shore just as Hexton reached it. The magician stumbled ahead and disappeared into the tall grass.

"Hexton's getting away!" Joe shouted.

"We'll have to let him go," Frank replied. "We can't let Vordo and Bleeker drown."

Chet, meanwhile, was too winded to speak, as he swam doggedly on with his heavy burden. Bleeker was a dead weight. The boys had almost made it to shore when a motor launch of the Air-Sea Rescue Service sped towards them.

"We received your distress signal," one of the crewmen shouted as the boat pulled alongside. "Anybody missing?"

"No," Joe shouted back. "One man made it to shore."

Vordo and Bleeker began to recover as they were hauled aboard the boat.

"We'd better tie up these two," Frank said. "They're jewel thieves." Rope was produced and the prisoners bound.

Joe and Chet helped McHugh, who groaned and

slowly got to his feet. Grief-stricken, he watched the tail of his plane disappear beneath the surface of the water in a bubbling sea of foam.

Joe began going through the prisoners' pockets. "Look!" he cried, holding out several sealskin pouches. They were crammed with jewels.

"Firsthand evidence," said Frank. "Hexton must have the rest. Now that his espionage work has been destroyed, he probably figures on living off the haul he made today."

"Let's ask these UGLI's a few questions," Joe suggested. He turned to Vordo and Bleeker. "How did you kidnap our father?"

The two men glared. "You're getting nothing out of us!" Vordo snarled.

"That's tellin' em, Vordo!" Bleeker snapped. "Too bad the mirror Hexton had you put on the road didn't work out and that Lou missed with that sandbag. We'd have been rid of these snoopers long ago! And it's a shame they have a crackerjack pilot who safely landed their plane after you loosened the fuel caps."

When the rescue ship reached shore, the prisoners were turned over to the authorities. The others proceeded to Prestwick in a car lent to McHugh by a friend. Regretfully the three boys bid goodbye to the brave pilot.

"You're tops," Joe added, and Frank said. "One of the best sports I ever met!" Chet nodded.

McHugh smiled. "You're the finest lads I ever knew. Come again sometime and have a ride in my new plane."

"We'll do that," Chet answered.

After the pilot had left them, the boys went for a bite to eat. Joe expressed his frustration that Hexton had escaped.

"Where do you think he'll go?" Chet asked. "Ireland, like he said?"

Frank shook his head. "My guess is New York."

Joe's eyes lighted up. "And maybe on Flight 101! It leaves tomorrow morning."

Chet snorted, "An UGLI secret agent on Flight 101!"

"We're going to be on board, too," said Frank. "If he's there, we'll nab him."

The boys informed Inspector Clyde of their plan. They could hardly wait to take off. Next morning they watched intently as the passengers filed aboard.

"Hey!" Joe exclaimed, nudging his brother. "There's that same man we saw on our last flight to New York— the one with the dark glasses and whiskers and cane."

"Well, he can't be Hexton in disguise," Frank commented. "This man's heavier set."

"I don't see *anybody* that looks like Hexton," Chet lamented.

They observed another elderly bewhiskered man with a cast on his left leg hobble up on crutches. A steward helped him into the plane.

The boys were the last to go aboard. During the flight the boys studied the other passengers but saw nothing suspicious.

When the wheels screeched down at Westboro, Joe stretched his arms wearily. "Guess we drew a blank this time." He sighed.

At the Great Circle Airways ramp, the passengers began to disembark.

"Let's keep our seats until everybody's out," Frank whispered. "Watch carefully."

The plane emptied until only the two elderly men, the three boys, and the steward were left. The man with the cast eased himself on to his crutches and started down the aisle.

Joe stiffened. "Hey! Did you see that?" he whispered excitedly. "That old man was walking on his injured leg! I'll bet he's a fake."

"I saw it too," Frank replied. He bolted out of his seat and called, "Wait a minute! We want to talk to you!"

The man stopped abruptly. Then he swung one of his crutches at Frank as the youth darted towards him. The other elderly man sprang from his seat and dealt him a blow with his cane that sent him stumbling up the aisle.

"Steward," bellowed the man with the cast, "keep these guys away from me!"

"That voice!" Joe yelled. "It's Hexton's!"

The steward was about to pounce on Frank, when Chet cried out, "This man's wanted by the police!"

Frank leaped at Hexton as the magician again swung his crutch. The young sleuth ducked and lunged forward, crashing into his opponent's midriff. As Hexton fell, his cast struck a seat and broke open. From it, a cascade of jewels spilled into the aisle. At the same moment several men poured in through the passenger door.

Among them was Kenneth Dell. "Looks as if you fellows already have things under control."

Chet picked up two sections of the cast. "It's light

plastic," he said, "and looks as if it's made to come apart."

Frank yanked the magician to his feet, and whipped a wig from the man's head. Then he ripped off Hexton's false eyebrows and whiskers.

Joe whistled. "Amazing what a little disguise can do to change a man's appearance!"

"You're right!" said the other elderly man.

"We want to thank you, sir, for your help," Joe said gratefully.

"That's all right, Joe," the man replied, chuckling.

Joe! As the boys looked on in amazement, the man removed his dark glasses and a false beard.

"Dad!" the young sleuths exclaimed, overjoyed to see their father.

Then Frank whispered to him, "So you were the secret agent for SKOOL on Flight 101!"

"Yes," Mr Hardy said quietly. His "aged" slouch was gone, and he pulled himself to his full height. "Sorry to keep my whereabouts a secret. But the job was so dangerous I couldn't risk telling anybody where I was."

"You never were in South Africa?"

"No."

Hexton was livid. "You haven't heard the last of me!" he snarled.

"Save your breath," Joe retorted. "You'll need it when the authorities begin questioning you and the other members of UGLI."

Federal agents arrived to take custody of Hexton. The boys learned that Mr Hardy had cabled Dell to have the agents on hand because he suspected who the "injured" passenger on the flight was.

"I wanted him captured on U.S. soil," the detective said.

"Tell us, Dad," Frank asked eagerly, "how Hexton managed to spirit you away in that vanishing-man device?"

"It was quite a simple trick," Mr Hardy explained. "The bottom of the plank I was strapped to was a highly polished mirror. After setting it in the frame, the frame was rotated so the mirror side of the plank was angled towards the audience. In this position, it reflected the roof of the enclosure, which was made of the same material as the draperies forming the rear wall. To an observer it looked as if the plank had vanished, including the subject. Meanwhile, a man of the same size and build wearing the identical clothes appeared from the wings."

"That was Lou, then," said Joe. "Bert's double. Chet, old pal, you were right about the trick.

Chet beamed modestly. "It was nothing."

"In my case," Mr Hardy went on, "Bleeker was hiding in a secret compartment in the base of the device. When Hexton closed the curtain, he popped up and jabbed me with a needle containing a powerful drug. UGLI members always carry these hypodermics for emergencies. I passed out in seconds."

"How did you escape from the lighthouse?" Joe asked.

Fenton Hardy grinned. "I had a lucky break," he said. "Vordo and Bleeker handcuffed me to the metal railing of the spiral stairway, with my hands behind my back. Fortunately I spotted a short piece of baling wire on the floor. It was a tough job, but I managed to get the wire to stick to the heel of my shoe. Then I bent my leg back far enough so I could reach the wire with my fingers."

"And you picked the lock of your handcuffs!" Joe guessed.

"Yes," Mr Hardy replied. "It took me hours. Then I sneaked out while Vordo and Bleeker were sleeping and borrowed their dinghy. I had almost reached the mainland when I heard their powerboat coming from the islet. So I capsized the dinghy and swam the rest of the way."

Frank grinned. "You hoped Vordo and Bleeker would find it and think you had drowned."

"Exactly," his father answered. "At least it would keep them guessing."

Mr Hardy then described his investigations of the Great Circle stewards he suspected. "I used several disguises including a blond wig."

Chet asked him why he had tripped Ross.

"I thought maybe he had a small package of jewels in his sleeve or under his coat, and it might fall out when he fell. But I was wrong. I also slipped the note into Joe's suitcase."

"What about Mazer, the pilot of the STOL?" Joe inquired.

"I believe he was a victim of circumstances," Dell replied. "The authorities are going to let him off with a year's suspension of his pilot's licence."

The group got out of the plane and Mr Dell said goodbye. "See you on the next case, Fenton," he called, and hurried off.

Frank and Joe fervently hoped they might be included, but soon they were involved in another case—*The Tower Treasure.*

"Now, fellows," Mr Hardy said with a grin, "I suggest we call Jack Wayne and have him fly all us SKOOL boys home."

"SKOOL *boys?* What do you mean?" Chet asked.

The secret agent grinned. "I think you've all earned places in the organization as junior members!"

**Peter May** was born and raised in Scotland. He was an award-winning journalist at the age of twenty-one and a published novelist at twenty-six. When his first book was adapted as a major drama series for the BBC, he quit journalism and during the high-octane fifteen years that followed became one of Scotland's most successful television dramatists. He created three prime-time drama series, presided over two of the highest-rated serials in his homeland as script editor and producer, and worked on more than 1,000 episodes of ratings-topping drama before deciding to leave television to return to his first love, writing novels.

He has won several literature awards in France, received the USA's Barry Award for *The Blackhouse* – the first in his internationally bestselling Lewis Trilogy; and in 2014 *Entry Island* was awarded the ITV Specsavers Crime Thriller Book Club Best Read of the Year, as well as the Deanston Scottish Crime Book of the Year. May now lives in south-west France with his wife, writer Janice Hally.

Also by Peter May

FICTION

**The Lewis Trilogy**

*The Blackhouse*
*The Lewis Man*
*The Chessmen*

**The China Thrillers**

*The Firemaker*
*The Fourth Sacrifice*
*The Killing Room*
*Snakehead*
*The Runner*
*Chinese Whispers*
*The Ghost Marriage: A China Novella*

**The Enzo Files**

*Extraordinary People*
*The Critic*
*Blacklight Blue*
*Freeze Frame*
*Blowback*

**Stand-alone Novels**

*Entry Island*
*Runaway*
*Coffin Road*

NON-FICTION

*Hebrides* (with David Wilson)

# PETER MAY

# CAST IRON

riverrun

First published in Great Britain in 2017 by riverrun
This paperback edition published in 2017 by

riverrun

an imprint of
Quercus Editions Ltd
Carmelite House
50 Victoria Embankment
London EC4Y 0DZ

An Hachette UK company

A CIP catalogue record for this book is available
from the British Library

MMP Format ISBN 978 1 78206 231 8
OME Format ISBN 978 1 78429 975 0
EBOOK ISBN 978 1 78429 976 7

10 9 8 7 6 5 4 3 2 1

Typeset by CC Book Production
Printed and bound in Great Britain by Clays Ltd, St Ives plc

In memory of my friend and mentor,
Dr Richard Ward

Keep your friends close
and your enemies closer

*Paraphrased from Niccolò Machiavelli's* **The Prince**

# PROLOGUE

## WEST OF FRANCE, 1989

*It smells of animal here. Dead animal. Something that has been hung to ripen before cooking. Hundreds of years of fermenting grapes have suffused the earth with odours of yeast and carbonic gas, stale now, sour, a memory retained only in the soil and the sandstone and the rafters. Like all the forgotten lives that have passed through this place, in sunlight and in darkness.*

*It is dark now and another life has passed.*

*Dust hangs in the pale light that angles through the open door, raised by the act of pulling her dead body from dark concealment to the wash of cold, colourless moonlight that bathes a face once beautiful and animated by youth. A face made ugly now by the blood that has dried in her golden hair, on her porcelain cheek, a tiny river of it following the contour from her temple to her ear. By the eyes that stare in unnatural stillness into the deep shadow that hangs overhead like a shroud. Blue eyes, lit once by the light of life, turned milky and opaque by death.*

*His tears fall like the first raindrops of a summer storm to splash heavy and hot on her cold skin. His shadow falls over her as he kneels*

1

by her side, and for a moment obliterates the sight of what he has done – a consequence of love and anger, those two most volatile of emotions. To gaze upon her is almost unbearable. But regret is useless, for of all the things in life that cannot be undone, death is the most immutable.

He reaches into his jacket pocket to pull out the blue plastic bag he has brought to hide his shame. Carefully, as if afraid he might damage it, he lifts her head from the dust and pulls the bag down over her face, hiding at last the accusation, recrimination and the sense of betrayal he imagines in the gaze he cannot bear to meet.

He ties it at the base of her neck with the short length of plastic string that came with it, and now tears fall on plastic to punctuate the silence. A moment of madness, a lifetime of lament, and he can never tell her now just how much he loved her.

His hands are trembling as they close around her neck, and he closes his eyes tight shut as his thumbs sink into soft flesh and he feels bone breaking beneath them.

# CHAPTER ONE

## LOT-ET-GARONNE, FRANCE, 2003

The cool air that came with the night was dissipating along with the early morning mist. Already he could feel the heat rising up through the earth, and soon the sky would be a burned-out dusty white. Like yesterday, and the day before, and the day before that. He had read in *La Dépêche* that the death toll was climbing, the elderly worst affected by temperatures now soaring into the mid-forties. Eleven thousand and mounting. This summer heatwave had scorched the earth, killing trees and bushes, burning leaves brittle and brown to tumble like autumn in August.

It was some months since he had come down to the lake, a primal need to sit in solitary silence with a line in the water, caring not in the least whether the fish would bite – though they usually did. His baby boy was just two days old, and both he and his mother were still in the hospital after a difficult birth.

He glanced west across a shimmering landscape, seeing the

undulations of burned fields and the skeletons of trees beyond, to where the caves in these chalk hills once provided refuge for resistance fighters when the German occupiers came looking for them.

The slope here was steep, fallen leaves crackling beneath his feet as he made his way through the trees. And then he saw it, shocked for a moment, and stopped. The lake simmered a chemical green in light already thick with heat, and was half or less its usual size. He stepped through dry, breaking undergrowth to his habitual spot, and saw that the water was four metres down, perhaps more. From here, he walked out on to cracked sloping mud, where his line had once snagged fish, and gazed down at the water below.

All the streams that ran into the lake had long since dried to a trickle, but the farmers, with more need of water than ever, had continued to draw on it, sucking it dry. Unless this *canicule* broke soon, there would be nothing of it left. And he wondered if the fish it supported would last the summer.

He started tracking west around the perimeter, a great swathe of exposed lake bed, parched and brown, cut deep into the land like a scar. All manner of detritus was exposed, both natural and man-made. The carcasses of long-dead trees. The skeleton of a pram.

In all the scorched mud and desiccated slime, a flash of blue caught his eye. Pale and bleached by water and sun, just above the new waterline. He stumbled over uneven ground, drawn by the incongruous flash of colour in all this withered landscape.

There were streaks of white in the baked mud around it, and he saw that it was a blue plastic bag. Only half of it was visible, the rest of it set solid in the mud.

He laid his rod and his bag on the ground and crouched down beside it, curious. There was something inside. The plastic was brittle with age and tore easily beneath his fingers, and he found himself looking down into the black sockets of a skull that had once held eyes. Long, yellowed teeth were exposed in a ghastly grimace, grinning out at him as if amused by his shock. He recoiled at once, and sat down heavily. And it was only then he realised that those white streaks set into the dry lake bed around him were the remaining bones of a human skeleton.

# CHAPTER TWO

## PARIS, OCTOBER 2011

In all the years that Enzo had been coming to Raffin's apartment in the Rue de Tournon, someone, somewhere, always seemed to be playing a piano. Scales and exercises, stuttering renditions of Chopin and Beethoven – those tuneless pieces that music teachers inflicted on their hapless pupils. And, in all those years, the pianist had never improved.

Enzo glanced distractedly into the inner courtyard below, the huge chestnut at the far side of it dropping big dried leaves on wet cobbles. But his eyes were drawn by an elegant lady in black whose heels clicked on those same cobbles beneath finely turned ankles, and he wondered if the day would ever come when his interest would not be aroused by an attractive woman. After all, he could see sixty now, looming not far beyond the horizon.

'Are you listening?' Raffin's voice was sharp, admonitory, irritated by Enzo's distraction.

'Of course.' Enzo turned his eyes back to the table, and the

6

papers and photographs that were strewn across it. Raffin's book was open at the sixth and penultimate murder of the seven cold cases he had written about in *Assassins Cachés*. He had slid his clenched fist between the pages, breaking the spine to keep it open at the desired place, and Enzo had drawn breath sharply. He hated to break the spine of a book. It seemed to him like vandalism.

'Lucie Martin was just twenty years old when she went missing,' Raffin said. He always liked to brief Enzo before the big Scotsman embarked on one of the cases from his book. And, for his part, although he had read Raffin's book many times, Enzo appreciated the briefing. It gave him access to the background research Raffin had done which never actually made it into the text. And he liked to hear the facts, rather than just read about them. Somehow that helped them stick. Raffin reached for the bottle of Puligny-Montrachet, running now with condensation, and refilled each of their glasses. 'But that was fourteen years before the discovery of her body. Her disappearance in 1989 was inexplicable. She hadn't run away. Or, if she had, she had left everything behind – her whole life and all that she owned. And, anyway, why would she? She was the loving daughter of doting parents. Her father, Guillaume, was an appeal court judge, her mother a former nurse. There was absolutely no evidence of foul play, and no one, apparently, with any motive for doing her harm.'

Enzo sipped his wine reflectively. 'She was still living at home, wasn't she?'

'Only at the weekends. During the week, she stayed at a studio apartment in Bordeaux. She had a job in town working for a charity called Rentrée that helped newly released prisoners reintegrate into society.' Raffin raised a sceptical eyebrow, and an element of sarcasm crept into his voice. 'Some kind of religious organisation.'

'And that's where she met Régis Blanc?'

'Briefly, yes.' He was irritated again by the interruption, and Enzo wondered – not for the first time – what it was his daughter saw in him. He was a good-looking young man. Though not quite so young anymore. More than forty now, perhaps. Like Enzo himself, he had aged during their six-year collaboration, and never been the same man again after taking, full in his chest, the bullet that had been meant for Enzo. Vanity was apparent in the careful arrangement of his hair and the cut of his designer clothes. Enzo had never taken to him.

'Anyway,' Raffin continued, 'she had arrived home for the weekend on the Friday night. Her mother went off to visit relatives on the Saturday, and that afternoon she told her father she was going for a walk.'

'The Martins have quite an estate, don't they?'

'About a thousand acres, most of it overlooked by the château at the top of the hill. Well, they call it a château, but really it's just a very large house, extended to a number of outbuildings. Been in his family for generations. He spent a lot of money restoring it all in the seventies and eighties.'

'So she went for a walk on the estate.'

'That's what she told her father. Only she never returned. When her mother got back that evening, Guillaume Martin was in a state.'

'But they didn't call the police immediately?'

'No. Not until some hours later. Martin knew the police wouldn't respond until she'd been missing for a certain period of time. She was, after all, an adult. But it was going through her room that night that her parents found the letter from Blanc.'

Enzo reached for the photocopy of the letter lying among the papers on the table. He had read it many times, and he cast his eye again over the scrawling, illiterate hand that had striven to convey emotions the man so clearly found difficult to express. He had signed it, simply, *Love, R.* And something about that suggested to Enzo an unlikely intimacy. It had always troubled him. 'Of course, they could have had no idea then that Blanc was just about to be revealed as one of France's most notorious serial killers.'

'Quite,' Raffin said. 'He was arrested on the Monday for the murder of those three prostitutes and within two months had been sentenced to life at the high-security *maison centrale* at Lannemezan. Lucie had met him first at Rentrée when he was released from Murat some months earlier, just after he'd completed a nine-month stretch for serious assault. The man was a pimp, and well known for his violent temper. Lucie's father was convinced that he had also killed Lucie. But there was

nothing to link him to Lucie in any way, apart from the love letter. And he has always claimed he wrote that when he was drunk and giving vent to an ephemeral infatuation.'

'But there was no doubt about him having murdered the prostitutes?'

'None at all. In fact, the defence didn't even deny it. Just argued that he'd been depressed after the break-up of his marriage and that he'd been under the influence of drugs and alcohol at the time.' Raffin ran a hand back through light brown hair that was greying at the temples, and perhaps thinning just a little on the crown. 'Hardly a mitigating factor. And, anyway, no one believed that the calculated way in which he had strangled each of those women, and then dumped their bodies, was anything other than the action of a cold-blooded, entirely sober serial murderer.'

Raffin's mobile phone rang and vibrated on the table. He turned it towards him to see who was calling.

'I have to take this,' he said. And he lifted the phone and raised it to his ear as he wandered across the *séjour*, through double doors and into his study. Enzo heard him say, 'No, no, it's alright. Nothing important.' And then the door closed and his voice became muffled.

At the same moment, Enzo heard the door of the apartment open, and he stood up, turning expectantly toward the hall. He heard the chortle of a child, the creak of a pram, and then Kirsty came in holding baby Alexis in her arms. She was wearing a long black coat, her chestnut hair and a red scarf

draped over her shoulders, face pink with exertion and the chill autumn air. She was momentarily surprised to see Enzo, then her face lit up.

'Papa! What are you doing here?' Although born and raised in Scotland, she had started adopting the French informal address for her father.

He took three strides towards them. 'Am I not allowed to drop by and visit my daughter and grandson?' And he kissed them both, eyes filled with love and affection for the six-month-old baby. The child gazed back at him, and his little round face broke into the broadest of smiles.

'God!' Kirsty gasped. 'Women and babies! They all fall for you, don't they?' She caught sight of the mess of papers and photographs scattered across the table, and gave her father a look. 'And, if I didn't know better, I might be tempted to think that the real reason for your visit is a briefing session with Roger on the Martin case.'

Enzo grinned. 'Oh, that . . . just a pretext.'

She smiled her scepticism. 'Here. Hold Alexis while I get out of this coat.' When she had hung it up in the hall, she took Alexis from his grandfather and laid him in a carrycot by the table, then sat down to pour herself a glass from the remains of the bottle Enzo and Raffin had been sharing. 'Mmmh,' she said. 'This is good.'

'It ought to be. It cost an arm and a leg.'

'*You* brought it?' Kirsty seemed surprised.

'Have to keep Roger happy.' And something in his tone took

a little of the shine off her pleasure at seeing him. She knew her father didn't care much for her fiancé. 'Set a date yet? he said.

She avoided his eye. 'No, not yet.' They had been going to marry before the baby was born, but hadn't, and never explained why. She followed his adoring gaze towards his grandson. 'Does it ever bother you?'

He looked at her, surprised. 'What?'

And perhaps she regretted having started down that road. 'Well, you know . . . that he's not your blood.'

His smile was fond, and he reached out to touch her face with the tips of his fingers. 'He's your son, Kirsty. How could I ever think of him as anything other than my flesh and blood?'

She raised her hand to catch his and held it for a moment.

He said, 'Do you ever see Simon?'

'No.'

'Why not?'

Her eyes blazed briefly. 'After the way he broke it to you, deliberately to hurt you . . . well, as far as I'm concerned, he lost all his rights as my real father. I only have one papa, and that's you.'

Almost embarrassed, Enzo looked back toward the cot and made some silly baby noises to attract his grandson's attention. But the boy didn't respond.

Kirsty said, 'We think he has a hearing problem.'

Enzo turned concerned eyes towards her.

'We noticed quite early that sometimes he just didn't seem

to hear things. I mean, if I clap my hands loudly, he'll turn in response, but quite often when I speak to him, he just doesn't hear my voice.'

'Have you had him checked?'

'Oh, yes, we've been to several doctors. None of them can agree on anything except that, while he's not deaf, he does have a problem. My own doctor's asked for an appointment for us with a consultant who is reckoned to be the top hearing specialist in France.'

'That'll cost a bit.'

She nodded. 'Unfortunately the doctor is based in Biarritz. So it's a bit of a trek.'

'Roger owns property down that way, doesn't he?'

'Yes, just south of the town. It was his wife's family home. She inherited it when her parents were drowned in a boating accident. She and Roger couldn't live there, but she couldn't bear to sell it. So she turned it into a kind of exclusive *chambres d'hôtes*, converting it into several apartments, one of which she kept for their own personal use. Obviously, Roger inherited it when Marie was . . . well, when she died.'

'Her family were pretty wealthy, weren't they?'

'Filthy bloody rich, from all accounts. I mean, they bought this apartment for their daughter. Imagine how much that must have cost. Two hundred metres from the Sénat. One of the most prestigious addresses in Paris. Who knows what it's worth now?'

'And I suppose Roger inherited everything from Marie?'

Kirsty didn't respond. 'Makes you wonder why he even bothers working.'

'Oh, he doesn't have to. He just wants to. Money's not everything.'

Enzo smiled. 'Say people who have lots of it.'

But Kirsty didn't return the smile. 'Anyway, Alexis and I will stay over at the apartment in the Biarritz house when we go down for the appointment. I've never been before.' She clouded a little. 'It's just a shame Roger can't go with us.' She pulled a face. 'Work.'

Enzo frowned. 'When is it?'

'Sometime next week. I'm waiting for them to confirm a day and time.'

'Well, why don't I go with you? Moral support. I suppose there'll be more than one bedroom.'

Kirsty's spirits lifted visibly. 'Oh, would you, Papa? That would be a great relief. I was kind of dreading going on my own.'

'Well, Sophie's planning a birthday party for me in Cahors next week. If the timing works out, we could go down to Biarritz afterwards.'

Kirsty nodded. 'Yes, I know about the party. Sophie's been in touch. Trying to get the whole family together, she said.' She hesitated. 'She wanted me to ask Charlotte to come, and bring Laurent.'

Enzo stiffened a little. 'Oh, did she?'

'But I'm not going to.' She seemed determined, and Enzo feigned indifference.

'I don't blame you.'

'You should do it.'

He flashed her a look.

'Papa, Laurent's your son. And Charlotte . . . well, I don't know what she is to you anymore. But you must have done something together to make a baby.'

He made a face at her. The last thing he wanted to do was talk to his daughter about his sex life with Charlotte. And he was rescued from the embarrassment of it by the return of her fiancé.

Raffin emerged from his study with a purpose of step and what, to anyone else, might have seemed like a smile on his face. To Enzo, it was a smirk of self-satisfaction. He barely acknowledged Kirsty, stooping momentarily as he passed to plant a perfunctory kiss on her head, and completely ignoring his son. The bottle of Puligny-Montrachet was in his hand even before he had sunk into his chair, and he refilled his glass. He sat back and raised it to his lips, sipping appreciatively before smiling at father and daughter. 'That was Jean-Jacques Devez on the phone,' he said, adding, quite unnecessarily, 'the Mayor of Paris.'

'Yes, we know who he is, Roger,' Kirsty said. 'The question is, what was he after?' And Enzo got the immediate impression that his daughter was not altogether fond of the Mayor of Paris. Raffin seemed oblivious.

'It looks like he's almost certain to win the UMP nomination for next year's presidential election.'

Enzo knew that Raffin, and presumably now Kirsty, saw Devez socially. A friendship between the Raffins and the Devez family that dated back to when the young politician was just embarking on his meteoric rise to political stardom. Marie, apparently, had been friends with Devez's wife from some private school they had both attended.

Kirsty said, 'The papers have been predicting that for months.'

Raffin sipped a little more of his Chardonnay. 'Yes, but I think he must have had the nod from the powers that be. There's to be an announcement within the next two weeks. And when it's made public, he wants me to be his press secretary.'

Neither Kirsty nor Enzo knew quite how to respond. If he accepted, and Devez were to become president, it would put Raffin at the very heart of power and influence in France. And there was no doubt that his family, along with Enzo's mission to solve the cold cases in his book, would take second or even third place.

'And?' Kirsty said.

But Raffin just shrugged, as if it were a matter of indifference to him. 'I haven't decided yet.'

Enzo said, 'Well, I hope it's a decision you'll take in consultation with Kirsty. After all, it's going to affect you both.'

'Of course!' Raffin flicked Enzo a look of irritation, and everything about his tone said, *It's none of your damn business!* He pulled his open book towards him. 'Now, where were we?'

'The lack of any real link between Blanc and Lucie,' Enzo prompted him.

'Ah, yes . . .' Raffin sifted through some of the papers in front of him until he found what he was looking for. 'But here's the strange thing.' He ran fingertips over a colour photograph of the spot in the lake bed where Lucie's skeleton had been found. 'The girl's body would have been reduced to bones very quickly, all flesh and soft tissue almost certainly eaten by the fish in the lake. Apparently there are carp, roach, rudd and catfish in those waters. They would have made pretty short work of her. Her skeleton would have disintegrated quite early on, and you would expect there to be some missing pieces. Not least those three tiny bones that make up the U-shaped hyoid in the neck. At twenty, they would not yet have fused into one single piece. We are usually thirty-five or older before that happens. The likelihood of recovering them after fourteen years in the water would have been very remote. Only, for some reason, her killer had tied a blue bin bag over her head, and the hyoid bones were caught up in the plastic.'

He pulled another photograph towards him. The three pieces of the hyoid bone were laid out separately on a sheet of grey paper. The main body of it at the base of the U, and the two horns on either side. One of the horns was broken. Raffin stabbed at it with his forefinger.

'This one was fractured.' He dropped the photograph back on the table. 'Blanc's modus operandi was strangulation. So violent that the hyoid bones were separated in all three victims, and actually broken in one. So it would appear that Lucie Martin was murdered in exactly the same fashion.'

Kirsty said, 'So why wasn't Blanc charged with her murder as well?'

Raffin sat back and quaffed more wine. 'Because there was no evidence at all to connect him to it.'

'Apart from the letter,' Enzo said.

'Apart from the letter,' Raffin conceded. 'But he was nowhere near Duras or the Martin family estate the day she went missing. He had a cast-iron alibi. And he was arrested for the other killings within thirty-six hours of her disappearance. The authorities never took the idea very seriously.' He washed the Puligny-Montrachet around his gums, and drew it back over his tongue with an intake of air through pursed lips. 'So what do you think, Enzo?'

Enzo sighed. 'I think, of all the cases we've addressed so far, we've never had quite as little as this to go on.'

# CHAPTER THREE

It was almost dark by the time Enzo got to the Rue des Tanneries. The narrow street was deserted. This was a commercial and industrial rather than residential area, in a corner of Paris once famous for its Gobelin tapestries and the tanneries that polluted the River Bièvre. The nearby market, 'La Mouff', in the Rue Mouffetard, derived its name from the word *mouffettes*, a slang term describing the putrid exhalations of the river. But the smells and dyes and the pollutants from the tanneries were long gone, and it was here, in a former coal merchant's, that Charlotte had made her home and set up her *cabinet*, dispensing wisdom to those wrestling with their inner demons.

He had not called in advance, because he did not want to give her the opportunity to tell him she was busy, or had company, or was simply somewhere else. And so he was taking a chance on catching her at home, alone and off guard.

He pressed the button on the door-entry system and waited to hear her voice.

'*Oui?*'

'It's Enzo,' is all he said. There was a long silence, and he could almost hear her thinking, before the buzzer sounded and the lock on the door disengaged.

It was cold in the little downstairs entry hall. A door off to the left, he knew, led to the indoor garden, with its tiny stream and paths and trees and bushes, a glass roof thirty feet overhead that let light flood in during the day. It was where she practised her skills as a psychologist, conducting *séances* with her patients in an incongruous and wholly unexpected environment.

He felt the cold retreating as he climbed the staircase to her apartment, and then the rush of warm air as she opened the door to let him in. To his relief, Janine, Laurent's nanny, had left for the day and Charlotte was on her own. He looked around for some sign of Laurent, and Charlotte said, 'I've already put him down for the night.' Which Enzo took as being her way of telling him he couldn't see his son.

'I'll just go and take a look,' he said, mounting the steps from the tiny kitchen to the living room, then down on to the grilled metal gallery that ran beneath the glass roof to the bedrooms at the far end.

He heard her hurrying along behind him. 'It's really not convenient,' she said.

He kept walking, his footsteps clattering on the grille. 'It never is.'

A light glowed beyond the glass walls of Charlotte's bedroom, where Laurent still slept in his cot.

'Enzo . . .' Her voice was shrill.

He turned and put a finger to his lips, softly shushing her, and pushed open the door to the bedroom. The sight of her bed, still unmade, made his stomach flip over. How often had he made love to her between those sheets? How often had they lain talking in the dark, overheard only by the imagined ghosts of the Italian soldiers killed and buried in the cellar by the previous owners on the liberation of Paris? It was the bed where Laurent had been conceived, and a bed Enzo had not slept in for more than two years.

He quickly turned his attentions towards the cot and the sleeping child. Laurent was twisted up in his woollen blanket, lying on his side, his thumb in his mouth. The gentle rasp of his breathing seemed to fill the room.

Enzo gazed down with unglazed love at the son he hardly ever saw, luxuriant black hair curling around the boy's ear, and he leaned over to brush his head very lightly with soft lips.

When he stood up and turned around, Charlotte was standing almost silhouetted in the doorway. Tall and willowy. Long curling black locks, shot through now faintly with silver, tumbled over square shoulders. She was dressed simply in a long-sleeved black T-shirt, jeans and sneakers. And, even without a trace of make-up, he still thought her beautiful, black eyes like polished coals reflecting light in the dark.

A flick of her head towards the gallery made it clear she wanted him out. He pushed past her into the light, and she pulled the door shut, following him then back along the

walkway to the steps that took them up to the living room. Computer screens set on a work desk displayed video of the garden below from cameras mounted on the walls. She recorded all her sessions for later review. She closed the door. 'What the hell—?'

'I have a right to see my son.'

She controlled her anger and her voice by clenching her teeth. 'You call me first.'

'Oh, sure. To be told that, well, you're busy. Or you're just about to go out. Or you're not at home. You're at a conference somewhere with Janine along to look after Laurent. Or – and I've had this a few times – it's just not convenient.'

'Well, given how rarely you're in Paris, it's hardly surprising that I can't just drop everything at a moment's notice simply because you're in town. If you really were interested in seeing your son, you might have thought about moving to the capital.'

'You know I can't do that.'

'Oh, no, of course. I forgot.' Her words oozed sarcasm. 'They can't do without you at Toulouse. A big fish at a silly little university.'

Enzo was stung. 'The forensics department at Paul Sabatier is the biggest in the south-west.'

'Like I said, big fish, small pool. How was it they described you in their brochure? Scotland's leading forensics expert? Specialist in blood pattern and crime-scene analysis?' She laughed. 'Scotland? Well, now, the pools don't come much smaller, do they? And when was the last time you practised any

of these dark arts? As far as I'm aware, you've been teaching biology to giggling girlies for the last twenty-five years.'

Enzo kept his voice low and steady. 'I've resolved five out of Roger's seven cold cases. The best efforts of the French police failed to crack one of them.'

'Yes, well, you know what I think about the French police.' She swanned past him and dropped into an armchair by the huge window that overlooked the street below. 'But don't flatter yourself, Enzo. You've had Roger, and me, and several others to help you on more than one. And you still have two to go before you win your silly bet.'

There must have been something in his expression, and he saw realisation dawn suddenly on her face. '*That's* why you're in Paris. Roger's been briefing you on the Lucie Martin case.'

It irked him that he should be so transparent. But then, Charlotte and Raffin had been lovers at the time Raffin was writing his book, and so she was intimately acquainted with each of the seven cold cases, and had followed the resolution of every one with more than a passing interest. For some reason that Enzo had never quite understood, Charlotte and Raffin had remained confidants, even after the fractious break-up of their affair, and it was probably true that, these days, she was closer to Roger than to Enzo. Something that seemed to Enzo even more extraordinary in light of the warning she had once given him: *There is something dark about Roger. Something beyond touching. Something you wouldn't want to touch, even if you could.*

Enzo was defensive. 'I have other reasons for being here, too.'

But she wasn't interested in those, at least not for the moment. 'So what do you think?'

He frowned. 'About what?'

'The Lucie Martin case, of course.'

And he recalled what he had said to Raffin. 'There's not much to go on.'

'No.' She ran long, elegant fingers back through her hair to take the fringe out of her eyes. 'A skeleton stripped clean by fish. Death by strangulation. A broken hyoid. The signature of a serial killer who was nowhere near the scene of her disappearance at the time. And not a single suspect. Is that about right?'

'Yes.'

'So where will you begin?'

He was annoyed by this digression. They were in danger of straying well away from the purpose of his visit. 'With the family.'

'You'll go to see the Martins?'

'Yes.'

'And then?'

He shrugged. 'I have no idea.'

She smiled. 'Well, that sounds like a promising start.'

He decided to take back the initiative. 'I want you to come to Cahors next week. And bring Laurent.'

The sudden change of tack caught her off balance. 'Why?' Perhaps if she'd had more warning, she might have been able

to lie about a previous engagement, or a trip to Angoulême to see her parents, or some other such concoction.

'Sophie's organising a birthday party for me. Originally it was supposed to be a surprise. But – you know Sophie – she can never keep a secret. She's trying to get the whole family together.'

Charlotte frowned. 'It's not your sixtieth, is it?'

'Fifty-sixth.'

'Yes, I didn't think you were quite *that* old.' She paused. 'It's not a particularly auspicious birthday. Why the party?'

He shrugged. 'Sophie turned twenty-five this year. I paid for a big bash for her and Bertrand. I guess she's just trying to return the favour.'

She smiled. 'Except, of course, you're the one who'll be picking up the tab.'

Enzo was unable to prevent a wry smile crossing his lips. 'Of course.'

'So, what other reasons?'

Which took him by surprise. 'What?'

'You said you had other reasons for being here in Paris – other than Roger's briefing and asking me to your birthday party.'

He shrugged. There were no other reasons.

'Perhaps you have a secret lover you're not telling me about. Some child, half your age, beguiled by the Celtic charm she hasn't yet seen through.'

He hid his hurt. 'There's no one else in my life, you know that.'

'I know nothing of the kind. All I know about is the succession of younger women you have somehow persuaded to share your bed. Star-struck students and God knows who else.'

His voice was raised in anger for the first time. 'I have never had a relationship with any of my students. And you know perfectly well that, if you hadn't pushed me away, I would never even have looked at another woman.'

'You can tell yourself that all you like, but I know you, Enzo. And I know you are not fit to be the father of my son. Grandfather, maybe. At a stretch. But, even then, what kind of example would you set? A drinking, womanising old hippy who left his wife and child in Scotland and never had a serious relationship in his life.' She quickly raised a hand to pre-empt his protests. 'And don't tell me about Pascale. I'm sick of hearing about how Sophie's mother was the love of your life. If only she hadn't died in childbirth ... How long do you think the relationship would have lasted if she hadn't? Really. I mean – be honest, Enzo – your track record's not that great.'

Enzo felt the cold blade of her cruelty slide between his ribs and into his heart. And he remembered again the awful night that Sophie was born. Climbing the hill above his hometown in south-west France and weeping in the dark. It was for Pascale that he had left Kirsty and her mother in Scotland and come to France to begin a new life. A life, it had seemed to him then, that ended the day she died. Charlotte had been the first woman in twenty years to touch his heart, and now

she was turning her blade in it. Deliberately inflicting pain. And she wasn't finished.

'So, next time you want to come and see Laurent, you call me first and I'll tell you if it's okay.'

'I have a right to see my son!' He repeated his refrain of earlier.

'*Your* son? Is he?' Her words struck him like bare-knuckled fists swinging out of the dark.

'What do you mean?'

'I mean, how do you know I wasn't seeing someone else?'

His heart seemed to be trying to escape through his mouth. 'Were you?'

'Actually, I was. But then, you wouldn't have known, would you? You were never around.'

'Are you saying—?'

'I'm not saying anything, Enzo. I'm telling you. Don't take anything for granted.'

He stood, gazing at her, filled with pain and uncertainty. Thoughts flashed through his mind like the frames of a movie spooling backwards. Words, pictures, memories. All too fast to catch and register. He felt sick.

She stood up. 'And I'm afraid Laurent and I won't be able to make it to your birthday party. We're much too busy.'

The Métro was full of Parisians out for the evening, heading for cafés and restaurants and to queue at cinemas. Enzo pushed his way through them, up the steps and into the Boulevard Saint

Germain. He bumped and jostled shoulders as he ploughed west, head down, oblivious to the protests of people around him. But no one was seriously going to challenge this big, ponytailed man with a white stripe through his greying dark hair. He was well over six feet, and built like a man who had played rugby in his youth – which he had, at Hutchesons' Grammar School, in Glasgow. His cotton jacket was open and flew out behind him, tangling on one side with the canvas satchel slung from his left shoulder. His cargoes were crumpled and gathered around heavy brown lace-up boots, his stride lengthening with every step, fuelled by the anger that simmered inside him.

He barely registered the young people sitting under canopies outside cafés, smoking and drinking coffees and cognacs, or the restaurants, full and noisy behind steamed-up windows, or the lights of a Carrefour Contact spilling out into the Rue Mazarine, late shoppers buying last-minute items to eat at home.

His mind was full of a dread fear. That Charlotte had not just been idly bating him. That Laurent really wasn't his son. He could hardly bring himself to entertain the thought. It had never before occurred to him that Charlotte might have had a relationship with someone else. Who? She had never given any indication. And yet, how would he have known? He was in Toulouse, she in Paris. Although, how different that might have been if only she hadn't constantly kept him at arm's length. She valued her independence too much, she

had said. She simply didn't want another relationship – it was too demanding. And now she was telling him there had been another man. Hurtful enough, but with its inherent implications regarding Laurent's paternity, Enzo felt wounded.

He turned into the Rue Guénégaud. The Café le Balto lay in unexpected darkness, and he pushed open the door to the neighbouring apartment block, climbing wearily to the first floor, fumbling to get his key in the lock. This tiny studio was where he always stayed in Paris. An apartment owned by a very elderly man passing his final days in a residential care home, and loaned to Enzo by friends in Cahors. When their uncle died, they would have to sell to pay the inheritance tax. Enzo wished he had the money to buy it, and, not for the first time, hoped that the old man would live forever.

The studio smelled of old age and was full of souvenirs collected during years spent travelling the world. All that remained of a life almost spent. Light fell in from the street-lamp outside and Enzo opened the windows for some fresh air. He let his bag fall to the floor and dropped heavily into a worn leather armchair.

He remembered Charlotte coming to him on the Île de Groix to break the news that she was pregnant. She had made it clear then that she did not want Enzo to have any part in her child's life, and threatened abortion if he made legal demands. Might that have made some kind of twisted sense to her, if she had known that Enzo was not the father? Try as he might, he could not see the logic in it. Because, just as suddenly, she had

relented. She would have the baby, and she would allow Enzo access, but wanted complete control of his upbringing. And most confusingly of all, she had called the child Laurent. The French equivalent of Lorenzo. Of which 'Enzo' was a shortened form. A name that owed its own origins to his Italian mother.

Enzo sat in the dark, feeling confused, and hurting like an old injured stag. Why would she have called him Laurent if he were not Enzo's child?

He reached for a bottle of whisky on the table, pouring himself a stiff measure into the glass he had used the night before, and drizzled liquid gold back over his tongue. The only certainty on this dark autumn night was that the bottle would be empty by morning.

# CHAPTER FOUR

It was like therapy being back in Cahors, this ancient Roman town set into a loop of the River Lot in south-west France where he had raised Sophie on his own for all these years. If there was anywhere on this earth that he could call home, this was it.

Soft sunlight washed over him as he stepped from the train and felt the air warm on his skin. Autumn was not yet so advanced in the south, and the plane trees on the road outside still held their leaves. Diners lingered over lunch beneath parasols on the terrace of the Hotel Terminus, and Enzo wished that life might be that simple for him, too.

He walked the fifteen minutes through town to the Rue Georges Clemenceau. The covered market opposite his apartment was shut for lunch and there were tables still occupied on the pavement outside the pizzeria. He glanced up at the red-brick facade of his apartment block with its brightly painted blue shutters, geraniums in late bloom cascading from flower boxes hung along the wrought-iron balustrades outside his windows. And he ached to hold Sophie in his arms. Comfort

and reassurance in the certain knowledge that she really was his daughter.

But he was disappointed to find the apartment empty. He threw his overnight bag into his bedroom and pushed open glazed double doors to the *séjour*. Sunlight angled in from the square outside, and he saw the twin domes of the cathedral shimmering in the warm afternoon. He threw open the French windows to let in air and the sound of life from outside, and breathed deeply. When he turned back into the room, he saw the letter lying on the table. He recognised her handwriting immediately and crossed quickly to tear it open.

Dear Papa,

Sorry not to be here to welcome you back. ☹ Bertrand and I decided to take an apartment at Argelès sur Mer for a week to profit from this lovely Indian summer we are having. The late-season prices were a real bargain and we couldn't resist — don't worry, Bertrand's paying. ☺ We're right on the beach, so I'm bound to have a perfect tan for your birthday. We'll be back in plenty of time for the party. Nicole's promised to set things up in my absence. I've told her she can have the spare room. I hope that's okay.

Love you,

Sophie

Enzo groaned audibly. Nicole was the last thing he needed. And it was just typical of Sophie that she should decide to

have a party, then disappear and let everyone else do the work. All his warm feelings towards her quickly dissipated. And his heart sank as he heard the door opening out in the hall. A familiar voice called, 'Monsieur Macleod?'

He sighed. 'Through here, Nicole.'

Her breasts preceded her as she emerged from the dark of the hall into the sunlit living room. Enzo blinked and tried not to look. She undoubtedly regarded them as her best asset and was never shy about displaying them. Today they were encased in a clinging, low-cut cotton top. Nicole was a large girl, of sound farming stock. She was endowed with what Enzo's mother would have described as good child-bearing hips. She had a pretty face and long, silken brown hair that cascaded over broad shoulders, and was Enzo's star pupil in the forensic-science department at Paul Sabatier University. Now in her final year, she had been an invaluable assistant to him in solving several of Raffin's cold cases, particularly when it came to use of the internet.

Her face lit up when she saw him. 'Monsieur Macleod!' And she kissed him enthusiastically on both cheeks before standing back to look at him. 'You've lost weight. Have you not been eating?'

'Yes, Nicole. I've been eating. And drinking. And doing all the things you warn me against.'

She pulled a face. 'Well, it's a good thing I'm here to take care of you now. Honestly, I don't know what Sophie's thinking. A few good square meals and we'll get you back up to optimum

weight in time for your party.' Nicole invariably saw people like farm animals in need of fattening. She twinkled. 'Sophie's got a little surprise planned for you, and we want you looking your best.'

'I'm afraid I'm not staying, Nicole.' It was a spur-of-the-moment thought.

'Why ever not?'

'I've started work on the next case.'

Her eyes opened wide. 'The Martin girl?'

'Yes.'

'Well, that's great. I can help!'

'Nothing for you to help with yet, Nicole,' Enzo said, and he saw her face fall. 'I'm just about to call her parents and arrange to drop by and see them. And I might take the opportunity to visit some of the other locations involved in the case, primarily in Bordeaux. So I may be gone for a few days.'

'I could come with you,' she said hopefully.

He shook his head solemnly. 'I wish you could. But Sophie's relying on you to set everything up for the party . . .' He held out open palms, indicating his helplessness in resolving the situation. 'Sorry.'

Nicole glowered.

# CHAPTER FIVE

Château Gandolfo stood on a hilltop in rolling country just east of the small town of Duras, on the very edge of the Bordeaux wine-producing area of western France. The commune had its own appellation, Côtes de Duras, producing wines with which Enzo was unfamiliar. He was better acquainted with the reds of Saint-Emilion, just a few kilometres further west, but had to confess that the gently undulating hills and green forests of this stunning part of the Lot-et-Garonne were much more interesting than the endless fields of vines that shimmered in the distance across the Saint-Emilion valley.

He was in Aquitaine now, that whole slice of western France which had once been a part of England before finally being annexed by the French at the end of the Hundred Years' War. The influence of the English was still apparent everywhere. In the names and the architecture, the religion and even the culture. As Enzo knew from his Scottish upbringing, it was not an easy thing to erase the pervasive traces of the English.

The single track that turned off the main road wound its way through trees in red, gold and yellow autumn splendour,

deep into the hills, before Enzo took a steep chalk track that cut its way up the slope to the château at the top of the hill.

It had been dry for several weeks, and a plume of dust rose up in his wake. Impossible to approach without being seen. The château itself seemed comprised of three separate buildings, with shallow-pitched, red roman-tiled roofs. Two towers stood at one end, and Enzo assumed that they had originally been *pigeonniers*, providing nourishment for the fields from their guano, and meat for their owner's table from a plentiful supply of pigeons. Four tons of meat a year, the average *pigeonnier* was calculated to produce.

The two storeys of the main building stood centrally between the others, its white stonework betraying a history of renovation and extension that probably went back centuries. Shutters were painted a faded blue, and half the building had been taken over by various vines and creepers that burned dazzling red and purple now, as summer transitioned to winter.

Enzo turned into a gravelled parking area near the lowest of the three buildings. A pergola stood on the terrace outside arched and glazed double doors, but Enzo couldn't see beyond them because of reflections. The building itself had almost vanished beneath red and green creeper with white flowers.

As he stepped out of his carefully restored Citroën 2CV, a voice in perfectly accented English said, 'That's my office. Or used to be. It's my den now – my escape from life.' A chuckle. 'And the wife.'

Enzo turned to see an elderly man walking down the tiled

path from the main house to greet him. He was of medium height and build, unstooped by age as he extended a confident hand to shake Enzo's warmly. Piercing blue eyes were set in a face that was tanned and deeply lined, contrasting starkly with the thick silver hair that grew in such abundance above it. He wore moleskin trousers that gathered around sturdy walking boots, and a quilted vest over a chequered shirt with the sleeves rolled up. He might easily have stepped straight out of a country estate anywhere in England.

He smiled at Enzo's surprise. 'My ancestors were Italian and English. There's very little about me that's French.' He grinned. 'Except, of course, for my entire cultural upbringing. And my name.' He paused. 'Guillaume Martin. And you're Enzo Macleod, I presume.' He looked Enzo up and down. 'A Scotsman.' It sounded more like a statement than a question.

'The last time I looked.'

'And how is your French?'

'I've lived here for twenty-five years, monsieur,' Enzo said in French. 'I have taught science to university students and raised a daughter who is as French as frogs' legs.'

Martin tipped his head in acknowledgement. 'Then let us speak French. I am always more at home in my native tongue.'

They walked up to the main house. Martin said, 'There used to be a Roman road running along here, between the watermill at the foot of the hill and the windmill at the top.' He waved his hand across half an acre of neatly trimmed lawn towards an infinity pool built into the hill and looking out over the view.

'That's where my Italian ancestor, Gandolfo, built a massive greenhouse for the Duke of Duras to house his exotic plants. In return for the duke gifting him the château and the estate.'

'Why would the duke do that?'

'Oh, it was all part of an attempt to repopulate the area and reinvigorate the economy. Gandolfo was a renowned wine grower in Italy, and he brought his enormous family with him.' They stopped outside the main door of the house. 'Plague and the Hundred Years' War had laid waste to this whole area, Monsieur Macleod. There wasn't a living soul for miles around. The Desert Lands, they called it. And, for the next two hundred years, they brought in foreigners and folk from other parts of France to breathe life back into it.' He turned to look up at the house. 'Gandolfo put a second floor on this part and a new front on it, making it pretty much as you see it now. And when there was no further use for the greenhouse, they knocked it down and used the materials to build the *chais* – or wine cellar, I suppose you'd call it – and the barn. Come in and meet Madame.'

Madame was a mouse of a woman, tiny and fragile, and Enzo was afraid to shake her hand too firmly when she offered it, in case he broke bones. Her hair was fine, spun silver, and she had skin as smooth and unlined as a twenty-year-old. Her smile spread across a face still handsome in spite of the years, and soft brown eyes met his with candour and warmth.

'What peculiar eyes you have,' she said.

Enzo smiled. 'One brown, one blue.' He ran a hand back over

the crown of his head. 'And a white streak in my hair – slowly disappearing, now, as it greys. They used to call me Magpie.'

She frowned. 'Is there a connection?'

'Between the eyes and the hair? Yes. Both symptomatic of a genetic condition called Waardenburg syndrome. But don't worry, I've had it all my life and I haven't died of it yet.'

She laughed. 'Would you like tea, Monsieur Macleod? I would have offered coffee, but I know you English like your tea.'

'He's Scottish, Mireille,' Martin said. 'You'll offend him if you call him English.'

Enzo grinned. 'Not at all. But coffee would be fine.'

They sat around an enormous wooden table in the centre of a vast kitchen that had clearly been designed to cater for a very large family, and probably servants and farm workers, too. An old Belfast sink stood beneath the window and piles of old tea boxes were stacked up against the far wall, beside one of two cookers. The second, a wood-burning range, was set into the long wall where an arched fireplace must once have stood. Worktops and cupboards ran along either side of it, and the place was filled with warm cooking smells and soft light.

While Madame Martin busied herself with the coffee, her husband lit up a small cheroot. 'You don't mind, do you?'

Enzo didn't see how he could.

'Damned smoking laws,' Martin said. 'They'll be banning it in the privacy of our own homes next.' He tilted his head

back and breathed blue smoke at the ceiling. 'So, Monsieur Macleod. You have amassed yourself quite a reputation. Are you going to find who killed our Lucie for us?'

'I certainly intend to try, Monsieur ... I'm not quite sure how to address you. Is it Monsieur le Président, or Monsieur le Juge?'

Martin's eyes crinkled in amusement. 'I am long retired, Monsieur Macleod, and was never one to stand on ceremony outside of the courtroom, anyway. "Monsieur" will suffice. And "Guillaume", if I decide I like you.'

'Well, I have already decided that I do,' said Madame Martin as she brought coffee pot and cups to the table on a tray. 'You have an honest face, Monsieur Macleod.'

Enzo smiled. 'Thank you, Madame.'

'Oh, "Mireille" will suffice.' And she flashed twinkling eyes at her husband. But just as quickly the twinkle faded and a shadow crossed her face. After a moment she looked at Enzo again. 'Sometimes I forget for ten or fifteen minutes. Even an hour or two on occasion. Once or twice, even for a whole day. And then I feel terribly guilty. Someone killed our lovely Lucie, monsieur. She would have been in her forties now, and with luck might have given us grandchildren. She had a whole life to live and someone took it from her. I have never felt I deserved the right to laugh or take pleasure in simple things since the day she went missing.' She could no longer meet his eye and occupied herself with pouring the coffee.

Enzo glanced at her husband and saw his glazed expression

as he stared, unseeing, at the floor. Some memory filled his thoughts and his eyes, his lips pressed together in a grim line. And, as so often happened, Enzo was reminded that this was not just some mystery to be unravelled, a puzzle to be solved. These were real people, with real lives and real sorrow. 'Tell me about the day she went missing,' he said.

Martin pulled the door shut behind them as they stepped outside. He had avoided discussing Lucie in front of his wife while they drank their coffee, telling Enzo that he would go through it all with him on the walk down to the lake where she was found. He turned to Enzo now. 'I'm sorry,' he said. 'She still gets very upset.'

'Of course.'

He quickly changed the subject himself, waving a hand towards a collection of crumbling outbuildings. 'Those were originally part of the house,' he said. 'An oven for drying prunes and meat, and a bread oven. They date back to the sixth century and still function, although the earliest date we could find for the house itself was on an old quoinstone: 1456. Come and see the *chais*.'

They walked around the house to the old, stone wine cellar, and Martin pushed open one of the huge, arched double doors. The wood was grey with age, deeply lined and knotted, and protested noisily. Inside, it was dark and fusty, and it took several moments for Enzo's eyes to adjust. It was a big empty space with rafters high overhead, cobwebs hanging in great

loops as if freshly fired from a designer's web-gun to dress the set of a horror movie. The effect was emphasised by Martin turning and pointing to the wall above the lintel, where there was a pattern of what looked suspiciously like human bones set into the stonework.

'Back when Lucie was still just a child, we started digging out the floor of the *chais* with a view to laying concrete and converting the building into guest rooms. We had only gone down about twelve inches when we came across bones. Human remains. An old grave, I thought, and as a kind of memorial I set them into the wall above the door there. But as we kept digging there were just more and more of them, and, in the end, I gave up the idea altogether.'

'What was it? Some kind of burial ground?'

'Oh, almost certainly a plague pit. People were dying in their thousands back then. Best left undisturbed, I decided.'

As they set off down the hill behind the château, the old man lifted his head towards the sun sinking in the west. He said, 'The light goes so early these days. Better be quick, or it'll be dark by the time we get back.'

The path that cut down the hillside led them into woodland, the last sunlight of the day slanting through branches and backlighting leaves in glorious autumn technicolour, like stained glass. Rising up to their left, jagged white rock pushed through earth and fallen leaves.

'The old quarry,' Martin said. 'Employed hundreds of people for centuries, right up until the 1920s. That's where they

quarried the stone to build the great château in Duras, and almost certainly Château Gandolfo, too.'

By the time they reached the water's edge, the sun had vanished over the horizon, and a purple dusk, like dust, settled on the land. The water came right up to the limit of the woodland, and several trees around its perimeter were growing out of the lake.

They stood and gazed across still water reflecting the last light in the sky. Enzo was impatient to hear Martin's story, but reluctant to press him, and so he waited for the old man to tell it in his own good time. For a long time, Martin stood simply staring out over the lake. Until finally he said, 'She was a beautiful girl. Took after her mother. The love of my life. There wasn't anything we wouldn't have done for her.' He turned to look at Enzo. 'And I don't mean we spoiled her. But she was as precious to us at twenty as she had been the day she was born.'

Enzo saw light reflecting in moist eyes, and the old man blinked rapidly several times.

'She cared deeply about her job.' He chuckled ironically. 'After years on the bench I had very little time for the pimps and prostitutes and petty criminals that populate our world, Monsieur Macleod. But Lucie always saw the humanity in them, no matter how deeply buried it was. She saw them all as victims – of society, of their upbringing, or just of fate. And something about her innocence touched them, too. Many of them, anyway. She was cut out for that kind of work.' He

smiled. 'Whereas her old dad would have locked them all up and thrown away the key.'

He pointed west, where the lake emerged from the trees into open ground.

'That's where they found her, and I suppose that's where her killer must have dumped her body, originally. It's one of the deepest parts of the lake. Probably weighted down, the police thought. Tied to a boulder or chunk of masonry that would stop her floating back to the surface. No trace of any rope left, of course. No doubt rotted away, or eaten by the same fish that . . .' He stopped and swallowed hard, doing his best to compose himself and regain control of his voice before he spoke again. 'He could never have imagined that fourteen years later there would be such a drought that the level of the lake would fall by as much as four metres and expose his brutal handiwork.'

He glanced at Enzo once more.

'Do you remember the year of the *canicule*, Monsieur Macleod?'

Enzo nodded. Two thousand and three. It had been a heatwave like no other he had ever known. It had begun in early March. Day after day after day of sunshine, and no rain. The heat building through the spring until, by early summer, temperatures were in the forties. Classes at university had to be cancelled. Students were fainting. Back home in Cahors he had been forced to keep all the windows shut. The air outside was hotter than in. He had set up fans on tables and chairs in every

room, but even then the temperature had been unbearable. Sleep was elusive – some nights impossible. More than 13,000 people around France had died that summer, just from the heat. He said, 'The Saturday that she disappeared . . .' It was his cue to Martin to tell him about that day.

The old man nodded. 'She'd been unusually subdued when she came home from Bordeaux the previous night. Normally, she would sit at the dinner table and chatter away, telling us all about everything that had happened during the week. Always so bright, never with anything negative to say.' He drew a long, slow breath. 'That night she ate in silence. Lost in some world that she wasn't inclined to share with us. I don't mean she was deliberately shutting us out. I think she was just deeply disturbed by something. Distracted. Mireille and I exchanged frequent looks, but we didn't dare say anything. And eventually she brightened a little, making an effort for us. But it didn't last long. She said she was tired and wanted an early night. It wasn't even nine o'clock when she went to bed.'

'Did you and Mireille speculate on what it was that might have been troubling her?'

'No, monsieur. We had no idea what it might be. It was so uncharacteristic. There was nothing for us to speculate about. But it left us both troubled ourselves. Not sure what to say, even to each other. I suppose we arrived at an unspoken agreement between us, simply not to mention it. As if, by not talking about it, we might make it just go away.'

'And the next morning?'

'She was late down to breakfast. But cheerier. Or so it seemed. Then she went back to her room. Mireille called up to her when she was leaving, late morning. Her sister lives in Duras, and she quite often has lunch with her and stays the afternoon. The woman's widowed, so I never go with her. One man, two women – just doesn't work. Lucie called down, telling her mother to say *bonjour* to her aunt. And that was the last exchange Mireille ever had with her.' He shook his head. 'She's never forgiven herself for not at least having kissed her goodbye. Silly. But there you go. You can't help but feel what you feel.'

Somewhere out on the lake a fish jumped. They heard it rather than saw it, but the rings from its point of re-entry reached out in ever-widening circles towards them, catching the last light of the day.

'And you?' Enzo said. 'What was your last interaction with Lucie?'

Martin kept his eyes on the rings that broke the surface of the water. 'She didn't come down for lunch. Said she wasn't hungry. I ate on my own in the kitchen, then retired to my study. I have a television down there. I was having a cigar and watching the rugby when she rapped on the door. I looked up and saw her through the glass, but I couldn't hear what she was saying. She wouldn't come in, and I had to get up and open the door. I'd swear she'd been crying, Monsieur Macleod. Those clear blue eyes, red-rimmed and blurred by the spilling of tears. I'm sure she hadn't wanted me to see her like that.

All she said was, "I'm going for a walk, Papa." And she turned and headed off down the hill.' He took a moment. 'I never saw her again.'

'Was she in the habit of going walking?'

'On her own? Never. Not that I can recall.'

'Do you think she might have been going to meet someone?'

Martin shrugged. 'Who can know? Usually she was so bright and transparent. But that day she was –' he searched for the right word – 'closed. Like a pebble held in your fist.'

Enzo raised his eyes towards the far shore. 'What is there beyond the lake?'

Martin nodded towards the east end of it. 'There's an artificial dam. You can cross the lake there. It leads up to a farm track on the other side. There's a vineyard, and beyond that you rejoin the single-track road that comes up from the D708.'

'So, if she'd had a rendezvous she didn't want you to know about, she could have met someone there who had driven up from the main road by car?'

Martin shrugged. 'Possible, I suppose.' But he didn't seem engaged by the idea. Perhaps, Enzo thought, he had been through every possibility so many times over the years that anything and everything seemed likely, or unlikely. When you are not in possession of the facts, speculation is both endless and pointless. Martin said, 'We should go before it gets dark.'

Enzo followed him along a dry animal-track made treacherous by knotted roots. It wound up through the trees before emerging on to a wide, open slope that climbed back up the

hill to the château. This, Enzo imagined, was the way that Lucie must have come, if she had gone straight down the hill from her father's study. He would have been able to see her all the way to the treeline, had he stood and watched. But Enzo didn't ask.

A nearly full moon had risen over the far horizon, washing the hillside in its bright, colourless light and throwing long shadows of the two men towards the west. Despite his age, Guillaume Martin was fit and took long strides up the hill, which Enzo found hard work to match.

A little breathlessly he said, 'When did you first become concerned about her?'

Martin stopped. 'It was March, monsieur. Just before the clocks went forward. So it was still dark quite early. I suppose it must have been about seven when I realised that she hadn't come back. I was in the kitchen preparing dinner, as I always do when Mireille has been at her sister's. I hadn't been aware of Lucie returning, so I called up to her room, but there was no response. Couldn't find her anywhere and started to get worried.'

'Did you go looking for her?'

'Yes, I did. Pulled on my wellington boots and set off down the hill. But it was pretty hopeless – almost completely dark by the time I got down to the lake. I called out her name. Several times. And I could hear it echoing away across the open water. In the end I gave up and went back to the house – and checked again, just to be sure she hadn't returned while I was gone. Mireille got home about half an hour after that. By then I was

pretty much beside myself with worry. I had the most dreadful sense that something awful had happened.'

'But you didn't call the police?'

He shook his head vigorously. 'Mireille wanted me to. But I knew they wouldn't do anything. Lucie had only been gone a few hours, and we had no reason to suppose anything had happened to her. It wasn't until we went to search her room, later that night, and found the letter from Blanc that I thought we should report it to the police.'

'What was it about the letter that convinced you, finally, to do that?'

'Because it was obviously from one of the criminals she'd been dealing with at the charity, and from the tone of his letter he was clearly obsessed by her.' He ran both hands back through his hair and sighed in exasperation. 'Little did we know then exactly what kind of a man he was.'

'You think he killed her, then?'

The old man swivelled to face Enzo, eyes blazing. 'I know he did, monsieur.'

'How can you know it?'

'You've read the letter. The man was deranged. Somehow he persuaded Lucie to meet him. She was such a damned innocent. And he strangled her, just as he had already killed those three prostitutes before her. And then he dumped her body in the lake.'

'But he had what police described as a cast-iron alibi for that afternoon.'

Martin's mouth tightened. 'I didn't spend all those years sitting on the bench, monsieur, without coming to the realisation that alibis can be fabricated. People vouch for family and friends all the time, for any number of reasons. Love, fear, money. Régis Blanc killed my Lucie, Monsieur Macleod, and I would very much like you to prove it.'

Lights around the outside of the château came on with a timer, sending warm yellow light cascading down the slope towards them, and they walked the rest of the way up the hill in silence. When they reached his 2CV, Enzo took out his keys. 'Please thank your wife for the coffee, Monsieur Martin. I'll need to do some thinking about all of this. Go and speak to some of Blanc's associates.'

Martin shook his head in consternation. 'Well, where are you going?'

'I have a hotel room booked in Duras.'

'I won't hear of it. You'll stay here, of course. I'll phone and cancel.'

'Oh, I couldn't possibly—'

'Nonsense, man,' Martin cut him off. 'Mireille has prepared dinner. And besides, there are some folk I want you to meet.' He glanced down the hill to see the beams of headlights raking the dark as they climbed towards the château. 'In fact, that looks like the first of them arriving now.'

# CHAPTER SIX

Several of the beachfront restaurants had already shut down for the season, but there were still plenty to choose from, and the good weather had brought a late rush of holidaymakers, so they were all crowded.

Sophie and Bertrand sat beneath the canopy of one that served barbecued meat and fish on hanging skewers. Their table was right down on the promenade, just feet away from the soft, golden sand that sloped away to the gentle wash of the Mediterranean. You could almost hear it breathing in the night, the lights of Argelès riding the black swell of the incoming waves in fractured shards.

It was getting dark faster now, and the couple had eaten earlier than usual. Their first-floor apartment above a bicycle-hire shop was just a hundred metres further along the beach, and they were looking forward to a night of undisturbed pleasure, windows left wide, net curtains billowing in the sea breeze, the sound of the sea itself accompaniment to their lovemaking.

It was unusual for them to have time alone together like this. Bertrand still lived with his mother. She was elderly and

frail now, and he was reluctant to leave her on her own. Sophie still stayed in her father's apartment, which seemed always to play host to a procession of visitors and rarely offered privacy. So they had jumped at the chance of this late-season booking to escape to the coast and indulge themselves a little in each other.

Bertrand poured the last of the wine into their glasses from a bottle of Collioure Puig Oriol from Domaine La Tour Vieille. It was a heady local wine, a rich blend of Syrah and Grenache noir, 14.5 per cent alcohol that slipped only too easily over the tongue. The two young people were mellow and easy in each other's company. Laughing at silly things and revelling in their freedom. This, they thought, is how it would be when they were finally together, free of family responsibilities, free to live life exactly as they wanted.

They paid up and left the restaurant to walk hand-in-hand along the promenade, the chatter of diners receding behind them, the air filled with the sound of the sea breaking on the slope of the beach. Bertrand untangled his hand from hers and put his arm around her shoulders, drawing her towards him. She slipped her arm around his waist and rested her head on his shoulder, the faintest streak of white running back through her long dark hair, just visible in the moonlight. She sighed her contentment. This was heaven.

Bertrand said, 'Will you marry me?'

Sophie stopped dead in her tracks, and he had taken two further steps before he could stop himself and turn back. She

was staring at him, open-mouthed, eyes wide with excitement. 'You're kidding?'

'You want me to get down on one knee?'

She laughed. 'Don't be silly.' Then composed herself. 'You'll have to ask my papa, though.'

Bertrand turned his head away, towards the sea, expelling air. 'You're not serious?'

She raised a coquettish eyebrow. 'I am. What? Are you scared of him? He didn't like you much at first.'

'Of course I'm not scared of him. Enzo's the finest man I ever met.' He turned to look at her and she saw just how much he meant it. For some reason it brought tears to her eyes. Her father and her lover had got off to the worst of all possible starts. Then Bertrand had saved Kirsty's life, and Enzo had financed the rebuilding of Bertrand's gym after it had been burned down. There was such respect now between the young buck and the old stag that it filled Sophie's heart to bursting with love for them both. 'Okay, I'll ask him,' Bertrand said. 'But what am I going to tell him your answer is?'

She shrugged. 'Maybe I'll have to think about that.'

'Sophie!' Bertrand growled at her and she grinned.

'Yes, of course. Yes, yes, yes!'

And they embraced and kissed in the moonlight, not caring who might see them. He grabbed her hand. 'Come on.' And they ran the rest of the way back to their holiday let. Bertrand stood by the shuttered window of the bicycle shop, fumbling with his key to open the door to the stairwell. Then they rushed

inside and up the stairs, barely able to contain their love and lust for each other. He struggled again, with trembling fingers, to get the key in the lock of the apartment door, but it simply swung open. A sudden stab of misgiving pierced his happiness.

'Idiot!' Sophie said. 'You forgot to lock the door.'

But Bertrand was standing perfectly still. 'I didn't.'

'You must have.' She pushed past him before he could stop her and flicked the light switch. But the room remained in darkness, divided into slats by the moonlight that fell in through the shutters. And, for the first time, she became aware of an alien scent. Something that didn't belong.

Two figures detached themselves from the dark. They were dressed all in black, ski masks drawn over their heads. And Bertrand saw the whites of their eyes catching the light. One of them grabbed Sophie from behind, a gloved hand immediately around her face to stifle her scream. The other came for Bertrand, but could never have imagined the strength or ferocity with which his attack would be met. All the hours spent pumping iron in the gym were concentrated in the fist that Bertrand smashed into his attacker's face. He felt teeth and bone breaking, and heard the man's pain in the cry that gurgled through the blood in his mouth as his legs buckled beneath him.

The second man hurled Sophie away across the room, and Bertrand heard the sound of her crashing into the kitchen table. The whole weight of his second attacker descended on him. And this was a big man. Bertrand went down, all the air

exploding from his lungs as the man landed heavily on top of him. The first man was on his knees again now, cursing, and his fist caught Bertrand on the side of his head. Bertrand's world became filled with pain and light. He tried to wriggle free, but a second punch almost crushed his larynx, and he found himself choking and unable to breathe.

A scream filled the air as a shadow flew through the darkness and knocked the big man off him. Sophie was all legs and clenched fists, striking out at anything and everything. The man whose nose and teeth Bertrand had broken swung around, and Bertrand saw his fist make an arc before connecting with Sophie's face. Her dead weight hit the floor. Bertrand tried to get to his feet, but a heavy boot sank itself into his midriff, bringing bile bubbling into his mouth, and a second blow to the head brought darkness.

# CHAPTER SEVEN

They had all arrived within fifteen minutes of each other, in five cars parked out front, alongside Enzo's, engines ticking as they cooled in the night. And now they sat around the big table in the Martins' kitchen, all eyes turned expectantly towards the Scotsman.

Martin had introduced them in turn. Monsieur and Madame Linol; Monsieur Klarczyk and his daughter, Karolina; Madame Robert; Monsieur and Madame Bru; Monsieur Edward Veyssière. All were guests for dinner, and Enzo was the centre of attention. He was embarrassed and confused as Madame Martin served up a cold starter of foie gras and salad, with strips of smoked duck breast, while Martin poured chilled sweet Bergerac wine into all their glasses.

'You must be wondering what all this is about, Monsieur Macleod,' he said.

Enzo nodded. 'Yes, I am.' He was feeling ambushed, and just a little resentful.

Martin took his seat. 'We are a group of parents . . . relatives . . . of girls who either disappeared or were murdered in

the weeks and months leading up to the arrest of Régis Blanc. Each and every one of us is of the firm belief that Blanc was responsible. But, in most cases, the police never even examined the links between Blanc and our girls. They'd got their man for killing those prostitutes. Why bother going over old ground to convict him for more murders when he had already been sent down for three?'

Enzo ran his eyes around the array of faces turned in his direction. 'Are you saying that your girls were also prostitutes?'

Martin seemed uncomfortable. 'Not at all. Lucie certainly was not.' But he glanced awkwardly towards the others.

Monsieur Klarczyk looked to be a man in his sixties. He spoke with just the hint of an accent. 'Karolina's sister had been working as a waitress in Bordeaux for several months before she disappeared.'

Karolina, whom Enzo gauged to be in her forties, had no trace of an accent whatsoever. She said, 'We're pretty sure she'd been working for an escort agency.' She avoided her father's eye, and Enzo saw that he was blushing. 'Well, I know she was, because she told me. She usually came home once a month. Then, one month, she didn't. We never saw or heard anything of her again. She was well behind in paying for the apartment she'd been renting, but all her things were still there, and nobody had seen her in weeks.'

Enzo found his interest engaged. 'What was her connection with Blanc?'

'None that we know of,' her father said.

And Karolina cut in. 'He was a well-known *souteneur*. A pimp, Monsieur Macleod. Veronika was a prostitute, and she vanished at almost exactly the same time that Blanc killed those other girls.'

Her father lowered his head and couldn't lift his eyes from the table.

Their stories were all remarkably similar. Girls who had been working in Bordeaux, away from home, telling parents and loved ones that they had jobs in restaurants or bars, one claiming to be an actress. Only one of them, other than Lucie, had turned up dead. She was Monica, the daughter of Madame Robert.

Madame Robert carried her sadness about her like something she might wear; a veil, a cape, a black shawl of mourning. It was almost visible, and only too apparent in her eyes and the tragic set of her face. She had been a single mother, doing her best to bring up her daughter on her own in the provincial town of Poitiers. But Monica had been a headstrong and argumentative teenager and run off at the age of seventeen.

'I searched in vain for her, Monsieur Macleod. Some friends and I raised a little money for a poster campaign. We had no idea, of course, that she'd gone to Bordeaux. And the press weren't interested. They ran her photograph a couple of times in the local paper, and once on regional television, and then other things caught their interest.' She examined her hands on the table in front of her. 'I was always waiting for the knock on the door, but it still didn't make it any easier when it came. Four

years later. They'd found her stabbed to death in some seedy hotel bedroom in the red-light district of Bordeaux. Naked.' She bit her lip. 'Her killer had done terrible things to her.'

There was absolute silence around the table. Enzo felt her pain. He said, 'I take it there were no arrests?'

She shook her head. 'They said they thought it had probably been a client. Maybe drug-related.' She took a moment to compose herself. 'She was a heroin addict, apparently. And infected with HIV.'

'And the connection with Blanc?'

'She was one of his girls, or had been. He claimed he'd let her go months before because he didn't like his girls taking drugs. And, of course, he had half a dozen people who vouched for where he was the night she was murdered.'

'Sally was one of his girls, too.' It was Monsieur Linol who cut into Madame Robert's story. Enzo swung his gaze across the table to take in the small, bald man who sat with his wife at the far end of it. He was dressed in a grey suit, worn shiny in places, and tightly buttoned over a white shirt with curled-up collar. His wife seemed even smaller. You could see that she had been a pretty woman once, but her face had collapsed with the years and her skin was the colour and texture of parchment.

'What happened to Sally?' Enzo said.

'Vanished,' Madame Linol said. 'Two days before the first of those girls that Blanc killed was murdered. She knew them. Everybody said so. But there was no trace of her, Monsieur

Macleod. Nothing. Her apartment had been cleared out, but no one saw or heard anything of her ever again.' She drew a deep breath. 'We're convinced that man killed her, too. They just never found the body.'

Enzo looked around the assembled faces. 'I don't understand. How did you all get together like this?'

Madame Bru said, 'We all became familiar with each other's cases while we were trying to get the police to do something about our own.'

Monsieur Veyssière, whom Martin had introduced as a widower, said, 'It seemed natural that we should get together, pool resources, since we were all so obviously interconnected.' He glanced towards Guillaume Martin.

Martin said, 'I suggested that we form a group to bring pressure to bear on the police. We managed to get quite a bit of publicity at the time. But the media never sustains interest for long, and the police resented our intervention. So, in the end, we resorted to hiring an investigator of our own.'

Enzo raised an eyebrow. 'Who?'

'The man who arrested Régis Blanc for the murder of the three prostitutes.' He nodded acknowledgement of Enzo's surprise. 'Commissaire Michel Bétaille. It was his final case before retirement, and I knew from having spoken to him that he was never entirely satisfied with the circumstances surrounding the murders and Blanc's arrest.'

'In what way?'

'Well, perhaps, Monsieur Macleod, if you were to pay him

a visit, he could tell you that for himself. Suffice it to say that he jumped at the chance of re-examining the whole case, and following up on the connections to our missing and murdered girls.'

'And what did he find?'

Silence fell around the table once more, and nobody was keen to meet anyone else's eye. At length, Martin said, 'He didn't find anything. He worked for nearly two years on the case, and charged us a considerable amount for his time. The trouble was that none of his former colleagues seemed anxious to help him. They denied him access to evidence and statements. In the end, he simply gave up, and we were no further forward than we had been two years before.'

'You're our last chance to find out the truth, Monsieur Macleod.' This from Madame Bru, and Enzo's heart sank. He hated being anybody's last chance. She reached down to retrieve a folder from her bag, which seemed like a cue for all the other families around the table, including the Martins, to do the same. Six folders in shades of blue and red and yellow and green, tied with black ribbon and held with elastic, were pushed towards Enzo.

He raised his hands defensively. 'Woah! I can't take on all these cases,' he said. 'I'm here to look into the murder of Lucie Martin. I don't know that any of these are even connected to it.' He looked around the table for their understanding, but saw only their sadness. The silence stretched from seconds to a minute, or more, before someone began picking desultorily at

their starter. Someone else took a sip of wine, then more eyes turned without relish towards the food on the plates in front of them. Before lifting again to look at Enzo. He sighed. 'Listen, I'll take a look at them, alright?' And he could barely believe he was hearing himself say it. 'I can't promise anything. But if something jumps out at me . . . well, I'll look into it further.' He felt absolutely trapped. 'It's the best I can offer.'

But it was an offer met by more silence.

Madame Martin began ostentatiously to clear away their starters, most of which had barely been touched. 'I'll just serve the beef now,' she said, colour high on her cheeks. She avoided Enzo's eye.

Enzo reached for his glass and took several gulps of the Bergerac, fervently wishing that he were somewhere else. He gathered the folders towards him and made them into a neat pile at the side of his place. The Lucie Martin case was on the top, and he opened it to see photographs and documents. Newspaper cuttings, a photocopy of Blanc's letter to the murdered girl. He looked at the old judge and said, 'Would you, by any chance, have the original of the letter that Blanc sent to Lucie?'

Martin looked puzzled. 'You've got the photocopy there. And surely you've read the text of it already, in Raffin's book?'

'Yes, I have. But I'd like to see the original, if it's available.'

He shrugged. 'I'll get it for you.' And he stood up.

But before he left the table, Enzo said, 'How do you know that it really was from Blanc?'

'What do you mean?'

'How do you know it was Blanc who wrote it?'

Martin appeared slightly embarrassed, as if he had been caught in the act of something illicit. He shrugged. 'Michel Bétaille obtained samples of Blanc's handwriting. Don't ask how.' He paused. 'I paid for a graphologist to compare them with the letter.' He raised an eyebrow. 'There was no doubt, Monsieur Macleod. They came from the same hand. It was Régis Blanc who sent that letter to my Lucie.'

# CHAPTER EIGHT

When Bertrand regained consciousness, he opened his eyes to disorientating darkness. Then his first awareness was of Sophie's face next to his, her lips, her breath, her whispered words, 'Oh, thank God. I thought they'd killed you.' And yet it all seemed to come to him once removed, as if through gauze.

Pain followed, searing inside his head like a red-hot poker. He tried to sit up, and winced from the bruising in his midriff. Well-developed abdominal muscles were all that had saved him from serious internal injury during the repeated kicking from heavy boots.

He tried to adjust his position and reach out to Sophie, but his hands were tied behind his back. More pain. Rough plastic cord cutting into soft flesh around his wrists.

Next came the realisation that they were moving, and he heard the roar of an engine. They were in the back of a vehicle of some sort.

'Where are we?' he whispered in despair.

'I don't know.' Sophie's voice sounded ragged. 'They put

sacks over our heads and tied us up and threw us in here. We've been driving forever.'

'Why? For God's sake, what do these people want with us?'

'I have no idea.' And he could hear that she was close to tears.

He said, 'It can only be some terrible mistake.'

He manoeuvred himself next to Sophie, so that they could at least take some comfort and warmth from one another. For a long time, then, he listened to her sobbing. Before it eventually tailed away. Crying brought neither comfort nor resolution, and eventually the body abandoned its expression of fear and pain through tears. It was just too exhausting.

They almost rolled on to their sides as the vehicle swung suddenly to the right, and then the rhythm of the wheels on the road beneath them changed. A different surface, pitted and bumpy. They found themselves tossed around the empty space in the back of the van as the driver made no allowance for the change of road, dropping a gear and accelerating left and right into several successive bends. Then there was a long straight stretch before they slowed almost to a stop and turned through what must have been a narrow opening, and on to a gravel surface that crunched beneath their tyres. This was no proper road. It was peppered by potholes that the driver negotiated carefully to avoid breaking an axle.

They lurched from side to side before swinging unexpectedly on to a smoother surface and drawing abruptly to a halt. Bertrand's heart rate increased. While he might have prayed for

the discomfort of their journey to come to an end, they were at least safe as long as they kept moving. Now that they had stopped, the unknown kicked in once again, and fear returned.

'Stick close to me,' he whispered to Sophie. 'Don't let them separate us.'

He felt her lean in hard against him. But, in the same moment, doors flew open and rough hands reached in to pull them apart and drag them from the vehicle. Bertrand landed heavily on the ground and dropped involuntarily to his knees. He found himself hyperventilating, almost suffocating behind the hood they had tied over his head. He felt the air around him cooler on his skin, but none of it seemed to be reaching his lungs, and he had a sudden fear of throwing up inside the sack, choking on his own vomit.

'Bertrand!' he heard Sophie wailing, and he tried in vain to free himself of the hands that dragged him to his feet.

'It's alright, I'm still here.'

'Shut up!' a voice breathed in his ear.

Their captors were whispering to one another in the dark, and he had the clear impression that there were more than just two of them now. Someone held him by the collar and propelled him forward until he nearly tripped on the first of a flight of steps. He staggered up them, uncertain when they would come to an end. But there were only half a dozen. He tripped again on the sill of a door, then heard the whispering voices, and their footsteps and rasping breath echo all around some cavernous space.

A tiled or stone floor clattered beneath their feet, and they were led forward to a door that scraped open, and then down a flight of steps leading into a smell of damp. Bertrand shivered in the cold, fetid air. He heard light switches being thrown, and muted yellow electric light filtered through the weave of his hood. They seemed to go through a room and then into a corridor before, some ten or fifteen feet further on, they were pushed through an open doorway into an empty space.

Bertrand heard Sophie scream with fright, and then hands on his hood ripped it away to leave him blinking in the harsh light of a single electric bulb that hung from the ceiling. He screwed his eyes up and, through his pain, saw Sophie standing in the middle of the room, her hair tangled around a bruised face with dried blood around her lip. Her eyes were black with fear.

There were two men in the room with them. Both still wearing ski masks. One stood by the door, a baseball bat dangling from a gloved hand. The other wielded a box cutter, and for a moment Bertrand thought the man was going to slash him with it. Instead, he turned Bertrand around before cutting his wrists free. The rush of blood back into his hands was almost as painful as the cut of the cord. The man pushed Bertrand towards the back wall, then turned to free Sophie. She stumbled to clutch the young man who had proposed marriage to her only two hours before, and he felt the trembling in the fingers that grabbed him. Her handbag and his shoulder bag lay in the middle of the room, on a dusty concrete floor.

The masked men turned and left without a word. The door slammed shut. A heavy, panelled wooden door. And they heard a bolt slide into place and a key turn in the lock. Footsteps receded down the corridor. Another door banged, and then there was silence.

For several long moments, Bertrand and Sophie stood holding each other, bodies trembling, breathing in short, tremulous bursts. Confusion and disorientation and fear breeding inertia.

'You okay?' he whispered finally, not quite sure why he was whispering.

'Oh, sure,' she said. 'Never felt better.'

And Bertrand almost smiled. Battered and bruised and deeply distressed, Sophie was still possessed of the withering sarcasm he knew she'd inherited from her father.

He cast his eyes around the room, but there wasn't much to see. Naked walls, painted a pale hospital green and scarred by the years. A concrete floor. And high up on the wall opposite the door, a window big enough for a man to crawl through, but too high to reach, and barred on the outside. The glass was caked with grime and it was well-nigh impossible to see beyond it.

In the corner lay a worn-looking mattress with a couple of grey woollen blankets folded one on top of the other. Bertrand's spirits dipped even lower. They were clearly expected to sleep here, and the provision of a mattress suggested that it was going to be for more than just one night.

'What the hell do these people want with us?' he said, abandoning his whisper, and his voice seemed inordinately loud in the confined space of the room which had become their prison.

But if Sophie heard, she wasn't listening. She detached herself suddenly from him and dropped to her knees in the middle of the room, grabbing her handbag and rifling through it in an almost hysterical frenzy. 'Shit!' She threw it aside and grabbed Bertrand's shoulder bag. But she chucked it away after the briefest of searches. 'They've taken our phones!'

Which came as no real surprise to Bertrand. Their captors would hardly have gone to all the trouble of kidnapping them and bringing them here, only to leave them with phones to call for help. There was a sickening sense of professionalism about the whole thing, and he slid down the wall to sit on the floor, pulling his knees up to his chest and folding his arms around his shins in despair.

# CHAPTER NINE

Enzo's bedroom was at the top of the house, looking out towards the swimming pool and the broad sweep of the valley beyond.

He had made his excuses and retired before the parents left. For a while, he had stood at the top of the stairs and listened to their animated and sometimes heated conversation in the kitchen below. They had waited until he had gone before giving full expression to their feelings. Although he could not hear what was being said, he could discern the frustration, perhaps anger, and certainly disappointment in the tone of their voices.

He sighed and went to his room, shutting the door and then standing in the dark by the window, watching as finally they all spilled out from the front door and made their way down to where the cars were parked. He was annoyed that Martin had set him up without warning, though he couldn't help but feel for the parents who had lost their daughters. While four of them were only 'unaccounted for', after more than twenty years without word, they were almost certainly dead. And all their parents really wanted now was closure.

He watched the cars leave one after the other, headlights following tail lights down the hill, before gradually being swallowed by the night and the mist that was rising from the river and the lake. They carried their pain off into the darkness, where it would stay with them for the rest of their lives. There was nothing, he was very nearly certain, that he could do for any of them.

Wearily, he undressed, splashing his face with icy water and brushing his teeth, before climbing between the cold sheets of his bed. Although physically and mentally tired, he knew that sleep was still a long way off, and so he sat propped up against two soft pillows, with the multicoloured array of folders laid out on the quilt in front of him.

One by one, he sifted through their contents. Police reports and official correspondence. Newspaper clippings, private letters. But most poignant of all were the photographs. And Enzo found himself looking at the faces of six young women, all of them long dead, he was sure. There were several photographs of each. Family snaps of smiling teenagers in happier days. Strips from photo booths. Faces serious and sad and sometimes silly. A portrait. This was the girl who had claimed to be an actress, and maybe that had been her ambition. But how often was it that unfulfilled dreams led to failed lives, a slide into despondency or despair, or sometimes simply an acceptance of a life less special than childhood hope had dared to imagine? This was a girl with fine, high cheekbones, lips lush with the promise of soft kisses, dark eyes reflecting light, hope and

innocence in equal measure. Inestimably sad. Enzo slipped it back into its folder with a deep sense of depression.

The murdered girl from Poitiers had been photographed in death – eyes open, skin touched by blue. A face ravaged by drugs and aged by an endless procession of men in her bed, using her for sex without any sense of the human being she was. Her clients had cared about nothing but sexual gratification. One of them might even have given her the virus that would eventually have killed her, even if the man with the knife had not.

Enzo found himself thinking about his own girls, Sophie and Kirsty, and how he would feel if anything were to happen to them – thoughts he could not even contemplate without pain. And his heart went out to all those poor people who had sat around the Martins' dinner table tonight, almost overwhelming him with a sense of obligation that he knew he could never fulfil.

He looked down and saw that he was holding yet another photograph in his hands. It showed a young woman with short blond hair, dyed and streaked through with a darker brown. This was the daughter of the Linols – Sally – the one they claimed had known the murdered prostitutes. She had an impish smile and glittering green eyes. A photograph taken somewhere on a sunny summer's day. The cut of her white T-shirt revealed the brown curve of her neck, and exposed the tattoo of a feather that ran from her collar bone to the lobe of her ear. The tattoo had been professionally done in fine

blue lines that created an illusion of softness, and Enzo might almost have thought it beautiful, if he had not considered all tattoos to be acts of self-mutilation.

He was glad he had fought Sophie's teenage wilfulness, and forbidden tattoos on pain of death. She had got her revenge by taking up with a boy who had them everywhere on his body. Before falling for Bertrand, a young bodybuilder whose facial studs and piercings would have set off security alarms at any airport in the world. Fortunately, Bertrand had grown out of his 'metal' phase and proven himself to be much more than met the eye. And Enzo was relieved that Sophie had stuck with him in the end.

He looked again at Sally and her feather, and wondered what had really become of her. Had Blanc killed her like the others? If so, why had she never been found, and why would Blanc have bothered to clear out her apartment?

Pointless questions to which he knew he would never find the answers.

Finally he lifted the photograph of Lucie. A professional head-and-shoulders taken on her nineteenth birthday. Her father had spoken of her innocence, and it was apparent in her wide, blue eyes and open, smiling face. Not a beautiful face, but pretty. Golden curls softening angular lines. A face that would have aged well, like her mother's. Enzo laid it down on the bed again, and found himself sick of it all. Of death and crime scenes, of blood spatter and DNA. An endless parade of dead faces and horrific injuries. He'd had enough. When he

had resolved the final case in Raffin's book, he was going to give it all up. Maybe he could take early retirement. Travel a little. Read. And then he recalled that the final murder in the book was that of Raffin's wife. The unresolved murder that had motivated Raffin to write the book in the first place. And it would not be without its own peculiar and very personal pain.

He sighed, slipping Lucie back into her folder so that he no longer had to gaze on that pretty, dead face in the knowledge that finding her killer was the reason for his being here.

Instead, he lifted the original of Blanc's letter that Martin had given him. This, he knew, was the one great enigma in this whole case. Martin claimed that it proved beyond doubt the link between Blanc and his daughter. And, of course, it did. But it did not, to Enzo's reading, suggest that there was anything in Blanc's mind other than the expression of his love. And if that, indeed, was how he felt about Lucie, why would he have killed her?

It was written on a page torn from a spiral notebook and dog-eared from constant handling. There was the hint of a cigarette burn in one corner, and what might have been a coffee stain. The handwriting was spidery and childish.

My dearest Lucie,

I know I don't deserve to even share the same space with you. I am a man who has known and did terrible things. I know you know it's not my fault, but people hate me for the things I've done. And you don't. You make me feel like I am someone else.

*No . . . like I could BE someone else. The man you would WANT me to be. I can only try and earn your love in return. Please forgive me. I really hope you will.*

*Love R*

It was a curious mix, Enzo thought, of the lyrical and the illiterate. Here was a hardened criminal, a man who ran prostitutes and had just served a prison term for violent assault, prostrating himself in front of a girl not much more than half his age. It seemed so entirely out of character. And the intimacy of the sign-off – *Love R* – as if they might have known each other for half a lifetime. It was troubling.

Enzo gathered everything together and dropped it on to the floor before turning out the light and curling up beneath his duvet in the certain knowledge that these girls would haunt the days and maybe weeks ahead, and that, tonight, sleep would not come easy.

# CHAPTER TEN

Retired commissaire Michel Bétaille lived in a modest two-bed apartment in a modern block in Bordeaux Bastide, near the botanical gardens just off the Quai des Queyries. From a front room with sliding glass doors on to a narrow balcony, he had a view across the slow-moving pewtery waters of the River Garonne to the Quai Louis XVIII, where *négociants* had built grand offices along quays from which barrels of Bordeaux wine were once loaded on to the boats that took it all around the world.

Bétaille was younger than Enzo had been expecting. A man in his mid-sixties, and yet he had retired more than twenty years ago. He smiled when Enzo asked him about it. 'Retired from the police,' he said. 'Not from life, or work. As a commissaire I saw too much of the worst of folk. Bad bastards, death and blood. Ruined and wasted lives. Lies and deception. You either get inured to it, or it breaks down your humanity and marks you for life. I was somewhere between the two, and knew that I had to get out before it destroyed me.'

He waved Enzo into a seat by the window.

'Can I get you a coffee?'

'Thank you.'

The kitchen, dining and living areas were open-plan. Comfortable living for one. A squeeze for two. Bétaille disappeared behind his kitchen island and primed an espresso maker.

'You live here on your own?' Enzo asked above the noise of beans being ground.

Bétaille smiled. 'Yes. Saw too many marriages fail among my fellow officers, so I was never tempted. Police and families don't mix. Besides which, I probably just never met the right woman.' He chuckled. 'And then you get to a certain age and, you know how it is. You don't want someone else filling your private space, moving your things around, interfering with your routine.' Pause. 'How about you?'

'Divorced once, widowed once.'

Bétaille glanced towards him. 'I'm sorry.'

Enzo shrugged. 'It was all a long time ago.'

Bétaille nodded, and when his machine had forced water at pressure through the freshly ground beans, he brought small black cups of it to place on a coffee table between them, with sugar lumps and spoons. He said, 'Help yourself.' Then, 'I've been half expecting you for some time.'

'Have you?'

He shrugged and sipped his coffee. 'I've been following your progress in the press, Monsieur Macleod. You've done an exceptional job on Raffin's unsolved murders. I knew you

would get to Lucie eventually, and that she would probably lead you to me.'

Enzo smiled. 'Nothing if not predictable, then.'

Bétaille cocked an eyebrow. 'There must be a couple of killers out there getting pretty nervous by now. If I were you, I'd be watching my back.'

'Oh, I do. There have already been three attempts on my life.' And he remembered that dark night in the gallery of the château in Gaillac where someone had tried to stab him to death. The serendipitous quirk of fate which had led to Raffin taking the bullet meant for him in the Rue du Tournon. And, most painful of all, the woman called Anna who had been sent to kill him – a woman he had slept with and who had stirred long-dead emotions. Someone out there was very anxious to see him dead. He laughed it off. 'So far I've led a charmed existence.' He stirred a single cube of sugar into his coffee. 'Tell me why you took on the parents' group.'

He made a moue with his lips. 'The Bordeaux Six, as the press called them. Referring to the number of girls, of course, not parents.' He paused and looked like he might be wondering how to frame his next statement. 'I wasn't satisfied with the original investigation into the Blanc murders.'

Enzo watched him carefully. 'Why? Blanc was guilty, wasn't he? He killed those three girls?'

'Yes, he was, and he did. But I was never satisfied that I knew why.'

Enzo sipped his coffee. 'The Chinese would say the *why* is

not important if the accumulated evidence leads conclusively to the killer. And it would seem that it did in this case.'

But Bétaille shook his head. 'You have to understand your man. I'm sure you know that from your own experience, Monsieur Macleod. There was nothing in Blanc's background, past or present, that would have led you to believe him capable of murdering those women.'

'And yet he did.'

'Yes. But here's the thing . . . Although I was satisfied that we had got our man alright, like I said, I was never happy that I knew his motive. So I started digging around in his history, his connections, his friends, searching for some kind of understanding.'

'And?'

'I wasn't just discouraged by the folk upstairs, I was told to stop it. In no uncertain terms.'

'Did they say why?'

Bétaille breathed his frustration. 'A waste of police resources on a case already resolved.' He shook his head. 'And who could argue with that? Blanc had admitted the murders in court and been sent down for life. No one was going to fund one man's *feeling* that something wasn't quite right.' He drained his cup. 'And I suppose that precipitated my decision to take early retirement. It was time to get out.' He smiled. 'But then, of course, along came the Bordeaux Six, and I couldn't resist the chance they presented me to have another look at the whole thing.'

'You spent two years on it?'

'Off and on, yes.'

'And did it bring any greater clarity?'

Bétaille gazed into his empty cup. 'No, it did not.'

'What about the six? The parents tell me you found no connections there, either.'

'No, I didn't. And I don't believe there are any. I mean, apart from the obvious. But I don't think Blanc killed any of those girls.'

'Why not?'

'As far as three of the missing were concerned, I couldn't find a single connection at any level with Blanc or any of his known associates.' He shrugged. 'People disappear all the time, Monsieur Macleod. Usually because they want to, for whatever reason.' He stood up. 'Would you like another coffee?'

Enzo declined.

'You don't mind if I do?' But he didn't wait for an answer and busied himself preparing a second espresso. 'It didn't help, of course, that I was getting the cold shoulder from my former colleagues. I had anticipated at least some access to inside info. But they shut me out, Monsieur Macleod. People I'd worked with for years, done favours for, helped up the ladder –' a bitterness crept into his voice – 'wouldn't give me anything. Not a goddamn thing!' He clattered his cup into his saucer. 'I suppose they'd been warned not to. But I thought, you know, that I'd get at least a nod and a wink. I almost had the sense that they were scared to talk to me.' He flashed a look

towards Enzo. 'Why would police officers be afraid of talking to a former colleague?'

Enzo just shrugged and shook his head, and wondered if perhaps Bétaille had read more into it all than there really was. Frustrated by his lack of progress in the investigation he had taken on for the Bordeaux Six, it would have been only too easy for him to blame his failure on lack of police cooperation, informal or otherwise. Enzo wanted to keep him on track. 'What about the other three?'

Thick, black coffee gurgled into Bétaille's cup. 'It was well established that Blanc had met Lucie at the offices of Rentrée. But you know, of course, that Rentrée was a Catholic charity for helping newly released prisoners back into society, so she would have met all sorts of criminals in the course of her work. The difference was that Blanc was the only one who wrote her a love letter.'

'Quite a letter it was, too,' Enzo said. 'And, if you asked me to guess, I'd say there had been others before it.'

Bétaille cast him a curious glance as he resumed his seat and sipped his coffee. 'Why?'

Enzo shrugged. 'Instinct. Something to do with its intimacy. You don't achieve that in a single exchange.'

But Bétaille did not seem impressed. 'Well, there was no other letter found, monsieur. The two would have met just a handful of times at the offices of the charity. Blanc himself admits to having developed an infatuation for her, and claims to have written the letter while he was drunk in a bar.'

'And the girl with the feather tattoo?'

'Sally Linol?' Bétaille shook his head. 'Yes, she was one of Blanc's girls. Well in with him, apparently. Known to all the others. But I don't think he killed her. She cleared out her apartment and left. And that was before any of the murders. She just moved on. A fresh start somewhere else.'

'What about Monica Robert? The one who was murdered.'

'Oh, she had been one of Blanc's alright. But ties had been severed several months before. She was working for some horrible, drug-dealing little pimp that operated out of a backroom in a café in the red-light district. She was found mutilated in a hotel room. A frenzied, sexual murder. Just not Blanc's style. He had no history of violence towards women.'

'And yet he strangled three of his girls.'

'Which brings me back to my original point, monsieur. Why? It was totally out of character. He was a man's man. He got drunk and into fights. He was a pimp, yes, but everybody said he was good to his girls. There was a soft, maybe even romantic side to him. Well, you've read his letter to Lucie. He *liked* women. Treated his prostitutes with a respect that none of them had been used to from other pimps. So why would he suddenly murder three of them? And here's the oddest thing of all. Never made public. Even at the trial, because the man pled guilty.' He paused. 'All three of those girls had been sedated. Rohypnol, or "roofies", as they called them on the street: the old date-rape drug. But he never interfered with them sexually, and the chances are all three were unconscious when he

strangled them. So they wouldn't have known anything about it. He didn't *want* to hurt them.'

'Just to kill them.'

'Yes.' He drained his second cup. 'Without rhyme or reason, monsieur. I understand his motivation no better now than I did twenty-two years ago. And it still troubles me.' He stood up and thrust his hands deep in his pockets, gazing out at sudden sunlight playing on the river. 'Of course, he's been visited in prison by a procession of psychologists and psychiatrists over the years, and he spins them all the same bullshit. His mother was a whore, you see. And, one time, the story goes, when he was in the back of the car, he saw her giving a client a blow job.' He turned withering sarcasm towards Enzo. 'So naturally, he was killing his mother each time he murdered one of those girls.'

Enzo smiled. 'Psychology for dummies.'

Bétaille nodded. 'You said it.'

'But he killed those three girls for a reason, and you think that the Bordeaux Six are completely unconnected?'

'That's exactly right.'

'So who killed Lucie?'

'I haven't the faintest idea, monsieur.'

Enzo felt this thread of his investigation starting to slip away from him. 'Were there ever any other suspects in the frame for her murder?'

'Well, I don't know about suspect, but her boyfriend was interviewed at the time of her disappearance.'

'And?'

'There was nothing to connect him to it in any way. He was in Paris the weekend she went missing.'

Enzo had left his 2CV in the station car park at Libourne and taken the train into Bordeaux. It was a half-hourly service and easier than driving into the city. The journey time back was less than thirty minutes. He picked up his car again and nosed the old Citroën through the narrow streets of Libourne and out on to the D670. Using the GPS in his phone he set a course south-west to Lucie's medieval hometown of Duras, where she had gone to school with the boy who would become her lover.

Richard Tavel lived with his wife and two young children in a house he had inherited from his parents. It was a solid, square, nineteenth-century house on three floors, on the outskirts of Duras, just off the Route de Savignac, and no more than five kilometres from where Lucie had lived with her parents at Château Gandolfo. It was late afternoon when Enzo got there. The day was beginning to fade, and electric lights already burned in windows on the ground floor of the house.

Enzo parked in the street and climbed half a dozen steps to the front door. He heard the sound of ringing somewhere distantly inside the house when he pressed the bell push. After a few moments a shadow appeared beyond the glass, and a woman in her mid-to-late thirties opened the door. She was a plain-looking woman, not unattractive, with thick brown hair drawn back in a severe ponytail. She wore jeans and a T-shirt

and not a trace of make-up. She looked at Enzo with enquiring brown eyes. '*Oui?* Can I help you?'

'I'm looking for Richard Tavel. Do I have the right house?'

At the far end of the hall behind her, a dishevelled-looking man appeared out of the shadows. 'Who wants to know?'

'My name's Enzo Macleod.' Enzo pronounced his name as the French do – *Mac-lee-odd*.

The man had stepped into the light by now, and Enzo saw his face pale immediately. He was tall and rangy, a woollen jumper hanging loosely on his angular frame. He didn't fill his cargo pants either, and they concertinaed around bare feet.

'Oh, yes . . .' he said uncertainly. As if he should have known. 'You'd better come in.'

His wife looked at him, surprised, and from somewhere at the back of the house Enzo heard the burble of a TV and the voices of children. But Tavel made no attempt to explain to her, and Enzo saw his reluctance even to meet her eye. He also saw her reluctance to let this stranger in. So he forced the issue and squeezed past her into the hall.

'What's all this about?' she said.

Tavel forced a smile. 'I'll tell you later, Magalie.' And to Enzo, 'We can talk in my study, monsieur.'

Enzo followed him up the stairs, aware of Magalie's eyes on them, until a child's cry of pain sent her running through to the back of the house. The first-floor landing was dark, and Tavel pushed open the door into a large, square room and turned on the light. His study was sparsely furnished.

An antique desk and captain's chair, and a couple of worn leather armchairs stood around on polished floorboards. A large mirror hung above the fireplace, the walls festooned with framed family photos. He closed the door and said, in a voice tight with tension, 'I just knew you were going to turn up on my doorstep one of these days.'

'Then, you should be well prepared,' Enzo said.

Tavel drew a deep breath. 'My wife knows nothing about this, and I'd like to keep it that way.'

Enzo frowned. 'Exactly what is it she knows nothing about?'

'My connection to the disappearance of Lucie Martin.'

Enzo raised an eyebrow. 'Oh? And what is your connection to her disappearance?'

'None! Absolutely none. And if you understood anything about what happened, you'd know that.' He wandered off towards the window, wringing his hands. He was in a state of some considerable agitation when he turned back to face Enzo. 'I am a happily married man now, Monsieur Macleod. I have a young family. Magalie's from the Aubrac and knows nothing about Lucie's murder, or my relationship with her. I'd like it to stay that way.'

'Well, I won't tell her if you don't.' Enzo smiled. 'Always assuming, of course, that you are prepared to answer my questions.'

'What questions? She's been dead more than twenty years, and everyone knows I had nothing to do with it.'

'Do they?'

'The police interviewed me only once, for less than an hour. They let me go as soon as they were able to confirm that I really was in Paris the weekend she went missing.'

Enzo nodded. 'It's amazing how mud sticks, though. I remember a cinema manager being questioned by police about the murder of a young girl in Glasgow. They grilled him for forty-eight hours before letting him go. Everyone assumed he'd done it, and that the police just couldn't prove it. Didn't matter that they caught the real killer three months later. By then that cinema manager had lost his job, his wife had left him, and he ended up committing suicide.'

Tavel sighed heavily. 'What do you want to know?'

'Tell me about you and Lucie.'

Tavel perched, then, on the edge of one of the armchairs, leaning forward, feet crossed one over the other, still wringing his hands in his lap. He stared into an abyss of time and tragedy. 'I'd known her from primary school. Then in our first year at the *lycée* I took her to the end-of-term dance. I'd always, you know, had a kind of soft spot for her. She was so pretty, with those blue eyes and soft golden curls. Goodness knows where she got them from, because her dad was always going on about their Italian heritage.' He glanced up at Enzo, but his eyes flickered quickly away again. 'We started going out regularly. All through our teen years. Childhood sweethearts, I suppose you could say we were.'

'And when you finished school?'

'I got a place at Bordeaux University, and Lucie didn't. Not

that she wasn't bright enough.' He seemed to feel the need to apologise for her. 'She just wasn't interested in continuing her education.'

'But she still ended up in Bordeaux.'

'Yes. A job with the prisoners charity, Rentrée. Took it to be close to me. Or so she said. My folks weren't that well off . . .' He flicked his head towards the house. 'They inherited this place from my mum's parents. So I was in digs with half a dozen other students in a pretty seedy apartment block near the university. Lucie's dad bought her a studio.' This said with what Enzo perceived to be the green monster of envy sitting on his shoulder. 'There was money in the Martin family, and her father was happy to indulge her in whatever took her fancy.' Again he darted a look at Enzo. 'In anything and everything except me. He never really liked me very much. Not good enough for his daughter. Didn't say it in so many words, but made sure I knew in other ways.'

'And you never stayed at her studio?'

'Oh yes, I did. All the time. Except when I had a lecture first thing in the morning. Her place wasn't exactly close to the uni. It was amazing, those first few months. Free from parental constraints. Free to do exactly as we wanted, when we wanted.'

Enzo watched him closely. 'I sense a "but" somewhere in the not-too-distant future.'

Tavel shrugged, and the tiny laugh that slipped from his lips was entirely without humour. 'She dumped me.' His fingers seemed locked together and his hands made a single fist, as

if he was indulging in some desperate kind of prayer. 'Not immediately. I mean, there was no "It's finished" speech. It just became "inconvenient" for me to stay over. We saw less and less of each other, and I could feel her slipping away.'

'Did you have any sense of why?'

Tavel simply shrugged. 'She'd found someone else.'

'She told you that?'

'No.'

'So how did you know?'

Tavel was avoiding eye contact with Enzo again. 'Educated guess.'

A tiny gasp of exasperation escaped Enzo's lips. 'Because, God knows, it couldn't possibly have been that she'd simply lost interest in you.'

Tavel looked sharply at Enzo, the implication of vanity had not escaped him, and Enzo saw a little spike of angry pride pierce his agitation. 'I saw her with him.' Tension levelled his voice.

'Where?'

And Enzo saw embarrassment, and maybe shame, cloud his anger. 'I waited outside the offices of Rentrée one night and followed her. She met this man, an older man, in a café. I can't tell you how shocked I was as I saw her reach up and kiss him when they met. Just a brushing of the lips. But it was so casual and intimate, you could tell immediately that this wasn't some new relationship.'

Enzo watched him replay the scene in his mind's eye.

'They slipped into a stall at the back of the café. It was dark and I couldn't see too well. And I couldn't go in without being seen myself. But I saw them holding hands across the table.'

'And how did that make you feel?'

Tavel's knuckles whitened. 'Hurt. Angry.'

'Did you recognise the man?'

There was an almost imperceptible pause, but Enzo didn't miss it. 'No.'

'So you had no idea who he was?'

'No, I didn't.'

Enzo stood watching him in a silence that went on for so long that Tavel was finally compelled to lift his eyes and look at him. Almost immediately, they heard his wife calling up from downstairs. 'Richard! The boys are waiting for you to help them with their homework.'

Enzo said, 'You know, this is material evidence in a murder case. Evidence that you withheld from the police.'

Fear widened Tavel's eyes. 'I didn't think it was important.'

'I'm sure you'll be able to explain that to them when they take you in for questioning again.'

'Richard!' His wife called once more, and Enzo could hear the irritation in her voice.

There was almost panic in Tavel's. 'Be down in a minute.'

'So,' Enzo said, 'you had absolutely no idea who this man was?'

Tavel sucked in his lower lip and bit down on it, getting to his feet and turning away towards the window. 'No, I didn't,'

he said, and Enzo could see his anguished reflection in the window in front of him. 'Not at the time.'

Enzo frowned. 'But you did later?'

Tavel nodded. And after a long pause, 'When Blanc was arrested for the murder of those prostitutes his picture was all over the papers.'

And Enzo knew he was just a breath away from a break-through in the Lucie Martin case. 'It was Blanc she met at the café?'

Tavel turned, then, an appeal for understanding in his eyes. 'I didn't want to get involved. There was no point in telling the police I'd seen her with Blanc.'

'Because that would mean admitting you'd been following her. And the press would have had a field day with the whole story, wouldn't they? Childhood sweetheart jilted for serial killer.'

'If it was Blanc who killed her, he got locked up for those other killings anyway, so what difference would it have made?'

'The difference is, Monsieur Tavel,' Enzo said slowly, 'it would have given you a clear motive for murder.'

'Except it couldn't have been me. I was in Paris!' There was an almost hysterical edge to Tavel's voice now.

And Enzo recalled what old Guillaume Martin had told him: *I didn't spend all those years sitting on the bench, monsieur, without coming to the realisation that alibis can be fabricated.* He said, 'You might have had an alibi for the weekend she vanished. But

who knows when she was murdered, or where you were at the time?'

And every last drop of blood drained out of Tavel's face.

When the door closed, Enzo knew he had left behind him a house fibrillating with tension. He stood for a moment on the top step, wondering how Tavel would explain him to his wife. What new lies he would fabricate to conceal a past filled with self-perceived shame. And – who knew? – maybe even guilt.

The moon was already rising in a clear sky, although it was not yet fully dark. The day was hanging on, reluctant to give way to the night. Enzo reached his car, pulling his keys from the pocket of his cargoes, and saw the note pinned to his windscreen beneath the wiper. A single white sheet, folded once. He lifted the wiper to retrieve it and opened it up. Four words. *Meet me at the château.*

For a moment he wondered which château. Did the writer of the note mean Château Gandolfo? Or the château right here in town? He lifted his head and saw the dark shape of Château Duras, with its circular tower pricking the sky, silhouetted against the western horizon, and realised it was there that he was meant to meet with the author of this message. What he couldn't divine was why, or who that author might be. And he remembered Michel Bétaille's words in Bordeaux: *There must be a couple of killers out there getting pretty nervous by now. If I was you, I'd be watching my back.*

# CHAPTER ELEVEN

It took him no more than two minutes to drive through the narrow arteries of the old town and emerge into the Place Jean Bousquet, which sloped down to where Château Duras stood in a commanding position above the valley below. A couple of cafés spilled light out into the evening, but there was no one sitting at the tables outside. It was getting too cold now, even for the smokers.

He parked his car under some trees and walked the rest of the way to the foot of the square where the château rose into the night and the lights of a tourist shop fell in rectangles across the paving stones.

The entrance to the château, through an arched gateway, was blocked by wooden fencing, and the château itself simmered in darkness beyond it. Access was gained through the tourist shop, which sold tickets for tours. But the note had said *at* the château, not *in* the château, and so Enzo shuffled impatiently on the cobbles outside, stamping his feet against the cold and watching warily for anyone approaching on foot or by car.

He was almost rigid with tension, and wondered again who had left the note, and why. He had the most awful sense of it being a trap, and yet he couldn't see what anyone could do to him in plain view like this. Although, as he looked around, there was not a soul in sight. He began to think that he should not have come at all. And yet, if there was a chance of at least throwing some light on the murder of Lucie Martin . . .

He decided to go into the shop and ask if someone had left anything for him there.

A bell tinkled as he pushed the door open into the light. Shelves were lined with books and brochures and maps and tourist guides. A till stood on a counter immediately to his left as he went in. But there was no one there.

He called out, 'Hello?' And waited. Then called again. But there was no response. He walked around to the far end of the counter and saw another door leading out to the other side of the fencing that sealed off the castle. This was clearly the entrance to the château that tourists took when they had bought their tickets. He stood awkwardly for a moment, hoping that someone would appear, before opening the door and heading out into the tall, arched passageway that led into the castle forecourt. One half of the huge metal gates that guarded the entrance stood open, and he passed through the arch and into a cobbled square flooded with the light of a moon rising in a sky studded now by stars.

'Hello!' His voice echoed around the courtyard. Walls on either side of it dropped away twenty feet or more into what

might once have been a moat, but was now a bank of freshly mown grass. At the far side a flight of steps led up to a stone terrace with doors opening into the château itself. There were no lights on anywhere that he could see, except for those that twinkled distantly in the vast swathe of countryside that fell away below.

One of the doors leading into the castle stood partially open, and he found himself drawn unaccountably towards it. The soles of his leather boots scraped on the stone of the steps as he climbed to the terrace. Moving more cautiously now, he pushed the half-open door wide and stepped into a grand salon, empty apart from the slabs of moonlight that fell across the tiled mosaic floor from the windows all along the side of it. There were three vast fireplaces, one on the facing wall, and one at either end. Each had a portrait hanging above it, and Enzo imagined a great table running the length of the room, all three fires blazing, and a banquet in progress, peopled by, among others, the faces in the portraits. But in the blink of an eye the image was gone, leaving only scaffolding at the far end, and loops of red silk draped between chrome poles barring the doors that led to the rest of the château. And silence. A quiet so profound that Enzo found himself holding his breath in case he disturbed it.

And then a noise outside filled him with sudden fright and apprehension. How foolish had he been to come in here on his own? He threw the door wide and stepped out boldly on to the terrace, prepared to confront whoever might be there. But the terrace was empty, as was the courtyard below.

Which was when he noticed that the lights in the tourist shop beyond the arch had gone out, and the gate through which he had entered was firmly shut. In sudden panic he ran down the stairs and across the cobbled yard, moonlight casting his shadow off to his right as he ran. He reached the gates, hands grasping the cold metal of iron uprights and shaking them as hard as he could. They barely moved, and he saw that a thick chain wound around the old lock was solidly padlocked. Someone had locked him in, damn it!

Across the road, a car started up. Then headlights raked across the square as it turned and accelerated towards the top end of the Place Jean Bousquet, where a narrow road led away to the south.

'Shit!' Enzo cursed under his breath. He reached into his pocket for his mobile phone and felt his heart sink as he pictured it still sitting in its dashboard holder where it had been in use as a GPS. Idiocy compounding idiocy! He rattled the gate again in anger and frustration, and shouted, 'Help!' He heard his voice echo away across the square, but there was no one to hear it. Letting his eyes close, and taking a deep breath, he bellowed as loudly as he could. 'Help! For God's sake, is there anybody there?' The lack of any response told him that there almost certainly wasn't, and he felt himself slump in despair. What was wrong with these people? Where were they all? Why did people in rural France all vanish the moment darkness fell? He felt sure that if he waited long enough, some smoker would eventually step out of one of the cafés for a cigarette,

and then they would surely hear him when he shouted. He waited and waited, for what seemed like endless minutes, and no one appeared. What an inconvenient moment, he thought angrily, for everyone in the world suddenly to give up smoking. He threw more imprecations at the night and turned back into the shimmering moonlight of the cobbled courtyard, walking briskly towards the left-hand wall. There, he peered down into darkness, shadow cast by the moon, and knew that it was far too big a drop to risk jumping.

He turned back into the courtyard, trying to stay calm. There had to be an office somewhere, a place for administrative staff. And there would be a telephone, so that he could call for help. Even if he had to kick a door down to get to it.

He headed back towards the steps leading up to the grand salon, and noticed for the first time that there were steps at the side of them descending into the cellars. It was profoundly dark down there, and it took several moments before he decided to risk it. What else was he going to do?

With fingers tracing his progress along the wall, he took one step at a time down into darkness. When he reached the foot of the stairs he saw light spilling out into a narrow corridor from an open door. On the wall outside the door a plaque read, Salle 'Emmanuel Félicité'. Beware of the stairs. There was a yellow square, and the numbers "1 . . . 9". With a sinking heart Enzo realised this was some kind of numbered and colour-coded tourist trail through the château. The light came from a window inside the room of Emmanuel

Félicité, moonlight divided into squares by panelled glass. In the centre of the room, raised on a plinth and protected by glass, was a model of the château itself. Beyond it a door opened on to a railed corridor. There was an arrow on the wall, a yellow square, and the numbers 2 . . . 9. The next point of interest on the tour. No office, no phone, no way out.

Enzo's sense of despondency increased, and he turned out into the corridor again to retrace his steps and climb back up to the courtyard.

Moonlight shadows and whispers came tumbling down the steps to meet him. Two men moving with great caution towards the stairs. Although he could not yet see them because of the arch that led to the steps, their shadows almost reached his feet, and behind their whispers he could hear the scrape of their shoes on the cobbles. Then he saw the shadow of an outstretched arm, a gun in its hand, and sheer panic gripped him. He turned and ran back into the Salle Emmanuel Félicité. All he could think to do was follow the yellow squares on a circuit that would surely take him away from these men, who could be intent on doing him nothing but harm.

Black railings led him down stairs to a dog-leg that took him to a further flight, descending even deeper into darkness. A sign told him that he was heading for *La Boulangerie*. And, in an absurd moment of fleeting incongruity, he realised that they must have made their own bread in the castle, back in the day.

Behind him, he heard footsteps clattering on stone. The men, who had so cautiously approached the stairs above him,

had now given up any attempt at subtlety. They knew he knew they were there, and were openly hunting him down.

Enzo ran into the *boulangerie*, moonlight flooding in through the window, and nearly died of fright as he saw a figure standing by a long wooden table, wielding the paddle with which bakers of old would have slid uncooked bread into the wood-burning oven. A short, sharp involuntary cry broke from his lips before he realised that the figure was a mannequin. A dummy surrounded by fake props, recreating the bakery as it must once have been. And this was a dead end.

He turned back into the corridor and out through an arched door into a long gallery lined by photographs. A sign pointed him towards *La cuisine 'aux Cent fagots'* and he sprinted down the length of the gallery, aware of the breathing and footsteps and voices of the men on his tail, just moments behind him. In desperation he turned into the old kitchen and collided with yet more mannequins. A plastic whole roast pig rotating on a spit in a cold fireplace. Yet another dead end. Fleeing back into the gallery, he caught sight of his pursuers running into the *boulangerie*, and he turned and sprinted in the opposite direction. Past the Room of Secrets, up stairs, turning left and right in blind panic, crashing into women in long aprons populating the Second Kitchen. A glass case of crockery toppled and smashed on the floor, splinters of porcelain exploding across the stone flags.

He had lost all sense of where he was now, the tourist itinerary long since abandoned. He found stairs leading up and

took them, two at a time. Reaching a landing, and then a room, then following the spiral ever higher until he emerged into a rectangular inner courtyard, open to the sky far above, and surrounded by stone galleries that looked down on him from all sides.

The heavy breathing and footfalls of the chasing men followed him up the stairwell, and he ran across the courtyard to yet more steps on the far side. Here, he entered a hallway mired in darkness, and felt his way along a wood-panelled wall, knocking over a standing sign before stumbling through a doorway into even deeper gloom. He was completely disorientated and felt once more for the wall, fingers connecting with a rocker switch that triggered a sudden explosion of light from the far side of the room, glass walls rising up into a void high overhead. Behind the glass, ghostly figures in white wailed and screeched into the night. All the hairs stood up on Enzo's neck and he fled in panic, tripping over the fallen sign and sprawling full length on the floor. As he scrambled to his feet he saw, by the reflected light of the room he had just left, an arrow beneath the legend *Salle aux Fantômes* – the Ghost Room.

He ran. Blindly. Back out into another gallery of some kind, and up steps to where an open door led on to a balustraded walkway high up on the side of the castle. At the far end of it, he found an opening on to yet another spiral stairway. The opening was narrow and, as he turned into it, he felt something snag the band that held his ponytail in place, pulling it free, and his hair cascaded down over his shoulders.

He forced his way on to the stairs, which twisted endlessly upwards, narrowing at every turn. On a tiny landing, he swung into an even tinier room with a low ceiling and arched windows set into each corner, overlooking the red-tiled roofs of castle buildings below. No way out. So he turned back, squeezing himself into an impossibly narrow spiral, climbing ever more steeply upwards, steps almost too short, even at their widest, to accommodate his feet. And he thought, People running away always go up. Something an old policeman had told him once. How stupid! Because there would always come a point when you could climb no higher.

His jacket tearing on ragged stonework, he finally pushed himself out from the top of the stairwell into the open air of a large, stone-flagged, balustraded circle. And this was it. The point at which he could go no higher. He realised with an inner sense of despair that he had just emerged on to the top of the tower. The only way down was over the edge, and certain death. Or back the way he had come, to meet his pursuers on the stairs.

The moon-washed landscape that fell away all around him shimmered into the distance, the lights of the town twinkling to the south, occasional clusters of light in villages and farms punctuating the plain that stretched off to the north and west. He saw a couple of rugby pitches, green and inviting under floodlights, not that far away. The tiny figures of rugby players in training, running and throwing the ball and shouting to each other.

And from the stairwell behind him, the sound of leather on stone and breath rasping in lungs. In a moment of sudden calm, Enzo turned to face them, determined not to go down without a fight. 'Come on, you bastards!' he shouted at the night, as two overweight and perspiring gendarmes tumbled, one over the other, from the stairwell, clutching their pistols and gasping for breath. They stared in amazement at the big, mad-eyed man with hair tangling wildly over his shoulders, and it would have been hard to say who was the more astonished – the gendarmes, or Enzo.

# CHAPTER TWELVE

Enzo sat, dishevelled and dispirited, in the interview room of the gendarmerie. With an elastic band found in his bag he had tied up his hair again, but strands of it still hung loose. He had been here for more than two hours, questioned relentlessly for the first of them by a humourless and po-faced officer demanding to know how he had broken into the château and why. No matter how many times Enzo told him it was all a misunderstanding, and that he had been accidentally locked in, he was regarded with patent disbelief.

Eventually, the officer had given him pencil and paper and asked him to make a list of people who might vouch for him, with phone numbers, if possible. Enzo had been forced to think about that. Locally, there was the retired judge, Lucie's father. In Paris, there was Roger, although he knew the police invariably disliked and distrusted journalists. And then, of course, there was Commissaire Hélène Taillard in Cahors. Who better to speak for his good character than a senior police officer? He just hoped that she didn't hold their nearly relationship against him. It had always, he recalled, been he who, in the

end, had shied away from going any further than friendship. To her obvious disappointment.

For the second hour he had sat twiddling his thumbs under relentless electric light, his backside growing numb on an unforgiving plastic chair. From somewhere else in the building he had heard the chatter of keyboards, phones ringing, the distant sound of muffled voices, but no one had come through the door for nearly an hour and a quarter. A window high up in the wall was barred. Beyond it, the darkness seemed so profound it was almost tangible.

He was beginning to think they had simply forgotten about him when the door swung open and his interrogator stood, glowering, in the doorway. He stuck out his jaw and jerked his head towards the corridor behind him. 'You can go.'

Enzo got up, surprised. Previous encounters with gendarmes had usually led to a blizzard of paperwork, forms in triplicate, complaints drawn up, disclaimers to be signed. But perhaps they were as embarrassed by the whole thing as he was and were happy simply to pretend it never happened.

'Commissaire Taillard has vouched for your good standing, and Monsieur Martin is here to collect you.'

Enzo felt an enormous wave of relief, but the gendarme stopped him in the doorway. 'Just the small matter of the damage at the château,' he said.

Enzo said, 'Tell them to bill me and I'll send them a cheque by return.'

The officer fixed him with a hard stare, then stood reluctantly aside.

Guillaume Martin was waiting in reception and cast curious eyes over him. Enzo realised he must present a somewhat bizarre figure, with his jacket torn and hair hanging in shreds. But Martin made no comment. The two men shook hands solemnly, and it wasn't until they were outside that the old man looked at him again and said, 'What on earth happened?'

Enzo explained about the note, and wandering into the castle only to find himself accidentally locked in. He said, 'Apparently someone heard me shouting from inside and called the police, who thought I was an intruder.'

Martin frowned. 'Who left the note?'

Enzo had no desire to go into all the previous attempts on his life, real or imagined, or his belief that someone, somewhere, wanted to stop his investigation in its tracks. So all he said was, 'I have no idea.'

'And what's your next move?'

Enzo sighed. 'I'll drive home, I suppose.'

'Nonsense!' Martin looked at his watch. 'Come and stay again at the château and Mireille will fix you something to eat. It's far too late and far too far to drive home now. Besides, I want to hear what progress you made today.'

The second glass of wine very nearly rendered Enzo unconscious. His long day, followed by his exertions in the château,

the interrogation and the interminable wait at the gendarmerie, had left him physically and mentally exhausted. Now, as he started to relax in the warmth of Mireille's kitchen, washing down her leftover but deliciously tender boeuf bourguignon with some fine Saint-Emilion, fatigue swept over him and he felt his eyes growing heavy.

But Guillaume Martin wasn't about to let him rest. He wanted to know exactly what Michel Bétaille had said to him, and listened attentively as Enzo related their conversation. It clearly didn't please him, and he threw his napkin on the table in disgust.

'Two years, we paid that man,' he said. 'And he came up with absolutely nothing.'

At least nothing, Enzo thought, that any of the parents wanted to hear. But he didn't say so, and decided to change the direction of their conversation. 'I'm assuming there was an autopsy, Monsieur Martin. On Lucie's body.' He immediately corrected himself. 'Bones.' And then glanced self-consciously towards Madame Martin, aware that she found talk of Lucie's murder difficult to deal with, even after all this time. The old lady kept her eyes on the table.

Martin seemed distracted, even annoyed by Enzo's switch of subject. 'There was,' he said.

Enzo knew that it wouldn't have been much of an autopsy. The collection of bones that they had recovered from the lake would have been very little for the pathologist to go on. But his years spent working as a forensic scientist had taught him

that every last detail counted, no matter how small. He said, 'I wonder where I might be able to get a copy of it?'

Martin placed his hands flat on the table in front of him. 'Well, that's easy. I have one.' He inclined his head a little. 'One of the perks of being a judge. One has a certain amount of influence. Or used to.'

'Could you make me a copy?'

'Of course.' He stood up, then paused. 'Who was it you went to see in Duras?'

Enzo was not at all sure he wanted to get into this right now, particularly in the presence of Lucie's mother, but he didn't see how he could avoid it. 'Richard Tavel,' he said, and both Martin and his wife looked at him in surprise.

'Why would you bother with that waster?' Martin said. 'I rue the day my daughter ever met him. He would never have been good enough for her, monsieur. That's the trouble with sending your children to state school. They mix with all the wrong people. We could have sent her to the private Catholic *collège* in Bergerac. But that would have meant her boarding out, and neither of us wanted that.'

'He was interviewed by the police at the time,' Enzo said.

'Yes, but he was in Paris the weekend she disappeared, so he couldn't have had anything to do with it.'

'Perhaps. But you told me yourself, experience has taught you that alibis are not to be trusted.'

Which stopped the old judge in his tracks. 'You mean he wasn't in Paris?'

'I didn't say that. According to the police, his story checked out. But he wasn't entirely honest with them in other ways.'

Martin sat down again, frowning. 'What do you mean?'

'About why Lucie had dumped him.'

The Martins exchanged puzzled glances. 'I don't understand,' Madame Martin said. 'Dumped him?'

And for the first time it became clear to Enzo that no one, other than Lucie and Tavel, knew that their relationship had ended. He said, 'Lucie had met someone else. But it wasn't until Tavel followed her one night that he saw her with him.'

'Who?' Colour flushed high on Lucie's mother's cheeks.

'He didn't know him immediately. Not until after his arrest.' He paused. 'It was Régis Blanc.'

Enzo was unprepared for the ferocity with which the old man hammered his clenched fists down on the table, making plates and crockery jump. 'Rubbish!' Spittle gathered immediately on his lips, and his face flushed red. He stood up suddenly and his chair fell over behind him, clattering on the tiles. 'There is not the slightest possibility that my daughter was having a relationship with that man! Not a chance in hell, monsieur!'

'Guillaume . . .' Madame Martin reached a calming hand towards him, but if he saw it he ignored it.

'That boy, Tavel, is a waster and a liar –' he stabbed a finger at Enzo – 'and if you go spreading scurrilous rumours like that to sully the memory of my poor dead daughter I can assure you, monsieur, you will get not one iota of cooperation from me.'

All of Enzo's fatigue was banished in an instant. He stood up, taken aback by Martin's outburst. 'I'm only telling you what Tavel told me.'

'So why didn't he tell anyone at the time? It's just lies. Lies!'

Madame Martin had rounded the table and placed both hands on her husband's arm, crooking her elbow around his and looking up with great concern into the old man's face. 'Calm yourself, Guillaume. Monsieur Macleod's just doing his job. I'm sure that nothing said between us will go any further than this room.' She glanced at Enzo for confirmation, and he shrugged noncommittally, hoping that Martin might interpret that as an affirmative. There was no way he could guarantee keeping any of his findings private. 'Now, you go and make that copy of the autopsy report for Monsieur Macleod, and I'll pour you a small cognac.'

Martin took a moment to control himself, breathing stertorously through his nose. And then he swivelled and strode out of the kitchen.

His wife took a deep breath and turned towards Enzo. 'I am so sorry, monsieur. Guillaume has always been inclined to a quick temper, and when it comes to anything to do with Lucie he'll not hear a word against her.' She righted Martin's chair and sat down where he had been sitting, gazing off into space. 'Personally, I always thought Richard was a rather nice young man.' She turned worried eyes on Enzo. 'Did he really say he'd seen Lucie with that man?'

Enzo nodded, and she lowered her eyes to stare at her hands in front of her. 'Oh dear,' was all she said.

Enzo sat down and reached for the bottle of Saint-Emilion, pouring another glass with slightly trembling hands. Martin's reaction, at the end of a long and difficult day, had caught him off balance and a little more alcohol seemed like a good idea.

'I'll pour us all a cognac,' Madame Martin said, and she stood and went off to get glasses and a bottle. When she returned, she poured generous measures into the glasses, and she and Enzo sat in awkward silence, waiting for her husband to return.

It was nearly fifteen minutes before Martin came back into the kitchen clutching a photocopy of his daughter's autopsy – a meagre document, which led Enzo to wonder what had taken him so long to copy it. All trace of his temper tantrum had vanished, and he handed Enzo the document as if nothing had happened. 'It's not very long,' he said. 'The *médecin légiste* had, in truth, very little to work on. And I'm not sure you'll find much illumination from it. I have read it many times. I keep imagining I'll see something I've missed. But I never do.'

'I've poured us a brandy,' Madame Martin said, holding out a glass towards him.

But he waved it aside. 'I've had enough tonight, Mireille. It's time for bed, I think. Don't you agree, Monsieur Macleod?' And no matter how much Enzo might have enjoyed a glass or two of cognac, his host was making it clear that their evening was over.

\*

For the second night running Enzo sat up in his bed at Château Gandolfo, unable to sleep. An hour ago he would have drifted away the moment his eyes closed, but Martin's outburst had brought the events of the day back into sharp focus, and he couldn't stop it all going round and round in his mind. Bétaille's cool assertion that none of the Bordeaux Six, including Lucie, could be linked to Régis Blanc's short, lethal and completely inexplicable killing spree. Richard Tavel's revelation that Lucie had dropped him for a relationship with Blanc – something that chimed very much with Enzo's reading of intimacy in Blanc's letter. His adventure, or misadventure, at Château Duras. Who had left him that note, and why had they wanted to meet him? And then Martin's extraordinary display of temper at the merest suggestion of a romantic link between Lucie and Blanc. What concerned Enzo most was that everything he had learned in the course of today had brought no greater clarity. If anything, he had simply stirred up more mud in the water.

He turned, finally, to the autopsy report lying on the quilt beside him. It weighed almost nothing as he lifted it. A life summed up in a few pages of observation gleaned from a handful of bones. And it didn't take long to read. Identity had been confirmed by comparing teeth with dental records. DNA had not been required. The three hyoid bones had been recovered individually, and it was impossible to tell whether or not they had been separated by force in the act of strangulation, or whether they had subsequently separated as the soft tissue

decayed or was eaten by fish. But there was no doubt that the left, greater horn, or cornu, had been fractured, as in one of Blanc's victims. Cause of death, however, was impossible to determine.

Enzo knew that a baby was born with 270 bones, some of which would gradually fuse together, leaving it with 206 as a mature adult. Lucie would not have reached full skeletal maturity at the age of twenty, and so she would have had more than 206 bones. Only 178 were actually recovered.

But what most interested Enzo was a fracture to the left side of the skull, which the pathologist had attributed to damage done when it was being retrieved from the mud. According to his report it had been necessary to dig the bones out of the dried silt in the exposed bed of the lake, and whoever had been sent to do it had been less than careful with the blade of his shovel.

Unfortunately, the photocopied photographs that accompanied the report were not clear enough to allow Enzo to examine the fracture. It seemed to him extraordinarily careless to have damaged the skull in that way, when the bones would almost certainly have been considered those of a murder victim. And yet in all likelihood it would have been a low-ranking gendarme without crime-scene training who had been dispatched to do the job. So was it really that surprising? Still, Enzo was troubled, and knew that he was going to have to pursue it further.

Finally, he slipped the report on to the bedside table and

switched off the light. He turned over on to his right side, pulling his left leg up into a semi-foetal position, his right leg stretched out towards the foot of the bed, and closed his eyes. Several minutes later he opened them again. Sleep was a long way off, and he knew it. And so he sat up, turned on the light again and pulled a book from his bag. There was nothing like a good book to fill those endless hours of a sleepless night, and a murder mystery by Scots author Val McDermid seemed like a good distraction.

He wasn't sure when sleep had finally crept up on him, but he woke at four a.m. with his book lying open on the floor and his neck stiff from sleeping at an impossible angle. The bedside light was still burning, and he thought he couldn't have been asleep for long. He turned it out and curled up again, as he had done several hours earlier. And again, within minutes, knew that he was not going to re-enter the land of nod.

With a sigh of frustration he sat up once more, swinging his legs out of bed and crossing to the window, moonlight flooding in across bare floorboards. It was a painfully clear night. With no light pollution for miles around, the sky was the deepest inky black, crusted by many more stars than he ever knew existed. The Milky Way was like a cloud brush-stroked into the fabric and texture of it. And suddenly he felt the need of air. He wanted to be out there, under that sky, free of the confines of this room, this château, these people. Free to think with clarity.

He dressed quickly and made his way tentatively down the stairs, careful not to make a noise. The Martins, he knew, slept in another part of the house, but he did not want to waken them.

The door in the hallway at the foot of the stairs was locked, but the key was still in it, and he turned it to let himself out. He felt the cold on his face immediately, and buttoned his jacket and turned up his collar.

He took the path that followed the original Roman road along the front of the house, and stepped on to grass that was silver with dew. If the temperature dropped any lower it would freeze, and the day would dawn in a few short hours to a landscape blanketed white with frost.

Retracing the route that he and Martin had taken the other day on their return from the lake, he descended the hill into the darkness of the woods. Fractured moonlight fell between myriad branches casting deep shadows in the undergrowth. But it was easy enough to follow the animal track that led down towards the water.

A sudden noise brought him to a standstill, and he listened intently. Nothing. And for a moment he began to doubt that he had heard anything at all. Then, there it was again. Something or someone moving through the trees, not twenty metres away. Slow, cautious steps. And Enzo felt his heart rate rising, perspiration beading his forehead in spite of the cold. Suddenly, those careful steps turned into a run and came crashing towards him, and he very nearly cried out. A white

stag materialised suddenly in the moonlight, stopping unexpectedly on the path, almost within touching distance.

Enzo gazed at it with a mixture of astonishment, and relief, and then pure awe. It seemed huge, breath bursting in condensing clouds from its nostrils, its coat washed almost silver in the moonlight. Enzo had never seen a white stag before, but he knew the legend. An old Scottish folk tale. That if you saw a white stag, someone close to you was going to die. And he stood transfixed, staring at the creature, which stared back at him with large, round, black eyes. Its antlers moved through broken light as it tilted its head, unblinking in its gaze, and Enzo could not imagine what it was thinking. Was it scared? Bemused? Angry at this night intruder invading its territory? It coughed into the night and scraped the path with its hoof, and Enzo could not bring himself to move. Then it turned, without another sound, and went crashing off through the woods, vanishing somewhere down near the lake, where Enzo could see flashes of broken black water reflecting the moonlight.

He stood, breathing heavily for some minutes, watching his own breath billowing in front of him. He was not a superstitious man, and he did not believe in the supernatural, but there was something about this encounter with the white stag in the dark of the woods, miles from anywhere, that left him feeling deeply unsettled. And a shiver ran through him that was not attributable to the cold.

Finally, he shook himself free of the spell that the stag had

somehow cast, and he carried on down towards the water's edge. When he reached the point where the trees opened out to reveal the expanse of still lake that filled the valley, he saw mist rising gently from its surface, like smoke, filtering moonlight through spectral gauze.

This was Lucie's final resting place. Her killer had dumped her body in the deepest part of the lake, never imagining that one day the water would dry up in the summer heat to reveal his handiwork. But how, Enzo wondered, did he know where the deepest part of the lake was? Was it just chance, or did it suggest local knowledge?

The relationships in this penultimate case from Raffin's book were endlessly complex. There were the Bordeaux Six, of which Lucie was one. Their links to the serial killer, Blanc, who might or might not have been responsible for their deaths or disappearances. Tavel, the jilted lover who was unusually anxious that his wife knew nothing about his involvement with Lucie, even though it was more than twenty years ago. The love letter from Blanc himself, which seemed so totally out of character with anything anyone knew about him. And then Tavel's assertions that Blanc and Lucie were involved in a secret affair that no one else appeared to know about. And, of course, Lucie's father, determined to defend her honour by denying the remotest possibility that Blanc and his daughter had been having an affair, despite it lending credence to his belief that it was Blanc who had killed her.

Enzo pushed his hands deep in his pockets and trudged around the edge of the lake to the man-made barrier at the west end of it, where he crossed to the other side. From there he climbed up a chalk track to a farm road that ran around the perimeter of a vineyard, its remaining leaves flaming red, discernible even in the colourless light of the moon.

Following the farm road, he came across the metalled single-track that climbed the hill from the main route into Duras, and he could see the lights of the town twinkling in the distance.

Richard Tavel and Lucie had been going out together for years. This would all be familiar territory to him. Local knowledge. If he had been up here before, perhaps many times, wouldn't he know which was the deepest part of the lake? And how easy would it have been to drive here, unseen from the main road below, just a handful of kilometres from where he lived in Duras? Except that he had been in Paris the Saturday Lucie went missing. Or so the story went. Impossible to disprove now, after all these years.

By the time he had made his way back down to the lake, the first light was dawning in the sky, and the mist rising from the water that filled the valley. As he crossed the lake, trees grew, wraithlike, out of the hillside, and Enzo imagined that this was how it all must have looked at the very dawn of time.

Climbing up through the trees, he kept a wary eye open for the stag which had so startled him in the dark, and the sense

of foreboding it had provoked returned to him now. But there was no sign of it.

When he emerged on to the open hillside he saw that it was frosted white, as he had imagined earlier, and he was struck by a sudden clarity which seemed forged out of the cold and his lack of sleep.

There was only one person alive who knew the truth about the relationship, alleged by Tavel, between Lucie and Blanc. Régis Blanc himself. And there was only one way to find out what he knew, which was to ask him. But since Blanc was still incarcerated in the high-security *maison centrale* prison at Lannemezan, Enzo also knew that getting access to him would be next to impossible.

When he got back to the house he saw lights on in the kitchen, and as he stepped inside breathed in the smell of warm bread and *pâtisseries*.

Martin looked up, surprised, when Enzo pushed open the door into the kitchen. He was brewing coffee on a worktop by the fridge. 'You're up early. Sleep well?'

'No,' Enzo said. 'Hardly at all. I've been out walking.'

Martin cocked an eyebrow. 'Cold out there. You could probably do with a coffee. And I'm heating some croissants in the oven.'

'That would be fantastic,' Enzo said, and he sat down at the end of the table, rubbing his hands to try to get the blood circulating in them again.

Martin delivered a basket of croissants to the table and

placed a mug of steaming hot coffee in front of Enzo, who gulped down a burning mouthful of it before dipping in the end of a croissant and filling his mouth with soft, buttery pastry. Martin watched him and smiled. 'You've been in France too long, monsieur!'

He pulled up a seat and dunked a croissant of his own. 'Mireille won't be up for a while yet. She's not an early riser.' A trail of drips fell on the table as he transferred the soggy pastry to his mouth.

Enzo eyed him a little warily, anxious not to arouse the ire of the previous night, but knew there were questions he still had to ask. He took another mouthful of croissant. 'What happened to Lucie's bones?'

Martin just shrugged. 'They're buried in the garden.' He took in Enzo's surprise, and explained, 'We have a family graveyard out there. Goes back about three hundred years. Most of my ancestors are buried in it.' He stood up. 'Come on, I'll show you.'

Enzo stood reluctantly. He would rather Martin just told him about it, so he could stay in here, in the warmth, with his coffee and croissant. But the old man crossed to the back door and opened it to let in a rush of cold air, and Enzo was obliged to follow him outside.

Beyond a stone terrace and a thick grove of tall bamboo in full leaf, a small graveyard nestled in the shadow of high hedges on three sides, and the ivy-covered wall of the old *chai* on the fourth. Fallen leaves, frosted and brittle, crunched

underfoot, and Enzo saw a shambles of moss-green gravestones set randomly into the ground.

Martin knelt down to scrape away the moss and lichen that covered the stone plaques on the gravestones, and took Enzo through the litany of ancestors who lay here, going all the way back to some of Gandolfo's earliest successors.

Some of the stones had circular holes set into them. As he stood up again, Martin explained, 'On the anniversary of each death, the descendants of the dead would come to the grave with a bottle of wine which they would share in a toast to the deceased. Then they would leave the remaining wine in the hole, here, so that the departed could have a drink with their also departed friends.' He grinned. 'They always had a good excuse for a drink.'

Then his smile faded as he turned to the most recent of the stones. It had been kept free of growth and discolouration, and the inscription on the plaque was clearly legible: *Lucie Martin, beloved daughter of Guillaume and Mireille (1969–1989)*.

'Just a handful of bones,' he said. 'That's all we had to bury.' And, with some rancour, 'They took away her whole skull for the dental comparison and we never got it back. I wrote several times and didn't even get a reply.' He turned towards Enzo, who could see him containing his anger with difficulty. 'I rather suspect they mislaid it. But we went ahead and buried her anyway. The skull is lost, and I wouldn't open up the grave again to bury it with the other bones, even if we had it. That would seem like sacrilege now. Let her rest in peace, I say.'

# CHAPTER THIRTEEN

The room was cold, and Bertrand and Sophie had spent their second night of captivity huddled together under the blankets they had been given, on a mattress that was lumpy and damp. Now, the first light of day was angling in through the bars set into the window frame high up on the wall behind them. But, as yet, it had brought no warmth.

Bertrand felt Sophie shivering in his arms. She had cried off and on during the night. The previous day they had talked for hours in desperate whispers. Speculating on why they were here, who their captors might be, what it was they wanted. But, when speculation was exhausted, bringing neither insight nor illumination, they had fallen silent, both slipping into a deep despond from which it was proving hard to rouse themselves. Their sense of complete helplessness was absolute. A feeling so alien to Bertrand that he was consumed by frustration and anger, much of it directed at himself.

A routine of sorts had been established during the course of that first day. The men would bring them food on a tray, shouting from the other side of the door that they should

retreat to the far wall before they would open the door. Bertrand didn't know how, but he was pretty sure their captors could see them, because the door would not open until they had done as instructed.

When the door was opened, one man would step in and crouch to leave the tray on the floor. A second stood in the doorway, watching. Both still wearing ski masks.

The food was poor-quality. Stale bread, tubs of yoghurt, mugs of bitter, stewed coffee and a scattering of sugar lumps. Still, they wolfed it down, hunger setting in again long before the next tray was delivered.

If either of them needed the toilet, they had to bang on the door and shout until someone came. Then they would be told, again, to stand against the far wall. When the door opened, one or other would be beckoned into the corridor and led off by two men to a filthy toilet at the far end. There was no lock on the door, and little privacy, and they were given minimal time to do what was required. There was no toilet paper. Only cold water was available in a cracked and dirty sink for washing hands or face, and there was no towel.

Sophie turned her head to look at Bertrand lying on the mattress beside her. Her face was pale, almost grey, deep shadows etched in half-moons beneath her eyes, and she seemed to retreat even further into the blankets. The look of abject misery in her eyes filled Bertrand with love and anger in equal measure. They had no right to treat his beautiful, innocent little Sophie like this. He tightened his arms around

her and drew her closer, wishing that he did not feel so utterly impotent.

'Against the wall!' The now familiar voice bellowed at them from the other side of the door.

Bertrand and Sophie scrambled stiffly to their feet, bones and muscles aching and joints frozen, and stood against the back wall below the window. Obedience meant food, and they were both weak with hunger.

They heard the key turning in the lock, and then the door was kicked violently open, slamming back against the wall. There was only one of them this time. Usually a second man would lean watchfully against the door jamb as the first laid the tray on the floor. But there was no second man, and the corridor beyond was dark and empty.

The man with the tray crouched to set it on the floor and Bertrand sprang at him, uncertain on what reserves of energy and strength he was drawing, but fuelled by the anger that had been simmering deep inside him. He caught the man full in the midriff with his shoulder as he stood up, and, behind him, heard Sophie scream as the two men crashed out of the room and slammed into the far wall of the corridor. A burst of rotten breath exploded in Bertrand's face, and he heard the man's involuntary grunt discharge itself through his mask. Bertrand balled his fist and went for the soft midriff again, only to feel pain fill his head. The power of a solid blow to the side of his face knocked him over. He sprawled heavily on the concrete floor, before hands grabbed him, swinging him

around to bang up hard against the wall. A forehead as hard as brick smashed into his face, and through his blood and tears he saw angry green eyes behind slits in a mask, and a voice hissed, 'Little fucker!'

Bertrand had no idea where the second man had come from, and guessed he must simply have been lingering a little further along the corridor. Attacking the man with the tray without a plan had been a bad idea, and he was paying for it now. The first man picked himself off the floor, cursing violently, and sank his fist into Bertrand's stomach. Once. Twice. Until Bertrand fell to his knees, retching. The second man kicked him over on to his side, and the two of them grabbed him and threw him back into the room.

Sophie was kneeling beside him in an instant, weeping almost uncontrollably, shocked by the blood oozing from his nose and mouth. The man who had brought the tray swung a foot at it, turning it over and spilling coffee and yoghurt across the floor. He spat into the dust and said, 'That's your breakfast. You want to eat, you can eat it off the floor.' And he pulled the door shut, the sound of it slamming closed echoing violently around the room.

# CHAPTER FOURTEEN

The Institut Médico-Légale in Bordeaux – or the morgue, as it might be described in detective novels – was part of the Groupe Hospitalier Pellegrin on the campus of Bordeaux University. Here, soulless concrete buildings in not quite fifty shades of grey congregated around a network of roads and flyovers carved out of the heart of what had once been old Bordeaux. The elegance of the past replaced by the functionality of the present.

Enzo waited a long time in a sterile reception area, breathing in antiseptic and sitting on a hard plastic seat watching the comings and goings. This was a busy place. Death was doing good business. A nurse behind the reception desk kept a watchful eye on him until eventually a young pathologist in a pristine white coat pushed through swing doors and walked towards him, hand outstretched. Enzo stood and the two men exchanged a cursory handshake.

'I'm told you're looking for Dr Bonnaric,' the pathologist said.

'That's right. You're him?' Enzo frowned. He seemed a little young to have carried out an autopsy in 2003.

'No. I'm sorry, Dr Bonnaric passed away a number of years ago. Before my time, I'm afraid.'

'Oh.' Enzo's heart sank. This looked like being another dead end. He fished in his shoulder bag to pull out Martin's photo-copied autopsy report, well thumbed and dog-eared now. 'He carried out this autopsy eight years ago.'

The pathologist took the document reluctantly, but kept his eyes on Enzo. 'And you are?'

'Enzo Macleod. I run the forensics department at Paul Sabatier University in Toulouse.'

The young man raised an eyebrow. Enzo knew he didn't look like someone who ran a forensics department and so fumbled in his pocket to find a business card. He handed it to the pathologist.

'I've been investigating a series of cold cases here in France. I'm currently working on the murder of Lucie Martin, daughter of the retired judge Guillaume Martin. She disappeared in 1989 and her remains were found in a lake in 2003.' He nodded towards the autopsy report in the young man's hands. 'Dr Bonnaric conducted that autopsy on her and retained the skull for the purposes of identifying the victim from dental records.' He paused. 'He never returned it.'

The pathologist frowned. 'Returned what?'

'The skull.'

'Oh.'

'The judge would like it back. Apparently he wrote several times, without response.'

'Oh,' the young man said again. And this time seemed a little embarrassed. 'Well, that's unfortunate.' He looked at the front page of the report. 'At least we have a case number here. I'll see if I can track it down. Would you like to come back in, say –' he checked his watch – 'a couple of hours?'

Enzo rode the tram east through town, standing room only, clutching an upright and watching the city spool past the windows of his carriage. Now that they had left the concrete campus behind them, the old city reasserted itself in all its eighteenth- and nineteenth-century glory. Ahead, he could see the tall spire of the elegant Cathédrale Saint-André, but stepped off the tram on the Cours Maréchal Juin to cross to the architectural curiosity that was the Palais de Justice. The courthouse was an ugly building with grey skeletal uprights supporting curved, overhanging eves above rows of blue slats – imitation shutters shielding the acres of glass from which the Palais seemed almost wholly constructed.

Its frontage abutted on to what looked like the original prison and sat elevated on a stone-clad plinth. Beyond a sign which read *Tribunal de Grande Instance*, steps led up over a water feature to a glazed public ambulatory, through which seven courtrooms could be seen rising in bizarre tapering towers, a grotesque parody of the medieval spires all around. The concept, Enzo imaged, was that justice was being seen to be done.

He waited on the steps with his back to the building, gazing by preference down a street of honey-gold stone and

black-painted wrought iron, and wondered what had happened to man's sense of the aesthetic. It seemed, these days, that concept was more important than character, and the result less than edifying. Sophie, he knew, would tell him he was just old and locked in the past. And maybe, he thought, she was right. Maybe it was time to pass it all on to the next generation and let them do their worst. After all, Enzo's lot had already done theirs.

'Monsieur Macleod?'

Enzo turned to find himself looking into a lugubrious face with wild, black, curling eyebrows beneath a shock of wiry white hair. It was a big, fleshy face, with silver fuse-wire growing out of nostrils and ears. It belonged to a large man standing on the step above Enzo and towering over him. He wore the long black gown of the French *avocat*, with its broad flash of white *col* hanging down from the neck.

'Maître Imbert?'

'Yes.' He shuffled impatiently. 'I don't have much time.'

'How on earth did you recognise me?' Enzo said.

'Monsieur, there can be hardly anyone working in the French justice system who does not know your face by now.'

Enzo smiled. 'Well, thank you for meeting me.'

There was no smile in return, and no handshake. 'Like I said, monsieur, I am pressed for time. What can I do for you?'

In the absence of any of Maître Imbert's precious time to soften the request, Enzo came straight out with it. 'I'd like you to arrange for me to see Régis Blanc.'

And for the first time the hint of a smile rearranged gross features. 'Monsieur, just because you have successfully resolved four of Raffin's cold cases does not mean that you are going to pin the murder of Lucie Martin on my client.'

'That's not why I want to see him.'

The eyebrows of the *avocat* gathered in a tangle above his nose as he frowned. 'Then why *do* you want to see him? Is this something to do with the Bordeaux Six?'

'No. Although I have met with the parents and looked at their files.'

'Time wasters and fantasists.'

Enzo found a seed of anger stirring inside him. 'Actually, those parents are just as much victims as their daughters.'

'Not victims of Blanc.'

'No, I agree.'

Maître Imbert seemed taken aback. 'Really?'

'If Michel Bétaille couldn't find any connections between Blanc and the disappearance or murder of those girls in two years of investigation, I'm inclined to think there aren't any.'

'So what do you want with Blanc?'

'I found his letter to Lucie oddly touching, Maître. I know he claims to have written it while drunk, but I doubt that. A drunk man, released from his natural inhibitions, would have expressed himself more freely, and perhaps more crudely. Blanc had real difficulty.'

Imbert's thick pale lips curled in what looked like a sneer. 'Blanc was not exactly what I would have called literate,

Monsieur Macleod.' He clearly didn't think much of his client.

'I don't mean the words he used. I'm talking about the emotions he expressed.'

Imbert sighed. 'Is there a point to this anywhere in our future?'

'New evidence has come to light suggesting that Lucie and Blanc had a romantic liaison.'

Now Imbert laughed out loud. 'Nonsense!'

'I have a witness.'

'Who?'

Enzo just smiled. 'They were seen together in a café, kissing and holding hands.'

The frown returned in another meeting of eyebrows. 'And you want to ask Blanc if it's true?'

Enzo inclined his head.

'He'll not tell you.'

'But you'll get me in to see him?'

'No, I will not. I'm far too busy to bother myself with a case that's more than twenty years old. Blanc killed those girls and now he's serving life, and that's an end to it.' He turned away on the steps, then paused and turned back. 'Why don't you ask your friend, Charlotte Roux?'

Now it was Enzo's turn to frown. 'Charlotte?'

'You and Raffin are pretty thick with her, aren't you? Certainly, if the papers are to be believed.'

'How could Charlotte get me access to Régis Blanc?'

The smile spreading the thick lips of the *avocat* was smug now. 'She's a regular visitor. I had to clear it with Blanc myself. One of a group of forensic psychologists doing some kind of study on the long-term effect of prison on lifers.' He paused, his smile widening. 'Didn't she tell you?'

Enzo walked back to the Institut Médico-Légale in a daze. He buttoned up his jacket against the cold and pushed his hands deep into his pockets, oblivious of his fellow pedestrians. Twice he crossed the road when the lights were at red, to a cacophony of klaxons.

Why wouldn't Charlotte have told him that she had visited Blanc in Lannemezan prison? But no matter how many times he asked himself, he could not come up with a satisfactory answer. She must have known that he would find out sooner or later – certainly as soon as he embarked on the Lucie Martin case. In addition to her training as a psychologist, Charlotte had spent two years in the United States studying forensic psychology. Her help was even solicited on occasion by the Paris police, when those particular talents were in demand, and so it was not unnatural that she should be participating in a prisoner study. What *was* unnatural was that she hadn't told him.

He drew long, deep breaths as he walked, to control his anger. It was not beyond the bounds of possibility that she was simply being bloody-minded. Where Enzo was concerned, it seemed she took great pleasure these days in baiting him. And

he could just imagine her supercilious response to his asking the question. But ask it he was determined to do. Besides which, it looked now like she might be his only way of getting to speak to Blanc himself.

He had walked off most of his anger by the time he reached the Hôpital Pellegrin and the young pathologist came to meet him in reception. He was carrying a square, cream cardboard box, which he set down on the chair next to where Enzo had been sitting. 'That's her,' he said. 'The box had been incorrectly labelled and misfiled in the *greffe*. It was pure chance that I found it.'

Enzo sat down beside it. 'May I take a look?'

'Of course.'

Enzo removed the lid and reached in to cup his hands carefully around the skull and lift it out. It had been wired together where separated and came out in one piece. Held in his hands like this, it felt incredibly small and delicate. The last trace on this earth of what had once been a vibrant, attractive young girl who, if Tavel was to be believed, had fallen in love with a serial killer. But the more he learned, the less inclined Enzo was to believe that it was Blanc who had killed her.

He looked into the large, dark, empty sockets from which her blue eyes had once viewed a world full of possibility, and gazed with love upon a man who had killed at least three times. Eyes which had seen her killer, filled perhaps with terror in the moments before her murder. He almost hoped that holding her skull like this might communicate something

of that to him. But all he felt was cold bone on warm skin, and something faintly sinister in the sense of cupping the head of a dead human being in his hands.

He turned it to examine the fracture on its left side, just above the temple. The bone was broken here, a piece of it missing, and Enzo realised how easy it would be to damage something so fragile.

The pathologist said, 'I read the autopsy report. Just out of interest. He was wrong, you know.'

Enzo looked at him, startled. 'Who?'

'Bonnaric. I don't like to speak ill of the dead, but he was no anthropologist.'

'I'm sorry, I don't understand.'

The young man smiled. 'Forensic anthropology. That's my particular specialty. Bonnaric wrote in his report that the damage to the skull was likely caused during the process of its recovery from the lake. That's not the case.'

Enzo looked in astonishment at Lucie's head in his hands and then back at the pathologist. 'How can you know that?'

He reached out for the skull. 'May I?'

Enzo handed it to him and stood up.

The pathologist turned the fracture towards them and ran his finger along the broken edge. 'There, you see?'

And Enzo saw immediately. He said, 'The edge of the break is stained.'

'Exactly. The broken edges would have got dirty during recovery, yes, but if Bonnaric had cleaned them properly, he

would have seen that they weren't just superficially dirty. The staining is deeply ingrained in the fabric of the skull.'

'So the fracture pre-dates the discovery of the body.'

'Indeed. And was therefore probably inflicted while the victim was still alive. If the damage had been done – by, say, a shovel – when it was being dug out of the mud, the break would have been clean and unstained.'

Enzo stared at it, absorbing the implications.

The young man smiled and said, 'It's like an ice-cream bar, really. If you break it and then dip it in chocolate, it's covered in chocolate even along the break. Compare that to an ice-cream bar dipped in chocolate and broken later. The break will be clean ice cream. *Et voilà.*' He shrugged. 'It's not rocket science.'

Enzo's mind was racing with all the new possibilities this development presented. 'So that means the blow that did this damage could have been the cause of death?'

'Very easily. Given the nature of it.' He handed the skull back to Enzo, who gazed at Lucie for several long moments before returning her to the cardboard box. Then he looked at the forensic anthropologist again.

'I wonder if I could ask you a very big favour?'

'What?' The young man inclined his head as if to say, *Have I not done enough?*

'One theory about how Lucie died is that she was a victim of the serial killer Régis Blanc, who murdered his victims by strangling them, separating the hyoid bone and breaking part of it in the process.'

'Which is how Dr Bonnaric thought Lucie might have died.'

'Exactly. But Blanc also sedated his victims with the date-rape drug, Rohypnol – Flunitrazepam – which is one of a class of benzodiazepines. I've read that it is possible to detect these drugs in bone, and not just the marrow.'

The doctor nodded. 'Yes. Easier in the marrow of fresh bone. But it is also possible to detect some drugs in cortical bone.' He glanced at Lucie's skull in the box. 'You would take a little bone and grind it into powder. If there were traces of Rohypnol in it, they would be detectable.' He looked at Enzo. 'You would like me to do that.' It was a statement, not a question.

Enzo nodded.

He sighed. 'I can't guarantee that I would be able to find the time or the resources.'

'No, I understand that. But if you could . . .' Enzo let his sentence hang. Then he said, 'You've got my card.' He paused. 'So, I'll leave Lucie with you.'

# CHAPTER FIFTEEN

Enzo left Bordeaux just after midday, arriving in Paris shortly before seven. He had stopped only once, and was stiff and tired when finally he left his 2CV in the car park at Rue Soufflot and walked to Raffin's apartment in the Rue de Tournon.

For once there was no piano playing as he crossed the shining wet cobbles of the interior courtyard and climbed wearily to the first floor. Somehow it always seemed to be raining in Paris in autumn. To his disappointment Kirsty and his grandson were not there.

'They've been away all afternoon visiting a friend of Kirsty's in the eighth,' Raffin said. He stood for a moment in the doorway before reluctantly opening it wide to let Enzo in. If there had ever once been warmth between them, it had long since dissipated.

In the *séjour* Enzo saw an almost empty bottle of Pouilly Fumé on the table, and a single glass with half an inch of honey-coloured white wine remaining in the bottom of it. There was a glassy quality, he noticed then, to Raffin's usually clear green eyes, and he spoke slowly, with the studied

concentration of a man trying to convince you that he had not drunk too much. Drinking too much had pretty well characterised Raffin since his shooting, here in this very apartment, and Enzo, though still nurturing a sense of guilt, worried for the future of his daughter and grandson. 'I've just driven from Bordeaux,' he said.

Raffin raised an eyebrow. 'That's quite a drive. I'm flattered you'd come all this way just to see me.'

Enzo gave him a look. 'Actually, I've come to see Charlotte,' he said, and saw Raffin stiffen. The journalist was still, inexplicably, jealous of Enzo's relationship with her, even although it had long since turned sour. Enzo dipped into his bag to pull out the folders given him by the Bordeaux Six, and his copy of Lucie's autopsy report. 'And I wanted to give you these. Or, at least, let you take copies for your files.'

Raffin glanced at them. 'Oh, yes. The Bordeaux Six.'

'I'm surprised you weren't tempted to include more of them in the book.'

Raffin shrugged. 'Lucie's was the only one of real interest. And four of them were just missing, still alive for all we know. Although, probably not.'

'And the girl stabbed to death in that hotel room?'

Raffin pulled a face. 'Again. Not very interesting. A prostitute murdered in a sexual frenzy by some lowlife client. Not the sort of mystery to engage my readers.' He flicked through them. 'But I'll take copies. You never know when you might find something interesting.'

Enzo followed Raffin through to his study, where the journalist ran off duplicates of the six files on his high-speed copier. He looked at Lucie's autopsy report.

'I haven't seen this before. Can't imagine there's anything very interesting in it.'

'Then you'd be wrong,' Enzo said, and for the first time he saw that Raffin's interest was piqued.

The two men went back through to the sitting room, and as Raffin spread out the contents of the six copied files on the dining table to examine in more detail, Enzo told him about the fractured skull, written off by the original pathologist as collateral damage and now reassessed as the possible cause of death.

Raffin looked at him, his eyes suddenly clear and shining. 'Well that changes everything, doesn't it? If a blow to the head was the cause of death, it means that her killer strangled her post-mortem to make it look like it was Blanc.'

But Enzo shook his head. 'She disappeared the day before Blanc was arrested.'

'Yes, but it was well publicised that those prostitutes had been strangled, that the hyoid bones had separated and fractured.'

'True – but until Blanc's arrest nobody knew it was him.'

'So the killer was simply trying to make it look like the work of whoever had murdered the prostitutes, without knowing it was Blanc.' Raffin was clearly irritated by Enzo's constant contradictions.

'Which would be an extraordinary coincidence,' Enzo said. 'Given that Blanc had written to Lucie, and that, according to her ex-boyfriend, he had been having a relationship with her.'

This set Raffin back on his heels. 'What? When did you learn that?'

'A couple of days ago.'

'He told you?'

Enzo nodded. 'Under a little duress.'

Raffin drew him a curious look, but his excitement at the revelation was patent. 'This is new. It's going to make a great story.' He paused. 'So you think that Blanc might have killed her after all?'

Enzo stroked his jaw thoughtfully and felt the bristles on his chin, realising he hadn't shaved for two days. He said, 'There's no way to know if that blow to the head killed Lucie or not. It might just have rendered her unconscious, and then she was strangled. After all, Blanc drugged his prostitutes with Rohypnol before strangling them. If you strangle someone, I guess you have to look them in the eye as you do it. And they look back at you. Maybe Blanc didn't like that.'

'So you do think it was Blanc?'

Enzo released a long, slow breath and ran his eyes sightlessly around the room, as if searching for inspiration in facts to back up his instinct. When he couldn't find any, he looked at Raffin and said, 'Actually, I don't.'

He was saved from having to provide a rationale for his instinct by the sound of the door opening out in the hall. Cold

air rushed in as Kirsty, with Alexis in her arms, manhandled a pushchair through from the landing.

'Oh hi, Papa,' she said, handing Alexis to Raffin before throwing her arms around her father. Enzo noticed that, although Alexis was six months old now, Raffin still seemed uncomfortable holding him. But Kirsty was looking over her father's shoulder at the mess of papers on the table. She stood back and, with a twinkle in her dark brown, liquid eyes, said, 'I see, once again, that Alexis and I were the reason for your visit.'

Enzo grinned. 'Always.' And he reached across to relieve Raffin from the burden of holding his grandson. Alexis chuckled and chortled as Enzo held him with the expertise of an experienced father and bounced him lightly up and down. Grandfather and grandson rubbed noses, and Enzo felt how cold the baby's face was.

Kirsty crossed to the table, divesting herself of coat and scarf, to look at the photocopied documents and photographs that covered it. 'Oh, by the way,' she said. 'We've got a date and time for the appointment with the hearing specialist in Biarritz.' She looked over her shoulder at Enzo. 'Two days after your birthday. Will you still be able to make it?'

Enzo said, 'Whatever else is happening, I'll make the time.' And he glanced at Raffin, who shuffled awkwardly in the knowledge that, unlike Enzo, he had made other things a priority.

Enzo turned back at the sound of Kirsty's voice. 'Who are

these girls?' She was lining up their photographs, one beside the other.

'Mostly prostitutes, either missing or dead,' Enzo said. He joined her at the table. 'Their parents think that Régis Blanc was responsible.'

'And was he?'

'Probably not.'

'Such sad faces,' Kirsty said, running her fingertips lightly over grainy facsimiles of once-living human beings. 'They'll be middle-aged by now.'

'If any of them are still alive,' Raffin said.

'And we know that two of them are dead,' Enzo told her.

Kirsty shook her head, almost unable to drag her eyes away from them. 'What a waste of lives.'

'Speaking of which . . .' Enzo turned back to Raffin. 'Did you know that Charlotte has been visiting Régis Blanc in Lannemezan prison?'

Raffin seemed startled. 'No, I did not. Why? I mean, why was she visiting him?'

'Some kind of study of long-term prisoners.'

Raffin shook his head. 'Then why didn't she tell us? She knew you would be working on the Martin case.'

Enzo's mouth set in a grim line. 'That's exactly what I'm on my way to ask her myself.'


'Because my life is my own and my work is confidential, and you have no rights of access to either.' Charlotte's words

were hostile, but her tone was indifferent, as if she didn't really care.

They were in the small kitchen, three steps down from the living area, in her sprawling home in the thirteenth. Charlotte sat back with a glass of wine, the remains of a light meal on the table in front of her.

'Don't you want to see Laurent? I've just put him down.'

'Stop trying to change the subject.'

'Ahhh,' she said, shaking her head. 'You see? Only when it suits you.'

But Enzo refused to be deflected. 'You knew I had started working on the Lucie Martin case, and yet you never thought to tell me that you had been visiting the man suspected of killing her. That you knew him personally. And given the number of times you've visited, probably know him better than anyone else in this world.'

She sat forward, angry now. 'In all the years I have known you, Enzo Macleod, you have never taken the least interest in my work. Except, of course, when it could be of some use to you. You're selfish and thoughtless and, frankly, with you there's always an ulterior motive.' She swallowed a mouthful of wine. 'Why would I even think of volunteering to provide you with information about my work? After all, if it was of any use to you, sooner or later you'd come looking for it.'

Enzo stood, face reddening, stung by her words. He was not so self-obsessed that he didn't realise there was some truth in them. 'I have never been anything but honest and totally open

with you, Charlotte,' he said. 'You're the one with the secrets. You're the one who guards your thoughts and emotions, the one who keeps things from me.'

She regarded him thoughtfully. 'And what is it *you're* keeping from *me*? The real reason for your visit, Enzo? The *ulterior* motive? I mean, you didn't drive all the way from Bordeaux to Paris just to accuse me of withholding information. Did you?'

Enzo reddened further. Charlotte always seemed to read him, like a large Métro map behind glass. Was his veneer really so transparent?

She smiled. 'I thought so. What is it you want this time?'

He took a moment to try to salvage, at least in his own mind, what was left of his pride. 'I want to talk to Blanc.'

A knowing smile spread across her face and she leaned back in her chair again. 'Of course you do. I should have seen that one coming.' She swirled the remains of her wine around in her glass, looking into it as if searching for enlightenment. 'To what end? To try and establish some kind of connection between him and Lucie Martin?'

'I don't have to establish anything. The links already exist.'

'Oh, do they? The famous letter that purports to be from Blanc to Lucie?'

'Oh, he wrote it alright. His handwriting. Confirmed by a graphologist.'

Which was clearly news to Charlotte. Her eyes lifted quickly from her glass to meet Enzo's. 'Really?' She thought about it for a moment. 'You said "links". Plural.'

'Lucie dumped her childhood sweetheart. He suspected a third party and followed her one night to see who.'

'Blanc?' Charlotte's eyes opened wide with amazement. And he could tell that, for the first time, he had really caught her interest. He could see her thinking rapidly behind guarded eyes. And she reached, it seemed, an equally fast decision. She drained her glass. 'Alright. I'll bring Laurent to your birthday party in Cahors. And if you can get someone to look after him, we'll drive down to Lannemezan the next day.'

'You can get me in to see him?'

'No guarantees, but I'll try.' She stood up. 'Will you stay over?'

Enzo was startled. 'What? Here?'

She shrugged. 'Of course.' Then paused. 'In the spare room, naturally.'

Enzo was stung, just as much as if she had slapped him, and he remembered the John Lennon song 'Girl', and just how easily Charlotte could manipulate him. He said determinedly, 'I'm staying over at the studio.'

She smiled with weary resignation. 'And he would pass up the chance to be with his boy, just so that he could snub Charlotte.'

He gave her a look. 'Snub Charlotte how?'

She raised both eyebrows. 'Did you really think I could bear to have you under my roof for a whole night and not also have you in my bed?'

# CHAPTER SIXTEEN

The trees in the Boulevard Léon Gambetta were finally beginning to shed. In just a few days, leaves had turned from yellow and green to orange and red, and a slight breeze rattling the branches sent them tumbling to gather in drifts along the pavements.

There was a chill in the breeze, too. Perhaps the first breath of winter to stir the air across the south-west. Enzo felt it when he stepped from his car in Cahors at the end of the second long drive in as many days. It was not the raw cold of a grey and humid Paris, but a crisper cold, like chilled wine on a summer's day. He loved the south-west in all its seasons, except winter. For when it came, finally, it stole away the softness of the light, and the land felt harsh and lifeless. And all that lay ahead were the long months of waiting for spring.

Leaves gathered, too, in the car park outside La Halle, the indoor market where Enzo bought all his fresh produce for cooking – just two steps from the door of his apartment. They crunched under his feet as he crossed the road and climbed narrow wooden stairs to the first floor.

'Hello?' he called, as he opened the door into the hallway. But there was no response. He glanced into the spare bedroom and saw that Nicole had made herself at home. A huge suitcase lay open on the floor, clothes strewn all over the bed. And Enzo wondered who she had enlisted to carry it up the stairs for her. He was glad not to have been around when she moved in.

He threw his holdall into his own room and went through to the *séjour*. Nicole had been busy. Every chair in the house, it seemed, was crammed into the living room. Occasional tables, card tables and footstools were scattered among them – laying space for drinks and nibbles. Beer mats covered every surface likely to be damaged by wet-bottomed glasses. Nicole was nothing if not fastidious.

Enzo had almost forgotten that his birthday was tomorrow. It had crept up on him so quickly, as birthdays seemed to do more and more with every passing year. But there had been other things on his mind during the long drive south, and he wanted now to write down all the thoughts he had been keeping in that crowded place that was his head. He moved several of Nicole's chairs and tables to clear a way to his whiteboard, which had long ago found a permanent place on the back wall of the living room. Sophie had objected, complaining that it ruined the room. But it was Enzo's way of visualising his thoughts. A graphic representation of them that he could take in at a glance.

He lifted a blue felt-tip pen and wrote *Régis Blanc* in the

centre of the board. And since Lucie was one of the Bordeaux Six, he wrote up each of their names around the whiteboard's perimeter. Above Blanc, he penned in the names of the three prostitutes he had murdered, and, below him, the name of Lucie's childhood sweetheart, Richard Tavel. These were the main players in the story so far, and he wanted to see what links there might be between them.

He drew an arrow between Blanc and Lucie, and then one back from her to him. Beside the first, he wrote *LOVE LETTER*. Beside the second, *MET AT RENTRÉE*. Then he drew arrows from Tavel to them both, noting his relationship to Lucie, and his claim to have seen Lucie with Blanc. There were plenty of other links, too. The most obvious of all between Blanc and the prostitutes he had strangled. The link between Blanc and the girl stabbed to death in the hotel room certainly existed, for he had once been her pimp. However, their connection was historical and therefore blurred, and so Enzo drew a squiggly arrow between them.

But the link that made the biggest impression on him was the one that led to the girl called Sally Linol, the one with the feather tattoo on her neck. She was connected not only to Blanc, but to the three dead prostitutes. Michel Bétaille didn't believe that Blanc had killed her, because she had cleaned out her apartment and vanished before the others were murdered. After all, why, when Blanc had dumped the other three in almost plain view, leaving clues that led directly back to him, would he have gone to the trouble of clearing out Sally's

apartment and hiding her body so well that it hadn't been found in more than twenty years?

But the big question was why had she run? Did she know or guess that something was about to happen to her friends? Was she scared that Blanc would have killed her too, and had simply gone to ground somewhere and never resurfaced?

Enzo guessed that, if he could find her, many of those questions would be answered. But, after all this time, he had no idea where to start looking. And, of course, there was no guarantee that she was even still alive.

Then he was struck for the first time by another question. Why had Blanc not made more of an effort to cover his tracks? He had murdered these three girls, dumping them on waste ground, where they were certain to be found. His fingerprints had been lifted from the necks of two of the girls, and were all over the purse of the third. He was known to be their pimp. He had no alibi. And police had found Rohypnol in his apartment, the same drug, Bétaille had told him, used to sedate the victims.

Enzo had always assumed that it was Blanc's crass stupidity or ignorance that had led to him being tied so quickly and easily to the murders. But Blanc could hardly have been a stupid man. He ran a successful prostitution ring, in the face of fierce competition. He was uneducated, perhaps, but streetwise, certainly. Why would he have made it such a simple task for the police to pin the murders on him?

Michel Bétaille had been obsessed with another why. Why

had he killed them, when it was so clearly out of character? He *liked* women, Bétaille had said. And yet he had never questioned the ease with which the evidence led straight back to Blanc, or why Blanc had never denied it in court.

Enzo gazed thoughtfully at his whiteboard and, in a circle next to Blanc's name, he wrote *DID HE WANT TO BE CAUGHT?*

'*Coucou!*' The sound of Nicole's voice crashed into his thoughts and dispersed them in random chaos to the four corners of his mind. Damn her! Just as he was coming close to some kind of epiphany.

'I'm busy, Nicole,' he called back, keen that she should hear the irritation in his tone.

But either she was oblivious, or chose to ignore it. She breezed cheerfully into the *séjour*. 'You're back.' As if he didn't know. 'I saw your car downstairs. It's got a parking ticket on it.'

Enzo closed his eyes and drew a deep breath, resisting the temptation, born of a Glasgow upbringing, to curse loudly.

'Oh, for heaven's sake!' Nicole's tone was chiding now. 'You've been moving things around in here. It took me ages to get this place set up.' And she started pulling chairs and tables back to where they had been, trapping Enzo at his whiteboard.

'Nicole, I'm trying to work.' Each word was enunciated slowly, through clenched teeth.

'And so am I. Your birthday's tomorrow, remember. I've been organising the food and drink. The *traiteurs* will be here in the morning.'

'Nicole, we really don't need caterers to celebrate an

unremarkable birthday. We could just go downstairs and have pizza.'

'Oh, don't be silly, Monsieur Macleod. You're only fifty-seven once.'

'Fifty-six.'

'Whatever. A lot of people are coming.' And, for the first time, she noticed his scribblings on the whiteboard, and stopped in her tracks. 'You've started on it.'

'I have.' And immediately he saw a way of deflecting her from party mode. 'And I could do with some help.'

Her eyes gleamed. 'Oh, what? Anything.'

'I need a detailed dossier on Régis Blanc. Personal history. Criminal record. Friends, family, known associates. Anything and everything you can get on him, Nicole.'

'When for?'

'As soon as you possibly can.'

'You got it!' And he could see that, straight away, she was just itching to sit down at a computer.

He said, 'When is Sophie due back?'

Nicole was already distracted. 'Tomorrow morning, I think. Just in time for the party.'

Enzo sighed fondly. 'Ye-es – just in time for everyone else to have done all the hard work.'

# CHAPTER SEVENTEEN

The tracks of Sophie's tears stained her face. The light was starting to fade on their third full day of incarceration and her sense of hopelessness was absolute. Both she and Bertrand had lost any and all control of their lives. Already the days were beginning to blur, losing shape and reason.

Bertrand looked terrible. She had done her best to clean the blood from his face, but smears of it had dried brown on his stubbled cheek and around his mouth. His shirt was covered in it. Yet more of it had dried solid in his nasal passages, making it hard for him to talk, and he was convinced that his nose was broken. His pain had morphed to a dull ache and then to numbness, and he had spent much of today sleeping.

He lay with his head in her lap, as she sat with her back to the wall, listening to him slow-steady breathing through his mouth.

At least their captors had relented and started bringing them food once more. Yoghurt, bread, coffee. Sophie had already decided that if she ever got out of here she would never consume any of these three things ever again.

While Bertrand dozed, and in between spells of self-pity and tears, Sophie had thought a lot about their situation. Bertrand had acted impulsively and alone in attacking the bringer of the food yesterday, driven by anger and frustration. Sophie had been taken as much by surprise as the man he attacked. Frozen by shock and fear and unable to help. If only they had discussed it in advance, thought it through, had a plan, the outcome might have been different.

And now, it seemed to her, it was no longer possible for them simply to sit and await the unfolding of events which appeared less and less likely to end well. It was time to become proactive. To do something before they both lost the will to resist.

She looked down into her lap and saw that Bertrand was looking up at her. She had no idea how long he had been awake.

'What time is it?' he said.

She shrugged. How could she know? They had taken their watches. 'Late,' she said. 'It'll be dark soon.' She paused, and lowered her voice. 'We've got to try and get out of here.'

He nodded. 'I know.' Stiffly, he pulled himself up into a sitting position. 'I'm sorry.'

'What for?'

'For not doing a better job of protecting you.'

She felt the temptation to weep again, but instead wrapped her arms around him and held him close. 'We'll do it together this time,' she whispered. 'I feel like doing these fucking people some damage.'

'Me, too.' He untangled himself from Sophie and got to his feet, stretching sore muscles and aching joints. It was important that he was both physically and mentally alert. 'I can take either of them, one on one,' he said. 'But not both at the same time.'

'What about your face?'

He grimaced painfully in a grotesque parody of a smile. 'They can't do much more damage to it than they already have.'

'No, I mean . . . are you fit for it?'

He flexed his fingers and balled them into fists at his side. 'Oh, yes.'

'And what are we going to do if we get out? We've no idea where we are.'

'Well, let's get a look at the lie of the land, then.'

Sophie pulled herself to her feet, frowning. 'How?'

'If I lace my fingers together into a stirrup, you can step into it and I'll hoist you up to take a look out of the window. But we'd better do it quick, before it gets dark.' He crouched, making his stirrup, and she put one foot carefully into it, pushing up as he straightened his legs, and sliding up the wall to clutch the window frame and peer outside.

The glass was very nearly opaque with dirt and mud spatter, but Sophie could see enough through the external bars to realise that the window was only just above ground level. There was a gravel path beyond it, then an overgrown grassy bank rising into deciduous woods that seemed to stretch away

into darkness. She could see a very tall pine tree on the edge of the woods, reaching high above the other trees, almost opposite the window.

When Bertrand lowered her to the floor she told him what she had seen, but in truth it gave them very little idea of where they actually were, and how far beyond the trees they might have to go to reach safety. *If* they got out.

'This is some kind of big house,' Bertrand said. 'Did you notice how cold it was when we arrived? Didn't feel like anyone lived here.'

Sophie nodded. 'And we're in the basement.' Then she lowered her head, shaking it, and felt tears welling up again. 'But what's the point? We know all this. We've been through it a hundred times. None of it means anything if we can't get past those two men at the door.'

'We can do that,' Bertrand said, his voice gently insistent. 'If we work together. But we have to be fast. I can grab the first guy. But I can only hold him for a moment. You'll have to disable him and free me up to go for the second guy. They won't be expecting it, so we should have surprise on our side.'

Sophie took a deep breath and lifted her head. 'You're right. My papa always says you'll never achieve anything if you can't visualise it.' She forced a laugh. Then, with her strongest Scottish accent, in parody of her papa, she said, 'If you can't see yourself sitting at the head of the table in the boardroom you'll never be chairman of the company.'

Bertrand managed a smile. 'If that's what you want to be.'

'No, but he's right. How can we be free if we can't picture it happening?' She looked at him. 'How do I disable him?'

Bertrand shrugged. 'Fingers in his eyes.'

But she shook her head. 'He'll be bucking and fighting against you. No way I can guarantee to get his eyes. Better a swift, hard kick in the balls. I hear that men don't much care for that.'

Bertrand grinned now. This was more like the old Sophie. 'Okay. So, I'll bang on the door and ask to go to the toilet. When they open the door I'll grab the first guy, back into the wall in the corridor and turn him towards you. You'll have one chance before the other guy's on us.'

The full enormity of what they were planning struck her suddenly, and she experienced a sharp, stabbing fear. It was madness. They could never do it. But she made herself close her eyes and visualise the alternative. Do nothing and meekly accept whatever fate these people have in store for them. Not an option. She opened her eyes again and nodded. 'What happens if only one of us gets away?'

'If you get away,' Bertrand said, 'keep running and don't look back. I can look after myself. Just bear in mind that these guys are working in shifts. There's at least four of them, so there'll probably be others somewhere else in the house.'

Sophie couldn't imagine a single scenario where she would leave Bertrand here on his own. 'And if you're the one who gets away?'

'I'll come back for you.'

'No, you won't,' she said, raising her voice. 'You'll go and

you'll get help. And then you'll come back for me.' Although the very idea of being left here on her own without him was almost unthinkable. It was one more scenario she absolutely wasn't going to visualise. And the hopelessness of it all descended on her again like a black mist.

'We should wait till it's dark,' Bertrand said. 'Then, if we get out, we have a better chance of getting away.'

She nodded and they sat down on the floor, backs to the wall below the window, to watch as the last light of the day slowly faded on the wall opposite.

After a long silence Bertrand said, 'You know we have to do this, right? We have to try. Even if we fail.'

She nodded. 'I know.' Though she couldn't help wishing there was some other way. She turned to look at him. His bloody face and broken nose – and she saw the determination in his eyes. 'I love you, Bertrand,' she said. His dark eyes grew moist, even as she looked into them, and she knew that apart from her papa, there was no one else in this world that she would trust with her life like she trusted Bertrand.

He tore his eyes away from her and saw that the shape of the window, made by the outside light on the opposite wall, was gone. The dull burn of the single bulb overhead now filled the room with its sad electric light. And it occurred to him that this room being in darkness would help their cause. He scrambled to his feet. 'Come on, I'll give you a punt up. Use your sleeve to protect your hand and unscrew the bulb. If it's dark in here they'll not be able to see in.'

'It'll make them wary,' she said, standing up to join him.

'Yes, but if they can't see where we are it'll still give us the advantage.' He crouched once more, interlacing his fingers to give her a stirrup, then slowly rose, straining to take her full weight as she reached for the bulb, one hand on his head to steady herself. He heard the scrape of metal on metal as it unscrewed, and then darkness as she jumped down clutching the bulb. He heard her smashing it on the wall, and by the last light of the day leaking in through the window above, saw her holding the jagged end of it in her hand, like a weapon.

'I hope I get the chance to stick this in one of their faces,' she hissed, and he could feel that the adrenalin was already pumping through her system.

He guided her to the right side of the door and stood her with her back to the wall, then took a deep breath before banging on the door and shouting. 'Toilet!' No point in losing the momentum of the moment.

They waited for nearly a minute, but there was no response. He banged again and kept shouting until they heard a door slamming somewhere in the house, and then footsteps in the corridor. Sophie closed her eyes and tried to control her breathing.

The footsteps stopped outside the door and there were several long seconds of silence. Then a voice. 'What's happened to the light?'

'The bulb burned out,' Bertrand said. 'Can you hurry, please, I'm desperate.'

'Stand back against the far wall!' the voice came from the other side of the door, and then they heard the scrape of the key in the lock. Another moment of silence before the door was kicked in, bursting open in an explosion of dust. Bertrand stood, braced and ready, and saw the owner of the voice standing in hooded silhouette against the lit corridor behind him, a baseball bat dangling from his right hand. The shadow of his companion was cast in elongated distortion across the floor.

Bertrand leaped on him before the man's eyes had a moment to adjust to the darkness of the room. The two of them crashed out into the corridor, Bertrand's muscled forearm like a steel rod around his neck. The baseball bat rattled away across the concrete. Bertrand backed into the wall and Sophie stepped into the light, driving her foot hard into the man's crotch. Bertrand felt the man's whole body judder, and the pain that exploded from his mouth was almost palpable. Then he went limp, falling to the floor, pulling his knees up to his chest in the foetal position and rolling around, whimpering in agony.

But Bertrand had no time even to move before the second man was on him, his fist smashing into a face already bruised and swollen from the headbutt of the previous day. And the two men fell to the floor. Bertrand was almost blinded by pain. He felt a fist slamming into his gut and forcing all the air from his lungs.

Then the man's whole body shook and went limp, becoming a dead weight on top of Bertrand. The sound of the baseball bat

striking his head had made the oddest hollow sound, like wood on a leather ball. Bertrand looked up to see Sophie standing above them, before a shadow rose up behind her, enveloping her almost like a glove and pulling her down. The first man had recovered sufficiently to rejoin the fight.

Bertrand fought to drag himself out from under the man that Sophie had struck with the bat, but the blow to his head had not been enough to disable him entirely, and he was already pulling himself to his knees as Bertrand rolled free. Bertrand could see the door ahead of him at the end of the corridor. But Sophie was down, and both men were now back in the fight.

'Run!' Sophie screamed at him. He hesitated, and she bellowed with all her might, 'Go! For God's sake, go!' And he turned and sprinted down the hall, towards the light at the end of it.

The sounds that followed him turned his blood to ice. Their wounded captors bawling with fury and venom. Sophie's scream echoing off cold plaster walls and concrete floors. He very nearly stopped and turned back. But he knew she would be furious with him. All this would have been in vain. A painful and pointless exercise.

The door at the end of the hall opened into a room that leaked warmth and cigarette smoke out into the cold of the corridor. In the middle of the room two chairs were pushed back from a table scarred with cigarette burns and scattered with playing cards. There had been a game in progress, and a

cigarette still burned in the ashtray. A kettle stood on a unit against the back wall, alongside a tray of food ready prepared to take along to the prisoners.

A door at the other side of the room opened straight on to a narrow staircase that led steeply up into darkness. Bertrand took the stairs two at a time, trying hard not to listen to the bedlam he had left in his wake. At the top, he fumbled in the dark to unlatch a door that opened into the tiled entrance hallway of what must once have been a grand manor house. Soft light burned in art deco uplighters. Wooden panelling, scarred by the years, and cream-painted walls that had seen better days.

At the far end of the hall, a rising moon was already casting colourless light through stained glass in the main door. A broad staircase rose behind him to a half landing, before dividing and leading up, left and right, to a gallery running all around the upper floor.

He didn't stop to think, but ran for the door, feet clattering on the mosaic of tiles beneath them. Past double doors that stood open. The light of a fire flickering in a hearth. And then men's voices shouting, and moments later, footsteps coming after him.

To his enormous relief, the front door was not locked. He threw it open and ran out into the night. Down a short flight of steps and on to a gravel driveway. Cold air caressed him like the chill touch of death, and he shivered as he ran past several vehicles parked in the drive, one of them almost certainly the van that had brought them here.

He could hear his pursuers not far behind him, but couldn't afford to turn and look. Immediately off to his right, trees threw deep shadows in the moonlight, and he plunged off into their embrace, finding himself immediately swallowed by darkness and wild, uncultivated woodland.

Briars and tangling shrubs snagged and tore at his trousers as he crashed through the undergrowth. His lungs were bursting now, but he was driven on by fear and sheer determination, arms pumping, legs straining every sinew as he forced them forward against the pain of each stride.

He could hear and feel that he was putting distance between himself and the men who were chasing him, and in a slash of moonlight he saw a bank of ferns falling steeply away from what looked like a deer track. Below was the sound of running water, and he saw moonlight coruscating on its broken surface.

Bertrand jumped the path and slid on his backside down towards the flickering reflections below until he felt cold water break over his feet and legs, and he tipped forward, suddenly, involuntarily, into the stream. The shock of it very nearly took his breath away. It was only a foot or so deep, the bed of it littered with stones worn smooth over eons, and he got to his feet, dripping wet, and stumbled forwards toward where a large fallen boulder cast its shadow on the water. He doubled up and rolled under the overhang and into the protection of its darkness. He came to a brutally sudden, gasping halt, pressed up against wet, cold rock, and tried to hold his breath, straining to hear above the running of the water.

Voices came to him in the night. Shouting. Angry, frustrated. They had lost him, without any idea that he had gone down into the stream. He waited for several trembling minutes, listening to their voices fade into the darkness, before he crawled out from his hiding place and scrambled, warily, back up the slope to the deer path. He could hear them distantly, still shouting to one another, as they spread out further into the woods. And he turned and limped back the way he had come, like a wounded animal, cold and wet and frightened, and almost consumed by guilt at having abandoned Sophie to her fate.

Sophie lay on the cold floor, sobbing in the dark, broken pieces of light bulb beneath her. They had thrown her immediately back into the room, and she had heard the door locking and their footsteps retreating along the concrete as they set off after Bertrand.

In her heart of hearts, she had always feared that, if only one of them got away, it would be Bertrand. It had been altogether too much to hope that they would both escape. She heard in her mind the echo of her own voice screaming at him to go. And she had seen his hesitation. She knew just how painful it must have been for him to leave her, but she didn't blame him. He was more likely to evade capture out there than she was. He was stronger, more resilient. He was their best hope.

Still, it did nothing to ameliorate the sense of total despair

that gripped her. She was on her own now, and if Bertrand succeeded in getting away she feared those men would take their anger out on her.

Somewhere in the outside distance she heard men's voices shouting, and then silence. A silence so thick and pervasive she felt she could almost touch it. She pulled herself up into a sitting position and leaned back against the wall. Looking up at the window, she could tell that there was moonlight out there, but it must have risen on the far side of the house, casting its light towards the woods, for none of it came directly into the room. Very slowly, her eyes accustomed themselves to what little light there was, until she could see her own hands trembling in front of her.

She prayed that Bertrand would get away. If they caught him, God only knew what they would do to him. She closed her eyes and thought about her father. It would be his birthday tomorrow, she remembered. And when she didn't turn up, they were bound to realise something was wrong. And if Bertrand escaped, he could lead them back here. She wanted nothing more right now than to feel her father's arms around her, his soft Scottish brogue, calm and reassuring as he held her, telling her that everything was going to be all right.

Then she heard rapid footsteps out in the hall, and she pulled herself up to her feet, heart pushing into her throat and nearly choking her. The key turned in the lock, and she stood, blinking painfully in the sudden glare of electric light from the corridor as the door was thrown open. There was just

the one man. Still hooded. With Bertrand gone, they clearly didn't think she posed the same threat.

He stepped into the room, and fingers of steel closed around her throat, almost lifting her off her feet. She could barely breathe, and his face came to within inches of hers, so that she could smell his sour breath through the fabric of the mask. 'Some boyfriend, eh? Leaving you here on your own. What a fucking hero.' He released his grip a little.

'Yeah, well, you would know,' she spat back at him. 'Easy to play the big man with someone who can't fight back.'

'Shut your fucking mouth, bitch!' And he took the open palm of his hand across the side of her face. A bruising, powerful slap that knocked her off her feet and sent her sprawling in the dust.

She rolled over on to her back, tears springing to her eyes, and saw his blurred figure stepping towards her. She said, 'Guess you're pissed off cos he got away.' Her words and voice sounded much braver than she felt. 'Well, he didn't leave me. He'll be back. With help.'

He leaned over and grabbed her by the hair, pulling her roughly to her feet. Again, he pushed his face right into hers. 'Yeah, he probably will. But you know what? We'll all be long gone by then. And your old man might get the message sooner than planned, but get it he will. Bitch!' And he threw her out into the corridor.

Bertrand watched the house from the cover of the trees, acutely aware that his pursuers would likely give up the chase

and come back this way very soon. One glance at the clarity of the sky overhead told him that they were nowhere near any village or conurbation. There was no light pollution of any kind, except from the moon itself, which shed its silver light across the land like frost.

The house was huge. Stone-built on three levels, and to Bertrand's eye looked nineteenth- or early twentieth-century. It had seen better days. Most of the windows were shuttered, and creeper grew freely up the walls and into the eaves. Juliette balconies all along the first floor were balustraded by rusted wrought iron, and the walls were stained where gutters blocked by leaves had overflowed and rainwater had run down the stone.

On the other side of the driveway he could see an overgrown lawn stretching away to a separate garage sitting in the shadow of a large chestnut tree which was in the process of piling its leaves up all around it.

From behind him, in the woods, he heard voices and the sounds of men slashing their way back through the undergrowth. He knew he had to move, and that he would have to break cover, exposing himself to the glare of the moonlight and full visibility to anyone watching from the house. But he could see a light in only one window, and nobody at it. So he sprinted across the gravel, past the vehicles parked there, and ploughed through the long grass of the untended lawn, already wet with dew.

To his surprise, when he reached the garage, he found that the door was not locked, and he slipped inside.

Moonlight spilled in through windows along the far side, and he could see three vehicles of some sort, covered over with dust sheets. The place smelled damp and fusty, as if it hadn't been in use for a long time, and, as he crossed to a heavy workbench against the near wall, dust rose up from his feet and hung in the silver light.

A toolbox lay open, some of its contents strewn across the worktop. Hammers and saws hung from hooks on the wall above it. He lifted a short crowbar, curved and forked at one end, and hefted it in his hand. It felt solid and heavy, and would make not only a good weapon, but an ideal tool with which to pry free the bars on the window to the room they had been kept in.

From the shadow of the garage, he peered out across the expanse of grass and saw his pursuers, three men, emerging from the woods and hurrying back into the house.

It had occurred to him as he crouched, shivering, in the water beneath the boulder by the stream, that he couldn't leave Sophie here. However long it took him to find and secure help, by the time he got back, their captors would almost certainly have gone, and taken Sophie with them. He had to get her out now.

As soon as his pursuers were inside, Bertrand ran, crouching, from the shadows to the near wall of the house. An overgrown path ran around it. And he followed it quickly to the back. There were extensions here, and a couple of outbuildings, but no sign of life, and he ran past the bins and the rear entrance

to the deep shadow that the moon cast on the far side of the house. Beyond lay the woods that Sophie had seen from the window.

She had described a tall pine tree that stood high above the others, and he saw it now, his marker to identify the window to the room in which they had been kept. There were several windows at path height along this side of the house, each allowing light into basement rooms. All were barred and lay in darkness. But even at a glance Bertrand could see that the bars were rusted, and corroded where their fixings were set into the wall. A simple matter to prise them free with the crowbar.

He eased his way carefully along the wall until he saw the faintest light falling out over the path from one of the windows. It was almost opposite the tall pine. This had to be it. He reached it and dropped to his knees, peering down into the semi-darkness of the room below. The door stood wide open, light from the corridor beyond lying in a long slab of yellow across the floor. He saw the mattress they had slept on for the last three nights, and their blankets lying in a tangled heap. But the room was empty.

Almost at the same moment, he heard the sound of vehicle motors starting up at the front of the house, and he cursed audibly with the realisation that he was already too late. He scrambled to his feet, clutching his crowbar, determined to do battle with however many of them he had to, and sprinted as hard as he could around to the front of the house. In time to see all three vehicles accelerating away along the drive, headlights

raking the darkness, one behind the other. Sheer frustration impelled him to throw his crowbar at their retreating brake lights and bellow into the night.

But they were gone. And they had Sophie with them.

They had left almost everything behind them in their haste to leave. Certainly they weren't taking any chances that Bertrand would return quickly with help. The room on the ground floor, where they had clearly spent much of their time, was littered with food wrappers and beer cans, and ashtrays full to overflowing. The freezer in the kitchen was stacked with frozen meals that they had been cooking in a microwave, as well as the part-baked bread they had been feeding to Sophie and Bertrand. There was at least a week's worth of yoghurt in the fridge. So they had been planning to be here for a few more days, at least.

There was a telephone in a back room, and for a moment Bertrand's hopes were roused. But the line was dead, and he could find nothing in the house that gave a clue as to where in the world it was.

He went down to the cellars, through the room where the men had been playing cards, and along the corridor to the open door of the place that had been his and Sophie's prison cell. He saw blood on the floor. Fresh blood, so he knew it wasn't his. And feelings of rage and frustration and guilt so consumed him that he could barely breathe. Tears sprang to his eyes, and he turned and ran back up the stairs, the world blurring around him.

His footfalls in the hall echoed back at him from the walls, and he felt the cold again as he ran out and down the steps to the drive. His clothes were still wet, and he realised that he felt no pain because his body was mostly numb. All he could think was that he had to get help. That somehow he had to get word to Enzo. If anyone knew what to do now, it would be Sophie's papa.

He fell into a long, loping stride as he followed the driveway through the trees and eventually out, through an open gate, on to a narrow, single-track road. Which way to turn? He tried to think back to their arrival in the van and the sharp turn into the drive, and he turned right.

The road was in poor condition, cracked and potholed, and took a long sweep around the perimeter of woods brooding darkly behind a high deer-fence on his right. On his left, flat, open country stretched away to an unseen horizon. He could see moonlight reflecting on fragments of water.

After fifteen minutes or so, his reserves of energy were starting to exhaust themselves, and his run had slowed to a walk. There were trees on both sides now, their shadows, cast by the moon, turning the ribbon of tarmac into a river of darkness, treacherous underfoot with its crumbling and pitted surface. Before suddenly he emerged into wide-open country, and in the far distance, away to his left, saw the headlights of cars on a road. A motorway, he thought, because they were travelling fast and straight. But it was a long way away. Three, maybe four kilometres, and there was no guarantee that the

road he was on would lead him to it. The only way to be sure of reaching the highway was to go cross-country.

This was rough land, once forested but now cleared and overgrown, roots and tangling creeper making progress difficult, and it didn't take Bertrand long, after leaving the road, to realise it could take him several hours to reach the motorway.

It was less flat than it had looked, and he found himself clambering over boulders and the remains of fallen trees. Then suddenly, in his haste, he pitched forward as the ground gave way beneath his feet. For a moment he felt the unconstrained freedom of falling through the air, before his head struck something very hard and he hit the ground with such force that, in the moments before he passed out, he was completely unable to draw a breath.

# CHAPTER EIGHTEEN

Sunlight fell across his bed, warming him even through the quilt. It had been a hot and restless night, in spite of falling temperatures outside, and now Enzo realised with a shock that he had slept until after nine.

He sat upright, blinking in the light of the bright southern sun that glanced off all the roman tiles of the rooftops beyond his window. His mouth was dry and his eyes gritty from too much wine consumed the night before. He slipped from his bed and walked stiffly into the bathroom to empty his bladder and splash his face with cold water. And as he pulled on fresh socks and underwear, and slipped into his trousers, he wondered why it was that age seemed always to be accompanied by pain – in muscles and joints and bones that had once moved freely and easily. As if it wasn't bad enough just growing older.

He stumbled barefoot through the hall and into the *séjour*. Beyond the dining area, through the arch, he smelled coffee and warming croissants coming from the kitchen, and thought perhaps there were some advantages to having Nicole around, after all.

But he was stopped in his tracks by the sight of a large young man, busy, beyond the breakfast bar, taking pastries from the oven. He was tall and built like a rugby player, with dark hair tumbling in curls over his forehead. He turned and smiled at Enzo.

'*Bonjour*,' he said.

It took Enzo a moment to realise that it was Fabien, the young Gaillac winemaker whose dislike of Enzo had once led the two men to a confrontation in his vineyard that nearly ended in fisticuffs. In the final event, however, he had saved Enzo's life, and so a truce had been declared, and each had a grudging respect for the other.

But seeing him standing there in the kitchen of his apartment, preparing breakfast, left Enzo at something of a loss. 'What are you doing here?'

Fabien smiled. 'Nice to see you, too, Monsieur Macleod.' He dished up warmed croissants and *pains au chocolat* into a basket and started pouring two large cups of black coffee. 'Nicole asked me to come and help with the party.'

Enzo had forgotten completely that Fabien and Nicole had formed the most unlikely of liaisons during his investigations in Gaillac, and it occurred to him that he had never asked Nicole if they were still together. But here, he thought, was his answer to the unasked question.

'Oh,' Enzo said.

Fabien pushed the basket of pastries towards him. 'Always happy to be on the receiving end of a warm welcome.'

'Sorry,' Enzo said, still recovering himself. 'Just surprised, that's all.'

'Ah, yes,' Fabien said, and he took a slug of his coffee. 'Speaking of which, Nicole has one for you. Something she's been saving to tell you on your birthday.'

And Enzo remembered that he had forgotten, once again, that today was his birthday. 'What?'

But Fabien just shrugged. 'Oh, it's not for me to say, Monsieur Macleod. Nicole would murder me if I spoke out of turn.'

Enzo could imagine only too well that she would. But he had no time to consider it further before Nicole herself bustled into the kitchen.

'Oh, you're up at last,' she said. 'I don't know what time of day you think this is to be getting out your bed.'

Fabien flashed Enzo a sympathetic smile.

'I've had a heavy few days, Nicole,' Enzo said.

'Yes, well, so have I. The *traiteurs* will be here any moment, and I don't want you two under my feet when they arrive.'

Enzo said, 'And what about this birthday surprise that Fabien says you have for me?'

Nicole swung a dark look in Fabien's direction, but the young man just shrugged and smiled. She turned back to Enzo. 'He wasn't supposed to say anything until later. But, since the cat's out the bag . . .' She drew in a deep breath. 'Fabien has proposed to me. And I've accepted.'

Sleep and hunger were immediately banished and Enzo opened his eyes wide. 'Really?' It didn't seem possible to him

that Nicole was even old enough to get married. Yet one more symptom of his relentless ageing. Because, as he reflected, she was probably twenty-two or twenty-three by now.

'Well, that's not quite the reaction I was hoping for,' she said, folding her arms in a huff.

Enzo said quickly, 'I'm sorry, I didn't mean it like that, Nicole. I should have said . . . Congratulations!' And he gave her a hug and a kiss on each cheek. Then turned to Fabien. 'To both of you.' And he shook Fabien's hand.

Slightly mollified, she said, 'I'm going to move in with Fabien's family and help in the vineyard. And my dad's going to sell the farm and join us.' She looked apprehensively at Enzo, who didn't seem to know what to say, and quickly added, 'Which means I'll not be finishing my course at the university.' She saw him about to open his mouth to speak, but cut him off before he could. 'Now, if you don't mind, I'll ask you two to drink and eat up and find yourselves something useful to do somewhere else. I have a ton of work waiting to be done here.' And, as an afterthought, 'Oh, and happy birthday, Monsieur Macleod.'

The indoor market was open, but it was still early, and the good citizens of Cahors had not quite shaken off the night before to embrace the new day. There were some cars already parked in the square, and shops were opening up along either side. At the top end of the Place Jean-Jacques Chapou, beyond the plane trees dropping their leaves on the cars below, Enzo saw the faithful leaving the cathedral after morning mass.

Where the Rue Saint-James ran off from the square, the Café Le Forum had its tables and chairs out on the pavement for the smokers to huddle in the early-morning chill over their *grandes crèmes* and *noisettes*. Hats and scarves and gloved hands holding today's *La Dépêche* open at the sports pages.

Enzo pushed the door open into its interior warmth and Fabien followed him inside. In silent accord the two men slipped on to bar stools at the counter, and Enzo nodded acknowledgement to Bruno, the proprietor, who was noisily nursing his espresso machine to produce a *grande crème* and a *chocolat chaud* for waiting customers in the back. They watched him for a long time in silence.

Then Enzo turned a grim face towards his companion. 'I suppose I should be ordering champagne, to drink a toast and congratulate you on your forthcoming nuptials.'

'Well, that would be very civilised of you,' Fabien said. 'But perhaps I should pay for it, since it's your birthday.'

Enzo flicked him a quick look, suspecting sarcasm, but saw none in the young man's face.

Fabien turned to Bruno. 'A bottle of your finest champagne, please, and two glasses.'

Bruno looked at him in surprise. 'You do know what time it is?'

'It's my birthday, Bruno,' Enzo said.

'Then you should be old enough to know better. It's a bit early to be drinking champagne, don't you think, Monsieur Macleod?'

But Fabien just shook his head. 'It's never too early to drink champagne.'

Bruno shrugged. 'Your funeral.' And he turned away to retrieve a bottle from the cold cabinet and find a couple of champagne glasses.

Fabien turned his head towards Enzo. 'Why do I get the feeling you disapprove?'

Enzo raised an eyebrow. 'Of you getting married?'

'Yes.'

'I don't.' He shrugged. 'Well, I mean, that's up to you. Nothing to do with me.'

'Nicole thinks the world of you, you know. The way you've looked after her. Got her that scholarship to stay on at university when her father couldn't afford to keep her there.'

Enzo stared at his hands in front of him on the bar, mildly embarrassed. 'She's the brightest student I've had in more than twenty years, Fabien.' He turned to look at the young man. 'It's not that I disapprove of her getting married. It's just . . . one more year and she'd have completed her course. A brilliant career in forensic science ahead of her.'

'I've tried to persuade her to stay on. But she won't have it. Her father's not fit to run the farm on his own anymore. And that's why she wants him to come and live with us. So she can look after him.'

The conversation was interrupted by the popping of their champagne cork, and crystal-white Mumm's frothed and bubbled in the glasses Bruno had placed in front of them.

Solemnly, the two men lifted them to chink together in a toast.
'Long life and happiness to you both,' Enzo said.

'And many happy returns to you.'

They both sipped the chill white wine, its bubbles bursting
in effervescence all around their lips. Enzo said, 'You'd just
better take bloody good care of her, that's all.' He paused. 'Or
you'll answer to me.'

A wry smile spread across Fabien's lips. 'I'm shaking in my
shoes, Monsieur Macleod.'

And Enzo grinned.

# CHAPTER NINETEEN

It took several moments for everything that assailed Bertrand's senses to register in his consciousness. First, it was low-angled sunlight shining directly in his eyes. That brought instant, sharp pain to a head which already felt as if it were gripped in a vice.

Then came the cold. A deep, numbing chill that penetrated his bones, and he realised he was shivering, soaked by a dew that had almost frosted in temperatures which had plunged overnight.

The final, and completely overwhelming pain that next gripped him came from his right leg as soon as he tried to move it.

He seemed to have no control over it, but any shifting of his body brought excruciating pain forking through the leg and up into his back. His brain was slow and fogged by exposure and pain, and it took several more moments for the realisation to dawn on him that it was broken.

He lay on his belly with his face in the dirt, and became aware of how shallow his breathing was. Then, gradually, it

came back to him why he was here, what had happened the night before. Sophie. They had taken Sophie. And the shock of recollection sent his heart rate soaring and produced a surge of adrenalin that enabled him to overcome the pain long enough to drag himself up into a semi-sitting position, giving free vocal rein to his agony as he did.

He heard himself call out, a disembodied voice, ragged with distress, that echoed away along the stony bed of what, it became clear to him now, was a dry river. As his cry died away, there was no other sound to replace it. He was, it seemed, the only living creature in this dead place. And then, very faintly, from some immeasurably far distance, he heard the almost imperceptible sound of traffic. A memory returned of the motorway he had seen the night before, and he realised that he could never reach it now.

He looked back up the slope he had fallen down in the dark, God knows how many hours ago, and it seemed almost insignificant to him in daylight. A stony bank, overgrown with wild grasses and shrubs, a drop of no more than five feet. If he could stand up, he would see over the top of it.

It was clear to him that going back the way he had come was the only viable option. The single-track metalled road could only be fifty or sixty yards distant. And, if anyone was going to pass this way, it would be on that road. Somehow, he had to get himself back up the slope and cover the distance to it. Because no one was going to find him here.

He had never been good with pain, but he was going to have

to overcome that now. His leg lay uselessly on the ground in front of him, the break halfway between knee and ankle, the shinbone snapped clean, its two halves lying at a sickening angle, one to the other. He couldn't even bring himself to look.

It took the next five minutes to manoeuvre himself into a position where he was supporting himself on his left knee, his broken leg trailing hopelessly behind him and to the side. There was no one around to see his shame as he vented his pain, crying out in the early-morning light, involuntary tears tracking through the dirt and blood on his face.

Now, using all his upper-body strength, he began pulling himself up the slope, using his good leg as an anchor and trailing the other behind him. Sweat joined the tears on his face.

Finally, he could see over the lip of the drop, back towards the road and the trees beyond it casting their shadows deep into the woods. It was going to take considerable effort – and some time – to get there, but just the sight of it gave him hope and strength.

He reached forward to grasp a rock half buried in the soil, to pull himself up, finally, out of the riverbed. And was caught completely by surprise as it tore itself free of the dry earth that held it, rolling back to strike him in the face. His other hand lost its grip, and he tumbled back down the slope, twisting as he went, indescribable pain forcing a scream from his lips. He was unconscious before he hit the bottom.

# CHAPTER TWENTY

By the time Enzo and Fabien got back to the apartment, they were both a little glassy-eyed. They had polished off the champagne and spent the rest of the morning in the Forum. Now, they realised, most of Enzo's birthday-party guests had already arrived.

Nicole greeted them in the hall, her face dark with anger. 'Where have you been?'

'You told us to get out from under your feet,' Enzo said.

She peered at them suspiciously in the gloom of the hallway. 'Have you two been drinking?'

Enzo and Fabien exchanged innocent looks.

'Us?' Fabien said.

And Enzo shook his head vigorously. 'Noooo, no, no, no, no. Just a little toast to your wedding.'

She glared at them. 'Nearly everyone's here, and they're all wondering where you are.'

'Then they need wonder no longer,' Enzo said, and he strode off into the *séjour*.

The first of the guests to greet him was Commissaire Hélène

Taillard, the town's chief of police, a statuesque woman, some-where in her middle forties. She had freed blond-streaked brown hair, normally pinned up beneath her hat, to fall in curls over her shoulders. She greeted him with a 'Happy birthday, Enzo,' and kissed him on both cheeks, her plump, rouged lips lingering overlong on his face. He breathed in the familiar scent of her perfume, and remembered with relief how they had once narrowly avoided having sex. He had been saved from his own libido only by the timely, or untimely, arrival of Sophie. How different might things have been now if she had not returned home when she did?

Kirsty was there, too, baby Alexis the centre of attention among the female guests. She gave her father a hug and a kiss. 'Happy birthday, Papa,' she said.

He looked around and turned to Nicole. 'Where's Sophie?'

But Nicole just shrugged. 'I don't know.'

'Happy birthday, old fella.' Préfet Jean-Luc Verne pumped his hand. It was his little joke, since he was several years Enzo's senior. Enzo attempted a smile. He and the chief adminis-trator of the *Département du Lot* were old friends, accustomed to intellectual sparring and the occasional game of chess. The state-appointed *préfet* was a graduate of the Ecole Nationale d'Administration, and a formidable intellect in his own right. It was he, along with Commissaire Taillard, who had called Enzo to task at a dinner party one night when the Scotsman had boasted that his forensic experience, coupled with the latest science, could easily solve the seven cold-case murders in the

book, then just published, by Parisian journalist Roger Raffin. Bets had been placed in the amount of 2,000 euros, and the following morning, in the cold light of day, Enzo had cursed his predilection for a glass or three of good Cahors wine and his foolishness in accepting the bet.

He did the rounds of all his guests. Neighbours and friends, colleagues from the university, and was surprised to see Nicole's father there. The old farmer had made an attempt to smarten himself up, his hair plastered to his head with some highly perfumed oil. He wore a jacket that was a size too small, and buttoned over an expansive belly which stretched out the creases of his white shirt. The knot on his blue tie was tied too tightly and Enzo wondered how he would ever get it undone. He recalled the day the two of them had rolled around on the floor in here, knocking lumps out of one another, when the farmer had believed Enzo to be taking advantage of his daughter. Now he shook Enzo's hand warmly. 'She's told you the news?'

Enzo nodded. 'She has.'

'I've tried to persuade her to stay on at the university, but she won't hear of it.'

'Then we'll have to get together and use our joint powers of persuasion.'

'*Oui, oui,* we will.'

Enzo saw that the man's glass was empty and reached for a bottle to refill it. 'Daughters, eh?'

'Enzo, are these your notes on the Lucie Martin case?'

Enzo turned at the sound of Hélène's voice to see her looking up at his whiteboard with Préfet Verne. He made his way across the room to join them. 'What powers of deduction you have, Hélène – given that her name is written up there in bold, blue letters next to Régis Blanc's.'

She cast him a withering look. 'One day,' she said, 'I'm sure you'll tell me all about the phone call I received from the gendarmerie in Duras the other night, asking whether a certain Enzo Macleod was someone I would think capable of breaking into a château.'

Enzo shifted uncomfortably. 'A misunderstanding.'

'I'm sure it was.' She lifted a sceptical eyebrow.

The *préfet* said, nodding towards the whiteboard, 'Are you making any progress with this thing?'

Enzo was guarded. 'Some.'

'Confident, then?' Hélène asked.

'As confident as I was with all the others.'

'Well, even if you do crack it,' Préfet Verne said, 'the final case – Raffin's wife – that seems to me to be the trickiest of the lot.'

And Enzo knew that it would be. There was almost nothing to go on. Marie had returned alone one winter's night to their empty apartment in the Rue de Tournon. Although there were no signs of a break-in, someone had been waiting for her there in the dark, and smashed her head in with a heavy brass ornament. There were no fingerprints, and in the absence of all forensic evidence – fibres, DNA – the police had been at a

loss. There was no apparent motive for the attack, and Raffin himself had been at an editorial meeting at the offices of the left-wing newspaper *Libération*. He had discovered her body on his return home.

However it would be tricky, not for any of those reasons, but because it was personal. She had been Raffin's wife, and Raffin was the father of Enzo's grandson. He and Raffin had never once talked about the murder, but Enzo sensed that it was still a raw and painful subject for him, the unsolved murder in his own life that had prompted him to research and write about the other six cold cases in his book.

All he said in response to the *préfet* was, 'I agree.'

'Of course,' Hélène said, 'you haven't always used your precious new science to resolve some of these cases. I'm not sure that should be allowable under the terms of the bet.'

'Sometimes new thinking is just as important,' Enzo said.

'Thinking outside of the box?' said the *préfet*.

'No,' Enzo said. 'Taking the box away altogether. Why put up walls to contain free thinking?'

The *préfet* said, 'Quite so.' And he looked around the room. 'I don't see your friend Simon here. I do hope he's still holding the money for our wager in his escrow account, and hasn't skipped off and spent it on a round-the-world cruise.'

'He's more likely to have spent it on some woman,' Enzo said darkly. Then forced a smile. 'I'm afraid he couldn't be here today.'

'Ah, the great man himself, engaged in debate no doubt about

the resolution of the Raffin murders.' Charlotte's voice, edged lightly with sarcasm, cut into their conversation. Enzo turned to see her, still in her coat, Laurent supported in the crook of her arm, and his heart lifted at the sight of his young son.

He took him immediately and kissed him, and bounced him gently up and down in his arms. 'I didn't know you were here,' he said to Charlotte.

'I've just arrived.' She turned her smile on the *préfet* and the chief of police. 'Aren't you going to introduce me?'

Enzo made slightly awkward introductions, trying hard to avoid Hélène's eye.

'Ah, yes, the second and third parties in the famous bet,' Charlotte said. And she smiled. 'You must be getting worried.'

'He still has two – very difficult – cases to go,' Hélène said.

'Perhaps. But who would bet against him now?' And she turned to Enzo. 'I need a word. In private.'

Enzo turned to look for Nicole and, as if by instinct, she materialised beside him, arms outstretched to take baby Laurent. 'On you go,' she said. 'I'll look after him.'

Almost reluctantly, Enzo let him go. He made his apologies to the others and he and Charlotte headed out into the hall. 'Let's go outside,' she said, and he followed her down the winding stairs to the studded door that opened on to the pavement. They weaved through the tables of the pizzeria to stand at the kerbside and she said, 'It's on for tomorrow.'

'Blanc?' Enzo's eyes opened wide in amazement. 'How did you manage it?'

'It wasn't easy, I'll tell you that. The prison authorities usually require several weeks' notice and prior security clearance. You'll need to bring your passport with you.' She paused. 'You'll be presenting yourself as my assistant.'

Enzo smiled wryly. 'A little old to be your assistant, amn't I?'

She returned a smile that never quite reached her eyes. 'Enzo, you are a little old for everything.'

The barb did not fail to draw blood, and his smile faded. He said, 'I've asked Nicole to look after Laurent until you get back.'

'Until *I* get back? That makes it sound like you won't be with me.'

'I won't. I'm going to ask Kirsty to follow us down to Lannemezan in her car, and then the two of us will head on over to Biarritz. She has an appointment with a consultant to discuss Alexis's hearing problem.'

Charlotte raised an eyebrow. 'Alexis has a hearing problem?'

'Apparently. They've seen several doctors. He seems to be suffering from partial deafness, but no one can explain why or what to do about it.'

'Oh dear,' Charlotte said, although there was not the least trace of sympathy in her tone. 'I suppose you'll be staying at Roger's place down there? In the apartment?'

'That's right.'

'It's a beautiful house,' she said, and Enzo realised immediately that she was letting him know that she and Raffin had stayed there. 'Used to be his wife's family home. Shame they turned it into a *chambres d'hôtes*. It's a special place.' She smiled

at him, eyes wide, satisfying herself that she had inflicted a little more pain. Enzo returned her gaze, marvelling at her ability to hurt him so easily. And she added, 'I must say, it was very convenient for Roger's wife to die the way she did.'

Enzo frowned. 'Convenient?'

'For Roger.' Charlotte hooked her arm around Enzo's and led him slowly along the pavement. 'Marie inherited everything after her parents died in a boating accident in Africa. Then, just five years later, she's dead, too, and it all goes to Roger. I would call that *very* convenient.'

'Not if you lose the person you love at the same time,' Enzo said. 'I wouldn't call that very convenient at all.'

'Perhaps. But there was no love lost between Roger and Marie, you know. They were still married, yes. But in name only. Had she lived, I think there might very well have been a divorce in the offing.' She stopped and sighed. 'I have often wondered just how closely the police examined his alibi.'

Enzo's brows creased in consternation. 'He was at an editorial meeting at *Libération*.'

'Apparently. But, as you very well know, Enzo, in such matters timing is everything.'

Enzo did, but found himself instinctively shying away from the implication that the father of his daughter's baby could have murdered his own wife. He searched Charlotte's eyes for some hint of the motivation that might have made her put the thought out there. After all, she had been Raffin's lover, too. But she just smiled and laughed and changed the subject.

'So, how are things progressing with the Lucie Martin case?'

He shrugged, and they turned and headed back along the pavement, casting shadows among tables that were rapidly filling up for lunch. 'There have been developments.'

She turned a look of curiosity towards him. 'Oh?'

And he told her about the damage to the skull, and the forensic anthropologist's suggestion that it could have been the cause of death. 'In which case,' he said, 'strangulation would have taken place post-mortem, ostensibly to make it look like she'd been killed by Blanc.'

Her face hardened. 'Obviously you knew this when you came to Paris the other day.'

'Yes.'

'But you never thought to tell me then.'

'You never asked. And, anyway, we had other things to talk about.'

He saw her jaw set. 'Yes, we did.' She stopped and turned to face him, almost confrontational. 'So why do you still want to see Blanc?'

'Because there's a connection between Blanc and Lucie that goes beyond the letter.'

'What the boyfriend saw?' Charlotte could barely keep the scepticism out of her voice.

'Not just that. The whole tone and content of his letter has always suggested to me that there was more to it.'

'Ah, yes, the famous Macleod instinct.' She pursed her lips thoughtfully. 'So you still think Blanc might have done it?'

'I'm keeping all options open.'

'And is there another suspect in the frame?'

Enzo nodded. 'The boyfriend, of course. Jilted by his childhood sweetheart for a lowlife ex-con, he kills her in a fit of jealousy.'

She frowned. 'From my recollection, he was in Paris the weekend she went missing.'

Enzo shrugged his shoulders very casually. 'As you very well know, Charlotte, in such matters, timing is everything.'

She glared at him for a moment, then her face cracked into a smile and she laughed. 'Touché, Enzo. Touché.'

'Monsieur Macleod!' Nicole's voice was raised to carry above the noise of the diners below. Enzo and Charlotte looked up to see her on the Juliette balcony outside Enzo's apartment, still holding Laurent. 'I just got a text from Sophie. Apparently the van's broken down on the motorway. They're not going to make it.'

Enzo gasped his frustration. 'Typical bloody Sophie!' he said.

# CHAPTER TWENTY-ONE

Sophie became aware of the rhythm of the wheels beneath her and, with a start, realised that she had drifted off to sleep. She was lying on her side on a cold, hard, metal floor, hands bound behind her back, a hood pulled over her head and tied at the neck.

They must have been driving for hours, and although she couldn't see anything, she was aware that it was light around her now, beyond the hood.

At one point during the night she had begged them to let her out to pee, and had suffered the humiliation of knowing that they were watching her as she squatted somewhere at the side of the road to relieve herself. There were, she had told herself with a great effort of will, worse things.

Now she managed to wriggle herself into a sitting position, knees pulled up to her chest, back against the side of the van. For the first hour or more she had fought the temptation to cry. She was damned if she was going to give them that satisfaction. But after so long in the discomfort of the van, she just felt numb. They must have travelled a

very long way in all this time, but she had no idea where.

For a while she could hear traffic around them on the road, vehicles overtaking at speed, and she figured that maybe they were on a motorway. Then they seemed to leave the traffic behind, and the road surface became bumpy and uneven. They turned left and right, slowing several times almost to a standstill. Before finally the van drew to a halt and the driver cut the engine.

She heard other vehicles draw up beside them on what sounded like a gravel surface. Car doors banging, the sound of voices. And whoever had been riding in the back of the van with her threw open the door and jumped out. There was a rush of cold air, and Sophie smelled sulphur in it, and iron. Pollutants. Atmosphere thick with them. Somewhere industrial, she thought.

Rough hands pulled her out and she stumbled and fell. The ground was wet, the air much colder than it had been at her last place of incarceration, and she realised she was not afraid. If they had been going to harm her, why would they have driven all this way to do it?

Forced back to her feet, fingers closed roughly around her upper arm, very nearly cutting off the circulation, and she was led across a flat area pitted with ruts and puddles. There was a fine rain in the air, and she felt it starting to soak through the thin material of her hood. They stopped, and she heard the scraping of a metal door sliding aside on rusted runners. The sound of it echoed off into a vast space beyond, and she found

herself pushed inside. Concrete suddenly beneath her feet, and despite them being indoors, water all across the floor, lying in pools that they splashed through as they walked.

There was no conversation among her captors, just a strangely forced silence as they led her over a huge empty floor area before finally reaching a metal staircase. Sophie felt it shake as they forced her to climb it, the sound of their footsteps echoing up into what seemed like a very high roof space. She was amazed at the pictures in her head that were conjured purely from the sounds and sensations around her. She envisaged a pitched glass roof, like a railway station, supported on a network of rusted girders. A sprawling, empty concrete floor that had once housed industrial equipment of some sort. This rattling old staircase leading up to a staging area, where there were maybe offices or workshops.

She was pushed across a grilled floor, then through a doorway and on to concrete again. The confines of a narrow corridor. There appeared to be just one man with her now, and she could hear his breathing and smell the cigarette smoke on his breath. They stopped. A key turned in a lock and a door swung open. Cold, stale air met her, and she was pushed violently forward, losing her footing and sprawling on the floor, hands still tied behind her back. She rolled on to her side and sensed her captor crouching down beside her.

'If you're a good girl,' he hissed, 'maybe we'll take off the hood and untie your hands.' She felt the flat of his hand run over the swell of her breasts, and she rolled quickly away. He

stood up and laughed. 'And maybe I'll have to teach you exactly what *good* means.'

She tensed, but he turned and walked out of the room, slamming the door behind him and turning the key once more in the lock.

All of the resolve that had seen her through the night dissolved in the tears that burned hot now on her cheeks.

Bertrand had lain in a state of semi-consciousness for some time before the world formed any coherence around him. It seemed impossible, somehow, that pain could maintain its intensity for this long. And yet it had. Relentlessly so. And he wondered how much more of it he could possibly take.

Rather than numbing his other senses, it seemed to have heightened them. Cold, hunger, fear, depression. He knew by now that he was suffering from exposure, and that even the toughest and strongest of men could be carried off by it.

The sun had gone behind thick cloud and it was impossible to see where in the sky it might be. The temperature had fallen, and he had no idea how long he had lain in the dry riverbed since sliding back down the embankment.

He felt himself succumbing to the temptation simply to close his eyes and drift away again into unconsciousness. At least that would bring some relief from his pain and misery. It was only the thought of Sophie and the need to reach Enzo that kept his eyes open and fuelled his determination to stay awake.

The sound of a car, motor purring, seemed suddenly very close, and he realised with a shock that there was a vehicle approaching along the single-track road. He had to get back up that slope, fast!

He gritted his teeth and forced himself to roll over on to his front, using his arms and his good leg to propel himself forward and drag himself back up the riverbank. As he reached the top of the bank, desperately searching fingers found and grasped the roots of some long-fallen tree. Summoning all his remaining strength, concentrated in muscles built during years of training in the gym, he pulled himself finally out of the dead river and rolled over among dried and browning ferns. In time to see a black Citroën gliding slowly by along the single track.

He bellowed at the top of his voice, hoarse now from crying out in pain, but felt hope and life draining out of him as the car kept going and receded into the distance. In less than a minute it was gone from sight, and the sound of it had faded to silence.

Bertrand lay on his back, succumbing to his misery and tears, and felt the first drops of rain falling from a darkening sky. He knew now that he was in real trouble.

# CHAPTER TWENTY-TWO

The party was drawing to a close. The *traiteurs* had provided a selection of tapas. From olives and stuffed prunes, to Iberico ham, prawns wrapped in bacon and frogs' legs in batter. And, as a main, Nicole and Fabien had reheated delicious *choux farcis*, served with cubes of roasted potato. Empty bottles of wine stood on all the tables, the ambience mellow and everyone gently tipsy.

It was late afternoon now and some of the guests were starting to leave. Enzo sat in his favourite armchair by the window, bouncing Laurent on his knee, not even daring to think that the child might not be his. Out of the corner of his eye, he could see Charlotte in deep conversation with Jean-Luc Verne.

He spotted his old acoustic guitar gathering dust in the corner of the room, and regretted that he played it so seldom these days. But he had consumed enough wine by now to contemplate the thought that he might just pick it up to serenade his remaining guests.

He was saved from what would probably have been the later

embarrassment of it by Nicole's return from the hall, where she had gone to answer a knock at the door unheard by almost everyone else. She cleared her throat and raised her voice to command the attention of the room, and announced, 'Sophie's birthday surprise for her dad has arrived.' And, as Enzo turned, he saw her step aside to reveal a young woman with chestnut hair and the warmest brown eyes, creased now by discomfort and self-consciousness. She was slight-built, not much taller than Nicole, and dressed simply in jeans and trainers, with a white T-shirt beneath a short denim jacket.

Enzo realised with a start who it was and stood up immediately, still clutching Laurent.

Nicole stepped quickly forward to relieve him of the baby. 'Here, I'll take him.'

And Enzo locked eyes with the new arrival, a sudden collision of butterflies in his belly.

No one knew quite what to say, and it was Charlotte's gently mocking voice that broke the silence. 'Another of Enzo's girlies?'

Which jolted Enzo out of his trance. He stepped towards the girl, his eyes still fixed fast on her. 'This is Dominique Chazal,' he told the assembled, 'the gendarme from Thiers, without whom I could never have cracked the Marc Fraysse murder.' And he paused. 'I had no idea you were coming.'

'It was Sophie's idea,' Nicole said. 'She and Dominique stayed in touch after everything that happened up there.' She turned to Dominique. 'Isn't that right?'

Dominique nodded, still clearly embarrassed to be the centre of attention. 'Yes.' She looked around. 'Is she not here?'

'Held up on the motorway,' Enzo said. And still he couldn't take his eyes off her. He took both her hands and kissed her on each cheek. 'Come in, come in.' He led her into the *séjour*, curious eyes upon them, and he avoided meeting the gaze of either Hélène or Charlotte.

The *préfet* said, 'They didn't make gendarmes that pretty in my day.' And Dominique blushed.

In truth, Dominique was not pretty in any conventional sense. Enzo had always thought her quite plain – but beautifully plain, in the way that sometimes the simplest things in life are the most beautiful. The touch of colour on her eyelids, and the merest hint of red on her lips, lifted her out of the ordinary. The deep pellucid brown of her eyes provided a window to her inner beauty, and revealed a vulnerability which had prompted Enzo's protective instincts. He remembered instantly the softness of her lips and the way every contour of her body had moulded itself to his.

'You must be hungry,' he said, and, without waiting to hear if she was, led her into the kitchen. They were momentarily on their own here, and Enzo had to resist the temptation to take her in his arms. Instead, he said, 'This is unexpected.'

'It was Sophie's idea.'

'But, still, you came.'

'If Mohammed will not go to the mountain . . .'

Enzo couldn't meet her eye, embarrassed. He glanced

towards the *séjour* and said, 'It's not even a particularly auspicious birthday.' He tried a smile. 'Just one more step closer to the grave.' Then paused when she didn't return his smile. 'You must have had to take precious leave.'

She shrugged. 'I haven't bothered much with leave in the last year or so. And, anyway, it's not an issue anymore. I've quit.'

'Quit the gendarmerie?'

'Served my time and had to make a decision. I could sign up again or try for a real life. I decided to go for the latter.' Her smile was brittle. 'So here I am, the new me, footloose and fancy free and trying to figure out what to do with a life that hasn't belonged to me for the last eighteen years.' She tipped her head to one side in recognition of the irony. 'It feels strange when they put it back in your own hands – sort of shop-soiled and used, and completely unfamiliar. As if you've been someone else, and only now realise that you haven't a clue who you are.'

Enzo reflected that that's how it must be for most people returning to civilian life after a career in the military. For it's what the gendarmerie was, just another regiment of the armed forces.

'Well, well . . . the famous Dominique Chazal.' Charlotte strolled casually through from the *séjour*, arms folded, and surveyed them both with smiling condescension. She was, Enzo thought, more defensive than he had ever seen her. 'So nice of you to drop by, all the way from . . . Thiers, was it?'

Enzo was awkward. 'This is Charlotte,' he said.

Dominique regarded her coldly. 'I think I could have guessed that.'

'Oh!' Charlotte mock-flinched. 'That sounds ominous. What on earth has Enzo been saying about me?'

Enzo recalled only too clearly telling Dominique about Charlotte's threat to abort their baby if Enzo did not agree to stay away. But before he could speak, Dominique said simply, 'Enough.' And Enzo felt the temperature in the room drop thirty degrees.

Charlotte's smile was equally frozen. 'I expect you two have kept in touch, then.'

Dominique said, 'I haven't seen Enzo since he left Thiers.'

Enzo shuffled uncomfortably, aware of the accusation in this.

'Well, then, it was good of you to come. I expect you two will have a lot of catching up to do.' Charlotte turned to Enzo. 'We'll have to leave early tomorrow. It's a two-and-a-half-hour drive to Lannemezan. I'll pick you up at eight.' And she swung a saccharine-sweet smile towards Dominique. 'Make the most of your time with him, because there won't be much of it.'

'All the more reason to appreciate it, then.' Dominique fixed her with a patently hostile and unblinking gaze, until Enzo saw Charlotte look away, unable to maintain eye contact in the face of such naked animus. He had never seen her this cowed before.

*

It was night in the square below now, though light still spilled out from restaurants and cafés, reflecting on dark cobbles littered with leaves. The party was over. Everyone had gone. The apartment was a mess, but Nicole had promised to tackle it in the morning. She was taking charge of Laurent for the night, and had already retreated with him in his carrycot to her room. Her father had left a couple of hours earlier, and Fabien had gone back to Gaillac.

Charlotte had pulled Enzo aside before leaving for her hotel. She'd hoped to have dinner with him tonight, she said. There were things she wanted to talk to him about. But when he reminded her that they would have nearly three hours to talk during the drive to Lannemezan, she had cast a surly glance towards Dominique and left with a bad grace.

Sophie had texted again to say that she and Bertrand had found a hotel to stay overnight, and Kirsty had decided to take Sophie's room, rather than stay at a hotel. She had retired with Alexis for an early night. And it had been some comfort for Enzo to know that his daughter, his son and his grandson were staying with him, all under the one roof, tonight. The only thing missing was Sophie.

Now Enzo and Dominique sat in the big old leather sofa which faced the French windows that looked out across the square. A slight breeze outside stirred the remaining leaves in the trees, to send flickering fragments of light from the streetlamps dancing across the darkness of the *séjour*. After some moments of awkwardness, they had fallen back into the

easy companionship they had discovered during his time in Thiers. She let her head fall on to his shoulder, and he slipped his arm around her to draw her closer.

Silence was easier than addressing the unresolved issues that lay between them, and so neither of them felt inclined to break it for a long time.

When finally she spoke, the quiet of Dominique's voice seemed to resonate in the room. 'You promised you would keep in touch.'

'I know.'

'You didn't.'

'No.'

More silence. Then, 'Why?'

Enzo sighed. 'I think you know, Dominique.'

'I'll tell you what I know,' she said. 'I know that I want to be with you. It's all I've wanted since you left. I've never met anyone like you, Enzo. You're sensitive, intelligent, and you were mine. Even if only for a few days. I've lost count of the number of nights I've lain awake thinking I was never going to see you again. Dying a little with every day that you never called or wrote. Scared to contact you for fear that I didn't mean to you what you meant to me.'

Enzo closed his eyes and felt the pain of regret at hurt given so casually, if only by default.

'And then I thought, For Christ's sake, girl, stop feeling sorry for yourself. If you want him, go and get him.' She paused. 'So here I am.' She turned quickly on the couch, placing a finger

over his lips to stop him from speaking. 'And don't tell me you're too old for me. I've heard it all before.'

He couldn't resist kissing her finger, then he turned his head towards her and smiled sadly. 'Trouble is, it's true.'

She sighed loudly and turned away.

'Dominique, I'm old enough to be your father. You're ... what? Thirty-five? Thirty-six? Young enough to find someone your own age and still have a full life ahead of you.'

'I don't want someone my own age. I want you.'

'I'm fifty-six today, for God's sake! In four years I'll be sixty. You don't know how it feels, Dominique. To reach a point in your life where the distance still to go is far less than the road already travelled. When you spend more time looking back than looking forward, because there is comfort in memory and only fear of the future. When I'm seventy, you'll just be turning fifty, and you won't want to be looking after some old man.'

She swung herself across the settee suddenly to straddle his thighs and sit facing him, taking his face in her hands. Her own face just inches from his. 'You're wrong, Enzo,' she said. 'I've thought so much about this. The past is ... Well, that's your history. It's a part of you. The memories that make you who you are. Good or bad, you can't change them. But the future is still yours to make. However long you've got. You told me once about Pascale, how she died giving birth to Sophie. She could never have imagined that. She thought she had a whole life ahead of her. You both did. Don't you see? You can't

look ahead and calculate the rest of your life by the law of diminishing returns. To live in fear, of anything, is not to live at all. You have to live for today, because you might be dead tomorrow. So damn well make the most of it!' And she kissed him, fierce with passion, and he felt the warmth of her tears on his face in the dark.

He slipped his arms around her and pulled her to him, feeling her body soft against his.

'I want you,' she said.

'I want you, too,' he whispered. 'I just—'

She kissed him again to stop him speaking. 'Just know that I am yours, Enzo, and that I want you more than I have ever wanted anyone. And that I am going to treasure every moment that I have with you, and not count them off as they pass.' She drew a long, slow breath. 'You don't spend a year thinking about someone, and missing them as much on the last day as the first, without realising that you must be in love.'

Her words dropped into his heart like molten metal into water, consolidating themselves into tiny bullets that pierced all the emotional armour he had so carefully built around himself for protection. He slid to the edge of the sofa and stood up with her in his arms, marvelling at how light she seemed. He grinned. 'Not bad for an old man, eh?' And he carried her through the darkness of the hall and into his bedroom.

Their lovemaking was not the frantic, lust-driven sex that might be expected of two people who had not slept together

in nearly a year. It was slow and tender, and so filled with emotional commitment that it left them both drained, spreadeagled on the bed. Not lying on it, but floating on it, not a ripple breaking the surface of their sea of post-sex tranquillity. And Enzo wondered if, finally, after all these years, he had found the woman who would make him happy for the remainder of his life.

Moonlight lay in angles and shadows across the rooftops, and poured like liquid through the window, splashing across their naked bodies.

For a time they dozed, drifting in and out of sleep, she turning to hold him, then turning again to let him spoon her. At some point she emerged from her sexually sated slumber to an awareness of Enzo lying on his back, staring at the ceiling, hands propped behind his head on the pillow. And she sensed something dark. 'What's wrong?'

'Nothing.'

'Lying to me is not a good way to start our relationship, Enzo.'

He rolled his head to one side to look at her earnest face in the moonlight and smiled. 'You're right.'

'Is it me? Us?'

'No. You are everything that is not wrong with my life.' He hesitated. 'It's Charlotte.'

He heard the tiny explosion of air that signalled Dominique's irritation. 'I don't know why you still give her the time of day.'

'Because she's the mother of my son, Dominique.' He closed

his eyes and ran the next words through his head several times before he spoke them. 'At least, I thought she was.'

Dominique pulled herself up on one elbow and stared at him in surprise. 'What do you mean?'

He found it difficult now even to form the sentence. 'She told me there had been someone else.'

'When?'

'She didn't say. But . . .' He was almost afraid to say it, in case speaking the words aloud would give them substance and truth. 'She hinted there was a chance that Laurent might not be mine.'

He was aware of Dominique going limp. 'What a bitch she is.'

Enzo said, almost as if apologising for her, 'She doesn't always endear herself to everyone.'

A silence lay between them, like the ghost of Charlotte herself. Then Dominique said, 'Where are you going with her tomorrow?'

'To the high-security prison at Lannemezan. To interview the serial killer Régis Blanc.' And he explained about the Lucie Martin case, and Charlotte's ability to get him access to Blanc.

Dominique listened in silence. She had played an important role in discovering who had killed the celebrity chef, Marc Fraysse. Now she said, 'Let me help.'

'How?'

'I'm a trained police officer, Enzo. I can be useful in the investigation. You know how it can sometimes throw more

light on a problem to have two minds working on it from different angles.'

'I can't take you with me to see Blanc.'

'No, but you can brief me when you get back. We can do this together.'

And for some unaccountable reason Enzo felt a huge wave of relief. Almost for the first time since Pascale had died he didn't feel alone anymore. Carrying the burdens of his life, his family and sometimes, it seemed, the whole world. All on his own. He turned to her again, suffused by a nearly overwhelming sense of affection, cupping the back of her head in his hand and drawing her to him to kiss her. He wanted to tell her he loved her. But he was scared to say the words. Three simple words, said too easily, that carried a weight far greater perhaps than any other three words in human history. He knew she wanted to hear them, but still they wouldn't come.

Suddenly she turned away and slipped out of bed. She leaned over to dip into her overnight bag and pulled out a sheer satin dressing gown. He heard the smoothness of it on her skin as she drew it around her. Then she held out her hand towards him. 'Come on.'

He shimmied across the bed and slid out to stand up beside her. She seemed so small next to him. 'Where are we going?'

'To lay your ghosts to rest. The only way to remove uncertainty is to know the truth.' She took his hand and led him across the room. He snatched his dressing gown from the door, black silk with embroidered dragons, and pulled it on as she

drew him out into the hall. There was not a sound from the other rooms. Streetlight lay in squares across the floor, divided and subdivided by the panes of glass in the double doors leading to the *séjour*. They stepped through them, avoiding the lines, almost like the games of peever Enzo remembered playing in the school playground.

Nicole had left a bag of Laurent's things sitting on the table. Dominique rifled through them until she found what she was looking for. A hairbrush with fine soft bristles, wisps of gossamer dark hair trapped between them. With thumb and forefinger, she teased some free and held it up to Enzo. 'You of all people, my love, should be able to use his DNA to test for paternity.'

Then he saw a shadow cross her face, as if a cloud had passed before the moon.

'But one thing you should know. I can't ever give you a son. Or a daughter. We tried, my ex and I, and failed. They tested us. He was declared fertile.' There was the slightest catch in her voice. 'And I was told I would never bear a child.'

# CHAPTER TWENTY-THREE

When consciousness returned it brought only darkness. Bertrand's eyes flickered open and saw nothing. Neither could he feel anything, except for the constant tattoo of rain on his chest and face. Where the raindrops touched his skin they felt like needles. His clothes were soaked and immeasurably heavy. Almost heavier than the limbs he seemed incapable of moving.

There was no sensation in his broken leg now, as if it had been amputated while he slept. He was unable to feel his feet. His hands seemed huge, swollen and clumsy.

But, even as he gazed into darkness, the world about him slowly began to take form. Shadows delineating shapes. The silhouette of a fallen tree. The bowed and sodden leaves of autumn fern. Hard black rock shot through with seams of marbled limestone. And they were moving. Slowly crossing his field of vision from right to left.

Then the sound of a motor. And, filtering through the fog that filled his head, the realisation that a vehicle was coming, the twin beams of its headlights raking this barren landscape,

a place that had somehow trapped him for a day and a night in its dead arms.

With an effort that robbed him of almost all his remaining strength, he rolled on to his side and found his right hand grasping the broken branch of a fallen tree. Strong enough to support his weight as he used it to get himself to his knees, pulling himself up to transfer that same weight on to his one good leg. He stood, trembling on it, swaying in the rain, using the dead branch to keep his balance.

What had begun as the distant sound of a vehicle's engine had turned into a roar that filled the night. Its headlights, set high in the cab of a tractor trailer dragging a huge container behind it, burned out the landscape like an over-exposed photograph. Bertrand levered himself forward, almost blinded by it, transferring weight between his left leg and the broken branch, his other leg dragging uselessly behind him.

By some light in the cab he could see the face of the driver, pale, focused, averted in that moment from the road, concentrating on something that he held in one hand. And it dawned on Bertrand that he was either sending or receiving a text on his mobile phone. He waved his arm uselessly and shouted at the huge, lumbering vehicle as he tried desperately to put himself level with the road. But even as he forced himself on he knew he was too late. The driver hadn't seen him, and the great sweep of its wheel arch caught him a glancing blow that

threw him back into the undergrowth, broken branches and briars tearing at his clothes and his skin, leaving him unconscious and barely breathing.

And still the rain fell.

# CHAPTER TWENTY-FOUR

The gap between carriageways of the motorway was on fire with leaves in full blaze of autumn colour. It had been dark when they left Cahors, and now a low sun was slanting through the rear windscreen as they headed west and south. Toulouse was behind them, and away to their left the Pyrenees cut a purple silhouette against the palest of clear blue skies. Some of the most distant peaks already bore snow.

Enzo glanced in the mirror and saw Kirsty keeping a measured distance behind them, her brown hair almost red, backlit by the sun.

For someone who had been so keen to talk to him the night before, Charlotte had stayed strangely silent for most of the last hour, gazing straight ahead at the lines counting themselves off beneath the car, lost in her own private world. She had handed her car keys to Enzo and insisted he drive.

Suddenly, apropos of nothing, she said, 'Why have Kirsty and Roger not married?'

Enzo was startled, both by the sudden sound of her voice and the question it had framed. 'I've no idea. I've asked

her about it myself, but she seems a little evasive. They were due to marry before the baby was born, but it never happened.'

'Good. Let's hope it stays that way. For Kirsty's sake.'

Enzo stole a glance at her, but her eyes were still fixed on the road ahead. 'Why? Are you jealous?'

Now she laughed, and her amusement seemed genuine enough. 'Good God, no. It was over with Roger and me a long time ago.'

'And yet you still maintain regular contact.'

She shrugged. 'What is it they say? Keep your friends close and your enemies closer?'

Enzo was surprised. 'You think of Roger as your enemy?'

She half turned her head towards him. 'Not exactly. But as I've told you before, I know him too well. I neither like nor trust him. I'd rather keep him in plain view in front of me than suddenly feel his knife in my back.'

And Enzo remembered the night on the terrace at Gaillac where she had expressed dark thoughts about him. He glanced in the mirror again at Kirsty, and the misgivings he had always had about Raffin came bubbling once more to the surface. Yet again he felt a stab of concern for his daughter, and Charlotte put his thoughts into words. 'Pity they had the baby. Children have a habit of tying people together more closely than marriage.'

And the irony in that was not lost on him. He glanced at her and their eyes met for a moment in unexpected communion.

He returned his gaze to the road. 'You know he's been offered a job by the Mayor of Paris?'

He felt her head turn towards him. 'Devez?'

He nodded.

'What kind of job?'

'Press secretary. If Devez gets the nomination for the presidential candidacy.'

He heard a tiny puff of air expel itself from between her lips. 'That figures, I suppose. With Roger's left-wing credentials and his association with *Libération*, it'll put the socialists on the wrong foot. Give the UMP a little street cred.' She paused. 'You know that Roger and Marie were great friends of Devez and his wife back in the nineties?'

'I do. Though I don't really know very much about Devez himself. Except that he's the front-runner for the UMP nomination.'

'Oh, he's a smart one, Enzo. A real smooth operator. Cut his political teeth in Bordeaux in the early days. He was deputy mayor for some years, with responsibility for finance, human resources and administration. One of the youngest ever to be entrusted with the job. I guess even then people saw him as a future star. Bright, intelligent, personable. But he had something else. That magic something you need to get to the very top. Charisma. The kind of charisma that marked out Bill Clinton as special. It shines through, even once removed, on television, or in press photographs.'

Enzo half smiled. 'Sounds like you've fallen for him.'

She laughed. 'Oh, he's an attractive man. There's probably not a woman in France who wouldn't be tempted to slip into his bed. Though he's happily married from all accounts. With a young adult family.'

Enzo said, 'It's a big leap from provincial deputy mayor to Mayor of Paris.'

'It is. But there was never any doubt when he made the move to the capital that that's where he was headed. Even though he was still just a baby, in political terms.'

'And now he has the presidency in his sights. Will he win?'

'If the party picks him, I think he will.' She turned to look at Enzo. 'Which will make Roger a very powerful man.'

Enzo nodded. 'Do you know him? Devez, I mean.'

He heard a tiny snorting laugh burst from her nostrils, her lips pressed tightly closed. Then, 'I've met him, yes. But know him?' She shook her head. 'Does anyone really know a man like that? Charisma is a wonderful and attractive quality, Enzo, but who knows what it conceals?'

# CHAPTER TWENTY-FIVE

Mist lay all across the plain, filling the contours of the land in swirls and eddies, and, from the slight elevation of the road, it looked like a lake.

The distant motorway was lost in it, but the man could see the faintest trace of fog lamps delineating its route along the horizon, and the sound of early-morning traffic reached him with an odd clarity, the way that sound travels across water.

The sky above was clear, and the southern sun was already spilling its warmth across the treetops to disperse the chill that had settled overnight with the mist.

The road was still wet from last night's rain, and his dog, a lively Scots border collie, took great pleasure in splashing her way from puddle to puddle. Turning back at frequent intervals to check that her master was still following, and to seek his approval.

As the road curved gently towards the west, she left the pitted tarmac and went bounding off through the tangle of creeper and briar that washed up on the very edge of the mist, like detritus on the beach after a storm. She snagged her fur as

she went, barking with excitement. The man imagined she had picked up the scent of a rabbit, or some rodent, or maybe even a fox. Suddenly she stopped and began pawing at the ground. He called after her. 'Fanny!' Unusually, she ignored him, snuffling and barking, and circling whatever it was she had found. 'Fanny!' He injected a tone into his voice that brought her head up to look at him. But only for a moment, before she returned to her new-found obsession.

He sighed. She was still young. This time he shouted, and still it had no effect on her. Leaving the road, he strode off through the tangle of dead undergrowth left behind in some distant past by the felling of trees. He reached her in a few short strides, and then stopped in his tracks as he saw what it was that had so focused her attention.

The body of a young man lay face down in the bracken, his right leg twisted at an unnatural angle. He wasn't moving or responding in any way to Fanny's barking. The man crouched down, with the dread sense that he was in the presence of death, and saw blood dried on the young man's forehead. Removing his gloves, he lightly brushed his fingers on the skin of the face. It was cold to the touch, and its pallor suggested that life might have departed some time ago.

Now he reached around to the neck, searching with his fingers for what he knew to be the jugular venous pulse. At first he could not find the vein, and when he did, no pulse. Fanny's constant barking produced a bellow from him that caused the dog to retreat, startled, standing off to stare at him

in bemused silence. And it was almost as if the silence itself found the life in Bertrand's prone body, and the man suddenly felt the faintest of pulses.

He stood up quickly, and with trembling fingers reached for his mobile phone.

# CHAPTER TWENTY-SIX

Lannemezan lay in the great southern plain that sprawled in the shadow of the Pyrenees. The high-security *maison centrale* and *centre de détention* was an ordered, modern prison complex behind a rectangle of concrete walls, built in the eighties and set in agricultural country outside the town itself. It was bounded on two sides by railway lines, and no doubt the 170 prisoners held within its cells could hear the trains that passed in the night, and dreamt of long-lost freedom.

It must, Enzo thought, as they turned off the main road and drove up to the entrance, be quite galling to look out from behind these bars to see the mountain range that was once the escape route for allied soldiers and resistance fighters fleeing the Nazis. The Pyrenees had long been a symbol of freedom, and he wondered if there was some deliberate irony in the choice of Lannemezan as the setting for a place to take it away.

Implacable prison guards watched them from behind glass in circular observation turrets at the top of concrete towers on each corner as the two cars drew into the car park. Kirsty would wait for them here, and she wound down the window

and unstrapped Alexis from his baby chair to sit him with her in the front.

Enzo followed Charlotte past a huge steel door set into a harled archway where vehicles came and went over the hump of a yellow and black ramp. Pedestrian access was at the far side of the entrance, leading them into an open reception area where electric lights reflected on shiny floors and hummed in the deep silence.

Enzo had visited prisons many times, and it always depressed him. There was something about stepping inside a place of incarceration that filled him with a sense of apprehension, and then on leaving, with relief and a gratitude for the freedom he had previously taken for granted.

At a long counter, unsmiling staff behind glass took his passport, which they copied and filed and told him they would hold in safekeeping until his departure. They gave him several forms to fill out and sign, before providing him with the black number six, printed on a white card, to pin to his jacket. They took his bag and the contents of his pockets and gave him a receipt to be produced for their safe return.

It was a procedure Charlotte had clearly been through many times, and she stood waiting patiently until Enzo was finished.

Finally, the door to the prison itself was unlocked and they were accompanied through the high-security wing by two guards in black uniforms with white stripes across their chests. The place smelled like a hospital. Of body odour and antiseptic. Floors were polished to a shine, and pale green

walls were punctuated at regular intervals by dark green bars that divided hallways into sections, like airlocks, gates behind them secured before gates ahead were opened. Overhead strip lights threw up glare from beneath their feet, and every sound seemed to echo back at them from every hard surface.

Finally they were led down steps, through a gate and into a room with reinforced glass walls on three sides. Régis Blanc sat behind a table facing two empty chairs. A door slammed behind them, a key turned in the lock, and they could see the guards who had brought them there through the glass, leaning back against a wall, arms folded, watching them with studied disinterest.

'*Salut, Régis. Comment ça va?*' Charlotte greeted him as if she had known him all her life and they were old friends meeting for lunch. But she didn't kiss his cheeks or shake his hand. Instead, she sat down and folded her hands on the table in front of her.

Blanc had been slouched in his chair. He wore a white T-shirt stretched tightly over muscles honed, perhaps, in a prison gym, or by isometric exercises performed in his cell. His jeans, too, were slim fitting to reveal well-developed thighs. He had about him the air of a man tightly wound and ready to spring. Like a cat on alert. Enzo knew that Blanc was two years younger than him, but he was probably fitter than a man half his age. He looked older, though. Much of his hair had gone, and what was left of it was the colour of metal filings. It had been shorn to a stubble across his scalp. His face was lean and lined, a dead

pallor pockmarked by teenage acne. But the most remarkable things about him were his eyes. They were the palest blue Enzo had ever seen. So pale they were very nearly translucent. And with pin-sharp pupils, and irises circled in black, they were like the eyes of some wild cat. A snow leopard or a tiger. And they were fixed on Enzo, suspicious and hostile, alert from the moment Enzo entered the interview room. He sat immediately upright, ignoring Charlotte's greeting.

'Who's this?'

Charlotte said, 'We had to indulge in a little subterfuge, Régis, to get him in. As far as the prison's concerned Enzo is my assistant.'

'And who is he really?'

'Enzo Macleod,' Enzo said, holding out his hand. Blanc made no attempt to shake it and kept his eyes fixed on Enzo.

'He's a former forensic scientist from Scotland,' Charlotte said. 'He's looking into the murder of Lucie Martin.'

Blanc was on his feet so quickly that Enzo was startled into taking a step back. Blanc's seat overturned and crashed to the floor behind him, and Enzo saw the prison officers beyond the glass pushing themselves off the wall, suddenly tense and ready to move.

There was a moment when it seemed that almost anything was possible, and Enzo calculated that Blanc could quite easily kill him before the guards had even unlocked the door.

Blanc snarled, 'You think I'm going to sit here and let you pin Lucie Martin's murder on me?'

'Cool it, Régis.' Charlotte's tone was calm, but there was an underlying sense of menace in it that drew his eyes towards her for the most fleeting of moments before they returned to Enzo.

With a surface calm that in no way reflected the way he felt inside, Enzo said, 'I'm not even going to try to do that, Régis. Because I don't believe you did. I think you were in love with Lucie. And that, very probably, she was in love with you. Or, at least, thought she was.' He saw consternation gather in the creases around Blanc's eyes.

Charlotte stood up and walked around the table to right Blanc's chair. 'Sit down, Régis,' she said. And like some schoolboy admonished by his teacher, he pulled his chair towards him and perched, sullen-faced, on the edge of it, still without taking his eyes from Enzo.

'What makes you think that?' His whole tone and demeanour was defensive.

'Your letter.' Enzo sat down so that they were all facing each other on the same level, and he was aware in his peripheral vision of the guards outside relaxing again.

'What about it?'

'I've written love letters in my time, Régis. The first one, all full of declaration. Love and intent. And the last one . . . Well . . .' And he smiled. 'That would depend on which of us was breaking it off.' He placed his forearms on the desk in front of him and leaned forward. 'But here's the thing. Yours doesn't fit either category. I don't believe that was the first, or

only letter. And it certainly wasn't intended to be your last. So I can only assume there had been others. Before, maybe after.'

Blanc sat back and folded his arms, and Enzo noticed for the first time the crude tattoos on his left forearm.

'That's quite an assumption, Monsieur . . . whatever your name is.'

'Macleod. But I know some people have trouble pronouncing that, so you can call me Enzo.' Enzo knew that he couldn't let his gaze wander left or right. He had to meet Blanc's eye with the same unwavering stare with which Blanc was fixing him. 'Anyway, maybe I'm cheating a little. Because I also know that you and Lucie were seeing each other.'

Blanc's whole expression changed. Incomprehension clouded the clarity of his eyes. 'How can you know that? Nobody knew that.'

'It's true, then?' Charlotte's voice broke like an intruder into their conversation, but neither of them paid it the least attention.

Enzo said, 'She'd been going out with a boy all through school.'

'Tavel!' Blanc spat out his name, and Enzo was amazed that Blanc both knew it and remembered it.

He nodded. 'When she threw him over he got jealous. Figured there was someone else. So he followed her one night. And guess who she met?'

This was clearly news to Blanc, and he took some moments to process it. Enzo could almost see the thought machinery

working behind eyes that were gazing into the past, making calculations and reaching conclusions. For once Enzo was not their focus. And then it was as if he had returned from some other place, and he looked at Enzo again. His eyes wild now.

'*He* killed her. It must have been him.' And he looked around the room as if searching for a way out. 'I'll fucking kill him. Even if I have to break out of here to do it.' He slammed the palms of his hands down flat on the table in front of him.

Enzo said calmly, 'There's no proof whatsoever that Tavel was involved. He was in Paris the weekend she went missing.' He paused. 'But, then again, what's an alibi, except someone else lying to protect you? You should know all about that, Régis. You always seemed to have an alibi when the police came looking for you.' Another pause. 'Except when it came to murdering those three girls.' And he thought about what he had written up on his whiteboard. *Did he want to be caught?*

For the first time, Blanc's unwavering gaze flickered away from Enzo, and when his eyes returned to him it was almost as if he accepted that Enzo knew the truth, whatever that might be.

'Tell me about your relationship with Lucie, Régis.'

Blanc sat back in his chair, folding his arms over his chest, and deliberately avoided a meeting of eyes. He glanced self-consciously towards Charlotte, and Enzo would have sworn that he blushed. Blood rose high on his cheeks to bring colour to his prison-pale complexion. He let his eyes fall, fixing his gaze on his own feet, stretched out under the table in front of

him. 'Hard to explain,' he said, 'what it was about her.' Even the tone of his voice had changed now, hushed, as if he were speaking in a church. 'When I first met her at the offices of Rentrée . . .' He laughed. 'I suppose I'd gone along to scoff. To be difficult. Rude and crude. Fucking Christian do-gooders! And then she came in the room and sat down opposite me, and I suddenly felt like a little boy. Tongue-tied and awkward. Didn't know where to look. But wherever I turned my eyes I couldn't seem to avoid meeting hers in the end. I'd never been in the presence of –' he fought for a way to describe it – 'such innocence. Ever in my life. It was so pure, and real. Like the first time you shoot up heroin. It feels so fucking amazing, you never want to be in any other state.' He shook his head. 'I never got addicted to heroin, but I got addicted to Lucie. Couldn't get enough of her.'

Now he sat forward, leaning on his thighs, clasping and unclasping his hands in front of him and staring at the floor. But he wasn't looking at it. Sightless eyes were transporting him back to another place and time. A place where the radiance of a young woman, real or imagined, had changed his life.

'My whole life I was surrounded by filth and evil. Lies and deceit. But something about Lucie shone a light into that life and made me realise things didn't have to be that way. That *I* didn't have to be that way.' He glanced up for a moment, as if searching for their understanding. 'And she saw it, too. She told me she did. That there was a better person inside me. Someone I didn't know was there. Someone I wouldn't

recognise, even if I did. She said she could help release him. The real me. The person trapped inside. That's what she said.'

Then he was overcome by self-consciousness and looked down at the floor again.

'I've thought about it often. That's the thing about prison, there's not much else to do but think. I wondered, looking back, if maybe she just saw me as some kind of a challenge. The triumph of good over evil. But that's not what she said in her letters.'

Enzo felt a tiny jolt run through him, like an electric shock. 'Lucie wrote to you?'

'We exchanged half a dozen letters or more over as many weeks. I could feel her in every word. Beautiful words. Words that made me realise how stupid and illiterate I was. Words that made me want to change. To be that other person she saw in me. She said . . .' He broke off, and Enzo was shocked to see the hint of tears in his eyes, tears that he lowered his head to conceal from them. But you could hear them in the tremble of his voice. 'She said that she had seen beyond the outer shell, to the soft, sensitive person within. And that she loved that person, and wanted to release him.'

Words, Enzo was sure, that Blanc had memorised from countless readings of her letters. And he found himself empathising with this serial killer sitting before him. A man robbed by death of something that might have transformed his life, but left him, instead, with only memories and regrets and the sense of a life unfulfilled.

'You know, I look back, and it's hard to believe it now. Knowing who I am, what I became. But I really believed Lucie could save me. Like Jesus fucking Christ. I'd have done anything for her. Anything.' He paused. 'Only . . .' And then he sat upright, folding his arms again, and Enzo could see him biting the inside of his lower lip.

'Only what?'

'There were things I had to do. You know. First.' This said with defiance, as if making excuses for not living up to Lucie's vision of him.

'What things?'

The colour was gone from his face again, and a shadow crossed it. 'Things. Obligations. Debts.'

'What obligations? What debts?'

But Blanc remained tight-lipped, staring at the floor, and Enzo saw an almost imperceptible shake of his head. It was clear that he wasn't going to say. So Enzo said it for him.

'Killing those girls, you mean?'

Blanc flashed him a look that was both dangerous and full of pain. His eyes flickered towards Charlotte, then back. 'These fucking psychiatrists,' he said, the contempt clear in his voice. 'They'll tell you that I killed them because my mother was a prostitute. That every time I killed one, I was killing my mother.' He snorted his derision. 'What bollocks! What they don't understand, any of them, is that it didn't matter what my mother was. She was my mother. I loved her unconditionally. And she loved me.'

'So why did you kill them?'

A sad, sick smile curled his lips and he shook his head. 'If I told you, they'd kill me.'

Enzo frowned. 'What do you mean? Who's "they"?'

Blanc's smile was smug now. A man who knew he kept a secret he wasn't going to tell, but was taking pleasure in dropping hints that would tease and tantalise without fulfilment. 'Trust me, there are worse things than death,' he said.

The silence that followed seemed to stretch from seconds to minutes, without Blanc being in the least aware of it. He was watching his hands in front of him, lacing and unlacing his fingers as if praying, then changing his mind. Enzo sensed that there was more to come and didn't want to break the moment. He willed Charlotte not to speak. Although she had said nothing throughout the entire interview, listening rapt to a killer's ramblings in mute fascination.

Finally Blanc looked up. His eyes moved from Enzo to Charlotte, then back again. The smile was gone. 'The thing is . . . sometimes obligations don't last a lifetime. Maybe one day soon I'll have my say.'

'About what?'

But he just shook his head. 'Why would I tell you?'

Enzo decided to chance his arm. 'You wanted to be caught, Régis, didn't you?'

Blanc shrugged. 'We all pay for the things we do. In this life or the next. But whatever awful things I've done, I know that Lucie would have forgiven me.'

'For killing those girls?' Enzo was genuinely surprised.

'Yes.' But he quickly changed his mind. 'Well, no. Not for killing them. I'm glad she never knew about that. I mean why I did it. She'd have understood that. She would.' He saw the question forming itself in Enzo's eyes, and he pre-empted the asking of it. 'But, like I said, I'm not telling you.'

Enzo nodded, sensing the finality in Blanc's words. 'And what about the Bordeaux Six?'

'Pah!' Derision exploded from Blanc's lips. 'That's just fucking incompetent cops trying to pin their failures on me. A convenient bloody scapegoat, already doing life. I don't know anything about what happened to those girls. That's just how it is, you know. People die, people get murdered, people run away. Who knows who or why or when? They come into your life and they go out of it again. Doesn't make you responsible for them.'

'What do you think happened to those other letters that you sent to Lucie? You know they only ever found one.'

He nodded. 'I've no idea.'

'But you denied any relationship with her at the time. Said you'd only written that one, and only because you were drunk.'

Blanc became almost agitated. 'Lucie was dead. No one would have believed what it was we had between us. And I wasn't about to drag her name through the mud along with mine.'

'And what about her letters to you?'

Blanc eyed Enzo warily now. 'What about them?'

'What happened to them?'

'Oh, don't you worry. I've got them safely hidden away. Somewhere no one will ever find them.'

Enzo said, 'You realise, if you could produce those letters, they are probably just about the only thing that could erase any suspicion that it was you who killed her?'

'I don't care,' Blanc said, verging on the hostile now. 'People can think what they want. I know I didn't kill her. And wherever she might be now, Lucie knows that, too.' He dropped his eyes to the number six pinned to Enzo's jacket, and a small smile of irony crossed his lips. '*Je ne suis pas un numéro, je suis un homme libre*,' he said.

Enzo frowned, then did the mental translation. *I am not a prisoner, I am a free man.* And he realised that he and Blanc were of the same generation, each sitting on either side of the English Channel, watching Patrick McGoohan in the cult sixties TV show, *The Prisoner*.

Enzo drew a deep breath as the prison gate shut behind them. It felt good to be out, breathing God's own pure, sweet air, chilled by the proximity of the Pyrenees, uncontaminated by big-city pollution or tainted by life behind bars.

It felt like emerging from some dreadful human laboratory where, for the hour they had spent locked in a room with a killer, they had found themselves looking deep into Nietzsche's abyss.

They stood in silence for several long moments, gazing out

across a pastoral landscape that shimmered off into a hazy blue distance that then took dark and brooding form in the ominous shape of the mountains.

Charlotte spoke first. 'I have never heard him speak like that before. No amount of prompting would ever induce him to talk to me about the murders. Or Lucie.'

Enzo glanced at her to see her face quite pale in the misted midday light. 'What did you talk about, then?'

'His childhood, mostly. His mother. God. Religion. I think he was always just glad to have someone to talk to. Today was different, though.' She looked at Enzo. 'He was a different man.' She hesitated. 'What do you think he meant when he said *they* would kill him?'

Enzo shook his head, equally mystified. 'I have no idea. He was . . . well, pretty enigmatic.'

'Except when it came to talking about Lucie.'

He nodded.

'You think he didn't kill her, then?'

'I'd put money on it.'

She smiled wryly. 'Enzo, do you not think gambling has got you into enough trouble as it is?'

His smile of resignation and the gentle inclination of his head signalled agreement. 'Very probably.' But he couldn't shake off the depression which had descended on him during his interview with Blanc, and he couldn't help feeling that there was something inestimably sad about the man. He kissed Charlotte on both cheeks and handed back her car keys. 'Thank

you for getting me in to see him. I'll let you know if there are any developments.'

'Please do,' she called after him, and before returning to her vehicle stood watching as Enzo got into the car with Kirsty to drive down the spur that would take them to the main road and back, ultimately, on to the motorway, heading west.

# CHAPTER TWENTY-SEVEN

Enzo was happy to sit back in the passenger seat and let Kirsty drive. The rhythm of the car had sent Alexis to sleep in his baby seat, and Enzo had spent half an hour or more lost in replay of his interview with Blanc. It seemed to him now that Michel Bétaille had been right to question Blanc's motivation for murdering those prostitutes. Blanc himself had scorned the reasons attributed by the psychologists to his sudden killing spree. But had very nearly admitted that it wasn't just some random notion. It had been a clear and conscious decision.

What was not clear, and what he wasn't saying, was why.

Neither had he denied Enzo's suggestion that he had wanted to be caught, attributing it to some Christian notion of paying penance. But Enzo didn't believe that Blanc was a very Christian man, in spite of what had very probably been a Catholic upbringing. His mother herself would have been the role model providing the lie that undermined the pretence of faith.

'I won't ask,' Kirsty said suddenly. She smiled. 'I'd love to know, but you can tell me in your own good time. We have a couple of days together.'

Enzo returned her smile. 'We have. And it's nice. A long time since I got to spend time like this with you on your own.'

She nodded towards the back seat. 'Not exactly alone.'

Enzo grinned. 'Ah, but Alexis is family.' And he saw the shadow that passed fleetingly over her face. They could pretend all they wanted that nothing had changed between them since the revelation that he was not her blood father. But it had. Not in any substantive way, but in some strangely amorphous sense of loss that neither wanted to acknowledge.

She said, 'I noticed that Dominique spent the night at the apartment last night.'

'She did.'

Kirsty flicked him a look. 'And I noticed that she didn't sleep on the sofa.'

'I could hardly ask the girl to doss down on that awful thing.'

She lifted an eyebrow. 'You're incorrigible, Papa, you know that?'

He grinned. 'Encourageable, Kirsty.'

'Is she . . . ?' And she left the sentence hanging.

'She's very serious.'

'And you?'

'I've been trying hard not to be.'

'Why?'

'Because she's not much older than you, Kirsty. There's no future in it for her.'

'Have you told her that?'

'I have.'

235

'And what did she say?'

'Oh, I got a great big long speech. Which I won't bother you with. But I told you, she's very serious.'

Kirsty took her eye from the road for just a moment to look at him very directly. 'And if it wasn't for the age gap?'

'Keep your eyes on the road,' he admonished her. And he thought about it for a moment before he spoke. 'She's the first woman I've met since Pascale died . . .' He hesitated. He always felt guilty at the mention of Pascale's name, and what it meant to Kirsty. If he hadn't met Pascale he might never have left Kirsty's mother and, by default, Kirsty herself. Although in his heart he always knew that, while he loved Kirsty with all his being, his marriage to her mother had been a mistake.

'Yes?' Kirsty prompted him.

'She's the first woman I've met that I would be happy to spend the rest of my life with. Even if I do turn into an old fart while she's still a young thing.'

'Papa, has no one told you? You're already an old fart.'

He grinned. 'Thank you, Kirsty.'

Her smile faded. 'And what about Charlotte?'

He expelled a slow, sad breath. 'She might have been the one. Only, I wasn't the one for her. Obviously.'

'Nobody seems to like her very much. Apart from you.'

'You shouldn't judge her by appearances, pet. Charlotte's a complex and, yes, difficult woman, and she tends to hide the real her.'

Kirsty shrugged. 'So who is the real her?'

Enzo smiled. 'Well, that would be hard to say. She had a pretty disturbed childhood. Discovered in her teens that she was adopted. Got obsessed by it and went looking for her birth parents. Only to discover that she was the love child of the celebrated political adviser and film critic Jacques Gaillard – whose murder, as you know, was the first case in Raffin's book that I investigated. Apparently her birth mother had been going to have her aborted. But Gaillard paid her a lot of money to have the baby, then farmed Charlotte out to a childless couple in Angoulême, retainers employed by his family. I think Charlotte was quite deeply affected by the sense of being unwanted, no matter how much her adopted parents loved her.'

Kirsty was less than sympathetic. 'And yet she was prepared to do exactly the same thing to her own child, when she was pregnant with Laurent.' She glanced at her father. 'Do you think she really would have had an abortion?'

Enzo thought about it. 'Yes, I do. Charlotte is a very determined and wilful woman. She'll do exactly what it is she wants to do, and never does anything without a good reason.' He paused and corrected himself. 'Well, a reason that she considers good for her.'

# CHAPTER TWENTY-EIGHT

A tree-lined drive of pale *castine* gravel wound through this lightly forested estate in the very south-west corner of France, before opening up suddenly on to a sweep of neatly cut lawn, and a view of the house where they were to stay, that very nearly took their breath away.

Although they knew it had only been built in the nineteenth century, it looked like a sugarloaf and marzipan château from some extraordinary medieval fairy tale. Cream-painted, with red-chequered stonework around arched and square windows and doors, it was topped off by a tower and a jumble of red-tiled roofs that raised themselves like eyebrows in surprise over dormers and balconies.

The whole was softened by exotic trees and shrubs, which grew all about it, and as the drive looped around to the front entrance, they saw the lawns that stretched away on the far side, to an oblong water feature with a fountain sparkling in the early-afternoon sun

In a long, tiled entrance hall they were greeted by an attractive woman in her thirties, black hair pulled back severely

from a sultry face and dark eyes that seemed to owe more to a Spanish than a French heritage. She wore a tight-fitting black business dress that reached the knee, and black shoes with impossibly high heels that emphasised the elegant curve of her calves. Long fingers, with perfectly manicured red-painted nails, and a simple pearl necklace completed the picture of the ideal hostess, always on hand to greet visitors to this exclusive manor house of half a dozen *chambre d'hôte* apartments.

So this, Enzo thought, was what Raffin had married into, and in the end inherited.

'I'm Rafaella,' the young woman said, shaking their hands. 'Roger told me to expect you.' And as they followed her along the hall and up the broad spiral staircase at the far end, Enzo found his eye being drawn by the sway of her hips and the way that her dress clung to a slim but curvaceous figure. He felt an elbow in his ribs, and turned to see his daughter glaring at him.

'Papa!' she admonished him in a whisper.

He shrugged and whispered back, 'I wouldn't be normal if I didn't look.'

She breathed her exasperation and shook her head.

On the first floor, Rafaella led them along a hushed and carpeted hall. At the end of it, she opened double doors into a sitting room filled with light from two enormous French windows overlooking the lawns at the back of the house. 'Bedrooms on either side,' she said, indicating doors to the left and right, 'each with their own en suite.' She looked at

their overnight bags, and Alexis in his carrycot. 'If you have more luggage in the car I'll send someone to fetch it.'

'No that's fine, thank you,' Kirsty said. 'I'm sure Roger must have told you, we're only here for the one night.'

'Yes, of course. There's a bar in the lounge downstairs. Just give me a call and I'll serve you whatever you would like. We've had the apartment airing. I'll send the housekeeper to close the windows and turn down the beds.' She smiled and exited the room backwards, pulling the doors closed.

When she had gone, Kirsty looked around in awe. 'Wow. I had no idea it was this grand.'

Antique furniture, cream-painted and upholstered in satin, languished in a big, square, high-ceilinged room. Soft silk cushions dressing settees and armchairs. A huge hi-def television was set, like a mirror, above an elaborate fireplace.

Enzo opened one of the French windows and wandered out on to a covered balcony. The air was soft here, almost warm, autumn retarded by at least three weeks. He looked down on to the terrace below and saw tables and chairs set out in the sunshine, and wondered if they were the only guests.

As if she had read his mind, Kirsty said, 'There's no one else here at the moment. They close down for the season at the end of the week. The housekeeper lives in and looks after the place during the winter.'

After she had fed Alexis and laid him down to sleep in his carrycot, Kirsty and Enzo went downstairs and had drinks on

the terrace. Both were a little overawed by the place.

'Imagine living here,' Kirsty said.

'It's where Roger's wife grew up, isn't it?'

She sipped her vodka tonic and shook her head in wonder. 'God, yes. Hard to believe it was a family home. I'm not surprised she didn't want to sell it. It's beautiful.'

'Must cost a fortune to maintain.'

'That's why they decided to do the *chambres d'hôte*, I think. To make it pay for itself.' Kirsty hesitated. 'I'm not sure I feel entirely comfortable staying in the apartment. Feels like . . . I don't know . . . trespassing on other people's lives.'

Enzo nodded. 'I know what you mean.' He took a mouthful of wine. 'What do you know about Marie? I suppose you and Roger must have talked about her?'

'We have. But maybe not as much as you would think. It's still a painful subject for him, so I can understand why.' She swirled her glass and listened to the chinking of the ice cubes. 'You knew she was a journalist?'

Enzo nodded.

'Roger said she was absolutely determined to make her name. Free herself from a life in the shadow of her parents. Privileged little rich girl. She needed to validate her own existence, not just for herself, but for a world whose eyes she thought were always on her.'

'Roger said that?' Enzo was surprised.

'Yes.' Kirsty smiled. 'He has a way with words. He's a journalist, too, remember.'

Enzo grinned. Then his smile faded. 'She never did, though, did she? I mean, find the success she craved.'

'Well, I think she was quite a respected journalist, but, no, never achieved the recognition she'd hoped for. Apparently she was working on something in the weeks and months before her murder that she point-blank refused to share with Roger, certain that it was going to make her name. He said she was obsessed. Secret meetings, disappearing sometimes for days on end, working into the small hours of the morning. Suspicious of him if he even asked her about it. He said it was as if she was paranoid, or scared that he might steal it from her.' She sighed. 'Roger and she hadn't been close for some time, but this weird, secretive behaviour was absolutely putting the nail in the coffin of their marriage.'

'And they never did find out what it was she had been working on,' Enzo said thoughtfully.

Kirsty shook her head. 'No.'

Enzo remembered the chapter about her in Raffin's book. How police had searched the apartment and her office, even the house here in the south-west, and found no trace of any story that she might have been about to break. No papers or letters, and since it pre-dated the internet, no emails. Neither her editor at *Libération*, nor Raffin himself, had been able to cast any illumination on the object of her obsession.

Kirsty said, 'It was during that time that Roger and Charlotte began their affair.'

'No,' Enzo corrected her. 'They didn't meet until he was

working on his book, which was some time after Marie was murdered.'

'No, Papa, you're wrong. Marie was still very much alive when Roger and Charlotte got together. A very secret affair, apparently. About six months before her murder. And afterwards, well, they agreed to just keep it that way. Secret. In case the police would see it as a motive for Roger to kill her. So they didn't tell anyone.'

Enzo frowned. None of this chimed with what Charlotte had told him when they first met. Then he said, 'Why would the police even consider Roger a suspect anyway? He was at an editorial meeting at the paper the night she was killed.' No sooner were the words out of his mouth than he recalled again, with a sudden sense of shock, the words of the old judge, Guillaume Martin: *I didn't spend all those years sitting on the bench, monsieur, without coming to the realisation that alibis can be fabricated*. And then Charlotte's words to him, only the previous day: *I have often wondered just how closely the police examined his alibi*. He glanced at Kirsty, concerned once more for his daughter. She was living with the man. She had borne his son, and it was still their avowed intention to marry.

They had decided to drive into Biarritz early to find something to eat and to check out the location of the specialist's consulting rooms in the quiet of the evening. The town lay only four kilometres away, and with a gentle breeze now blowing from the west they could almost smell the Atlantic.

They went back upstairs to prepare Alexis for going out and were startled to find the door of the apartment lying open. 'Hello?' Kirsty called out in alarm, and ran towards the open door of the bedroom where she had put Alexis down to sleep.

Enzo was right behind her as she stopped in the doorway at the sight of a middle-aged woman standing by the bed, bouncing the baby gently up and down in her arms. She was making faces at him and Alexis was lost in fits of giggles.

She smiled at Kirsty. 'I heard him crying from the other room when I came to turn down the beds.' And Enzo noticed that she was wearing a black blouse and skirt beneath a cream pinafore. The housekeeper that Rafaella had spoken of. She was a plain-looking woman who might once have been pretty. But the years had not been kind to her, and the absence of any make-up seemed only to emphasise the colourless quality of her skin. Lifeless, greying hair was pulled back in a severe bun. Alexis, however, had brought animation to her face, and her blue eyes sparkled with pleasure.

'Thank you,' Kirsty said, but nonetheless moved quickly to retrieve her baby from the stranger.

The woman stood awkwardly, then. 'You're . . . um . . . Monsieur Raffin's partner?'

'Yes.' Kirsty was clearly annoyed that Alexis seemed to want back to the arms of the woman who had been making him laugh. 'And you are . . . ?'

'Madame Brusque. The housekeeper. Been here for years.

I have rooms up in the tower.' She seemed suddenly self-conscious. 'Anyway, I'm sorry to disturb you. If there's anything you need at all, you can buzz me from the reception desk downstairs. Rafaella finishes at seven.'

'Okay, thank you,' Kirsty said, a little coolly, and Madame Brusque slipped out of the room, averting her eyes timidly as she passed Enzo.

When she was gone, he said, 'You were a little brusque with her.'

Kirsty made a face. 'Oh, very funny.' Then paused. 'I don't like people picking up my baby without permission.'

'I don't think she meant any harm.'

'No, neither do I. But still . . .' Then she frowned. 'You know, it's weird . . . I'm sure I've met her before, or seen her somewhere.'

Enzo shrugged. 'She didn't seem to know you.'

'No . . . She didn't look familiar to you?'

Enzo said, 'To be honest, I wasn't paying her very much attention. She's no Rafaella!'

Kirsty glowered at him. 'Oh, Papa!'

# CHAPTER TWENTY-NINE

Sunlight slanted into Bertrand's room at an acute angle through venetian blinds, and lay in stripes across the white sheet that covered him. Stripes that followed the contour of his leg, raised under the sheet and supported from below. The softness of the pillow beneath his head felt so luxurious that he had no real desire to come fully to the surface of what felt like a very deep sleep.

For the first time in a long time, there was no pain. No sensation of any kind. He might have been floating.

But gradually he became aware of an electronic beep that sounded at regular intervals, and it dawned on him that it was keeping time with the beat of his heart. With an effort he turned his head to his left, and saw a bank of electronic apparatus spilling wires and tubes across the floor to the bed. A drip almost directly above him feeding clear liquid into a vein in his arm, sensors stuck to his chest.

His mouth was so dry he could barely separate his tongue from the roof of it, his lips cracked and sore. He tried to swallow, but it seemed there was a boulder in his throat.

He heard a door opening and lifted his head a little to see an elderly nurse bustling into the room, her crisp white uniform swishing as she walked. She leaned over and looked at him with soft, kindly brown eyes. 'Good morning, young man,' she said. 'I'm glad to see you are finally awake at last.'

Morning, Bertrand thought. Morning? What morning? What day? Where on earth was he?

'How are you feeling?'

He struggled to find his voice, then finally heard it croak in the quiet of the room. 'Not bad.' What else to say?

The nurse smiled. 'Maybe now you'll be able to tell us who you are and where we can get in touch with your family.'

Bertrand was confused. Why would they not know who he was?

Then recollection returned like a sledgehammer and set the machine beside his bed beeping at an alarming rate. He sat bolt upright, and the nurse stepped back in surprise. 'You've got to get me a phone,' he said, suddenly finding strength in his voice. 'You've got to get me a phone, now!'

# CHAPTER THIRTY

'The ear is a very complex construction of multiple parts. The outer and inner ears, the middle ear, the acoustic nerve, the auditory system that processes sound as it travels from the ear to the brain.' Doctor Demoulin sat back, dispensing his expertise with the dispassionate disinterest of a man who has made the same speech many times. His consulting rooms were in an eighteenth-century provincial townhouse that sat up on the cliffs above the Boulevard du Prince de Galles, looking out across the bay beneath the town of Biarritz, once the playground of European royalty. The doctor himself sat at a large mahogany desk with his back to a double window, and, beyond yellowing vertical blinds, Enzo could see sunlight coruscating away across a crystal-blue sea.

The furniture in the doctor's consulting rooms appeared to be of the same vintage as the house. His office smelled of time and disinfectant, and entering it felt like stepping back a century.

Doctor Demoulin might also have come from the same era. He was a big man, his great balding cranium ringed by a tangle

of silver hair, like wire bursting from its sheath. The same wiry growth sprouted in abundance from his ears and nostrils. He wore a grey tweed suit and heavy brown brogues. His hands, Enzo noticed, were enormous, with more hair growing between the knuckles. He looked at the notes in front of him. Then raised his eyes towards Enzo. He gestured a hand back across the top of his head and nodded towards the Scotsman. 'Waardenburg syndrome?'

Enzo's own hand went instinctively to the white stripe in his hair. 'Yes.'

Demoulin looked at Kirsty. 'And have you inherited?'

Enzo and Kirsty exchanged embarrassed glances, and Enzo said, 'Kirsty is not my blood daughter.'

Demoulin cocked an eyebrow, then scratched his chin and closed the folder in front of him. 'Okay, so the fact that baby Alexis failed his newborn hearing test would not, in itself, have signalled a problem. Anything up to ten per cent of babies fail that test. Vernix in the ear canal, fluid in the middle ear . . . It's the follow-up confirmatory test which is the most important. And the fact that he failed that is the cause for concern.' He leaned over to smile at Alexis in his carrycot, and elicited a happy chortle from the baby. 'Nothing wrong with his sight anyway.'

Enzo could feel Kirsty's tension as, during the next hour, Doctor Demoulin donned a white coat and conducted a series of tests in a clinical room next door to his office. Miniature earphones were inserted into Alexis' ears and electrodes placed

on his head to detect brain response to the various sounds played. Then a microscopic microphone was placed in the ear next to a tiny ear bud to measure auditory echo.

A test that the doctor described as a 'brain audiometry evaluation' was a straightforward visual determination of changes in Alexis' behaviour in response to what sounds were fed into his earphones.

When he had completed his tests Doctor Demoulin stood thoughtfully, his lips pursed. 'That he has a hearing problem, there is no doubt. He is not deaf, but is what I would describe as hearing-impaired. It's not serious, but still a cause for concern.' He looked at them both, then focused on Kirsty. 'There's no history of deafness in your family?'

Kirsty shook her head. 'Not that I know of.'

The doctor nodded and stood up. 'Well, I'm going to have to take a little bit of blood from Alexis to send to the lab for testing. Then, perhaps, we'll be in a better position to make both diagnosis and prognosis.'

They stepped out into the street and the rumble of traffic, and Enzo sensed his daughter's disappointment. He said gently, 'It never was going to be settled here and now, Kirst. These things never are. But I think you came to the right man. I had a good feeling about him.'

Kirsty turned her face up towards him, concerned. 'Did you? I wasn't sure.'

Enzo nodded. 'He had a good way with Alexis, and you

don't get to be the number one specialist in your field without knowing what you're about.'

'It's just . . .' She shrugged. 'He gave so little away.'

'I'm sure he'll have plenty to say when he knows how things stand.' He put an arm around her shoulder and she leaned into him gratefully.

He felt his phone vibrate in his pocket. He had silenced the ringtone and ignored it while they were in with the consultant. Now he took it out and saw that there were several messages, all from Nicole. He hit the dial icon and waited. It barely rang once.

'Monsieur Macleod, where on earth have you been?'

'It doesn't matter where I've been, Nicole, I'm here now. What's the problem?'

Kirsty watched her father's face lose all its colour in the blink of an eye. He staggered, and for a moment she thought he was going to fall down. She clutched his arm. 'Papa? Are you okay? What's wrong?'

'Where?' she heard him say, and his voice sounded oddly hoarse. 'I'm on my way.'

He hung up, and she saw tears trembling on the lower lids of his eyes, a strange, wild look in them as he stared off into some unseen distance. Now she was scared.

'Papa! For God's sake, what's happened?'

He turned his head, as if in slow motion, and though his eyes were on her he didn't appear to see her. The first tears spilled on to his cheeks. 'Sophie's been abducted,' he said.

*

During the five and a half hours it took them to drive to Montpellier, Enzo barely spoke, and Kirsty knew better than to ask more than he had already told her. 'The bastards have taken her,' is all he'd say. And beyond briefing her that they were going to see Betrand in Lapeyronie Hospital, in Montpellier, he'd told her very little.

'Is he okay?'

He'd nodded mutely. Then, 'He'd be dead if they hadn't found him when they did.'

Kirsty had fretted about Bertrand the whole way. She was concerned for her half-sister, yes, though the two had never been the best of friends. But Bertrand had saved her life. Stopped her from drowning in the catacombs below Paris, and there had been a special rapport between them ever since. He had once told her that saving her life made it his responsibility for the rest of *his* life. And now she felt responsible for him. But she also knew that if anything were to happen to Sophie it would destroy her father. There would be no way back for him, no future, no life.

The *Département de Médecine d'Urgence* of Lapeyronie Hospital was in the north-east of the city, in the Avenue du Doyen Gaston Giraud. Parking was in a sprawling, tree-shaded area to the east of the hospital complex, off the Route de Ganges.

Enzo had insisted on driving, but now he abandoned both the car and his daughter and ran, following the red *Urgences* signs. By the time he had been directed to Bertrand's room, he could barely catch his breath. There were several uniformed

officers of the Police Nationale standing in the corridor outside, talking. The most senior of them put a hand out to stop
him. 'Monsieur . . . ?'

'Macleod. It's my daughter they've taken.' He leaned over,
supporting his weight with his hands on his knees, then stood
up. 'I've got to talk to Bertrand.'

'All in good time, monsieur. He gave us a statement, and a
description of the house they were taken to. It wasn't that far
from where the dog walker found him.'

'And?'

'Nothing there. They've left traces, of course. The *police sci-
entifique* are going through the place right now. We might get
lucky with fingerprints, or DNA, but from everything the boy's
told us, these were professionals. So I wouldn't go holding
your breath.'

Enzo said, 'I'd have to catch it first to hold it. Where's my
daughter?'

'I'm sorry, monsieur, we've no idea. According to the young
man, they drove off with her in a van three nights ago.'

'Jesus Christ, what's Bertrand been doing all this time?'

'He has a badly broken leg, monsieur, and was suffering
from severe exposure. Another few hours and he'd have been
dead. And we would have been none the wiser about any of
this.'

Enzo heard footsteps hurrying up behind him and turned to
see Kirsty arriving, pink-faced and breathing hard, with Alexis
in her arms. 'Is he going to be alright?' she said.

Enzo turned back to the police officer. 'Can we go in and see him?'

He nodded.

Bertrand turned his head as the door opened. He had been aware of voices on the other side of it and now, as he saw Enzo step into the room, he almost choked on his guilt. He tried to sit up.

'Stay where you are, son,' Enzo said. He pulled up a chair at the bedside and sat down. Bertrand saw Kirsty standing beside him, her baby in her arms, her face rigid with concern. She leaned over to take his hand and squeeze it.

Then he forced himself, no matter how painful it would be, to meet Enzo's gaze. 'I'm so sorry, Monsieur Macleod. I tried everything I could to protect her.' And tears gathered to blur his clear, dark irises.

Had Enzo been prone to uncharitable thoughts he might have felt that perhaps Bertrand could have done more. But he knew this young man. Knew that he loved his daughter. And that if Bertrand couldn't protect her, then no one could. His face was swollen and bruised, his nose broken and set in high-grip tape. Enzo nodded. 'I know. There's no blame in this, Bertrand. I just want to find her and get her back. Did they say anything – anything at all – that might give me something to work on?'

Bertrand shook his head hopelessly. 'They barely spoke to us, Monsieur Macleod. They grabbed us at Argelès. Two of

them waiting in the apartment. But I think there were four in all. They took us straight to that house, and just kept us there till I got away.' His lower lip was trembling. 'I went back to try and get her. But they took her. A van and two cars. Just drove off.' He closed his eyes, squeezing out tears. 'And I went and broke my stupid bloody leg in the dark.' He opened his eyes again, and Enzo saw the pain in them. 'Get her back, Monsieur Macleod. You have to get her back.' And Enzo knew that Bertrand was passing the baton of responsibility on to him.

Back out in the hall, the investigating officer of the Police Nationale said, 'Have you the least idea why someone would want to kidnap your daughter, monsieur?'

Enzo said grimly, 'Well, it's not for financial gain, I can tell you that.' He sucked in a deep breath to steady himself. 'I've been investigating a group of cold cases.'

The policeman nodded. 'I know, monsieur. We know all about you by now.'

'Then you'll know that there have been at least three attempts on my life. Someone really doesn't want me continuing with my investigations. And it looks now like they think they've found a way to stop me.'

'Then, with the greatest respect, monsieur, I suggest that's exactly what you do.'

Kirsty struggled to keep up with her father as he strode through the hospital. His breathing, stertorous and full of anger, echoed

back at them off all the shiny surfaces of the sterile corridors. By the time they got to the car she could see his fists clenching and unclenching at his sides. He stopped by the driver's door and turned towards a litter bin raised on a concrete coping between lines of cars. He kicked it with the flat of his foot, all of his pent-up and impotent rage channelled into the violence that sent it spinning away across the asphalt, spilling its contents over the car park.

'Bastards!' he yelled at the sky.

Alexis began to cry.

'Papa . . .' Kirsty said. But Enzo wasn't listening. His phone was issuing an alert. An incoming text. He grabbed it from his pocket and brought up the screen with fumbling fingers. As his eyes scanned the text he went very still, and Kirsty saw him suck in and bite his lower lip. 'What is it, Papa?'

Without a word, he handed her the phone. The text had come, ostensibly, from Sophie. It was from her phone, at least.

*Stop investigating the Raffin cold cases or you'll never see me again.*

Kirsty looked up with frightened eyes at her father. 'What are you going to do?'

His voice was barely audible above the roar of traffic from the Route de Ganges. 'I'm going to get these fucking people, that's what I'm going to do.' And he remembered all their attempts to stop him. At the château in Gaillac, in the mountains of the Auvergne, at Raffin's apartment. He remembered their attempt to kill Kirsty in Strasbourg. And the note left on

his windscreen, just the other day. Had that been yet another attempt to lure him to his death? But what could it possibly be about the apparently straightforward murder of a young woman twenty-two years ago that had driven them now to the desperate act of kidnapping his daughter?

'What if they kill her?'

Enzo turned wild eyes in her direction. 'They're going to kill her anyway, Kirsty. If they haven't already. I can only hope that somehow they believe keeping her alive gives them continued leverage.'

Kirsty looked at him helplessly, bouncing Alexis up and down to try to calm his crying. 'Doesn't it?'

'No. If I wasn't motivated before to solve the Lucie Martin murder, I damn well am now. Because only by finding her killer, or killers, am I going to find Sophie.'

'But what if it's not that murder they want to stop you looking at? What if it's the murder of Marie Raffin?'

Enzo closed his eyes and shook his head. 'I can only think in a straight line, Kirsty. If it's not Lucie, it's Marie. One or other of them is going to lead me to Sophie's kidnappers. Then there'll be another murder. Only, I won't be investigating it. I'll be committing it.'

He took several long, slow breaths, trying to calm himself, before looking at his phone.

'But first things first.' He tapped a dial icon and lifted the phone to his ear. He heard it ring three times before it was answered. But whoever was on the other end was saying

nothing. Enzo said, 'If you want me to stop coming after you, I need to know that she's still alive.'

Another long silence. He heard ambient sounds and a scraping noise, then what sounded like footsteps. A door opened, then a hand went over the phone to muffle voices. When it lifted away again, Sophie's voice nearly broke his heart. 'Papa?'

'Baby, are you alright?'

'Papa, they say they'll kill me if you don't stop chasing Roger's cold cases.'

He heard her voice breaking. A stifled sob.

'Don't worry, baby, I'm going to get you out of this.' Though he had no idea how.

'Papa—'

He heard the phone being snatched from her before it went dead.

Kirsty watched as his phone hand fell away from his ear, and she thought she had never seen him look so old, or so defeated.

# CHAPTER THIRTY-ONE

For the longest time Dominique just held him. She felt the pain in his silence, and in the tears she wiped from his cheeks. 'We'll find her,' she told him. 'We will.' And he nodded, grateful that for almost the first time in his adult life he did not feel completely alone. Even so, he was overwhelmed. By pressure and emotion. By love for his daughter and hatred for those who had taken her.

The drive back to Cahors from Montpellier had taken nearly four hours, and both Enzo and Kirsty were exhausted by the time they got to the apartment. Emotionally, physically and mentally drained.

Now Enzo and Dominique lay fully dressed in each other's arms on his bed in the dark. He realised that he had to remain focused, that he couldn't allow his emotions to drive his thinking or his actions. If ever he needed to stay cool and clear and calm, this was the time. But anger and fear, in equal measure, kept bubbling into his consciousness, like carbonated water fizzing and spitting and drowning out cogent thought. The only thing saving him from himself was Dominique.

All of his instincts were telling him that somehow Régis Blanc was the key. Not the killer, at least not of Lucie Martin. And not behind the kidnapping of his daughter. But somehow at the centre of it all. He recalled vividly the picture of him that he had carried away from the prison in Lannemezan only yesterday. Lean and fit, and with a tension inside him so tightly wound that Enzo had felt him capable of unravelling in violence at any moment. And yet he had controlled himself with a steely composure, keeping close those secrets he had hinted that one day he might reveal to the world. But not yet. Not to Enzo. And Enzo knew that somehow he had to get inside the man's head and find them for himself.

A soft knocking at the door interrupted his thoughts, and he heard Nicole's voice from the other side of it. 'Ready now, Monsieur Macleod.'

He and Dominique rose wordlessly from the bed, and she took a moment to wipe his face dry and kiss him softly on the lips.

They found Nicole settling herself in front of her laptop, which sat on the table in the *séjour* beneath a ring of light from the pull-down lamp. Kirsty sat opposite, a pen resting on the top page of an open notebook. Enzo and Dominique joined them in silence, faces set in grim resolve, floating on the edge of darkness. Any one of them could have reached out and touched the apprehension that sat among them. It was after ten p.m. But a night of inactivity through all the sleepless hours that would surely lie ahead was not an option.

Nicole said, 'I wasn't expecting to have to brief you on Blanc quite this soon. But I think I've pulled together just about everything about him that's out there in the public domain. There've been a lot of articles written on the man.' She tapped on her keyboard, and Enzo saw the changing light from the screen reflecting on a face fixed with dark determination. 'Do you want just the bones, or the detail, too?'

'Everything,' Enzo said. And he could barely recognise his own voice. He blinked several times to clear stinging eyes.

'He was born in 1957. Mother, Paulette Blanc, the daughter of a fishmonger and a seamstress. Father unknown. He had a half-brother, Jean-Paul, born three years later. Again, father unknown, but he died in infancy. Paulette lived in one of the Bordeaux slums that were cleared in the sixties. Prostitute, alcoholic. Used to bring her clients home when Régis was still a child. According to Blanc himself, she used to tell him to "keep an eye out" while she took her clients into a back bedroom. Though, apparently, he never quite knew what he was keeping an eye out for.'

Nicole navigated her way to a new screen.

'Anyway, when he was about twelve, Paulette got herself a regular man, who moved in with them and effectively took over the role of Régis's father. But he wasn't exactly the kind of role model you might hope for in a father. He was a pimp, but insisted that Paulette give up her night job and stay home. Again according to Régis, it was this man, Arnaud, who first introduced him to drugs. Cocaine, and

later heroin, though it seems that Régis had more of a taste for alcohol than drugs.

'Arnaud conducted his business out of a café near the station, and when Régis was a teenager used to take him along, so he got to know all of the girls that Arnaud ran, and all of his associates. Drunks and drug dealers and petty thieves.' Nicole looked up and shrugged sadly. 'You could almost say that Régis Blanc was destined for disaster.' She returned her eyes to the screen. 'At first he looked up to Arnaud. Respected him. Probably feared him. Certainly saw him as the father he'd never had. Until the man started beating his mother.'

Kirsty said, 'It hadn't always been an abusive relationship, then?'

Nicole shook her head. 'No. It seems not. But Paulette's addiction to gin went from bad to worse. The house was filthy. There was never any food, and it seems that Arnaud just lost patience with her. But raising his fists to her was the beginning of the end for his relationship with Régis. Blanc was nearly eighteen by then, and a real hard case from all accounts. Told Arnaud that if he didn't stop beating up on his mother he would have him to answer to. Arnaud didn't take him too seriously, and according to witnesses there were several confrontations when Arnaud made a fool of him in public, humiliating the boy in front of his mates.'

Nicole breathed deeply and pressed her lips together with distaste in anticipation of what was to come.

'One day Régis came home to find Paulette so badly

beaten up she had actually lost an eye and was in a coma. He rushed her to hospital, but she remained unconscious for two months before finally passing away. Arnaud was never charged. No witnesses, no proof. Two weeks after Paulette died, Arnaud was found dead on a railway siding on the south side of Bordeaux. Almost every bone in his body was broken and he was missing an eye. Everyone knew Régis had done it, but there was no physical evidence to link him to the murder, and he had a solid alibi.' She looked up from her computer screen and saw all eyes fixed on her. 'Arnaud had always groomed Régis to take over the "business" from him sometime in the future. And that's exactly what he did, only a little earlier than Arnaud had planned. Régis was just eighteen years old.'

It was, Enzo thought, a classic example of being moulded by your environment. Whatever good there might have been in Régis Blanc, he had never stood a chance. He became the mirror image of those who had corrupted him. And he wondered what it was that Lucie had seen in him. What it was that could possibly have attracted her, or suggested the possibility of redemption.

Nicole said, 'In 1985 he married a young woman called Anne-Laure Couderc. She had been one of his girls. But like Arnaud before him, he made her give all that up when she married him. Two years later she gave birth to a baby girl that they called Alice. From all accounts, Blanc was absolutely smitten by the child, but he and Anne-Laure weren't getting on, and

after he was sent to Murat for nine months in late eighty-eight she quit their apartment and got a place of her own.'

Dominique said, 'What was he sent to Murat for?'

'Aggravated assault,' Nicole said. 'Blanc had got away with murder, only to be sent down for getting into a drunken brawl. Made a bit of a mess of the other guy, apparently. The only time he was ever actually convicted of anything. Before he murdered those girls, of course.'

Her fingers rattled across the keyboard, and Enzo saw her eyes scanning the text that she next brought up on her screen. He saw the earnest concern in them, and the studied concentration as she read.

'A condition of his early release from Murat was that he attended sessions at Rentrée, the Catholic charity for the resettlement of prisoners. Which, of course, is where he met Lucie. He had come out of prison to find that Anne-Laure had left him, and maybe that was a contributing factor, but it seems he became besotted by Lucie Martin. And, well . . . the rest we know.' She glanced at Enzo. 'Do you want me to go through the murders of the prostitutes?'

But Enzo shook his head. It was all a matter of public record, and he had been over those killings many times. Blanc's story was not untypical of the lives of the petty criminals who inhabited that dark and dangerous underworld concealed by the wafer-thin veneer of civilisation that society papered over it. A world inhabited by criminals and cops alike, creatures found crawling beneath the stones we never want to lift. But it told

him nothing new, providing not even a foothold from which to advance the investigation. He felt the fingers of despair closing around him.

Dominique said, 'We should go and talk to his wife.' She looked at Nicole. 'Or is it ex-wife?'

Nicole shrugged. 'There's no mention anywhere of them ever getting a divorce.'

'Can you get us an address? We'll go first thing in the morning.'

'I'll try.'

Enzo reached down to retrieve a bundle of folders from his shoulder bag. He pushed them across the table towards Nicole. 'Those are the files on the Bordeaux Six.' He shook his head. 'I've been through them and through them. But a pair of fresh eyes . . .'

Nicole pulled them towards her. 'I'll go through them myself with a fine-toothed comb, Monsieur Macleod.'

'I'm going to have to take Alexis back to Paris tomorrow.' Kirsty's face said it all. 'I hate to leave you, Papa. But I'll brief Roger on everything that's happened.'

Enzo nodded, then the ringing of his mobile phone startled everyone around the table. He glanced at the screen and saw that the call was from Commissaire Hélène Taillard, and he was almost afraid to answer it.

'Hélène?' Everyone watched as he listened and nodded. He glanced at his watch. 'What are you doing there at this time of night?' His eyes grew moist at her response, and he blinked

furiously to clear them. 'I'll be right over.' He hung up and looked around the expectant faces. There was a break in his voice as he said, 'She's been at the *caserne* all evening. Taken personal charge of coordinating the investigation into Sophie's abduction. She has the forensics report on the house she was held in.' He stood up. 'I'll be back as soon as I can.'

Dominique got quickly to her feet. 'I'll come with you.'

Much of the police headquarters lay in darkness. It stood at the north end of the loop in the River Lot that contained the old town of Cahors, and was manned only by a skeleton night staff. An officer at reception led them back through a half-lit corridor towards a slab of yellow electric light that fell from an open door to lie across the floor and fold itself up the wall. They could hear Hélène's voice all the way down the hall. Rapid, insistent. One end of a telephone conversation.

Hélène hung up and rose from her desk as the officer showed Enzo and Dominique into her office. She took Enzo in her arms and held him close for several long moments before standing back. Enzo was almost shocked to see the hint of tears gathering themselves in her eyes. 'We'll get her back,' she said.

She was still in uniform, but had dispensed with the hat, her hair piled up and pinned neatly to her head. There was barely a trace of make-up remaining on her face after a long day. She looked tired. She shook Dominique's hand and turned to lift a folder from her desk.

'They emailed me a preliminary report.' She forced a smile. 'I know we're all supposed to be on the same side, but you've no idea how difficult it is to get cops from one *département* to share information with cops from another. You can thank the *préfet* for exerting his influence.'

And Enzo felt himself choked at the realisation that friends from all sides were stepping up to the plate to help him. She handed him the folder and he pulled out the three printed sheets from inside.

'There's not much to go on, I'm afraid. The house has been on the market and lying empty for nearly a year. The owners pay someone to check up on it occasionally. Air the house, cut the grass, that sort of thing. He says he was last there about two weeks ago.'

Dominique said, 'And he was the only key holder?'

Hélène shook her head. 'No. The house is with several estate agents, and they all hold keys. There have been eight or ten visits to the property by prospective buyers over the last few months. The last one just ten days ago. And apparently the keys from that visit have gone missing.'

Enzo looked up from the folder. 'Who were the last people to visit?'

'Don't raise your hopes, Enzo,' Hélène said. 'If it was the people behind the abduction, they wouldn't have given real names. But we're chasing it down.' She nodded towards the folder in his hands. 'And you'll see the forensics people haven't come up with much. The house is full of fingerprints,

of course. But probably none of them belonging to the people we're interested in. The one possibility is DNA.'

Enzo frowned. 'How so?'

'Saliva traces on cigarette ends. The ashtrays are all overflowing. Depends whether or not they're in the database, of course.' She paused and examined the big Scotsman with concern. 'How are you holding up?'

He shook his head. 'Not well.'

'If we were to take bets again, Enzo, I'd put money on whoever took Sophie being the same people who've been trying to kill you for the last three years.'

'Then we'd be betting on the same side. Pretty short odds, too, I'd say.' And he told her about the text from Sophie's phone, and calling it back.

'Enzo, there are ways of tracking phones down to locations these days.'

But he shook his head. 'I've tried it several times since. It's dead. Whatever else they are, these people aren't stupid.'

'So what will you do?'

He pursed his lips to contain his anger and frustration. 'Catch them.'

She put a hand on his arm. 'Leave it, Enzo, please. That's our job.'

'Yes, and you've been so good at it so far.' It was out of his mouth before he could stop himself, and he saw Hélène withdraw her hand, as if from an electric shock. Regret immediately rushed in to fill all his empty places. He reached out

and took her hand. 'I'm sorry, Hélène. That was unfair.' But he had hurt her, and hurt is something that is very hard to take back.

She pulled her hand away and rounded her desk. 'I should probably be getting home.'

Dominique felt the hurt and tension that lay between them and tried to bridge the gap. 'Speaking of DNA,' she said, and delved into her bag to retrieve the small plastic container with the strands of Laurent's hair that they had taken from his comb.

Enzo glanced at it and turned away. 'This isn't the time.' He reached for the door.

But Hélène's interest was piqued. 'The time for what?' She glanced at the hair sample and back at Enzo.

'It doesn't matter.' He opened the door.

Dominique said, 'There's a question mark over the paternity of Enzo's son, Laurent. We thought, maybe . . .'

Enzo avoided Hélène's eye, and tried to ignore the curiosity in the look she gave him. 'Like I said. This isn't the time.'

Hélène took the container from Dominique, but kept her eyes on Enzo. 'Well, since your DNA will still be in our data-base . . . I'll pull a few strings.' She paused. 'I'll keep you up to date with any developments on Sophie.' Another pause. 'If you'll do the same?' She raised an eyebrow and cocked her head.

Handling both his regret and his embarrassment at the same time was difficult for Enzo, and all he managed was a nod.

# CHAPTER THIRTY-TWO

Anne-Laure Blanc lived on the second floor of a seventies apartment block in the Bordeaux *banlieue* of Pessac, made infamous by La Cité Frugès, a self-contained housing scheme designed and built for workers in the 1920s by the Swiss-born architect Corbusier. Her one-bed apartment overlooked some of the concrete cubes intended by Corbusier's experiment to solve a twentieth-century housing shortage. All brightly painted now in orange and blue and green and red, and set in serried rows among trees shedding autumn leaves on empty streets.

In the two-and-a-half-hour drive from Cahors to Bordeaux, Enzo had briefed Dominique fully on the events of the past week and every tiny detail of his investigation into the murder of Lucie Martin. His eyes were stinging from lack of sleep, although he supposed he must have drifted off sometime shortly before the alarm brought him crashing back into reality and the sickening recollection of Sophie's abduction. Coffee had turned to acid in his stomach, and his mouth was dry and suffused with a bad taste that wouldn't go away.

Anne-Laure was happy enough to invite them into her tiny

apartment, and although she had filled it with bright paintings and photographs, and china ornaments of puppies and pixies, she had the demeanour of someone entirely consumed by loneliness. Even had they been the bearers of bad news, Enzo thought, she would still have greeted them with a smile, an offer of coffee and an invitation to sit on her best settee.

She had put on weight, Enzo imagined, since the days when she and Régis had married, and her red-dyed hair seemed sparse, thinning perhaps with an early onset of the menopause. She wore blue jog-pants that fitted where they touched, and a pink hoodie that looked like it might have been purchased before the weight had begun to accumulate.

The apartment was clean enough, but made smaller somehow by cheap furniture that was much too big for it. An electric fire was switched off and the room was cold. Enzo wondered if it was an attempt to save money. A woman who was at home mid-morning was unlikely to have a job, and he thought she was probably on benefits.

'I still go and see him sometimes,' she said. 'There's no hard feelings. We had our time. It was short, and it passed. But he's still a lovely man.'

Enzo and Dominique exchanged fleeting glances. It seemed an odd way to describe a triple murderer. She went off to retrieve a photo album from an ugly 1960s sideboard, and squeezed on to the settee between them to open it up. 'I should look at these more often. Everything's digital now, and nobody keeps photo albums any more. Which is a shame, because they

are lovely to look back on.' Everything, it seemed, in Anne-Laure's life was 'lovely'.

There were photographs taken in a bar somewhere of Régis and Anne-Laure raising glasses towards the camera. Both of them almost unrecognisable. Impossibly young, brimming with life and laughter, moments trapped in time and captured in the virulent reds and greens and blues of cheap 1980s film stock. Like the painted concrete blocks outside her window.

She flicked through the pages faster than they could take them in. Girls with the superficial glamour of the street-corner hooker, dyed blond hair and unthinkably short skirts. Men with broken-veined faces and glassy eyes leering at the lens. And then she stopped at a photograph taken in a park some-where, sunlight dappling grass through summer leaves. She and Régis were seated on a travelling rug spread out on the lawn, a picnic hamper between them and a baby held up by Régis above his crossed legs. Both he and Anne-Laure were burned out in places by patches of sunlight, but their happi-ness shone through, and there was such pride in Régis's smile that Enzo began to regard him as almost human.

'Happiest days of my life,' Anne-Laure said. Enzo glanced at her and saw that she was transported back to that time, a radiance in her eyes and her smile at the recollection of a life long gone. 'Being pregnant was the best feeling ever. Like it's what I had been born for.' Then a darkness crossed her face. 'Though I only ever had the one.'

Dominique said, 'Why did you leave him?'

She laughed, as if there were something funny in the question. 'Oh, Régis was never a one-girl man. I suppose I always knew that. But it wasn't until he went inside that I realised there was no future for us. If I wanted a life of my own, a real life, it wasn't going to be with Régis.' Her smile was rueful and filled with irony. 'And look where I ended up.'

Enzo said, 'What did you know about Lucie Martin?'

She frowned. 'Lucie . . . ?' Then recollection dawned. 'Oh, that girl who was murdered over in Duras.' She shook her head. 'That wasn't him. No doubt he had a thing for her. But that was just Régis. He'd never have hurt the girl.' She turned a look on them that was so honest and open it was almost startling in its innocence, and Enzo wondered if it was the innocence in Anne-Laure that had attracted Régis, just as it was in Lucie. She said, 'I never stopped loving him, I suppose. There was violence in him, but it was never directed at me. Or any other woman, as far as I knew. He always treated his girls well. They liked him. And that's rare for a man in his line of work.'

'Still,' Dominique said, 'he murdered three women.'

Anne-Laure's smile faded and became fixed. 'They say that, yes.'

'He's never denied it.'

'No, he hasn't. But it doesn't make him a bad person.'

She stood up, a little huffily, closing her photo album and returning it to its place in the sideboard where it would reside unopened for who knew how many more years.

'But don't take my word for it. Ask any of his girls. They all loved him, you know. Go and see Lulu. She'll tell you all about Régis. Still on the game, even after all these years. Past her sell-by, you might say. But, then, some men seem to like that kind of thing.'

'Where would we find Lulu?' Enzo asked.

'I don't know where she lives. But she still plies her trade on the Quai Deschamps,' Ann-Laure said. 'Any night after dark. Just ask one of the girls. Can I get you another coffee?'

'No, no, thanks.' Enzo stood up. This had been a waste of time. Whatever she might have told them about Régis, she wasn't going to discuss the murders. Or Lucie Martin.'

But Dominique remained seated. She said, 'What happened to your daughter?'

Anne-Laure lifted her chin and stared off into some unseen distance. 'Alice is lucky. She got away from all this.'

'She must be nearly twenty-five by now,' Dominique said. Then paused. 'She's not in Bordeaux anymore, then?'

'No. No, she's not.'

Enzo said, 'Does she ever visit her father?'

An almost pained look flitted across Anne-Laure's face. 'She's never set eyes on her father in all the years since ... well, since they sent him to prison. And never will.'

Prostitution around the Gare Saint-Jean had become a blight, with ladies of the night soliciting customers from the doors of churches and pharmacies, congregating in the underpasses. If

you knew where to look there were strip clubs and swingers' clubs, massage parlours and brothels, and places you could watch live sex shows caught on camera.

The Quai Deschamps was on the other side of the river. Derelict industrial properties and once grand mansions, like bad teeth in a grim smile. After dark, cars cruised the riverbank, girls appearing out of the shadows, catching headlights. Pale, painted faces, sometimes brown, sometimes Asian, long legs barely covered by miniskirts so short they verged on the obscene. Breasts spilling out of low-cut tops or unbuttoned blouses as they leaned in open windows, displaying their wares to potential clients.

Enzo and Dominique got off the tram at Stalingrad and walked south along the quay into darkness, past crumbling brick walls defaced by garishly coloured graffiti. Across the river, the black water reflected the lights of the city, another world away, where people went about lives uncontaminated by crime or a sex trade that bred only misery and disease. Where young women sold their futures for a handful of euros, and men exploited them to indulge their sad fantasies.

On a patch of waste ground they saw three white vans parked among the rubble, suspension tested by men exploiting the world's oldest profession, and women practising it. Vehicles cruised slowly by, hidden faces staring out in suspicion at the incongruous sight of a man and woman walking here together.

During the long hours of waiting in the hotel room they had taken near the station, Enzo had barely been able to contain

his frustration. Time, it seemed to him, was simply ticking away, and with it any hope of getting Sophie back. But he had no idea what else to do. For very nearly the first time in his life he was lost. He did not know which way to turn next. He was like a drowning man, struggling to keep his head above water, but losing the fight. And he felt himself being sucked under.

He had been determined to go to the Quai Deschamps alone. It was too dangerous, he had said, for Dominique. He couldn't guarantee to protect her. She had sat him down on the edge of the bed and told him that she was young, trained and fit, and the only reason she was going along was to protect him. And he had smiled, in spite of the darkness in his heart.

'Kinky!' A skinny young black woman stepped out of deep shadow where she had been standing behind a broken-down *portail* that opened on to the garden of a derelict gatehouse. Somewhere beyond the darkness, an old house rose in silhouette against a sky backlit by the city itself. 'Been a long time since I had a couple. First timers?'

Enzo said, 'We're looking for Lulu.'

Derision exploded from her lips. 'Oh, are you? What's she got that I haven't got, then?' She cackled. 'Apart from another fifty kilos of flesh.'

'Do you know where we can find her?' Dominique said.

The girl looked her up and down lasciviously. 'Not bad,' she said. 'Sure I can't change your mind? Just you and me. We don't need the old guy, do we?'

Dominique reached into an inside pocket and pulled out

an ID wallet that she opened up and thrust in the girl's face. 'You can tell us where we can find Lulu, or you can spend the night in a cell.' She snapped the wallet shut and thrust it back in her pocket.

'Oh, shit,' the girl said, all her levity displaced by disappointment. 'Fucking cops.'

'Well?' Dominique was insistent.

The girl nodded towards the south end of the quay. 'About a hundred metres down. Gates of an old tyre factory. She parks up on the concrete behind it.' She puckered up her lips. 'Give her a kiss from me, darling, would you?'

Enzo waited until they were twenty metres or so away before he said in a low voice, 'What the hell did you show her?'

'My old gendarme's ID. I was supposed to hand it in, but no one ever asked, so . . .' She shrugged. 'Thought it might come in handy.'

'Isn't it illegal to impersonate a police officer?'

Dominique smiled. 'But I'm so well practised, who could tell the difference?'

It was somewhere along here, Enzo knew, that one of Blanc's victims had been found. As they approached Lulu's van across a cracked concrete apron strewn with the detritus of discarded lives, a client was slipping out of the back of it. The man was short and middle-aged, and Enzo saw the panic in his rabbit eyes as he noticed them coming towards him, and he went skulking quickly off into the darkness like some resentful rodent.

Then Lulu swung into view from behind the van and cast cautious eyes in their direction. The placing of her hands on her hips, Enzo decided, was pure bravado. Telling them she was neither frightened nor intimidated. But no matter how long she had been at this game, it never became any less dangerous, and Enzo knew she would be feeling both.

'I don't do couples,' she said.

'Neither do we,' Enzo said. 'We just want to talk.'

Lulu looked at him as if he were some kind of pervert. 'Talk? I don't do talk.'

She was at least a hundred kilos in weight, but most of it still hung in the right places, and what wasn't on show was contained in a brightly coloured print dress with a crossed front that lifted and held her breasts unnaturally high. She had calves like a rugby player and shoulders to match, and teetered on strapless high-heeled sandals that looked both too small and too tight. Back-combed brassy blond hair was piled up high above a face so poorly painted it would not have been out of place in a circus. She was, Enzo thought, at least fifty. A raddled wreck of what might once have been an attractive woman.

'Anne-Laure Blanc suggested we talk to you,' he said.

And her face changed immediately. 'Anne-Laure? Is she in some kind of trouble?'

'She's in no trouble,' Enzo said. He took out his wallet and counted out fifty euros. 'We just want a few minutes of your time to talk about Régis. Will this cover it?'

Lulu snatched it so quickly from his hand that he almost didn't feel it leave his fingers. She tucked it into her cleavage.

Enzo said, 'Are you not a bit old for this, Lulu?'

She looked him up and down. 'Not as old as you, pappy. What do you want to know?'

They turned as a car cruised by out in the street. The driver's eyes, catching the light beyond the window, quickly averted themselves before the vehicle accelerated suddenly away.

Lulu said, 'You just lost me a customer.'

Enzo drew out another twenty note and it vanished to join the others in the generous depths of her cleavage. 'Anything at all you can tell us about him.'

She eyed them suspiciously, clearly wondering why they would come asking her about Régis Blanc after all these years. But she knew better than to ask. 'With Régis what you saw was what you got. You played it straight with him, he played it straight with you. No side to him. Never touched the girls, never laid a finger on us. And let me tell you, that's pretty unique in my world.'

Enzo reckoned she had probably been on the business end of a few fists in her time.

'Truth is, we all liked him. You couldn't help but like Régis. He was a good laugh. Always wisecracking, and never sold you short. Took what he was owed and nothing else. And see if anyone messed with you. A client, or another pimp, Régis would pay him a visit. And you never had no more trouble.' She shook her head, and her smile was one of fond recollection.

'Word gets round, you know. You don't fuck with Régis's girls.' She grinned. 'Unless you're paying. We felt safe. You know?' She spat on the concrete. 'Not like now.'

Dominique said, 'Those three girls he murdered must have felt safe, too. Until he strangled them.'

Lulu folded her arms beneath her breasts and shook her head vigorously. 'I still don't understand it. None of us did. At first we thought he'd been set up. Régis would never have done something like that. Then, when he didn't deny it . . .' She turned dark eyes of consternation on them. 'I'm still not quite sure I believe it.'

'Did you know them?' Enzo said. 'The dead girls.'

She shrugged. 'Everyone knew everyone back then. But I didn't *know* them. I mean, they weren't friends or anything.'

'You've heard of the Bordeaux Six?'

'Who hasn't?'

'You knew them, too, then?'

'Same way as I knew the girls he strangled. Except for Sal. We used to hang out. Do the occasional double act.'

'Sally Linol?'

'Never knew her second name. She had a tattoo of a feather on the side of her neck. Bitch just up and disappeared on me. Not a damned word. One day she's here. The next she's gone. I remember Régis asking about her. Seemed very keen to find her. Someone said she'd gone to Paris, but no one knew for sure.' She looked at Enzo and then at Dominique. 'I can't imagine what use to you any of my ramblings might be.

But you're running out of time. Unless you want to put more money in the machine.'

Enzo shook his head hopelessly. It was another dead end. Just confirmation of the enigma that was Régis Blanc. A man of impossible contradictions, who had murdered three prostitutes and fallen for an angel from Duras. But he hadn't killed her, Enzo was pretty sure, and he was starting to doubt that Blanc was anything more than a time-consuming red herring. Despair was beginning to seep into his soul. 'Thanks anyway,' he said.

'It's poor Anne-Laure I feel the most sorry for,' Lulu said suddenly. 'Left on her own without any financial support to look after that little girl. I drop in sometimes for a coffee and a chat. She's a poor soul. Must have been a terrible burden.'

'What?' Dominique frowned.

'Looking after that kid. What was it they called it? Pump, or Pompe's disease. Something like that. They said she wouldn't live for more than a couple of years. I remember Régis was devastated. I mean, really devastated. He thought the world of that little girl. Then, when he got sent down for the murders, poor Anne-Laure got left to cope with it all on her own.'

# CHAPTER THIRTY-THREE

Their hotel-room window looked out over a clutch of skeleton trees in a patch of scrubby grassland at a road junction. Opposite was a café, and further down the street, a Chinese restaurant. On the far side of the tram tracks, the Gare Saint-Jean stood in all its floodlit glory against a black sky, and the surrounding restaurants and bars were filled with people whose lives were untouched by Enzo's pain. Their laughter and pleasure in life and living seemed to mock him as he stood looking down at them, cocooned in his own internal misery.

Why had Anne-Laure not told them about the child's illness? It had loomed so large in their lives at the time. Only two years to live, Lulu had said. And yet Anne-Laure had spoken of Alice as if she were still alive. Now, it seemed to Enzo, the woman had been evasive when Dominique asked her about her daughter. *Alice is lucky. She got away from all this.* She was no longer in Bordeaux, she had told them. And then, enigmatically, *She's never set eyes on her father in all the years since they sent him to prison. And never will.*

'Found it.' He turned at the sound of Dominique's voice. She

had been huddled over his laptop on the dresser opposite the bed for the last ten minutes.

Enzo crossed the room to stand at Dominique's shoulder and look at the screen. She had found the American website of NORD, the National Organisation for Rare Disorders. *Pompe Disease* was emblazoned at the top of the page.

Dominique read aloud from the text: 'Pompe disease is a rare genetic disorder characterised by the absence of the lysosomal enzyme, GAA. This enzyme is required to break down glycogen and convert it into the simple sugar, glucose. Failure to properly break down this thick and sticky substance results in a massive accumulation of it in cardiac and skeletal muscle cells. The infantile form is characterised by severe muscle weakness and diminished muscle tone, and usually manifests within the first few months of life. Additional abnormalities may include enlargement of the heart, the liver and the tongue. Without treatment, progressive cardiac failure can cause life-threatening complications between the ages of a year to a year and a half.'

Enzo straightened up. 'That sounds horrible. No wonder her parents were devastated.'

Dominique scrolled down the page. She stopped and whistled softly. Then read, 'Treatment requires the coordinated efforts of a team of experts specialising in neuromuscular disorders. Paediatricians, neurologists, orthopedists, cardiologists, dieticians . . .' She sat back. 'God, a whole army of specialists.' She squinted again at the screen in the dark. 'And

more recently they seem to have developed some kind of enzyme-replacement therapy that has to be done every two weeks.' She swivelled in her seat to look up at Enzo. 'Régis could never have paid for treatment like that, Enzo. And Anne-Laure?' She paused. 'How can that child still be alive?'

Enzo lay awake, turning it over in his head again and again. It felt important, but he wasn't sure why. He and Dominique had decided to go back to ask Anne-Laure about the child first thing in the morning, which for Enzo only meant more hours of passive waiting, treading water, while Sophie was being held somewhere under threat of her life. *If* she was still alive. But that was a thought he could not bring himself to contemplate.

He was aware of Dominique curled into his side, her skin on his, her arm thrown carelessly across his chest, holding him like a child clinging to her father. And he felt the comfort of her warmth and her touch. He tried to visualise how it would be for him right now if he were on his own, but it was simply unimaginable. Somehow he would have had to cope, but could not see how. In almost no time at all he had picked up where he had left off with Dominique nearly a year before. And very quickly she had become his rock, his anchor. He trusted and needed her, and could no longer picture his life without her in it. If he believed in God, he might even have thought that He had sent her to him in his hour of greatest need.

He closed his eyes and tried to concentrate on breathing

slowly and deeply, despairing of ever again finding the escape of sleep.

And then the ringing of his mobile phone startled him awake.

Both he and Dominique sat upright, hearts pounding, as Enzo fumbled to answer it. He saw that it wasn't even midnight. And a glance at the screen told him it was Nicole calling. 'What's happened?' He breathed fear into the phone.

'Nothing bad, Monsieur Macleod. But go and wake up your laptop. I want to talk to you on FaceTime.'

Enzo and Dominique pulled on dressing gowns and drew up chairs in front of the computer. Enzo tapped the trackpad then entered his password. Almost immediately his FaceTime video-conferencing software began ringing. He clicked on the bouncing icon and Nicole appeared, full screen, a miniature screen in the bottom corner displaying the pale, bleary faces of Enzo and Dominique, illuminated only by the light of the computer. Nicole looked flushed with excitement, her hair all about her head in a tangle.

She said, 'I've been going through those files, Monsieur Macleod.'

'Which files?'

'The Bordeaux Six. And I've found something.'

Enzo almost held his breath. 'What?'

'It goes back to the murder of Pierre Lambert in Paris.'

Enzo frowned, and Dominique said, 'I don't know anything about that.'

'It was the third case in Raffin's book,' Enzo told her, though

he couldn't for the life of him see the relevance. 'Lambert was a rent boy in Paris, a homosexual prostitute found murdered in his apartment. I tracked down the killer, a professional hitman. But not who paid him. Why anyone would have hired a professional to kill someone like Lambert was always a mystery. And I've never got to the bottom of it. He was salting away a lot of money in offshore accounts, and the suspicion was that he'd been blackmailing someone. But who . . . ?' He shrugged.

'Yes, yes,' Nicole said impatiently. 'You can fill her in on all that later. The thing is, I've found a link between Lambert and one of the Bordeaux Six.'

Enzo felt his face stinging. 'What sort of link?'

'It was there in the book, but we never paid much attention to it at the time. You remember, you gave me Monsieur Raffin's notes to look over, and there was a little more detail in there. So it sticks in my mind.'

'Nicole . . .' Enzo prompted her, frustration creeping into his voice.

'I'm coming to it, I'm coming to it.' She breathed deeply and then it all poured out of her. 'The police interviewed all of Lambert's friends and known associates at the time. But there was a girl. Someone everyone said was his best friend. She'd just gone missing. Simply vanished. A prostitute. Lambert's fag hag. She spent more time at his apartment than her own. Like they were lovers. They even slept in the same bed together.' She paused. 'And they never did track her down.'

'And?' Enzo was still struggling to see the connection.

'Her name was Sally, and she had the tattoo of a feather on her neck.'

And all the hairs stood up on the back of Enzo's.

When Dominique woke, it was to see Enzo standing fully dressed at the window, staring gloomily out across the street as the first light of dawn painted the city grey. His hands were pushed deep into his pockets, and she could tell by the slump of his shoulders that he was hurting. She felt a surge of both pity and love, and slipped silently from the bed to cross the room and put her arms around him from behind.

He folded his arms around hers, still gazing from the window, and she said, 'Did you sleep at all?'

'Maybe. If I did, I wasn't aware of it. But you know how that can be.'

She nodded. 'What's the plan?' For she knew there would be one. He wouldn't have spent all these hours awake without planning some kind of schedule for the day ahead.

He untangled himself from her and sat down in front of the laptop. The first image on screen when he woke it from the sleep he had been unable to find himself, was the face of the girl with the feather tattoo. Nicole had scanned it and sent a jpeg by email. He paused for a moment, staring at it, as perplexed now as he had been when Nicole first told them about the link. It seemed inconceivable to him that it could simply be coincidence. But he had no other way of explaining it. Or even beginning to understand it.

He banished her image with a sweep of his fingers on the trackpad, and brought up a one-way e-ticket on the TGV to Paris. 'You're going to have to go and see Anne-Laure on your own. Take the car. I'm going to Paris.'

Dominique was disappointed. She didn't want to be separated from him. 'What will you do there?'

'I need to confirm that Lambert's girlfriend – fag hag, whatever . . . I need to know that she really was Sally Linol.'

Dominique said, 'Even if she was, Enzo. What does it mean?'

He closed the lid of his laptop abruptly. 'I don't know.' He stood up, frustrated and angry with himself. 'I really don't. But it must mean something. It has to. It's the only chink of light in all this darkness.' He turned towards her, letting his hands fall helplessly to his sides. 'What else can I do?'

She slipped her arms around him and pressed the side of her face to his chest. 'Where there's light there's hope.' And she looked up at him. 'When's your train?'

'In an hour.'

'Then let's get breakfast. You need to fuel up for the day ahead.'

The Café du Levant, opposite the Gare Saint-Jean, owed its origins to the Arabic countries of the Eastern Mediterranean, with an extravagant facade of coloured mosaic beneath a domed representation of a rising sun. The brasserie below, more prosaically, offered choucroute and oysters. And this early, Enzo and Dominique found themselves the only customers.

Staff were still cleaning up from the night before, and a bleary-eyed girl brought them coffee and croissants. The place was poorly lit, mirrors and brass rails and red velvet soaking up the light from globed chandeliers. Somehow it reflected Enzo's mood, and he toyed with his croissant rather than eating it, sipping only desultorily at his coffee.

Dominique watched him in silence, feeling his pain but not knowing how to assuage it.

Eventually he raised his eyes to hers and said, 'I have no idea if I am doing the right thing, Dominique. And Sophie's life depends on me doing the right thing.'

'Whatever we are doing,' Dominique said, 'right or wrong, is better than doing nothing. Think how much worse that would feel.' She put her hands over his on the table. 'What these people are scared of is that you're going to find something that will be a danger to them, whatever that might be. But if you can find that thing they're scared of, then at least you'll have some kind of bargaining power. And the only way we're going to find it is by looking.'

She sat back and drained the coffee from her cup.

'I'll see you off on the train. And when I've spoken to Anne-Laure I'll drive to Paris and meet you there. You're not alone, Enzo. We'll do this together.'

He looked at her and had to fight to stop tears springing to his eyes. Instead, he stood up and lifted her to her feet and put his arms around her, enveloping her almost completely.

They stood, swaying a little together, turning gently from side to side. And he whispered, 'I love you, Dominique.'

He felt her stiffen at his words, then relax again and hold him even more tightly. And he realised that the only reason he had said it was that he meant it. That it was what he felt. Words that had come spontaneously in a moment of need, from his heart, from his very soul. And he wished that everything else would just fade away, leaving him this moment with her. A moment he could never have imagined all those years ago when Pascale was taken from him.

He heard her whisper back, 'I love you, too, my darling man.'

# CHAPTER THIRTY-FOUR

Sophie had been through many phases. At first her overwhelming emotion had been fear. And then she had felt sorry for herself. But it was impossible to maintain such high-octane emotions for an extended period, and gradually, through despair and hopelessness, she had descended into an almost catatonic state of nothingness. She was completely numb.

She had lost count now of how many days and nights they had kept her here. Hours were endless. Light and dark came and went, but only on the outside. In this room, her cell as she had come to think of it, there was only electric light. The one constant in her life.

No sunshine reached into the room. For across a narrow lane a brick building rose high enough above her to block any view of the sky. The window stood at head height, but was barred on the inside. An iron frame hinged at one side, padlocked at the other. Beyond filthy glass, most of what might be visible on the other side of it was obscured. By standing on tiptoe she had been able to look down into the narrow,

potholed asphalt lane that ran between the buildings twenty feet below. Reflections in the puddles of the sky above were her only view of freedom.

Initially she had been anxious to learn as much as she could about where she was. She drank in every available glimpse of the place they were holding her when they took her downstairs to the toilet. A filthy hole in the floor with raised footings, cracked porcelain and the smell of broken sewers rising up from below. But at least here there was paper and soap.

Her impression of the place when she first arrived, blinded by her hood, had proved amazingly accurate. A pitched glass and asbestos roof, supported on a rusted iron superstructure, was broken in a dozen places and let in the rain to lie in pools and puddles across a vast, empty expanse of concrete floor. Huge sliding metal doors closed off the outside world, and she was being held in what had once been offices, reached by a metal stairway leading to a grilled landing.

The men seemed to come in shifts. Two at a time. And spent their days and nights in an office with a window that looked out over the empty factory beneath them. They played cards and smoked, and drank beer, and watched television. Sometimes, from her cell, she could hear them laughing. They were always hooded when they brought her food and led her to the toilet. And she took encouragement from that. If the intention was to kill her, why would they care if she saw their faces?

Her cell itself must once have been some kind of lockfast

room for storing valuable goods. The door was a heavy rein-forced steel, with dead bolts that went into the floor and ceiling.

They had brought in a camp bed and sleeping bag on her first night, and when she wasn't lying in it, she sat on the floor with her back to the window wall, or paced the cell, back and forth, conscious that it was important to exercise, and to keep oxygen flowing to her brain.

Now, as the door opened, she got to her feet. The hunger gnawing in her belly told her it was time to eat. The tallest of her captors, for she had got to know them by their height and their voices, pushed open the door and slid her tray into the room with the tip of his boot. This was the one who had threat-ened her when she first arrived. The one she most feared. Not just for the hurt he might inflict, but for other things, perhaps worse, that he had hinted might await her if she didn't behave.

She stood looking at him, waiting for him to go. But he remained, returning her stare, and although all that she could see were his eyes, she could have sworn he was smiling. The tray sat on the floor between them, but she wouldn't eat until he had gone. And still they stood, facing each other across the room, until an old, familiar emotion came bubbling back to the surface. Fear. For this was new. This was a departure. This was not good.

'What?' she said eventually. Almost shouting it at him.

Still he remained silent. Enjoying, she was sure, watching her panic. Before finally he said, 'Your father doesn't take a

telling, does he?' And now she could hear the latent violence in his voice. Anger, and something else that she feared even more. 'Doesn't seem to believe that we'll kill you if he doesn't give it up.'

'Or maybe he just knows that if you kill me you lose any power over him.' Defiance came from that same panic.

'Yeah, but how would he ever know?' And now she heard the smile in his voice and watched in horror as he peeled his mask back over his head to reveal the face of a man in his early thirties, unshaven, a smile dimpling his cheeks. Dark eyes twinkling. In any other circumstance she might have thought him good-looking. But here, and now, all she could see was her executioner. Why else would he have revealed himself? And he knew that she knew it. He said, 'Enjoy your meal. Because this one, the next . . . today, tomorrow, who knows? One of them is going to be your last.' He grinned. 'And I'll take real pleasure in seeing to that.'

He stepped out into the hall and slammed the door shut behind him. She heard all the dead bolts slot into place, and sank to the floor on trembling legs. She needed her fear now, to motivate her, to kick-start her brain. She could no longer accept her incarceration like some passive prisoner awaiting her fate. They were going to kill her. And she would not go gentle into that good night.

She looked around, panic still rising in her throat. She had to get out. She *had* to. But how? She looked at her tray. Yoghurt, an apple, a piece of cheese. Some bread. A mug of coffee with

the spoon still standing in it, two paper-wrapped cubes of sugar. And an idea born of desperation began to clot among the panicked thoughts free-falling through her mind. She lifted the spoon from the mug, ignoring how it burned her hand as she closed it around the hot metal, and she held it to her breast. Everything would depend on them not noticing it was gone.

# CHAPTER THIRTY-FIVE

Anne-Laure was not so welcoming this time. She held the door to her apartment half open and peered suspiciously out into the hall at Dominique. 'I've told you everything I know,' she said. And tried to shut the door.

Dominique stopped it with her foot and pushed the door wide, forcing Anne-Laure back into her apartment. 'No, you haven't.'

'You can't come in here like this!'

Dominique reached for her old gendarme's ID and thrust it quickly in Anne-Laure's face. 'I can do anything I damn well like. So either we do this the easy way or the hard way.' Which caused Anne-Laure to step back, and her pale face lost what little colour it had.

'You never said you were cops!'

'You never asked.' And Dominique noticed for the first time that Anne-Laure wore a little make-up this morning. Gone were the jog pants and the pink hoodie, to be replaced by a black skirt and white blouse. A coat lay draped over the back of the settee.

'Going somewhere, were you?'

'None of your business!'

'To see Alice, maybe?'

Which brought the older woman's defiance to an abrupt end. She wilted, almost visibly.

'Where is she?'

Anne-Laure avoided her eye, averting her gaze like a truculent child to look at the floor.

'Where is she, Anne-Laure? You know you're going to have to tell me sooner or later. One way or another. Sooner would be better, and this way would be easier.'

The woman turned resentful eyes on Dominique. 'You fucking people,' she said. 'You just never let us alone.' She looked at the wall, the floor again, then out of the window towards the ugly, painted concrete blocks that were her view of the world. Then finally back at Dominique, and the former gendarme saw resentment turn to resignation. 'She's in a special residential clinic. In the commune of Gradignan, just south of the city. Been there most of her life.' She controlled her breathing. 'They take care of her. She'd have been dead a long time ago without them.'

Dominique stared at her. 'That's twenty-four-hour care. How can you afford that?'

'I can't.'

'Who pays for it, then?'

Anne-Laure shrugged. Sulking now, surly-faced. 'I don't know.'

'How can you not know? It must be costing a fortune.'

'I'm sure it is.' She was wrestling with some inner resistance that was telling her not to say any more. But she knew there was no point in hiding it now. 'About a week after Régis was sent down, the head of the clinic in Gradignan came to see me and Alice. He was a nice man. So good with Alice, too. He said they could offer her specialised care, but that she would have to live in.' She sighed. 'It wasn't funny, but I laughed. I told him there was no way on this earth that I could afford to pay for that. And he said that I didn't have to. That it was all taken care of.'

'Who by?'

'I don't know.'

Dominique didn't believe her. 'You never asked?'

And a little of Anne-Laure's earlier defiance returned. 'No, I didn't. I didn't want to know. And I was afraid to ask in case it all turned out to be some terrible mistake and they would send her home again. To die.' Dominique was shocked to see tears welling in her eyes. 'I've visited her every other day for twenty-three years. Years she would never otherwise have had. And I wasn't about to do anything to risk that. Then or now.'

The Clinique des Cèdres stood discreetly behind trees off the Cours du Général de Gaulle, opposite a retirement home and a new-built block of apartments. An old stone mansion house had been home to the original clinic. But over the years it had been extended at the side and back, and rose three storeys into a grey, sultry autumn sky.

Dominique parked in the forecourt, and she and Anne-Laure waded through fallen leaves blowing in gentle eddies across the tarmac in a soft wind. Up stone steps and into a tiled reception area, where Anne-Laure was greeted like an old friend by uniformed nurses.

'Warm today, but I think it's going to rain,' one of them said with a shrug of her shoulders.

Anne-Laure's smile was strained. 'I have a visitor for Alice.'

The nurse smiled. 'Of course.'

They rode up in an elevator to the first floor and stepped out into a brightly lit corridor of green linoleum and yellow walls. Alice's room was halfway along it. A viewing window to the right of the door allowed them to see in without entering. Dominique was startled.

A young woman with spun gold hair splashed across a pillow lay on a hospital bed hooked up by wires and tubes to machinery and drips. Lights winked red and yellow. A green phosphor screen displayed a graph that followed the beating of her heart. A desk strewn with papers and books stood in a bay window. An artist's easel leaned against the far wall, and the walls themselves were plastered with paintings and drawings. Some, beautifully childlike. Others, extraordinary landscapes and portraits, in watercolour or pastel crayon. A comfortable, well-worn armchair sat beneath a wall-mounted television set, and was surrounded by books piled untidily on the floor.

On the bed, a threadbare toy panda lay close to her side, one of her hands crooked around it. But her eyes were shut

and her breathing seemed shallow. Her skin was ivory white, painfully thin hands and arms stretched out above the sheets.

'Welcome to Alice's world,' Anne-Laure said. 'Apart from short outings with me to the cinema or the park, she has spent nearly all of her life in this room. They say she'll be dead in a matter of weeks.'

Dominique glanced at the girl's mother and saw a kind of stoic dignity in her face as she gazed at her dying daughter.

'In the early years they were able to keep her mostly healthy. Then in 2006 they started using a new drug from America. Enzyme replacement therapy. And that extended her life by another few years. Though there was always going to be a limit.' She turned to look at Dominique. 'But it's been a life worth living, don't ever doubt that. She has revelled in it, lived it fully, in ways her father and I never could. Her disease has been both a blessing and a curse. The curse being confined to this room. The blessing being the happiness she brought to everyone who knew her. I've never known anyone as happy as my little Alice.'

Silent tears spilled from her eyes to roll slowly down her cheeks as she turned to gaze again at her daughter.

'They brought tutors in to educate her. She loved to read and watch movies. Very early, she discovered a talent for painting. You'll find her work all over the clinic. She painted portraits of all the staff, and everyone wanted their own. Her work is in homes and on walls all over this town. We never hid from her that her life would be short. She's always

understood that. Knew that she would have less time on this earth than others.'

She searched for a pack of tissues in her bag, and wiped away the tears from her cheeks.

'None of us knows how long we have, do we? And maybe that's how we can live without fear. But Alice has never been afraid of dying, just grateful for every day she was alive.' Her eyes met Dominique's very directly. 'So, you see, why would I even question the funding that made that possible? It has been an extraordinary life. And it has touched everyone who knew her.'

Dominique looked again at the fading girl on the bed. A serenity in her face. Her life reflected in all the paintings on her walls, and she felt guilty for intruding on her mother's pain. She placed a hand on Anne-Laure's arm and said, 'I'm sorry.'

Anne-Laure turned to search her face with sceptical eyes. 'Are you?'

Dominique took her hand away, resigned, and said, 'I'll leave you to your visit.'

At the elevator, she stopped and looked back along the hall. Anne-Laure was still standing gazing in at her dying daughter. She wiped her eyes again with a fresh tissue before composing herself and opening the door.

Dominique stopped at reception and smiled at the young nurse who had predicted rain. 'Might it be possible to have a word with the director?'

*

The director was a square-shaped woman in her middle forties, who wore a charcoal-grey skirt and white blouse. Hair streaked with silver was drawn back into a neat bun at the back of her head. She was evidently not the same director who had come to Anne-Laure's house twenty-three years previously. She had a pleasant face and smiled warmly as she rose from behind her desk to shake Dominique's hand. 'You're a friend of Anne-Laure's.' It was a statement rather than a question, so Dominique didn't contradict her. On the wall behind the desk she noticed a framed portrait of the director painted by Alice. It was a good likeness. The director waved her into the seat opposite. 'How can I help you?'

Dominique sat down and came straight to the point. 'The family would like to know who has been covering the cost of Alice's treatment all these years.'

The director frowned. 'I'm not sure I understand. You mean they don't know?'

'No, they don't.'

The director sat back, clearly surprised and considering how she should respond. 'Well, I'm afraid I wouldn't be at liberty to say, even if I wanted to. This is a private clinic. Our funding is confidential.' She lifted her shoulders in a shrug of consternation. 'And what difference would it make now, after all this time? That little girl's life has shone more brightly than any of us ever dared to hope. But the light is fading now, and she'll be gone within the month.'

*

The wind had stiffened by the time Dominique stepped back out into the car park, and leaves were falling like snow from the tall chestnut trees that were lined up along the outer wall. She could see no sign of the cedars from which the clinic had taken its name, and she slipped behind the wheel of her car to sit for some minutes in thoughtful silence. She reached into her jacket pocket for her phone and tapped the *Contacts* icon. After entering the name 'Bouthet', she sat looking at the contact details which had materialised on her screen, and had a momentary flutter of regretful recollection. Then she tapped the number to autodial.

A girl on a switchboard answered her call. 'Tracfin. How may I help you?'

'Could I speak to Franck Bouthet?' Dominique said.

'One moment.'

But it was several long moments before the phone ringing on his extension prompted Franck to answer it. 'Hello?'

Dominique felt the remnants of the butterflies he always used to give her resurrect themselves in her tummy. 'Franck, it's Dominique.'

There was a moment's silence, laden with a whole history. Then that familiar voice. 'My God! Dominique. You certainly know how to waken a man from his slumbers.'

'You're at work, Franck. You're not supposed to be sleeping.'

'My whole life has been in hibernation since we went our separate ways.'

She laughed. 'Hedgehogs and bears hibernate, Franck. Not policemen.'

'Emotionally, I meant. I'm just an automaton at work.'

'You're a damn genius. Which is why they pulled you out of the gendarmerie.'

She could hear him smile. 'Flattery will get you everywhere.'

'Good,' she said. 'Because I have a favour to ask.'

# CHAPTER THIRTY-SIX

Paris was wet and grey, and several degrees cooler than Bordeaux. Winter here, it seemed, had already got the city in the grip of its dead hand.

Jean-Marie Martinot lived beyond a gated arch in an apartment block called Villa Adrienne overlooking sumptuous gardens hidden from view off the Avenue du Général Leclerc in the fourteenth arrondissement.

Two of the three rooms he had once shared with his wife on the second floor were largely unused, gathering dust along with his memories, and he spent much of his life in one room with large windows that looked out over the gardens. It was a shambles. Settee and armchairs strewn with discarded clothes, half-eaten meals on plates gathering themselves on bookshelves and tables. Newspapers and wrappings accumulated in drifts on the floor.

'Excuse the mess,' he said as he showed Enzo in, but he seemed not in the least embarrassed by it. As if he had long stopped seeing it as the symptom of his loneliness that it was. The air was so thick with cigarette smoke that Enzo immediately wanted

to open a window, but Martinot was oblivious. He had a hand-rolled cigarette, stained brown by nicotine, burning between his lips, and ashtrays everywhere were overflowing. He lifted an old coat from the back of an armchair by the window where rain ran like tears down the glass, and he waved Enzo into the seat. He threw the coat on the settee and sat himself down opposite, across a cluttered coffee table.

He wore baggy dark trousers held by a belt at the waist, and a stained grey cardigan open over a white shirt frayed at the collar. A day's growth of silver bristles covered fleshy cheeks beneath a high forehead and a sweep of thick white hair. A big man once, age had diminished him in more ways than one. But there was still a twinkle in his clear blue eyes, even though Enzo noticed that he was wearing different-coloured socks.

'So,' he said, 'you're still on the Lambert case. I thought you'd got his killer?'

'Well, yes. The one who actually broke his neck. But not whoever paid him to do it.'

The old policeman shook his head. 'There are some cases that just never go away. The Lambert killing haunted me for damn near twenty years, even into retirement.' He gave Enzo a look of grudging admiration. 'But I could never have tracked down that killer the way you did. I'm just not up on all this new technology. In my day it was all about knocking on doors, tramping the streets and following your instincts.'

'There's still a lot to be said for that,' Enzo said. It was what he was doing himself. All the science and new technology in

the world was unlikely to save Sophie now. It was all boiling itself down to her father's instinct and intuition.

'How's that journalist doing? What was his name . . . ? Raffin?'

'He's pretty much recovered,' Enzo said, and he remembered very clearly stooping to pick up the note left by Raffin's cleaner in the journalist's apartment, only for Raffin to take the bullet meant for Enzo.

'A messy business.'

'It was.'

'Anyway, I'm glad to be of help again. Retirement is a much overrated thing, monsieur. Leads to atrophy of the brain as well as the body. I'd much rather be back at my old office on the Quai des Orfèvres than wasting away here waiting for my time to come. There's nothing quite like feeling there's a point to your life.'

He leaned forward to stub out his cigarette, and ash overflowed from the ashtray on to the table.

'Your phone call gave me a good excuse to revisit some old colleagues and retrieve my case notebooks from the *greffe*.' He laughed. 'Hah! Notebooks. Do cops these days even carry such things?' He opened a tin of tobacco and began carefully rolling another cigarette. 'Funny looking at your old handwriting, and remembering things that used to be important to you. I was amazed how much of it I did actually recall, though. Lambert didn't have that many friends. Nobody liked him very much. Apart, of course, from the girl called Sally.'

'But you had names for the others?' Enzo knew that the odds of this leading anywhere were extremely long.

The old man lifted an eyebrow. 'Of course. But there's only one, I think, that you'll be interested in. When we first went looking for Sally we learned that she had a friend. A girl called Mathilde Salgues. Another hooker. Her only real friend, apparently, aside from Lambert himself.' He shook his head. 'Strange relationship that.'

'Do you know where we can find her? Mathilde, I mean.'

'Well, she's not at the address she was back then.' Martinot lit his cigarette, and smoke seeped out of the corners of his mouth as he grinned. 'But there's still a little life in this old dog yet. I did a bit of checking. She's no longer Salgues. Seems she married into money, and up a class.' He fumbled in the pocket of his cardigan and pulled out a folded page torn from a notebook. He handed it across the table to Enzo. 'Lives in the Paris suburb of Orsay, and calls herself Mathilde de Vernal these days.'

Enzo unfolded the sheet of paper and looked at the address written in the old man's tight, neat hand.

'If it's not too much to ask, Monsieur Macleod, I'd very much like to come with you when you go to see her. Just a wee reminder of how it used to be. When I still had a life.'

With a name like de Vernal, Enzo had imaged Mathilde to be living in some grand nineteenth-century townhouse set behind trees in its own extensive grounds. Instead, the taxi

from the station dropped them off in the car park of a block of modern upscale apartments looking out over a sprawling area of parkland and lakes on the edge of *la ville d'Orsay*. Ash and sycamore, and lime and oak cast their shadows and their leaves on wet roads. A row of fir trees stood very nearly as tall as the apartments themselves.

It had taken only twenty minutes on the train to get here, and another ten in the taxi to the Rue de Valois. Old Martinot was in his element. He had listened intently on the train as Enzo explained why he wanted to talk to Mathilde, and fallen silent when he heard about Sophie's abduction. Now, as they left the elevator on the third floor and walked to the door of the de Vernal apartment at the end of the hall, he said to Enzo, 'I know it's a dreadful cliché, monsieur. But there never is smoke without fire. If we can confirm your link between Lambert and those murders in Bordeaux, no matter how tenuous, there's a reason for it. And it'll lead us somewhere. Mark my words.'

Enzo noticed Martinot's use of the word *we*, and took comfort from the sense of support gathering around him.

Martinot rapped on the door and said, 'You leave this to me.'

A shadow darkened the other side of the spy hole at eye level. And a woman's voice called from inside the apartment, 'Who is it?'

'Police, madame. Open up.' The old man turned and half-winked at Enzo. He had shaved and put on his best and shiniest shoes, and a long, dark winter coat. Enzo had persuaded him

that he should take a moment before they left to clean the food stain off the lapel.

Mathilde was a handsome woman, close to fifty Enzo thought. Recently coiffed hair shone almost blue-black, immaculately cut and cascading from a centre parting to very nearly touch her collar. The years had treated her kindly, and she had worn well, a strong jawline defining a well-structured face above an elegant neck that was only now beginning to show signs of age. She wore a cream blouse with a frilled lapel, and a pale blue pencil skirt that fell just below the knee. It would have been impossible to guess that she had once sold her body on street corners.

She looked out at them with concern, casting an appraising glance first towards Enzo, before turning it without apparent recognition in the direction of Martinot.

'Commissaire Jean-Marie Martinot,' the old man said, ignoring the fact that he had been retired for more than ten years. He half turned, but without looking at Enzo. 'My colleague, Monsieur Macleod.'

She glanced again at Enzo and frowned. Whatever else he looked like, it wasn't a policeman. But Martinot didn't give her time to dwell on it.

'We met in February 1992, you may recall, when I was investigating the murder of one Pierre Lambert, a rent boy working out of an apartment in the thirteenth.'

Colour immediately rose high on her cheeks, and she glanced quickly along the hall. 'Please, come in,' she said, and

held the door wide, clearly in a hurry for them to step out of public view, and the possible earshot of prying neighbours.

She led them into a sumptuous living room, expensive leather furniture set around a deep, white, shagpile carpet. French windows looked out beyond a balcony and the trees below, to the still waters of distant lakes reflecting the pewter of a wintery sky. There were no lights on, and the room seemed gloomy and faded somehow. She turned towards them, clearly agitated. 'I have two teenage children due home from school in ten minutes. I would appreciate it if you were gone before then.'

'That'll depend on how cooperative you are, madame,' Martinot said. He looked pointedly around the room. 'Seems like you married well. What is it your husband does?'

'Look . . .' She was almost ringing her hands. 'My husband knows nothing about . . . about my life back then. And I'd very much like it to stay that way.' She paused. 'What can you possibly want to talk to me about after all this time?'

'Your friend Sally,' Enzo said.

Mathilde frowned. 'Sally?' Then it dawned on her. 'Oh, you mean Sal?'

And Enzo remembered that 'Sal' was what Lulu had called Sally Linol.

'She disappeared,' Martinot prompted her. 'Immediately after Lambert was murdered.'

'Yes . . .' She seemed lost for a moment in recollection. 'They were a weird pair, those two.'

'And yet you and Sal were friends,' Enzo said.

'We used to work the same patch. Shared a pimp.' Somehow the memory of it was distasteful to her now. 'Even shared a studio for a time. Then she got herself some money and moved out. A place of her own. Though she still spent most of her time at Pierre's.'

'Where'd the money come from?' Martinot asked.

She shrugged and folded her arms defensively below her breasts. 'Who knows? She certainly never told me. Some of the girls said she'd caught herself a nice wealthy client who treated her well, but, if she did, I didn't know anything about it. It was just gossip.' She couldn't resist a glance at her watch, and she sighed theatrically. 'Look, what is this all about? Has she turned up, or what?' And then she was struck by a sudden thought. 'She's not dead, is she?'

'I hope not,' Enzo said. 'Did she ever tell you where she was from?'

She gave him a withering look. 'The girls don't talk about stuff like that. You don't tell, you don't ask.' But she paused then, realising this was not the answer they wanted. She thought for a moment. 'I don't know why, maybe it slipped out sometime. Bordeaux?' Then she shrugged. 'Could be wrong.' She glanced from one to the other. 'Listen, I'd really like you to go.'

Martinot said, 'She never got in touch again after Lambert's murder?'

A vigorous shake of the head. 'Never. And good riddance. Didn't even say goodbye.'

Enzo retrieved his laptop from his shoulder bag and kneeled down to open it up on a low coffee table by the window. He woke it from sleep and brought up, full screen, the jpeg image of Sally Linol that Nicole had sent him. The feather tattoo was clearly visible on the side of her neck.

Mathilde's hand flew to her mouth. 'Oh, my God! Where did you get that?'

'Is it her?' Enzo said.

Mathilde leaned over to trace the line of the feather with the tips of her fingers. 'God, yes. Even without that tattoo, I'd have known her anywhere.'

# CHAPTER THIRTY-SEVEN

Sophie had spent nearly an hour scraping the handle end of the spoon on the concrete floor to wear it thin enough to slip beneath the domed head of the bolt. Even then, it had not been easy. The bolt was rusted solid, and who knew how many years it might have been since these bars had last been un-padlocked and swung open on their hinges?

At first she had been afraid they might hear the scrape, scrape of metal on concrete, but the door was thick, and she could hear very distantly the sound of their television. They would never hear her above it.

Later she had watched with apprehension as one of them came to take away the tray from which she had removed the spoon. But it elicited no comment. And when the man returned several hours later with her next meal, there was another spoon in her coffee mug. She could only imagine that there must be several, and that one missing had gone, mercifully, unnoticed.

Now she stood on tiptoe, working assiduously at the head of the bolt, scouring away the rust which had almost welded

it to the hoop of the top hinge. Intermittently she used the lip of the spoon end to try to lever it up, but only succeeded in bending the spoon. Several times she very nearly gave up. But the thought of sitting doing nothing while meekly awaiting her fate was worse than the frustration of making no apparent progress with the bolt. At least that gave her a focus, and concentration relieved her fear.

It had been some time before it dawned on her that the small rectangle of pre-packed butter that they provided with each tray of food could be used as a lubricant.

With trembling fingers she had unwrapped the first of them and smeared it all over both hinges, around the tops of the bolts and the inset holes at the foot of each. Then she worked the spoon furiously into every tight space before squeezing in more butter.

The next tray had brought another pat of butter, and as she rubbed that into the hinges she began to fear that they would see how it was staining them dark. They seemed to scream out at her from the wall, *Look, look, look at me! Look what she's doing!* But when the short man with the gravelly voice came a little while later to take her down to the toilet, his eyes did not even wander in that direction.

She had lost track of how long she had been working on the top hinge when she got the first hint of movement from the bolt. With the spoon handle inserted between the top of the bolt and the hinge itself, she finally got it to turn a little. And that tiny movement was enough to set her off on a frenzy

of activity, working the spoon in and out, getting the head of the bolt to turn a little more each time.

The bolt was about three inches long, as thick as her little finger, and frustratingly stubborn. She twisted and turned the spoon, buckling it completely out of shape, until suddenly the bolt head lifted a quarter of an inch. She almost gasped in surprise, and stood back staring at it in disbelief. Before throwing herself at it feverishly once more, grasping the head between thumb and crooked forefinger. Turning and pulling until she drew blood, and her wrist and arm began to ache from the effort of trying to pull it out.

Then suddenly it came. In three short turns. And she stood breathing hard and holding the bolt in her hand. She slathered it in butter and started working it in and out of the hinge until she could slide it in and retrieve it easily again. God only knew how long she'd been working on it, but she understood that if she could achieve the same result with the lower hinge, she could swing the bars in their iron frame away from the window to hang from the padlock at the other side. Which would give her access to the window itself. Breaking the glass would be simple enough, but they would be sure to hear the noise, and she would have only a very short time to squeeze herself through it.

But then what? It was a twenty-foot drop to the lane below. She shook her head. She couldn't let herself think about that. One step at a time. If she got out of the window, that would be the time to start worrying about how to deal with the drop.

It was only at this point that she noticed a white SUV parked almost immediately below the window, tight in against the wall. She hadn't heard it arrive, and was certain it hadn't been there before. But she had no time to think about it. Footsteps in the hall forced her hurriedly to reinsert the bolt and slide her back down the wall to sit on the floor. She tried to control her breathing, but was sure that her cheeks must be burning pink. She dragged a forearm across her face to wipe away the sweat.

The footsteps came to a halt outside her door. And then silence. A silence that seemed to extend itself for a very long time. Before whoever was there turned and headed back the way they had come. Had they been able to see in? The thought set panic beating in Sophie's breast again.

She held her breath and listened intently. From the offices at the far end of the corridor, where her captors spent their time, she could hear very faintly the sound of men's voices raised in argument. Then a woman's voice, sharp and commanding. Sophie strained to hear, but there were no words taking shape. And then silence.

For a long time she heard nothing. Then a car door slamming. And she stood up quickly to press her face to the bars and peer down into the lane below. The SUV started up and drove away, but she could not get even a passing glimpse of the driver.

Now she stood breathing hard, the sense of time running out sending chills of apprehension through her body. And she set to work on the lower hinge with a ferocity driven by fear.

# CHAPTER THIRTY-EIGHT

The late-afternoon fever of Parisians dressed in winter black was building towards rush hour on the packed concourse of the Gare d'Austerlitz. People stood gazing upwards in impatient, ever-shifting crowds, at the electronic arrivals and departures display. Others gathered around tables outside cafés and in the stuffy, packed waiting room with its unyielding seats. Trains came and went from an endless line of platforms, engines revving and resounding along the quays, uniformed SNCF staff checking tickets and issuing refund vouchers to passengers spilling off late arrivals.

Enzo found Dominique in the crowd and the two stood locked in embrace, the rest of the world eddying around them, before reluctantly they let go to kiss with a short, desperate intensity. They hurried to grab a recently vacated table outside the café at the north end of the concourse. A harassed waiter swept away the crumbs and lifted empty, stained coffee cups before taking their order. It was cold, and their breath condensed in clouds, rising with the noise into the cavernous glass-roofed station.

Dominique had abandoned the car at Orléans and taken the train the rest of the way. Quicker, she had told Enzo on the phone, than driving into Paris in the rush hour. She listened in silence now, sipping her coffee, as Enzo told her about his visit to Mathilde de Vernal, and the confirmation that Pierre Lambert's great friend and confidant was, indeed, Sally Linol. The prostitute from Bordeaux with the feather tattoo on her neck.

'And she never resurfaced?' Dominique said.

Enzo shook his head grimly. 'Never.'

'So what does it mean?'

'I wish I knew.' It was the question that had been exercising his mind ever since dropping old Jean-Marie Martinot back at his apartment with the promise of keeping him up to date with any developments. He glanced at Dominique and saw the concern on her face. 'How did you get on with Anne-Laure Blanc?'

And she told him. All about Alice, and the clinic, and the secret funding of her treatment. Enzo's consternation grew as she spoke.

'But who would pay that kind of upkeep for the daughter of a serial killer?'

Dominique glanced at her watch. 'Hopefully we'll find that out in an hour or so.'

Enzo frowned. 'How?'

She smiled. A rare moment of sunshine on a dark afternoon, Enzo thought.

'An old colleague of mine,' she said. 'An ex-gendarme who

turned out to be a genius with figures. We always knew he had a special talent. He could make the most extraordinary calculations before you even had time to take in the figures. We used to try and catch him out, throwing him impossible sums, like a curveball at an unsuspecting kid. Additions and subtractions and multiplications that we didn't even know the answers to. But he never failed. Every one of them rattled off his tongue. And it would take us the next ten minutes to work it out on paper to see if he was right. And he always was.'

'*Ex*-gendarme?'

She nodded. 'He got headhunted by Tracfin.'

Enzo pursed his lips and shook his head. 'No idea what that is.'

'It's a government organisation set up five years ago to track and prevent money laundering, and to cut off the flow of finance to terrorists. They have absolute power to access financial records and bank accounts.'

Enzo sat back and raised an eyebrow. 'And you asked your friend to find out who's been paying for Alice Blanc's care?'

Dominique's smile was faintly smug. 'He owed me a favour.'

'That's some favour.'

She leaned forward, her elbows on the table, smile fading. 'I don't know why, Enzo. I just get the feeling that it could be the key to everything.'

Enzo noticed the car idling in the street outside Raffin's apartment. A large, black government car with a uniformed

chauffeur behind the wheel. Any other car that stopped here, just two hundred metres from the Senat building at the top of the Rue de Tournon, would have been moved on by traffic cops within minutes. But it looked as if it might have been there for some time, belching fumes into the rain and the gathering gloom, a rectangle of dry tarmac beneath it.

It wasn't until Enzo and Dominique reached the first-floor landing of Raffin's apartment block that he realised just whose vehicle it was.

Raffin was emerging from the apartment, pulling on his coat, accompanied by a tall, good-looking man who might have been in his early forties. The man wore a long black coat and a crisp white shirt with a red tie, and he had the unmistakable dyed and manicured coiffure of a typical *homme politique*. Enzo realised that he knew him, but couldn't immediately place him.

Raffin was startled to see Enzo. 'Oh.' His voice echoed down the narrow stairwell. 'Are you here to see Kirsty?'

'I'm here to see you,' Enzo said. 'There have been developments.'

Raffin looked uncomfortable. He glanced at his companion. 'Jean-Jacques, this is Enzo Macleod, and . . .' His eyes flickered towards Dominique.

'Dominique Chazal.' Enzo filled in the blank for him.

Raffin nodded and turned to introduce the other man. 'Jean-Jacques Devez.'

And Enzo realised now that they were in the presence of the

Mayor of Paris. He had seen photographs of him many times in the press, and in television debates and news items. The would-be future president. But he had not recognised him out of context. And yet there was something about him that seemed more familiar than a face seen on television. Something oddly, indefinably personal. In the smile. Or the impenetrable darkness of his eyes. The two men shook hands, and Devez nodded a dismissive acknowledgement towards Dominique. He was more interested in Enzo, and cast appraising eyes over him, his smile faintly sardonic. 'Ah, yes,' he said. 'The great Enzo Macleod. One hears so much about you these days. You're quite the celebrity.'

Enzo inclined his head a little. 'I didn't mean to be.'

Devez widened his smile. 'None of us ever do. A man like you would be a welcome addition to any government department dealing with crime. In an advisory capacity, of course. If I ever get elected, we must talk.' He turned to Raffin. 'I'll wait for you in the car.' And glanced at his watch. 'Don't be long. We're a little pushed.'

'I'll be right down,' Raffin said. And as the scrape of Devez's leather soles on the steps receded down the stairwell Raffin lowered his voice and turned to Enzo. 'What is it? I've got a really important meeting.'

Not even an enquiry about Sophie. Enzo bit back his annoyance. 'One of the Bordeaux Six, the girl with the feather tattoo on her neck . . . She was the best friend of Pierre Lambert.'

Which finally got Raffin's full attention. He stared at Enzo. 'You're kidding?'

Enzo shook his head. 'There's a link, Roger. I don't know what it is, but I know it's important. And someone's been paying a fortune to keep Régis Blanc's daughter in a specialised care clinic for the last twenty-three years.'

Raffin frowned. 'Who?'

'We don't know yet. But we hope to very soon.'

'Well, what's the connection?'

'I don't know that, either.'

Raffin glanced at his watch. 'Look, we'll talk about this when I get back in a couple of hours. I've really got to go.' He hesitated a moment, as if replaying what Enzo had just told him. Then repeated himself. 'Got to go.' And he hurried off down the stairs.

Dominique looked at Enzo. 'Any word on Sophie?' She mimicked Raffin's voice. The question he had failed to ask. Then she shook her head. 'So that was the great Roger Raffin. What a charmer.'

It was the first thing Kirsty asked when she let them in, anxious eyes searching her father's face. And when he shook his head, his disappointment was reflected in hers. She hugged him before turning with moist eyes to kiss Dominique on each cheek.

'Come through,' she said. 'Can I make you coffee? Or maybe you need something stronger?'

'Coffee would be good,' Enzo said.

Alexis was crawling around the floor amid a colourful clutter of plastic toys contained within a baby frame designed to limit

the extent of his wanderings. He didn't appear to hear them come in, but as soon as he saw Enzo his face lit up, and Enzo stooped to lift him high into his arms and rub the child's nose with his. A chortle of delight burst from the baby's lips, and he grabbed his grandfather's ears and held on tight.

Kirsty had just brought a cafetière of freshly made coffee through from the kitchen on a tray with cups and sugar cubes when the phone rang. 'I'll take that in the study,' she said, and left them to pour their own.

The gloom from the courtyard outside seemed to permeate the whole apartment, the dying of the light at the end of the day casting the corners of the *séjour* into darkness. Enzo found a switch for one of the uplighters and it threw light across the table as Dominique poured their coffee. The pianist upstairs was back to practising scales. Chromatic. Endlessly repeating semitone steps up and down. Stiff fingers still hesitant, even after all these years. And Enzo wondered what the point of it was. He felt depression settle on him like dust.

Somewhere Sophie was being held hostage to his investigation. Wherever she was the light would be dying, too. He closed his eyes and tried to imagine what it was she must be feeling. Only to unlock the horrors of his own imagination. He quickly opened his eyes again, and wanted to cry out. To throw his fists wildly about him, to hit anything and everything in his way. In his head he heard his scream, but the room remained silent. Invaded only by the distant sound of the piano.

He turned to find Dominique looking at him. She didn't ask. She didn't have to.

The door from the study opened and Kirsty emerged, as if in slow motion. Her eyes were lost in a focus somewhere far beyond the room they were in. Enzo saw how pale she was. All the blood had drained from her face, and she looked almost ghostlike in the gloom. 'What is it?' he said.

It took some moments for his words to cross the distance to that place her thoughts had taken her. Her delayed reaction to his words was startled, and she responded as if he had just spoken. 'What?' She seemed confused.

'Who was on the phone?'

'Doctor Demoulin. From Biarritz.'

Enzo stood up, immediately. Something was wrong. 'What did he say?'

Again his words appeared to travel a long way before they reached her. She looked at him. 'Alexis has a congenital condition. There's no treatment. Nothing that can be done.' She glanced at her son in his playpen. But he was oblivious, focused on trying to fit plastic shapes into the correct holes in a yellow board, before giving up in frustration to throw them on to the floor. Hand–eye–brain coordination not yet developed enough to fulfil the desire. 'He'll have to wear hearing aids all his life.'

Enzo said. 'The technology's amazing these days, Kirst. You won't even see them.'

Her eyes flickered back to her father. 'That's what Doctor Demoulin said.'

'See?' Enzo tried to force a smile. 'I told you he was a good guy.'

She suddenly took two steps towards him, bursting into tears and throwing her arms around him, just as she might have done as a child. She buried her face in his chest and he cradled her head in his hand and remembered all the times he had held her like this. Before a loveless marriage and a new-found love had torn them apart. The greatest regret of his life. She drew her head back and looked up at him, eyes filled with tears and a strange intensity. 'I love you, Dad,' she said.

No longer *Papa*, he was *Dad* again. And he felt tears running down his own cheeks, strangely hot in the cold of the apartment.

'I love you, too, pet,' he said, and held her all the tighter.

'He said he would put it all in a letter.' Her voice came muffled from his chest. 'A detailed explanation, along with a prescription for the hearing aids.' She drew away from him now. Wiping the tears from her cheeks with the flat of her hands. 'I've got to get out. Take Alexis with me and get some air. Time to think.'

'It's raining, Kirst.'

'Doesn't matter. He'll be fine in his pram.'

'Do you want me to come with you?'

'No,' she said, almost too quickly. 'I need time to myself. Besides, you have other things to think about.' She squeezed his hand. 'But you could get my coat from the wardrobe in the

bedroom while I get Alexis ready. The fawn one with the belt.'
And she went to lift her son from his playpen.

Enzo exchanged a glance with Dominique and saw the sympathy in her eyes. He wiped away his own tears, embarrassed, and went into the bedroom through glass-panelled double doors that led straight off the *séjour*.

The wardrobe was a big, antique *garde-robe* in polished walnut. A family heirloom, perhaps, from Raffin's family or Marie's. He opened both doors and searched among all the coats and jackets hanging there for Kirsty's fawn raincoat with the belt at the waist. People have their own distinctive scent, whether from the traces of perfume, or soap or aftershave, or from the oils secreted through the skin, earthy, musky, unmistakable. He could smell his daughter among these clothes, a scent as familiar to him as fresh air on a Scottish winter's day. And he could smell Raffin, too. Some aftershave or hair oil that he must always have been in the habit of using. Just behind Kirsty's coat he saw a pale green linen jacket with the breast pocket torn away, threads still hanging from it where the material had been violently ripped. The remnants of some crest or emblem embroidered into it were still visible along the inside edge.

Enzo stopped dead, and for a moment thought his heart might have stopped, too. In his head he tumbled back through time to an open gallery running around the roof of the château at Gaillac, where a shadowy figure had lured him in the dark and tried to drive a knife into his heart. Someone who had cut himself in the attempt, and fled in panic at the arrival of

Bertrand, leaving Enzo dazed on the floor, and clutching the bloodstained, torn pocket of a pale green linen jacket with a maker's emblem embroidered on it.

His breath was coming to him with difficulty now. It was Raffin! Raffin who had lured him up a stone staircase on that dark night and tried to kill him. And here was the jacket he had worn. Freshly laundered to get rid of the blood, but still missing its breast pocket.

Enzo's world was collapsing about him like a house of cards. If it was Raffin, then Raffin must have killed Marie. And somehow it was Raffin who was implicated in the murder of Pierre Lambert. Raffin who had kidnapped one of his daughters and was intent on marrying the other. Raffin, the father of Enzo's grandchild!

He had accepted Enzo's offer to use new science to resolve the cold cases he had assembled in his book. Because how could he refuse? But he could never have imagined just how successful Enzo would be. And it must have become apparent to him at a very early stage that sooner or later Enzo was going reveal Raffin himself to be the killer of his wife.

The implications were igniting in Enzo's mind like firecrackers on Guy Fawkes night, though there was still too much missing for him to make all the connections and see the whole display. He felt weak, and sick, and angry, but he knew that somehow he had to stay in control.

'Dad?' Kirsty's voice crashed into his thoughts from the other room.

'Coming.' He grabbed her coat, his mind still a mess of confusion, and hurried through to the *séjour*.

Alexis was wrapped up warm in her arms, his pram sitting out in the hall, ready to go. She passed him to her father while she pulled on her coat. And, as Enzo handed her the baby back, she looked at him quizzically. 'What's wrong?'

He had no idea how to be natural in this situation, and just shook his head. A forced smile, he was sure, appearing more like a grimace on his face. 'Nothing. Don't get cold out there.'

Still she looked at him oddly, before shrugging it off and heading out to the hall. 'Will you wait till Roger gets back?'

Just the mention of his name caused Enzo to quite involuntarily clench his fists. He would never tire of punching that bastard's duplicitous fucking face!

Dominique said, 'Actually, we have a rendezvous very shortly. But we'll come back.'

'Okay. See you later.' And Kirsty was gone.

Dominique stood up immediately. Their coffee had gone cold, untouched in their cups. And all her instincts told her that something was very wrong. 'What is it?'

Enzo turned and strode back into the bedroom, ripping the linen jacket from its hanger. 'This!' he hissed. And he could hardly find his voice to speak, his face dark now with anger and hatred.

Dominique looked at him, utterly bewildered. And he fought to control his breathing so that he could explain. Painting a picture for her of that night, high up in the roof of the château,

vivid and clear, when Raffin had tried to murder him in cold blood. 'I'm going to fucking kill him!'

The colour had risen high on her cheeks. But she put a hand on his arm and gripped it tightly. 'Enzo, you can't afford to do anything silly. We have the advantage of knowing what he has tried so very hard to stop you from finding out. But he still has Sophie, and we have no idea how any of this ties together. We have to play it smart.'

All Enzo wanted to do was inflict violence on the man who had done this to him. But he knew that Dominique was right, and was glad that she was there to moderate his more intemperate instincts. The quick emotions inherited from his Italian mother, and the even quicker resort to violence and swearing born of a tough Glasgow upbringing.

'Where is the bloodstained pocket now?'

'The police have it. Hélène had it run through the DNA database at the time, but of course it came up blank.'

'Good. So now we need a sample of Raffin's DNA for comparison and we've got him. At least for attempted murder. But I'm pretty sure the rest of it is just going to unravel from there.'

Enzo took a deep breath and nodded, and he turned and marched purposefully into the bathroom. His eyes scanned the sink and the bath, the shower cubicle. Then he opened the mirrored cabinet above the sink. 'There.' He reached in and retrieved Raffin's razor. A triple-bladed head that he detached from its handle. He held it up between his thumb and forefinger. 'More than enough bristle and skin, maybe even some

blood, to provide the bastard's DNA.' He was getting some of his control back now. He laid it carefully on the rim of the sink, took a fresh razor head from a dispenser in the cabinet, and snapped it on to the handle, replacing the one he had removed. 'He'll never know.'

Dominique followed him back to the *séjour* where he retrieved a small plastic evidence bag from the pocket of his shoulder bag and dropped the razor head into it. She said, 'If we FedEx that to Cahors tonight, Hélène will get it first thing in the morning. We can do that on our way to meet Franck.'

Enzo frowned. 'Franck?'

'The Tracfin guy. And you can call Commissaire Taillard to let her know it's on its way.'

# CHAPTER THIRTY-NINE

They met Franck at the L'Ecritoire, in the tree-lined Place de la Sorbonne. Smokers, mostly students, sat out of the rain under a red canopy that cast its gloom over the tables and chairs lined up along the pavement outside, yellow light and laughter spilling out into the darkening day. At the far end of the square, floodlit figures atop high columns flanked a clock set into the arch of a tall, stone building that dominated everything else around it. Fountains played in a rectangular water feature, lit along its length by concealed underwater lighting. The whole square resounded to the sound of voices. Student voices, animated by youth and aspiration and unbounded optimism. They made Enzo feel very old and tired.

Franck was a good-looking young man in his mid-thirties. He had a mischievous smile and rich brown hair that fell in luxuriant curls over quizzical eyebrows. He still carried about him the natural confidence of youth, and so seemed not at all out of place among all these students from the university. His black coat hung open and a red scarf dangled from his neck. A scarred leather satchel lay on the chair next to him.

He was waiting for them at a table at the back of the café, and rose to greet Dominique with a warm embrace and a kiss on each cheek. Then he looked at Enzo. 'Who's this? Your dad?'

Dominique gave him a dangerous look. 'This is Enzo Macleod. If you were even remotely in touch with the real world, Franck, I wouldn't need to make the introduction.'

Franck's liquid brown eyes opened wide with sudden recognition, and he pumped Enzo's hand enthusiastically. 'Monsieur Macleod. What an honour.' And Enzo wasn't sure if the younger man was mocking him or not. 'Sit down. What can I get you to drink?'

They ordered coffee, since they had never got around to drinking the ones that Kirsty had made, and Franck reached across the table to take both of Dominique's hands in his. To his annoyance, Enzo found a tiny seed of jealousy germinating inside him at such casual and not unfamiliar intimacy. Dominique blushed with embarrassment and avoided his eye.

Franck said, 'It's been too long.'

Dominique nodded. 'It has.'

He gazed into her eyes with unglazed affection. 'I still miss you.' He turned a smile of regret in Enzo's direction and sighed. 'Life, monsieur, is full of might-have-beens. The moments we missed, or didn't see until they were gone. Dominique is one of those. The one who got away.'

Dominique took back her hands. 'Oh, stop it, Franck.' She risked a glance at Enzo. 'He was always a fantasist.'

'A man's entitled to dream, isn't he?' He looked to Enzo for confirmation.

Enzo said, 'Sometimes the dream is all we're left with.' And somehow that stole away all the levity, leaving a moment of awkward silence among them.

Dominique broke it. 'So? Did you find anything?'

Franck said, 'I did.' The smile was gone now, and the twinkle with it. He sat back and looked at them thoughtfully. 'I don't know what you two are involved in. And I don't want to know. In fact, I'm beginning to regret I ever agreed to do this.'

'You owed me, Franck.'

Franck looked at her. The merest nod of his head and a downward turn of his eyes acknowledged it. 'I know.' He examined his hands for a moment, before looking up again. 'It wasn't that hard, actually. Money, even the electronic variety, leaves indelible traces wherever it goes. You just have to follow the tracks.'

'And?' Dominique could hardly contain her impatience.

Franck sucked in a deep breath, as if stealing himself to reveal some dirty little secret. 'That little girl's medical care has been paid for over the last twenty-odd years by money transferring automatically out of a private account in the BNP Paribas.' Again he paused, before adding reluctantly, 'A personal account belonging to someone who might conceivably be the next president of France. A certain Jean-Jacques Devez. The Mayor of Paris.'

# CHAPTER FORTY

They walked for some way in silence in the rain after leaving Franck in the Place de la Sorbonne. They were several streets away before Dominique slipped her arm through Enzo's and posed the question that had gone unasked in the café. A question that all three of them had assiduously avoided. Franck had been compromised enough as it was. 'Why would the Mayor of Paris be paying for the medical care of Alice Blanc?'

Enzo shook his head grimly. 'I don't know.' His mind was swimming and filled with the recollection of Charlotte telling him that Devez had begun his political career in Bordeaux. 'But I do know this. He was an *adjoint* to the Mayor of Bordeaux at the time Blanc was murdering those prostitutes there.' He thought some more about that conversation he'd had with Charlotte on the drive to Lannemezan. 'And Raffin and Devez are old friends. Charlotte told me that Raffin and Marie used to socialise with Devez and his wife.'

Dominique tightened her grip on his arm. 'And now that Devez is on the brink of entering the race for the presidency, he's offering Raffin a job as his press secretary.' Her frustration

billowed, like smoke, in condensed breath around her head. 'I don't understand it, Enzo. The more pieces of the picture we assemble, the more obscure the picture itself becomes.'

Enzo pulled her close. 'That's because we're missing something, Dominique. Something big. Something important. Something that's going to connect all the pieces and suddenly make the whole picture blindingly clear.'

'Which is exactly what they're trying to stop you from doing.'

He nodded, and thought once more with anger and pain about Sophie.

'So what is it?' Dominique said. 'This thing we're missing?'

'I haven't the least idea.'

Light from all the apartments around the interior square fell from countless windows to reflect on black cobbles. Raffin's apartment on the first floor was no exception. Evidently, someone was home.

The piano player had given up as Enzo and Dominique climbed the stairs to the landing, and so they were accompanied only by the sound of their own feet on the stone steps, and the exhalation of their breath in the chill air of the stairwell. Enzo rang the doorbell and after some moments it was Raffin himself who opened the door. He was in shirtsleeves and stockinged feet, his hair a little dishevelled, and he looked wild-eyed. 'Come in, come in,' he said, and headed back into the apartment, leaving them to follow and close the door behind them.

Dominique tugged on Enzo's sleeve as they crossed the hall and cast him a warning look. The revelation that somehow Jean-Jacques Devez was involved in all this had ratcheted everything up to a new and more potent level of danger. They had decided not to confront Raffin just yet. The razor head had gone off to Cahors, and Sophie's life might just depend on how things would unravel over the next twenty-four hours. But Enzo was containing himself with difficulty.

In the *séjour* Raffin had spread his files on the Bordeaux Six all over the table, and he returned to them now in a state of apparent excitement. 'It's a real development, Enzo,' he said. 'Blanc's running a prostitution racket in Bordeaux. Then, out of the blue, he ups and murders three of his girls. And, who knows, maybe Lucie Martin, as well. But one of his other girls vanishes just before the killings. Sally Linol. Who then turns up in Paris, where she becomes best friends with Pierre Lambert. Then, when he gets murdered, she vanishes again.' He picked up his photocopied image of Sally Linol, the tattoo on her neck blurred and darkened by the process of copying it, and he waved it at Enzo. 'She's the key. She's got to be the key.'

And Enzo realised, quite suddenly, that that's exactly what she was. The one common factor. The 'something big' they were missing that he had discussed with Dominique. And here was Raffin waving her under his nose, telling him that she was the missing piece of the puzzle. Almost flaunting her, as if he knew that it really didn't matter. And the only reason he could have such confidence in that was his knowledge that

Enzo would never find her. Because she was dead. Buried long ago in some dark wood somewhere, or lying in the bottom of a lake, a bagful of bones like poor Lucie Martin.

'Don't you see?' Raffin was saying. He dropped the picture back on to the table. 'There's a connection we had no idea ever existed.'

Enzo said, 'Which doesn't help us much with the Lucie Martin case.'

Raffin's eyes were still shining, and Enzo couldn't remember seeing him this animated in a long time. 'Maybe not. But it throws new light on the killing of Pierre Lambert. We always knew who did the deed, but not who paid him or why.'

'So,' Dominique said, 'all we have to do is find Sally Linol?'

Raffin smiled. 'Exactly.'

They all turned at the sound of the door opening into the hall, and Kirsty manoeuvred Alexis's pram in from the landing, bringing the chill damp air in with her. She was soaked, in spite of her waterproof, hair hanging in wet rats' tails about her head, and Enzo realised she must have been out walking the streets all this time.

She divested herself of her coat and lifted Alexis from his pram. The baby boy was fast asleep, and Enzo stepped towards his daughter, concerned, as she carried him into the *séjour*. 'Are you alright? You're soaked.'

'I'm fine. I just needed to think, that's all. It's a lot to take in.'

'What is?' Raffin crossed the room to take Alexis from her. And Kirsty told him about the phone call from Doctor

Demoulin. Enzo saw disquiet flit across his face. 'If he's not deaf, and the hearing aids are going to help . . .'

Kirsty nodded. 'I know, I know. I've just been trying to come to terms with that. As Dad says, the technology is so advanced you don't even see them nowadays.'

But no matter how hard she had been trying, Enzo thought, she was still a long way from coming to any kind of terms with it.

She changed the subject, self-consciously. 'How did you get on with Jean-Jacques?'

Raffin's face lit up. 'He's got the nomination. And my job offer's official.'

'And?'

He grinned. 'I said yes. The party's going to announce his nomination in the next two weeks, and I'll be the one up front doing it.'

'Oh, darling, that's wonderful.' Kirsty leaned in past their baby to kiss him, and yet Enzo couldn't help feeling that her delight was a little less than enthusiastic. But if Raffin was aware of it, he gave no indication.

Kirsty took Alexis again. 'I'll just put him down.'

'Congratulations,' Enzo said. His voice laden with all the insincerity he felt. But again, Raffin seemed oblivious. And a stab of anger at the man's apparent indifference to almost everything around him pushed Enzo to cross a line. 'By the way,' he said, 'Kirsty asked me to fetch a coat for her earlier, and I couldn't help noticing one of your jackets in the

wardrobe has had its breast pocket torn off.' He almost heard Dominique's intake of breath beside him.

Raffin frowned. 'Breast pocket?' He pushed out his lower lip and shrugged. Then recollection dawned. 'Oh, that's the green linen. Part of a suit, actually. Came back from the dry cleaners like that. Always meant to take it back and complain, but somehow never managed to get around to it.'

'Oh, my God!' Kirsty's exclamation startled them all, and started Alexis crying. She had stopped by the table on the way to the bedroom, and was standing holding the photograph of Sally Linol in her hand. She turned, still holding it, and looked at her father. 'I told you I recognised her.' She waved the photograph towards him, just as Raffin had done minutes earlier. 'That's the housekeeper at Biarritz. Madame Brusque. Twenty years younger, but it's her alright.'

'That woman didn't have a tattoo,' Enzo said, raising his hand to touch his neck without thinking. And he could feel the blood pulsing in it.

'She was wearing a high collar. And, anyway, you get make-up for masking tattoos these days. I'm telling you, Dad. It's her.'

Raffin's face was a mask of confusion. 'Madame Brusque?' He turned bewildered eyes towards Enzo. 'Marie appointed her after the death of her parents. I never saw any reason not to keep her on. How can she possibly be Sally Linol?'

# CHAPTER FORTY-ONE

The rain, the light reflecting on the shiny black wet of the road, the white lines that passed below them with such monotonous regularity; the rapid beat of the wipers on the windscreen, smearing the glare of oncoming traffic across the glass. It had all become impossibly hypnotic after only an hour on the motorway, heading south-west out of Orléans.

Enzo ached with fatigue. Every muscle hurt with every movement of the wheel, and just the sheer effort of will required to stay awake was, in itself, exhausting.

Dominique sat in the passenger seat beside him. Tense. Anxious to relieve him from the stress of driving. But he had been insistent. And she had been brooding in silence for some time before, finally, all her exasperation came bubbling to the surface. 'He was so fucking cool!' she said. 'One minute he's waving her in your face like she's the answer to everything. The next we find out she's been right under his nose the whole time.'

Enzo said, 'I don't think he knew. In fact, I'm certain of it. Because, if she really is the key to it all, Raffin – or Devez,

or someone else – would have got rid of her a long time ago. What I can't figure out is how Raffin's wife fits into all this. If she really is the one who employed Sally at the house, to work there under a false name, then it's almost as if she was hiding her there.'

'From what?'

'I don't know. Raffin himself, maybe.'

'Well, he seemed pretty shaken up.'

'He did.'

'So what do you think he's doing now?'

'I think he's organising someone to get to her before we do.'

'Well, if he thinks we're not leaving till tomorrow, he'll figure he's got time to fly someone down first thing.' They had told him they would spend the night at the studio in Paris and drive down to Biarritz in the morning.

Enzo shook his head in the dark. 'He knows we're on our way. Raffin may be many things, but he's not stupid. It's quite possible he could already have someone else on the road. Whatever we do, we've got to get there before they do.' He breathed deeply. 'As long as I can stay awake long enough.' The thrum of the tyres on the wet tarmac was adding to the soporific effect of driving weary in the dark and the rain.

Dominique glanced at his face, flitting between light and shadow, pale and washed out in the reflected headlights of other vehicles. They had taken the train to Orléans to retrieve the car, and now would be six hours on the *autoroute*, but Enzo's absolute determination was clear. Dominique knew

that he saw Sally Linol now as the best and only way of nego-tiating Sophie's safe release. If he had Sally, even if she knew nothing, or wasn't prepared to tell, he would still have bar-gaining power. Leverage over Raffin and Devez. Because, as Raffin himself had been only too keen to point out just a few hours earlier, Sally Linol was almost certainly the key to everything.

The sound of Enzo's mobile phone ringing startled them in the dark, cutting above the roar of the engine and the end-less vibration of the road beneath them. Enzo fumbled in his pocket to find it and handed it to Dominique. At 130 kph, in the dark and the wet, he didn't want to take his eyes off the road for a second. She answered it and put it on speaker.

'Monsieur Macleod?' Nicole's voice was razor-sharp, honed thin by the airwaves and the tiny speakers of the phone.

'What is it, Nicole?'

'Have you seen the news?'

'Nicole, I'm in a car on a motorway in the pissing rain. I haven't seen a television in days.'

If Nicole was perturbed by the tone of her irascible mentor, there was no hint of it in her voice. Perhaps, Dominique thought, she was just used to it. 'It's on the radio, too. All over the news.'

And Enzo was suddenly afraid for Sophie. 'What is?!'

'Régis Blanc. He's dead. Killed in a fight with another pris-oner in Lannemezan.'

# CHAPTER FORTY-TWO

All that Sophie could see in the window as she worked was her own reflection. Beyond it the darkness was profound. And still the rain fell, tears from heaven running in tracks through the dirt on the outside of the glass.

It was almost startling to see herself so close up and personal after all this time. Her face stained and streaked with dirt, her tan faded now to a blue-white pallor. Her hair was tangled and matted about her head. The wild-eyed creature that stared back at her from the glass was virtually unrecognisable. Certainly not the face she was accustomed to seeing every morning in the mirror above the bathroom sink, where she washed and plucked her eyebrows and applied her make-up.

But even as she looked at this strange creature gazing back at her, she saw the determination in her own eyes. An oddly dead-eyed determination that fuelled her nearly obsessive attempt to free the second hinge pin.

She had been working at it for much of the day, and now into the night. She had no idea what time it was, but darkness had fallen beyond the bars several hours ago. The bolt in the

lower hinge had been stubbornly determined not to budge. For some reason, it was more badly rusted than the other.

Her hands were greasy with the butter she had been using to lubricate it, and the spoon kept slipping through her fingers. It was bent and twisted unrecognisably, and she was beginning to despair of ever getting the bolt to move.

There was a gap between the top of the metal framework of the bars and the underside of the window frame into which it was fitted, and finally, in frustrated desperation, she rammed the heels of both hands hard up under the top of the frame. To her astonishment it slid up, and the gap vanished. She held the bars, then, in both hands and pulled down sharply. The frame moved again, and she was amazed to see that the lower hinge pin had stayed slightly raised, providing her with a quarter of an inch gap into which she could work the remains of the spoon with ease.

For the first time in several hours, hope returned. An almost debilitating depression had descended on her at regular intervals. With each fresh tray of food had come the fear that this could be her last meal. Then each time left alone, she had grabbed the fresh pack of butter to start working it again into the hinge. An emotional roller coaster that had taken her from the depths of despair to impossible peaks of euphoria and then down again.

Now she was on the way back up. There was movement in the bolt. She wiped the butter from her fingers on her jeans, gripping the head of the pin and twisting as she pulled with

one hand, grasping the bars with the other and shaking them violently.

And suddenly it simply came away. She stood looking at it in her hand, dumbfounded by the abrupt and unexpected success. She clutched it tightly, excitement rising in her throat and very nearly choking her. She slid the top bolt out of the upper hinge and stuffed both pins into her pocket. With trembling fingers she grasped the bars with both hands and pulled sharply inward. The whole frame came away, except where it was attached at the other side by the padlock. Hardly daring to breathe, she lowered the frame so that it rested against the wall below the window, suspended from the padlock, and reached for the window handle itself. To her astonishment the handle turned quite easily and the window swung open into the room. No need to break the glass.

Fresh air rushed into the stale warmth of her cell, stimulating and intoxicating at the same time. She pushed her face out into the darkness and felt the cold of the rain on it, like tiny chilled drops of freedom. And with a great effort she pulled herself up on to the frame of the window, crouching to very nearly fill it, and balancing herself to get a first real glimpse of the world outside.

About two feet to the left of her window, a rusted downpipe ran from a gutter ten feet above, to a drain set into the road twenty feet below. It was attached to the wall every few feet by brackets that had seen better days, corroded by time and weather. If she was going to escape this place, she was going

to have to trust her life to them holding long enough for her to slide her way down to the ground. Fear and hope filled her heart in equal measure.

Even just to reach the downpipe, though, would be fraught with risk. She would have to swing herself from the window, holding on to the nearside of it, until she could grasp the pipe. Then she'd have to let go and trust that it was going to take her weight while she grabbed it with both hands and used her feet to brace herself and stop herself from falling.

She breathed deeply, imagining everything that could go wrong, and the consequences of tumbling twenty feet to the ground. She leaned her back against the frame of the window and realised, for the first time, that she could see further than the brick wall opposite. The narrow road below opened out beyond the facing buildings into a vast area of industrial wasteland, pitted with lakes of milky green and the stumps of derelict buildings. Interlacing strings of old streetlights illuminated roads long fallen into desuetude. In the far distance she could see the lights of a city reflecting on the underside of low cloud, suffusing the rain-filled night with a disturbing orange glow.

And with that came the realisation that, even were she able to reach the safety of the ground, there would still be a very long way to go before she was free.

The sound of approaching footsteps out in the hall brought her back to her present situation with a sudden, stinging shock. There was no time to try to effect her escape now.

Even if she managed to get to the ground, they would be after her in moments. She wouldn't stand a chance. She needed a head start.

She jumped lightly back down into her cell and swung the window shut. With fumbling fingers she lifted the frame she had left dangling from the padlock and pushed it back into place. But there was no time to replace the hinge pins. She just hoped to God that they wouldn't notice.

By the time the footsteps had reached her door, she was lying on her camp bed, pulling the single blanket over her. Which is when she saw her wet footprints on the floor. The soles of her shoes had picked up rainwater on the outside sill of the window. Panic consumed her. All these hours of patient perseverance in loosening the hinge pins had gone to waste. Her captors could not fail to see her stupid damned footprints on the floor. She wanted to scream. But instead held her breath and listened as the footsteps passed the door and carried on down the hall.

She leaped off the camp bed and spread the blanket over the telltale signs she had left on the concrete, and sat on it, her back to the wall. In the silence that followed she could hear her heartbeat. She could hear the blood pulsing in her head. The sound of her breathing seemed to fill the room.

She waited, then tensed again as she heard the footsteps returning. Once more they passed without stopping, and she released a long, slow breath of relief, as if letting it out too quickly might make sufficient noise to bring those footsteps running back.

Sometime soon, she knew, they would come to take her to the toilet, and then they would leave her be for the rest of the night. That's when she would make good her escape. While they were sleeping and she had time to get out, and be a long way away even before they knew she was gone. She leaned her head back against the wall and closed her eyes.

The realisation that she had been asleep startled her awake. She sat blinking in the harsh electric light, without any idea of how long she might have slept. They had not come to take her to the toilet as she expected, and as consciousness returned she could hear the sound of voices from the room at the far end of the corridor. There was an argument in progress. A man was shouting. And then a woman's voice. As before, imperious, commanding. Followed by silence.

Sophie strained to hear as the conversation resumed, this time at a lower level. She got to her feet and crossed to the door, pressing her ear to the cold metal and listening hard. But she could discern nothing more than a murmur of voices, a soft vibration.

Alarm bells rang deafeningly in her head. Something felt wrong. Something was different. They had not come to take her to the toilet. The routine was broken. And everything about the last few days had been defined by routine. Suddenly it seemed that if she didn't go now she would never go at all.

She didn't stop to think, or reason, but acted on pure, naked instinct, crossing the room in three strides to wrench the

frame of iron bars from the window. As before, she let them dangle from the padlock, and hurriedly opened the window, pulling herself up to brace her feet in the crouching position she had adopted previously.

She glanced down and saw the white SUV there once more, almost immediately below the window. Again, she had not heard it arriving. On the wall opposite she could see her silhouette crouched in the square of light projected through her window and on to the facing brickwork.

Tentatively she manoeuvred herself into a position where her whole body was leaning out of the window, secured only by the grasp of her fingers on the window frame, and she reached for the downpipe. Infuriatingly, the length of her arm left her fingertips inches short. She felt the rain on her face and a sense of desperation so acute it seemed as if a hand, fingers spread, was squeezing her heart.

From inside the building she heard voices raised once more, and then those same footsteps coming back down the hall. Only, this time, it felt as if there was a sense of purpose in them that had not been there before. Adrenalin surged through her body, overcoming fear, and she drew herself back into the window before swinging into the night, letting go her grip of the window frame only at the last moment, reaching out with her other arm and trusting to God that her fingers would find the downpipe.

She felt cold, wet metal and closed her fingers around it. But even as she grasped the pipe with her other hand, she heard

the fixings tearing themselves free of the wall. She glanced up and in the light from the open window saw the gutter overhead peeling itself away from the roof. The brackets holding the downpipe to the wall above her sprang loose, and with the most awful sound of rending metal filling her consciousness, both gutter and pipe tore themselves away from the building.

Sophie swung her legs up to wrap around the downpipe and braced herself for the fall. But almost immediately the whole disintegrating structure came to a juddering halt. The downpipe and its attached gutter had bridged the gap between the two buildings, arcing between them and jamming at a point higher up in the facing brickwork. Sophie was dangling now in mid-air, still twelve or fifteen feet from the ground. She began to shimmy down the curve of the pipe, wet fingers desperately trying to maintain their grip, skin flaying and burning as she slipped one hand over the other.

Then, from the room above, she heard the bellow of a man's voice. They knew she was gone.

A quick glance down, then she simply let go of the pipe and dropped the rest of the way to the ground, landing heavily and tipping on to her side in the wet. She rolled over and slammed hard into the wall below the window. She flattened herself against it, hoping that she could not be seen from above.

Looking up, she could see the silhouette of a man leaning out of the open window, looking down into the darkness. She heard his oath filling the night air. 'Fuck! The bitch is gone.' And his shadow disappeared from the light.

Sophie looked around in a blind panic. If she ran, they would catch her. And there was nowhere to hide. She slid along the wall until she was level with the back of the SUV. She could hear its engine ticking in the dark as it cooled, and she reached forward to try the handle on the tailgate. It opened. The vehicle was not locked. Fleetingly she wondered if the driver might have left the keys in the ignition, but shouting voices from the far end of the abandoned factory stole away any illusion of time that she might have had. She lifted the tailgate and jumped inside, pulling it shut behind her and curling up in the foetal position, arms wrapped tightly around her shins.

She tried very hard to control her breathing as she heard the sound of several men running in the dark, splashing through the puddles in this cracked and pitted alleyway. She braced herself, waiting for the tailgate to be thrown open, angry hands reaching in to pull her out. But they passed her by and continued on down between the buildings. More raised voices and angry shouts. It seemed so obvious to her that she was hiding in the boot space of this SUV that she couldn't believe they would not think to look.

Now she heard the woman's voice again. Just the tone of it, not the words. Angry, ugly and abusive. Someone smacked a fist or a boot into the side of the SUV and the whole vehicle shook. They were all gathered just outside. Just a touch away. Sophie held her breath for so long she thought her lungs would burst.

Then the driver's door opened and someone slid in behind

the wheel. The door slammed angrily and the engine coughed to life, revving violently before the vehicle pulled away with a spinning of tyres that sent Sophie rolling back to slam into the tailgate. The driver was oblivious, picking up speed across the broken tarmac, lurching side to side and front to back, tossing Sophie around the boot like some tattered little rag doll.

After less than a minute they seemed to find the smoother surface of a proper road, and the driver accelerated hard, off into the night.

# CHAPTER FORTY-THREE

Dominique glanced at the digital clock for the fourth or fifth time in as many minutes. *04:56.* Again she felt her eyelids grow heavy, and a comforting sense of nothingness began to steal her away. Then her whole body convulsed from what felt like an electric shock, as consciousness shouted in her head that she was falling asleep. She blinked furiously at the road ahead caught in her headlights. The endless white lines flashing past on either side. Her heart was hammering against her ribs. She adjusted the drift of the car, but oversteered it and had to correct.

She glanced at Enzo, asleep in the passenger seat. God knows, he needed his sleep, and she didn't want to waken him. But she knew she couldn't carry on much longer. All she wanted to do was to pull over on to the hard shoulder and close her eyes. Just for a minute. Just for one wonderful, stressless minute when she could let her mind and her body go.

Concentration and focus wavered again, and she forced herself back from the brink. It was no good. She had to stop.

Like manna from heaven, a large blue and white road sign

ballooned into her headlights. Services in two kilometres. Just two kilometres. She could hold out for that long. She stretched each arm in turn, then flexed her neck and rubbed a hand over her face. Anything to keep herself awake for the next minute and a half.

Three hundred metres to go. She began to indicate. At least the rain had stopped, and there was almost nothing else on the road at this hour.

She crossed the broken white line and decelerated into the curve, following the signs for *Essence* and services. A floodlit forecourt simmered emptily before the rows of vacant parking bays that welcomed her, and she pulled on the handbrake and switched off the engine.

She released a long, slow breath, closing her eyes and letting her head fall back on to the rest.

'Why have we stopped?'

She turned her head to see Enzo rubbing his eyes. 'I was falling asleep. I need a break.'

'I'll take over.'

'No, you need a break, too. Let's get a coffee and stretch our legs. Then just shut our eyes for ten minutes. Just long enough to get us back on the road.'

For a moment she thought Enzo was going to argue, but if he was he thought better of it and nodded.

There was almost nobody in the cafeteria, and a wan-faced girl with sleep in her eyes served them short, sweet, black coffees.

For a long time during the night, the death of Régis Blanc had exercised their thoughts.

*Sometimes obligations don't last a lifetime. Maybe, one day soon, I'll have my say,* he had told Enzo. Had someone had Blanc killed to stop him having that say? Or was it just Fate laughing at them all. Cruel and deceptive, determined to hide the truth until the last? Or maybe forever.

Impossible to know, and Enzo had realised very quickly that it was pointless to fret about it. The man was dead. A man who had killed people and sold women's bodies for money. The world was a better place without him. And, whatever the truth, he had surely carried it with him to the grave. Which led Enzo full circle to the thought that just maybe he had been murdered for that very reason.

They finished their coffees and walked twice around the car park, gulping down the fresh, cold night air, then back at the car Enzo slid into the driver's seat. He looked at Dominique. 'Ten minutes,' he said. 'No more.'

When he next opened his eyes there was the faintest light dawning in a leaden sky.

'Shit!' He sat up, startled, and Dominique stirred in the seat beside him, blinking blearily into the first grey light of the day. He checked his watch. 'Two hours!' he said. 'We've been asleep for two fucking hours!' He leaned forward and started the car, reversing fast out of the parking bay.

The first trucks were already leaving the lorry park, and

Enzo weaved his way through them to accelerate on to the feeder lane and back on to the motorway.

'I'm sorry,' Dominique said.

'Not your fault.' Enzo's denial of blame was grudging. It was someone's fault. Maybe Dominique's, but most probably his, and he was cursing himself for ever closing his eyes in the first place. 'We've still got three hours to go. If we had a head start we've lost it now.'

Even as he spoke, the heavens opened, and rain like stair rods beat its tattoo on the roof and splashed up from the road in a white mist.

# CHAPTER FORTY-FOUR

The marzipan house, with its sugary red roof and quizzical eyebrows, looked as if it might dissolve in the rain. Mist rose up from the ground around it like steam. A veil of gauze concealing all its detail and reducing it to a blur of colour and shape, like some impressionist painting.

Tall conifers stood dripping darkly in the rain as Enzo turned their car through the gates and they caught their first sight of it. The time was a little before ten a.m. He followed the sweep of the gravel drive to the parking area in front of the main entrance where there was a single car parked. A green Renault Clio. All the windows and doors were shuttered for the winter, except for a couple high up in the tower, where Enzo knew that Madame Brusque had her private rooms.

He and Dominique stepped out into the rain and climbed steps to try the front door. It was locked. They followed the path, then, around the side of the house, past shuttered bay windows and large shrubs shedding leaves on the gravel, to a porticoed side entrance. Water poured from the sloping roof above its steps where a gutter was broken, a curtain of water

that they slipped through quickly to squeeze into a tiny porch. A glazed door looked into a narrow, stone-flagged entrance hall.

Enzo tried the handle and the door opened into the hall. He and Dominique stepped inside, dripping second-hand raindrops all over the flags. It was gloomy here, and the house beyond lay brooding darkly in silence. A narrow staircase led off to their right and Enzo leaned forward to peer up into the stairwell. Somewhere at the top, cold light spilled in from a hidden skylight. This was the tower.

'Hello!' His own voice sounded strangely remote as he called up the stairwell. Disconnected from him, somehow. 'Is there anyone there?'

They waited in silence and exchanged glances before Enzo called again. 'Hello!'

The sound of a door opening somewhere high up in the tower travelled down the stairs to meet them. Then a ghostly pale face peered over the banister. Its spectral effect was emphasised by the lifeless grey hair that hung in lustreless loops to her shoulders. Hair that had been pulled back into a severe bun when last Enzo had seen her.

'What do you want?'

They could hear the apprehension in her voice.

'It's Enzo Macleod, Madame Brusque. I was here the other week with my daughter, Roger's fiancée.'

'Oh,' she said. 'Yes.' And now they heard apprehension morphing to indifference. 'What do you want?'

'Can we come up?'

'I'm not really prepared for visitors.'

'Won't take long,' Enzo called back. 'I promise.'

She hesitated, and clearly wanted to say no. But this was the father of her employer's fiancée. How could she refuse? 'Alright.'

She watched Enzo and Dominique all the way up the stairs, until they drew level with her on the landing. Enzo seemed to tower over her. A quilted pink dressing gown gathered itself around a long, diaphanous nightdress, and she wore grey and pink slippers. She might very well still have been in bed when they came calling.

'Has anyone been in contact?' he said.

She frowned. 'In contact? What do you mean?'

He shook his head. 'Obviously not. It doesn't matter.'

The woman looked beyond him at Dominique. 'Who's this?'

'My colleague.'

Again the woman frowned, and Enzo couldn't help but notice that her once glittering green eyes were faded now, and almost grey like her hair. 'Colleague?' She seemed confused. 'Are you here on business?'

'I'm afraid we are.'

Now he saw the return of apprehension, perhaps even fear, in her eyes. 'What sort of business?'

Dominique said, 'The business of catching killers, Sally.'

And what little colour there was in Sally Linol's face vanished, leaving it almost transparent. Dominique stepped

forward and pulled away the upturned collar of her dressing gown. There, starkly etched on white skin, was her feather tattoo. Sally took a step back, eyes wide with fear. 'What do you want?'

'To keep you safe, Sally,' Enzo said. 'There are people on their way here to kill you.'

Even her lips were bloodless, eyes darting, panic-stricken, towards the open door of her apartment, and then the stairs, neither offering any real means of escape. And suddenly it was as if her fear, something sick and malign that had possessed her for nearly two decades, had left her. Enzo saw the slump of her shoulders, the resignation that settled on her, cutting deeper lines into a face shaped by angst and uncertainty over all the lost years of her life.

Enzo said, 'What we need to know, Sally, is why.'

She nodded. 'You'd better come in.'

They followed her into the tiny apartment at the top of the tower. A single room with a kitchen and breakfast bar. A small round table in the window looking out over the gardens. A couple of armchairs gathered around a TV set. Through an open door they could see an unmade bed, and another door off the bedroom, leading to a shower room. Régis Blanc had spent all the years of his life sentence in Lannemezan. Sally Linol had spent hers here. Both of them prisoners of their own making.

She slumped into a chair by the window and gazed sightlessly out at the view she must have seen every day for the nearly seven thousand of them she had spent in this place.

Then she put her elbows on the table in front of her and dropped her head into her hands, shaking it in despair.

'I always knew that someday, somehow, they would find me.' And she lifted her head to look at Enzo, an appeal for understanding in her eyes. 'It's been no life at all. Just a living hell.' She ran her tongue over dry lips. 'It'll be a relief, at last, to tell somebody the truth.'

Enzo felt Dominique's tiny tug at the sleeve of his jacket, and he half turned. Dominique tipped her head towards the door. She wanted them to go. Everything in her face and her eyes said they had no time.

But Enzo's frown and the slightest shake of his head said, *Not yet*. This was a defining moment. Sally Linol, after years of silence, wanted to tell her story. To tell it to them. The last thing he wanted to do was break the spell. In other circumstances, away from here, when she felt safe, it was perfectly possible that she might decide to keep it to herself after all.

He stepped away from Dominique and sat in the chair opposite the woman who had once sold her services on the streets of Bordeaux and Paris, and shared a bed with the murdered rent boy, Pierre Lambert. He slipped his phone from his pocket, tapping its *Record* icon and setting it on the table between them. She was oblivious. Enzo said, 'I've met your parents, Sally. They're both still alive. And still hoping to find you alive, too.'

Those green-grey eyes flickered towards him, and he saw the pain behind them, before tears blurred their sharpness.

'The last thing I ever wanted to do was hurt them. You know? They were good people. I couldn't have asked for a happier childhood. Only . . .' Time and distance glazed her eyes now, and Enzo knew that she had left him, transported back to another place and time. Memories, regrets, all those fears and fantasies that we shut away in lockfast boxes in the darkest corners of our minds. 'They didn't have the money to put me through university in Bordeaux. Tuition fees, books, an apartment, food, transport. My dad was a farm worker. He barely made enough to cover their own living costs.' Her breath trembled as she drew it in. 'So I told them I had a job. And I did. But not the job they thought it was.'

The first of her tears splashed on to the shiny surface of the table.

'In the beginning it was almost fun. Wealthy older men who liked young girls. Sugar daddies with wandering hands and generous wallets. A friend introduced me to it, and you know pretty quickly you get used to the money. You buy things. You move into a better apartment. You meet people. And then the money dries up. You're a little older and the sugar daddies lose interest. You start to get desperate. You'll do anything for cash. And that's when you begin to lose control, when it all starts slipping away from you, and you find yourself mixing with pimps and junkies, getting yourself into hock and standing on street corners to pay your debts.'

'How did you meet Régis Blanc?'

'I was at a club with a client one night. He got really drunk,

and he wasn't nice with a drink in him. He started beating up on me, and this guy steps in and kicks the shit out of him. That was Régis. He was like that. Hated to see any of his girls treated badly. Not that I was one of his girls.' A pale smile flitted across her face. 'Not then. But it wasn't long before I was. He was really good to me, especially after what I'd been through the previous six months. But he was good to us all.' She raised her eyes to Enzo 'We loved him, you know. Régis was special. All the girls felt really bad for him when his little girl was born with that . . . whatever it was. Some kind of congenital defect. And I suppose, in a way, it changed him. He adored that baby. Really adored her.'

Dominique said, 'But he murdered three girls.'

Sally's eyes darted towards her, then quickly away again, as if embarrassed. 'Régis had some kind of a deal going with this rich guy. Well, I don't know that he was rich, but he liked to have working girls in his bed, and certainly had the means to pay for it. He had this little apartment in west Bordeaux. His little love nest, he called it. There were four of us that Régis used to send there on a regular basis. Sometimes two at a time. The guy wasn't violent or anything. But he was pretty weird. Young, too. Liked us to do some pretty strange things.'

She went silent for a moment, and the knuckles of her inter-locked hands turned white with tension on the table in front of her. Enzo guessed that she was recalling some of those strange things.

'Anyway, one of the girls found out that our weirdo was

married, with a very young family, and was some kind of politico at the *mairie*. I mean, none of us ever read the papers, or watched TV, but apparently he was all over the news. Youngest ever *adjoint* to the mayor.'

Enzo sat back. 'Jean-Jacques Devez.'

Rabbit eyes darted a frightened look in his direction and Sally nodded.

'So you blackmailed him.'

Resentment flared briefly in the one-time prostitute. 'I didn't, no! But the other three figured he would probably be willing to pay to keep our sordid little sessions permanently under wraps.' She shook her head. 'I didn't want anything to do with it. He was a weirdo, yes, but he paid good money. Why risk that?'

'So what happened?'

'They went to see him, all three together, and he went ber- serk. Smashed up the furniture, threatened to kill them if they breathed a word to anyone. They were pretty shaken up, and I thought, Shit! Time to get out of here. Packed up my stuff and left. Didn't tell a soul. Just got the hell out of there as fast as I could. Seemed to me you don't go messing with people like that. We're little people, know what I mean? We don't control much of anything in our lives. And people like him . . . Well, they have power and money. They control everything, and they're dangerous. Get away with anything, too.'

'Like murder,' Dominique said.

Sally nodded and stared at her hands.

'Only Devez didn't kill anyone,' Enzo said. 'Régis did it.'

Sally swung her head slowly from side to side, and it was clear that she still found it difficult to believe. 'When I heard the news, in Paris . . .' Her face was a mask of consternation as she lifted it towards Enzo. 'It just didn't seem possible. Régis? He would never have laid a finger on his girls.'

Dominique said, 'But he strangled your three friends.'

'I can only think that Devez forced him to do it somehow. Had some kind of, I don't know, power over him, or hold on him.'

Everything was falling into place for Enzo now. 'Or made him an offer that he couldn't refuse. An inducement.'

All the lines around Sally's eyes gathered themselves in a frown. 'What possible inducement could he have offered Régis to make him do a thing like that?' But it wasn't a question Enzo needed to ask. He knew the answer.

He said, 'So you went to Paris.'

She shrugged. 'Where else would I go?'

'And resumed your –' he searched for the right word – 'career.'

She glowered at him. 'It was never my intention to go back on the game. I wanted to make a clean start.' Her indignation faded almost as quickly as it had fired itself up, and she sighed with sad despair at the memory. 'Only it's not that easy. In the end you do what you know, you do what you can do.'

'And that's when you met Pierre?' Enzo saw in her eyes,

then, a kind of acceptance that somehow they knew everything about her.

She nodded. 'Best friend I ever had. I loved that man. You know? I mean, really loved him. Not in a sexual way. Cos, well, that wasn't ever going to happen. Though I'd have slept with him in a heartbeat if he hadn't been gay.' She looked away self-consciously, staring into the empty void of recollection beyond the window. 'We were, you know, total confidants. Told each other everything.'

'Including the story of Devez and the three dead prostitutes?' Dominique said.

Sally dragged her eyes away from the window and looked from one to the other. 'I never in my wildest imagination thought he'd go blackmailing Devez. I mean, Jesus, the man was a fucking superstar by then. Followed me to Paris. Well, he didn't, but that's what it felt like. Rising star in the town hall. Tipped to be the next mayor. You just don't fuck with people like that. Christ, he'd already had three girls killed. Why wouldn't he do it again?'

'So you didn't know anything about it?' Enzo said.

She shook her head. 'All I knew was that suddenly Pierre had money. Lots of it. And he was generous, you know. Splashed it around. Spent a lot of it on me.'

Dominique folded her arms across her chest. 'And you never thought to ask him where it came from?'

'He said it was a wealthy client who'd fallen for him big time, liked to indulge him.'

'And you believed that?'

'Well, maybe not. But, you know, some things you don't ask.' She sucked in a long, slow breath then expelled it quickly, as if summoning her courage for the final revelation. 'Then, one night, he told me. He was drunk. And scared. Something had spooked him. I was . . . incandescent. I can't begin to tell you. I'd have killed him myself if I could. But, you know, he'd a way of wrapping me around his little finger. Calmed me down. Told me he was setting up one last payment, and then that would be it. He and I would get out of Paris. Set ourselves up somewhere else, enjoy the fruits of the payouts Devez had already made.' She stopped, eyes staring into the abyss. 'And then he was dead. Murdered in his apartment. And I knew they'd be coming for me.' She looked up, reliving the horror of it. 'I had no idea what to do, where to go. I was sure they would find me. No loose ends. These people never leave loose ends.'

Dominique drew up a chair and joined them at the table, curiosity written large all over her face. 'So what did you do?'

A sad smile flickered across her face. 'I was rescued by an angel.'

Enzo said, 'Marie Raffin.'

Sally looked up, surprised. 'How did you know?'

'Educated guess.' He paused. 'What was Marie's involvement in all this?'

'She was a journalist, you know? I'd never met her before, had no idea who she was. Only she turns up at my door within twenty-four hours of Pierre getting murdered and says that if

I'm prepared to help her, she can keep me safe.' She gasped. 'Jesus, I nearly bit her hand off. Seems she was working on some kind of story about Devez. An exposé. Something she'd been at for months, something linking him to the murders in Bordeaux. I don't know what her source was, or how she knew, and I didn't ask. She was just there, offering me an escape. And I jumped at the chance. She brought me down here, set me up as housekeeper under an assumed name. Showed me how to use make-up to cover my tattoo. She said it would only be for a short time and that as soon as the story had broken I would give a statement to the police, and they would put me in protective custody. Devez would go to jail and I'd be safe.'

She breathed her exasperation, irony turning her mouth down at both corners. 'But, then, as you know, Marie herself was murdered. I can't tell you how scared I was then. Absolutely certain they would come for me. But they never did. And here I am, twenty years on, a middle-aged spinster living on her own in the tower of an upmarket *chambres d'hôtes*, changing the sheets of wealthy fucking guests and cleaning their shit out the pan when they're gone. My whole fucking life wasted.'

A life, Enzo thought, configured by fear and mired in regret.

She looked at him almost defiantly. 'So what now? A statement to the police and protective custody? Just like Marie Raffin promised all those years ago?'

Enzo nodded. 'Something like that.'

Sally snorted. 'And what makes you think you'll be any more able to deliver it than she was?'

Enzo slipped his phone back in his pocket. 'We get you away from this place, I can pretty much guarantee it.'

Dominique stood up. 'You need to get dressed fast, Sally. And put whatever you need in an overnight bag.' She glanced at Enzo, then back at the older woman. 'We'll wait for you downstairs.'

There was a chill pervading the darkness of the house, and a smell of damp that Enzo had not been aware of on his previous visit. They wandered through into the main hall, where the double doors to the large sitting room stood open. Light leaked in around the edges of all the shutters, casting deep shadows in the gloom. Enzo found the rocker switch for an electric roller blind on the French windows and half raised it to bring some real light in from the outside. But it was a grey light, suffused with rain and pessimism. In the distance, yet more rain pitted the surface of the rectangular water feature set into the lawn, but the fountains had been switched off. There was enough water falling from the sky.

Enzo's thoughts were full of Sophie. There had been no news of her for days. But as soon as they had got Sally Linol safely away from this place he could begin to open negotiations. He glanced at his watch, anxious now to be gone.

Dominique said, 'So Raffin must have killed his own wife to protect Devez.'

Which dragged Enzo back from gloomy thoughts. 'I suppose he must have. Although I can't figure out why. We know by now what it was that Devez offered Régis by way of inducement to murder those girls. Blanc sacrificed them, and himself, for his daughter. But what kind of hold must Devez have had over Raffin to make him do something like that?'

Dominique shrugged. 'Who knows? But maybe the offer to take him on as his press secretary is some kind of sop, now, to keep him sweet.'

Enzo kicked a footstool and sent it clattering away across the floor, the sound of it resounding around the house. 'To think I trusted that bastard. That my own daughter gave him a child!'

Dominique crossed to the door and listened for Sally on the stairs. 'He won't come himself, will he? Raffin, I mean. He must know by now that we've figured out his part in all this.'

'Whoever comes,' Enzo said ominously, 'it's not just Sally Linol they'll be wanting to silence.'

Dominique flashed him a look of apprehension. And she, too, glanced at her watch, as if it might tell her when Raffin's unwelcome emissaries would arrive. Under her breath she muttered, 'Come on, Sally. Hurry up!'

The ringing of Enzo's mobile phone in the deep silence of the house made them both jump. Enzo fished it out of his pocket and looked at the display. 'Hélène Taillard,' he said and set it to speaker. Dominique crossed the room to listen in.

Hélène's voice was tinny, and seemed inordinately loud in the hush of this grand salon. 'Enzo, I got the sample you sent

first thing this morning. Raffin's razor. I had it couriered immediately by motorbike to the lab in Toulouse with instructions
to give it priority over everything else. They just faxed me the
results.'

Enzo was aware that he had actually stopped breathing.
'And?'

'There's no match, Enzo. The blood on the torn jacket pocket
is not Raffin's.'

For a moment it felt as if not only his breathing, but his
heart, too, had stopped, along with a world which had ceased
to turn. He was drowning in a sea of confusion. 'But . . . it must
be. If it's not Raffin's blood, whose is it?'

There was a laden silence at the other end of the line that
lasted perhaps a second, maybe two. To Enzo it seemed like
an eternity. Then Hélène said, 'Let me put it this way, Enzo,
there's good news and bad.' Another pause. 'There was some
kind of mix-up at the lab. A misunderstanding about what
samples were to be run against the database. I'd already sent
them that sample of Laurent's hair that you gave me to check
for paternity.'

Enzo frowned. His confusion was deepening with every
word of Commissaire Taillard's that his mobile brought to
him across the ether. He glanced up to find Dominique's brown
eyes open wide and watching him closely. She shrugged.

'I don't understand,' he said, and he heard Hélène sighing
softly.

'They ran both Raffin's DNA *and* Laurent's against the

database. The good news is that you are definitely Laurent's father.' Enzo barely had time to absorb this before she added, 'But they also found a familial match for Laurent's DNA.'

He frowned. 'A match with what?'

'The blood on the jacket pocket.'

Enzo's confusion morphed now from incredible to surreal. How could that possibly be? 'I don't understand,' he said again. Three words wholly inadequate to communicate his complete stupefaction.

Hélène's voice took on a hard edge as she spelled it out for him. 'It's his mother's blood that's on the pocket, Enzo. It was Charlotte Roux who tried to kill you in the château that night.'

Now Enzo's entire universe had come to a stop, as if somehow God had pushed the pause button, and all known things had fallen into a state of suspended animation.

'Enzo . . . ?' Hélène's voice came to him as if from some distant planet. He saw the look in Dominique's eyes. He saw the dust suspended in the light that fell through the half-raised roller blind. He knew that he had died and woken up in the place they called Hell.

And then the sound of a car door slamming crashed through consciousness, and everything wound up to speed again with the revving of a motor and tyres spinning on gravel.

Dominique was at the door before him, and he followed her, running in a daze of bewilderment through the darkness of the main hall and into the corridor that led to the side entrance. The door stood open.

They ran out into the rain and the mist in time to see Sally's green Renault Clio skidding on the gravel at the end of the drive and slamming, side on, into a white SUV which had just turned in from the gate through the trees.

Steam rose up from a fractured radiator. Dominique sprinted up the drive towards the cars and Enzo chased after her, still dazed and numb, and praying that sometime very soon he would wake up from this nightmare.

The door on the driver's side of the Clio swung open, and Sally, in jeans and trainers and a camel coat hanging open, fell out into the drive, blood streaming from a gash on her face. She crawled for half a metre before managing to stagger to her feet. The driver's door of the SUV opened and Charlotte stepped out into the rain. Her dark coat fell to below the knees, her face chalk white by contrast. Within moments her black curls were glistening with raindrops. She took three swift paces towards the dazed Sally Linol and ripped away the collar of her coat and her blouse to reveal the feather tattoo on the side of her neck. In one single movement, she drew a pistol from her coat pocket and shot the one-time prostitute in the head at close range. Even before Enzo could summon the breath to scream NO!

He saw the blowback from the shot spray fine blood in her face, red-speckling the white. Black saucer eyes swivelled then towards the approaching figure of Dominique. She turned her gun to aim it at the chest of the former gendarme, and Dominique stopped abruptly. Enzo drew up by her side seconds later.

Charlotte's arm was fully extended towards them, the gun trembling in her hand at the end of it. Her eyes were wild in a way that Enzo had never seen them before. This woman, the mother of his child, who had just shot Sally Linol dead in cold blood. Who had tried to kill him high up in the dark of a château in Gaillac. Whose bed he had shared on countless occasions. A whole kaleidoscope of memories spun through his head. A million fragments of light and colour. Laughter and love. Moments in time, shared over years. And he was almost blinded by it all. He felt tears burn hot on his cheeks. He couldn't even find his voice to ask why.

But he heard the quivering in hers. 'Roger called me last night. To tell me about your little discovery.' She inclined her head slightly towards the prone form of Sally Linol, lying on the drive, her blood soaking with the rain into the gravel. 'He thought I would be interested. He had no idea just how much.'

Finally, words forced their way beyond Enzo's lips as his brain wound back up to speed and a million pieces of an impossible puzzle started dropping into place. 'You killed Marie Raffin!'

She gave the most imperceptible of shrugs. And although she was trying hard to project cool, Enzo could see that she was shaken to the core.

'Why?'

'Many years ago, in science class at school, I learned that for every action there is a reaction. Consequences. All the things that have happened in the twenty-two years since my

brother took the first steps on his road of no return have left me picking up the pieces in his wake. Everything I have done has been to protect him.'

'Your *brother*?' Enzo was incredulous.

But she ignored him, and almost as if she were trying to persuade herself, she said, 'He had a weakness, and he made a mistake.'

Dominique said, 'Murdering three women is hardly a mistake.'

Charlotte could not even meet her eye. Her gaze flickered in Enzo's direction. 'He was young, immature. Married with a young family. And, yes, he had certain . . . predilections.' Enzo saw her mouth curl in distaste as she found a euphemism for his perversion. 'But he is also a genius. He has intelligence, vision, charisma. Everything that is lacking in the generation of politicians who run this country today. I couldn't allow the errors of youth to deny France the special gifts that he has to offer. And, God knows, we are in dire need of them now.'

Enzo had difficulty both breathing and thinking. He said again, 'Your *brother*?' And he saw some of her arrogance return as she focused her scorn on him.

'The great Enzo Macleod.' She shook her head. 'You had no idea, did you? That when I went looking for my birth parents, not only did I discover who my real father was, but that I also had a brother. A twin brother. Not identical. But born thirty minutes before me. And while I was given for adoption to the Gaillard family retainers in Angoulême, Jean-Jacques went to

my adoptive mother's cousin, also afflicted by the family curse of infertility. All my years growing up, I only knew him as my second cousin, meeting at family get-togethers. Christmas, Easter, summer holidays.'

Enzo saw fond recollection cloud her dark eyes, like cataracts.

'During all those long summers spent at the family cottage in the Corrèze we were inseparable. Understood things in a way that others did not. Sharing thoughts and secrets. Writing to each other when we were apart. I admired him, adored him, maybe even fell in love with him a little. And then I found out why. We weren't cousins at all. But brother and sister. Flesh and blood. One and the same. Each of us a piece of the other.' Her eyes cleared in a moment of anger. 'They had no right to separate us. To break us up like that. They should have known. Blood is thicker than water.'

Her hair was hanging in wet ropes now around her face.

Enzo said, 'And it was you who tried to kill me in the château at Gaillac.'

Something almost like a smile flitted across her lips. 'That was a mistake. Reckless. And nearly cost us everything. I had one of Roger's suits in my apartment. I had picked it up for him from the dry cleaner's some months earlier and forgotten to return it. It was still hanging in my wardrobe. There seemed to me to be a certain irony in it, you see. To kill you in the guise of Roger. Stupid. I know that now. When I finally returned it to him, I suggested that perhaps it had been damaged at the

cleaner's. If it was ever traced back, it would point the finger at him, not me.'

She looked down again at the body lying on the drive. 'She was the one loose end that's been hanging over us all these years. I knew you would find her in the end, Enzo. You're so bloody relentless.' She turned angry eyes back on him and he saw them soften. 'But fortunately, you also led me to her. And now that she's been taken care of, that leaves only you. And your little piece of . . . stuff.' She cast a disparaging glance at Dominique. 'You always did like them young, didn't you, Enzo?'

He felt a constriction of all the muscles across his chest, like a great weight bearing down on him. 'What did you do to Sophie?'

Charlotte shrugged. 'She's dead, of course. You never did learn to do what you were told.'

And almost everything that Enzo was or had ever been died in that moment. He closed his eyes, remembering the white stag he had encountered in the woods at Château Gandolfo, and willed Charlotte just to pull the trigger. There was no way, he knew, that he even wanted to go on living. When he opened them again, he saw Charlotte smiling, and he knew, finally, that she was quite insane.

She said, 'And now it seems like such a shame to deprive an old man of his little piece of skirt, when I have already taken away everything else.'

The roar of her gun in the still of the morning was deafening

as she fired a single shot into Dominique's chest. Enzo heard the bullet strike her. A soft, sickening thud that sent her spinning away and falling to the ground. His cry of anguish pierced the damp air as he dropped to his knees beside her, to turn her over in the wet. Blood oozed from her mouth, and spread quickly into the fabric of the T-shirt beneath her jacket. The pain and hurt and anger that filled him was unbearable, and he cried again, like some wild animal howling for the dead. He half turned in time to see Charlotte lowering her gun to level it at him.

'Seems wrong, somehow, to kill the father of my child. I told you once about keeping my enemies close.' She sighed. 'Sometimes it's the only way to stay in control. I got involved with Roger when we discovered that Marie Raffin was sniffing around Jean-Jacques' affairs, asking questions in the wrong places, trying to access his accounts. And you . . . ?' And now he saw affection in her smile. 'I kept you too close, Enzo. Much too close.' Then affection gave way to something much colder. 'But Laurent . . . Well, that really was a mistake. Though I suppose I'll just have to live with it. At least he'll always be a reminder of you.'

He could see her finger tightening on the trigger and he braced himself for death. But the slightest scrape of a shoe on wet gravel made her turn as a dark figure rose up behind her in the rain, and struck her down.

Charlotte's gun went clattering away across the drive as her legs folded beneath her and she fell to the ground, blood

streaming from a gash on her forehead. And Sophie stood over her, dripping wet in the pouring rain, a wheel brace dangling from her hand.

'Fucking bitch!' she said, looking down at the prone form of her father's would-be killer, her lower lip trembling with raw emotion. And Enzo was struck by the strength of her Scottish accent as she said, 'Never actually did get round to killing me, did you?' Despairing eyes found Enzo's. 'You'd have thought by now she'd have learned that you don't fuck with a Macleod.' And her face crumpled to dissolve in a mess of tears.

# CHAPTER FORTY-FIVE

He had been waiting for hours, and it seemed like a lifetime. Overhead lights dazzled off polished hospital floors. The sound of voices, always hushed, permeated the corridors. Porters passed with patients on trolleys, on their way to or from theatre. Nurses gave him sympathetic smiles as they walked by, plimsolls squeaking on shiny linoleum.

For the longest time possible he had focused on simply not thinking. About anything. For every time he did he was unable to stop the tears. Tears for the woman he had once loved, a woman who had given him a son and who would spend the rest of her life in prison. Tears for the horrors poor Sophie had suffered because of him. And Bertrand, with his broken leg and battered face, still lying in a hospital bed in Montpellier. And, most of all, tears for the young woman who had taken a bullet in her chest for the singular crime of being his lover.

The only glimmer of light in the whole foul business was that Kirsty had not, after all, borne a murderer's son. Raffin, whatever else he might be, was neither corrupt nor a killer. He was as much a victim as the rest of them. And

Enzo felt guilt for the hatred he had harboured for him in his heart.

'Monsieur Macleod?'

Enzo jumped to his feet as the young surgeon approached. He wore a long white coat over jeans and white tennis shoes, his hands and nails scrubbed almost painfully clean. Skin scarified by the scouring demanded before entry to the operating theatre. But it was nearly twenty-four hours since he had operated on Dominique. Enzo searched his face for light or hope.

'She's awake, finally,' he said. 'To put it crudely, we sewed up the lung and put in a tube to drain the blood. There is a broken rib, but fortunately no tracheobronchial damage. The bullet missed the heart and, by some miracle, all of the arteries. If it hadn't lodged in the rib it might well have entered her spine. Best prognosis ... She's a strong young woman. She should be on her feet in four to six weeks. Full recovery, four to six months.'

Enzo's legs nearly folded under him. The young doctor put a hand on his arm to steady him as he staggered slightly.

He said, 'She's still heavily sedated. But you can have a few minutes with her. It'll be good for her morale.'

Sunlight bled in around the blinds that darkened her room, and the sense of something shining bright out there in the world beyond them offered hope and optimism for the future.

There was a hush in here, broken only by the beeping of the equipment that monitored all her vital signs. The air was sickly

warm and smelled powerfully of disinfectant. She turned her head a little as he came in, and the tiniest smile stretched dry, cracked lips. She was deathly pale, eyes red-rimmed and distant. Her right hand reached tentatively for his as he pulled up a chair at the bedside. He took it, feeling how small it was, and squeezed it gently.

Her voice was pared thin and clotted by the mucus in her throat. 'When I was lying there,' she said, 'with the blood bubbling into my mouth, I thought I was going to die . . . and my only regret was that I would never see you again.'

'Well,' Enzo said, and he grinned in spite of the hurt he felt inside, 'twenty years from now, when you're wiping my arse and heaving me into a bath chair, maybe you'll regret that you did.'

'Oh, stop it!' She laughed and winced from the pain. Slowly the smile faded, and she put all her effort into concentrating on his face. 'I love you, Enzo Macleod.'

It was all he could do to stop the tears from coming again. 'I love you, too, Dominique Chazal,' he said. He blinked furiously and reached for his back pocket, pulling out the copy of today's *Libération* that he had folded into it. He opened it up to show her the front page. 'Look.' There were photographs of both Charlotte and Jean-Jacques Devez, and smaller inset pictures of the three murdered prostitutes from Bordeaux. The story, beneath the headline, *DEATH OF A DREAM*, told of the arrest of the secret twins. An explosive story threatening a political earthquake that would shake the country to its

foundations. Raffin had been busy since Enzo's call to him yesterday morning.

She forced another smile. 'You'll win your bet now, then.'

But he shook his head. 'Not quite.' He paused. 'There's still the question of who murdered Lucie Martin.'

She blinked clarity into her eyes and frowned a little as she focused them on him. 'And do you know who that was?'

He sighed. 'I have an idea. But no proof.' Then he thought about it. 'Yet.'

# CHAPTER FORTY-SIX

Enzo had driven behind the ambulance all the way from Biarritz to the *Centre Hospitalier de Cahors*, to see Dominique safely installed in her own room where he could visit her every day to help her through the long and difficult process of recovery. Or *re-education* as the French called it.

Now he parked in the square below the cathedral and walked past the covered market. He saw familiar faces on the terrace outside the Café Le Forum. He waved but didn't stop. Everything surrounding him was familiar, and yet he felt like a displaced person in a foreign land. He knew, of course, that while the world around him remained the same, the only thing that had really changed was him. Everything about him. Everything he had known and understood. Everything he had been. Everything he was and might be in the future. The very bedrock on which he had built his life had fallen away beneath his feet. And the only thing that kept him from sliding down into the abyss was Dominique. The way she felt about him. The way he felt about her. She would need him to be there and be strong. How could he fail her after what she had suffered for him?

He climbed the stairs wearily to his apartment. It seemed painfully empty, haunted by the ghost memories of a happier past. Sophie had gone to bring Bertrand back from Montpellier.

He remembered holding her in the rain that morning at the house in Biarritz, as the ambulance rushed Dominique to the hospital and the police led Charlotte away in handcuffs. Traumatised and barely able to stand, she had been trembling in his arms, the deepest of sobs shaking her whole body. The little girl that Pascale had bequeathed him, the child he had raised and loved all those years on his own, the daughter he had thought was dead, and who, in the end, had saved his life. How could there ever be any life for him without her?

And then there was Laurent. The son Charlotte had given him so reluctantly, and who now had only him. A father who was old enough to be his grandfather. While his mother was someone about whom he would only ever feel ashamed. Arrangements would have to be made to go to Paris to take custody of him. Kirsty had retrieved him from the care of the nanny Charlotte employed, and he was staying temporarily with her and Raffin at the Rue de Tournon.

The hall simmered in semi-darkness, light spilling from half-open bedroom doors. The door to the spare room stood wide. Nicole had changed the sheets and made the bed. Everything was in its place, dust-free and shining in the sunlight that fell in across the roofs. She would make Fabien a good wife, but Enzo mourned for the career she might have had, the person

she might have been. And yet, if it was Fabien who made her happy, who was he to pass judgment?

He moved stiffly through to the *séjour*, throwing open the double doors and breathing in the familiar scents of a life he had once known. Again, he had the sense of being a stranger haunting his own past. Beyond the French windows, in the square below, life went on as it always did, flowing past him as if he were no more than a rock in the river. Tiny, insignificant, the most minor of impediments to its swift onward passage.

Nicole had left the mail piled neatly on the table, and he began sifting through it absently. Bills mostly, and bank statements, and junk mail, the detritus of a life that seemed somehow less important. He paused over a white envelope embossed with the official stamp of the Institut Médico-Légale in Bordeaux. The address was handwritten and he opened it with a powerful sense of knowing exactly what was inside. And he was right. The letter was from the young forensic anthropologist at the Bordeaux morgue. He had found no traces of Rohypnol in Lucie's cortical bone. The final affirmation, if it were needed, that nothing about Lucie's death fitted with Régis Blanc's modus operandi.

He let the letter fall to the table and saw a white padded envelope addressed to him in a large, childish hand. He tore it open and inside found two further envelopes. Both were sealed. His name was written on one in a scrawling, oddly familiar handwriting. The other, fatter envelope was blank. He opened the one with his name on it and took out a single

folded sheet. Unfolding it, his eye fell to the sign-off at the foot of the page. It was from Régis Blanc.

*Monsieur Macleod,*

*I knew as soon as I learned some weeks ago that little Alice did not have long left in this world that I would not be safe. Chances are I might even be dead by the time you get this. There are things, monsieur, that I will take with me to the grave. But I wanted you to have these. Anne-Laure will have fetched them for me from a secret place where we both kept things safe. She doesn't know what's in the envelope, and I'd be pleased if you never told her. I hope, in some way, they might help you to catch the bastard that killed poor Lucie.*

*Régis*

Enzo felt a shift in the stream of life rushing by on either side. A tiny shift, but enough to cause the water to foam and eddy a little, albeit briefly.

His hands shook as he carefully opened the second envelope. Inside were half a dozen letters, folded over and held together in a perished elastic band that broke the moment it was stretched. The letters themselves were written on pale blue stationery in a darker blue ink that had faded just a little with the years. Somehow the handwriting felt feminine. Each began, *My Dearest Régis*, and they were signed simply, *Lucie*.

Whatever might have become of his letters to her, these were hers to him, and Enzo stood reading them, transfixed.

Earnest entreaties of love from a twenty-year-old innocent to a man fifteen years her senior who traded in women for sex. Letters from one dead person to another, memories from the grave returning to haunt an ill-informed present. But more, much more than that, they told Enzo who had killed her. Confirmation, for him at least, of a long-held suspicion.

# CHAPTER FORTY-SEVEN

The light was fading by the time Enzo's 2CV toiled up the hill to the Château Gandolfo. The ground was still sodden from the recent rain, and so there was no plume of chalk dust rising in his wake this time. But the sky had cleared, and only a few dark clouds bubbled up on the distant horizon as stars appeared faintly in the darkest blue, presaging the coming night.

Lights burned in windows below the red-tiled roman roof, and the twin *pigeonniers* stood in stark silhouette against the sky.

Enzo parked in front of the wing that housed old Guillaume Martin's study. He peered in the window and saw a light burning at the former judge's desk, but there was no one there. He turned and walked instead around the back of the house, past the old bread and prune ovens, to where squares of light fell from the kitchen door and windows. He knocked on the door and through the glass could see Madame Martin busy at the stove. She turned at the sound of his knocking, and wiping her hands on her apron hurried to see who was at the door.

Her face lit up in pleasant surprise when she saw Enzo. 'Monsieur Macleod. Come in, come in,' she said. And he stepped into the warmth of the kitchen. Until now, he had not been aware of just how cold it was outside.

'I'm looking for your husband,' he said. 'Is he at home?'

'Oh, yes, Guillaume's out in the *chais*, the old wine shed. He spends a lot of time out there. I think perhaps he's still hankering after the idea of converting it into guest rooms.' She laughed. 'As if we needed any more.'

One of the old wooden double doors stood ajar, a dull flickering yellow light from inside stretching long across the path as Enzo went around the side of the house to the *chais*. The door creaked loudly as he pulled it open to step inside, and Guillaume Martin turned, startled, at the sound of it.

'Monsieur Macleod?' His face was half lit by an old oil lamp hanging on a wire from one of the rafters. The surprise that initially registered on his features changed as sharp eyes searched Enzo's face. And something like resignation settled on him.

Enzo said, 'What did you do with the rest of Blanc's letters to Lucie?'

The old man turned away, unable to face his accuser, and he pushed his hands deep into his pockets. 'Destroyed them, of course. I can't begin to tell you how every word made my skin crawl.' He breathed deeply. 'I had to keep one, of course. The one that would best point to Blanc's singular obsession with my daughter. An obsession not shared by Lucie.'

'Except that it was,' Enzo said. 'I have her letters to him. It was no singular obsession, Monsieur le Juge.'

Martin's head came around, eyes blazing with defiance and denial. But he could find no words of rebuttal. If Enzo had her letters what point would there be?

Enzo said, 'There's no accounting for love, monsieur. And I don't pretend to understand it. But your daughter loved that man.' He hesitated. 'In her letters she tells Blanc about the day you found his letters to her. Your absolute fury at the disgrace she would bring on her family. Her defiance, and the dreadful rows that followed. How she threatened to leave home for good and tell the world about her love for Régis.'

Martin pulled his hands from his pockets and clenched his fists as his sides. 'I did not mean to kill her.' He gave each of the words its own emphasis, as if underlining them. As if lack of intention would make the act of murder somehow accept-able. 'The last thing in the world I would have wanted to do was hurt her.'

'Then why did you?' Enzo was unable to find even an ounce of sympathy for the man, and that must have conveyed itself to Martin, because he spun around, voice raised.

'Because she was going to do it. She was going to leave.' His breath was coming in short, rapid bursts along with a memory he had probably spent more than two decades trying to bury. 'She came looking for me out here that Saturday afternoon, when her mother had gone, and she told me she had made up her mind. She was going to pack her things and, when she

returned to Bordeaux on the Monday, she wouldn't be back. We had the most horrible row. I'd never seen her like that. Shouting and scornful, almost goading me into trying to stop her. That man had contaminated her somehow. Sullied her.'

He fixed Enzo with pained eyes, as if pleading for understanding.

'This was my little girl. My lovely little girl, with her golden locks and pigtails, who used to sit on my knee and tell me she loved me. My little Lucie.' Silent tears poured down his cheeks. 'And there she was, standing there, shouting in my face. Telling me that I knew nothing about love, knew nothing about her, knew nothing about a man who pimped prostitutes for a living.' A sob caught his throat. 'I couldn't stand it. I just couldn't stand it. It had to stop, monsieur. I had to make it stop.'

'So you killed her.'

'I didn't mean to. I didn't. There was an old wooden haft of a pickaxe leaning against the door, and suddenly it was in my hand and I was lashing out.' His eyes were wide, staring, reliving the horror of the moment. 'When I realised what I had done, I wept over her body for what felt like hours. On my knees, holding her hand. I would have given anything to take back the moment. Anything.'

His own words drew him back to the here and the now, in the dark of this dimly lit old wine cellar, and he looked at Enzo. 'And then I knew there was no way I could tell Mireille that I had killed our baby. I panicked. I hid her body and cleaned

away all traces of her blood. But I had no idea what to do next. When Mireille got home, I told her Lucie had gone for a walk and hadn't come back. It was all I could do to persuade her not to call the police right there and then. When she still hadn't returned, hours later, I suggested we search her room.'

'And found the letter that you'd left there from Blanc.'

He nodded. 'It was never going to be enough, and when they started searching for her, they were sure to find the body.' His eyes wandered involuntarily towards a dark corner at the back of the *chais*, and Enzo wondered if that was where he had put her. 'Then it was as if God had stepped in and offered me a way out. Blanc was arrested on the Monday for the murder of those three prostitutes, and I knew what I had to do.'

Enzo said, 'You came down here in the dark that night and strangled your own daughter, post-mortem, so it would seem like Blanc might have done it, if ever she was found. Then you carried her down to the lake, weighted her body, and dropped her into the deepest part of it.' Enzo paused, biting his lip to contain his anger. What this old man had done was simply unforgivable. 'Your own daughter!'

The old man lifted eyes filled with shame. 'What happens now?'

'You should know,' Enzo said. 'You must have sat in judgement of people just like you many times.' He controlled his breathing. 'You should get a coat and we'll go together to the gendarmerie in Duras. You can make your statement there.'

*

Madame Martin knew that something was wrong, but the old judge did not have the courage to tell her. 'I'm just going to get my coat and hat,' he said, 'and Monsieur Macleod and I are going for a short drive. We won't be too long.'

He headed out to the old Roman path that led down to his study.

The old lady looked at Enzo with fear in sad eyes, and he wondered if, somewhere behind them, perhaps she knew what it was that was wrong. 'Where are you going?'

Enzo was acutely embarrassed. Here was maybe the only innocent in this whole sordid story. A woman who, inexplicably, had lost a daughter, and was soon to discover that the man she loved had killed her. For Mireille Martin it was the worst of all possible outcomes. He said, 'We're just going into Duras.'

'Why?'

She was spared his answer by the muffled sound of a distant gunshot. Frightened eyes immediately sought Enzo's for clarification. For his part, he knew exactly what had happened. He hurried through the house and out on to the Roman road, old Madame Martin trailing along behind him. The door to Martin's study stood open. Martin himself was spreadeagled in his captain's chair, most of the top of his head missing where he had shot himself through the roof of his mouth.

The sound of the scream that tore itself from Madame Martin's throat was one, Enzo knew, that would stay with him for the rest of his life.

# CHAPTER FORTY-EIGHT

## PARIS, SPRING 2012

For Enzo, spring was the best time of the year in Paris. All the flowers in bloom, trees laden with blossom, the air still fresh from the winds of winter, as yet unadulterated by the heat and the pollution of the summer months to come.

Soft clouds were scattered thinly in a blue sky, the morning light bright and clear in the spring sunshine. The Luxembourg Gardens were busy. Couples strolling hand in hand, mothers pushing prams, students gathered together on park benches, laughing and smoking, or reading study books for upcoming exams. At the far end of the circle, the Sénat building glowed almost white beneath imposing slate roofs. Palm trees in huge pots stood around the faux lake, newly recovered from their winter hibernation in the great greenhouses that served the park.

Enzo pulled up a couple of pale green-painted chairs for them near the grass, and Dominique manoeuvred Laurent's pushchair into a position between them where he could see

them both, as well as the sunlight coruscating on the water beyond. He was toddling now, but not to be trusted on his own. Released from his pushchair he would be off like a bullet, little legs carrying him forward at a furious pace until he stumbled and fell. Which was not a good idea near water. But he was happy enough, for the moment, in his pushchair.

In the months that had passed since the events of the previous autumn, Laurent had accepted Dominique, unquestioningly, in the role of his mother. But there had been a special bond forged between father and son during those months, too. They had spent hours and days and weeks together, Enzo leading him through an early exploration of the world around him with all the time and patience of a well-practised dad.

They sat for some minutes, just watching life flow around them. Then Dominique said, 'Don't you ever get upset at the injustice of it?'

He looked at her, surprised. 'The injustice of what?'

'Solving all those murders, and yet still losing the bet.'

He shrugged. 'I know I won. That's all that matters. And what's two thousand euros among friends?'

She laughed. 'Tell me that when the next tax bill comes in.'

'Anyway,' he said, 'if people want to believe it was Blanc who murdered Lucie, so what? More important, I think, that old Madame Martin was spared the truth.'

'You really think she doesn't know?'

'Oh, probably. In her heart. But there will always be a part

of her that can believe something else. Another version of events. And maybe that's what you need to survive.'

Dominique leaned across the pushchair and put her hand over his. 'You're a good man, Enzo Macleod.'

He chuckled. 'Maybe. But I could probably be better.' He glanced at his watch, and she saw a flicker of apprehension cross his face.

'You really have no idea why it is Kirsty wants to see you?'

'None.'

'And you don't think it's strange that she specifically asked you not to bring me?'

He shrugged. 'What's wrong with a daughter wanting to see her dad on his own?'

Dominique lifted one eyebrow to signal her scepticism. 'Sure you're not keeping something from me?'

He held up two fingers. 'Scout's honour.' He looked ostentatiously at his watch again. 'Look, I'd better go.' And he stood up. 'Will you two be okay here on your own? I shouldn't be too long.'

'We'll be fine.' Dominique stood up to kiss him, and he noticed that there was still the slightest stiffness in her movement. But, if there was any pain, she steadfastly refused to admit it. She said, 'Will you tell her that we're going to get married?'

He nodded and held her by the shoulders, looking directly into the concern in her eyes. 'Don't worry, she's going to be nothing but happy for us.'

'I hope so.' Dominique sat down again and watched anxiously as he headed off towards the Senat and the top of the Rue de Tournon.

Raffin's apartment was a place so full of bad and painful memories for Enzo, that he had been delighted when Kirsty told him that they were going to move. A bigger, brighter, more modern apartment in the fourteenth arrondissement. It would be, she had thought, a better place to raise Alexis.

But, for the moment, they were still in the first-floor apartment that looked out on to the cobbled courtyard at the back of the buildings on the east side of the Rue de Tournon. The chestnut tree was already in full blossom, always the first to have its fat green buds burst into leaf, and the first, too, to shed them.

Enzo climbed the stairs with a heavy heart. It was on this first-floor landing that he had met Jean-Jacques Devez for the first and only time, puzzled by a sense of familiarity, later explained only too brutally by events. It was here that Raffin had been shot, an assassin's bullet meant for Enzo. And it was here, in this apartment, on a hot summer's evening, that he had first met Charlotte. An encounter that had changed his life in ways he could never have imagined.

The pianist who had provided the stuttering accompaniment to the last six years was playing now, on the same tuneless piano, in an apartment somewhere on one of the upper floors. Handel's Gavotte in G minor. A favourite exercise dished out by piano teachers to talentless pupils. It seemed to Enzo that

this particular student was still struggling with Grade One.

Kirsty greeted him at the door and held him in a way she had not done since she was a child, very nearly squeezing the breath from him. She stood back then, eyes shining, her mood strangely bright and brittle.

'Come on in, Dad. I'm so pleased you were able to come.' She took him by the hand and led him into the *séjour*. Sunlight splashed in through tall windows and lay in patches across the floor. It seemed as brightly over-lit as Kirsty. Enzo looked around. 'Where's Alexis?'

'Oh, Roger took him out for a walk.'

Enzo cocked an eyebrow. 'You really did want to see me on your own, then.'

She just smiled and led him to the table where green tea stood infusing in a Chinese teapot, with ceramic cups gathered around it on a tray. 'Sit down.' She waved him towards a chair. 'Would you like a cup?'

'Sure.' He examined her more closely as she poured. There were the beginnings of crow's feet around her eyes, a well-defined jaw showing the first signs of age. Even your children grow old, he thought. He said, 'How are things with you and Roger?'

'Good.' She nodded enthusiastically. 'We've had a lot of stuff to work through since ... well, since everything that happened. But we're better for that. Closer now than we have been for some time. He's more like the Roger I first knew.' She paused. 'We're going to be okay.'

Enzo forced a smile. 'I'm happy for you.' Though, in his heart, he knew that he would never be truly happy about her liaison with Raffin.

The doorbell sounded, and he saw her stiffen, as if she had just received a tiny electric shock.

'Are you expecting guests?'

She looked at him, and could barely hold his eye. 'Just don't hate me for this. It's taken me a long time to pluck up the courage.' And she hurried off into the hall, where he heard the door opening and then voices greeting her in English. Familiar voices. A man and a woman. He stood up, heart pounding, and felt as if he had been ambushed.

Kirsty came back in, eyes to the floor, avoiding his. She was followed by Enzo's boyhood friend, Simon, her blood father. He seemed strangely old. Most of his hair had gone now, and his beard was shot through with more silver than black. Right behind him was a woman Enzo felt as if he might have known in another life. She was small and middle-aged, carrying more weight than was good for her. Hair that should have been allowed to go gracefully grey was dyed a shiny blue-black, and served only to emphasise the ageing quality of her skin. It was her eyes that remained unchanged. A deep, startling green, ringed by black. And Enzo realised with a shock that she was Kirsty's mother, his ex-wife, Linda. The woman he had left for Pascale, and not seen once in the more than twenty-five years since.

It was evident from their faces that they were as shocked to see him, as he was to see them.

Simon looked at Kirsty. 'What the hell's going on, Kirst?' And Enzo found himself resenting the use of his one-time friend's shortened pet name for her.

But Linda's gaze was still fixed on Enzo. 'You've worn better than I have,' she said, rancour in every word. 'The good life in France, no doubt.'

'No doubt.' Enzo summoned his smile with difficulty.

'Kirsty?' Simon wasn't giving it up. Beyond his first sight of Enzo he hadn't looked at him once. His eyes were on Kirsty.

She said, 'I'm sorry if this seems a bit overdramatic. But it felt like the best way to deal with things. Everyone here at once. A single telling of the tale, then an end to it. If I've been a little sparing with the truth in getting you all here, then I apologise.'

Her mother looked at her for the first time. 'What are you talking about, Kirsty?'

Enzo saw Kirsty draw a deep breath. 'You all know that Alexis has a hearing problem. Some months ago Dad and I went to see a specialist in Biarritz. He took blood from Alexis for testing and diagnosed a congenital condition that will require him to wear hearing aids, probably for the rest of his life.' She paused. 'What I didn't tell you, any of you, is that mild sensorineural deafness is only one of the symptoms of his condition. It is likely that it will manifest itself in other ways as he grows older.'

'Like what?' Linda was clearly concerned.

Kirsty looked at Enzo. 'Well, for example, a white streak through his hair.'

And Enzo felt all the hairs rising up on the back of his neck.

His right hand lifted involuntarily to touch the white streak through his own hair, just as he had done in the doctor's office in Biarritz. He felt the others looking at him, but kept his eyes on Kirsty.

She said, 'Alexis is suffering from Waardenburg syndrome. It can manifest in many ways. Different-coloured eyes, a cleft palate, a white streak in the hair. Deafness. It's an inherited, genetic condition. From which, I think, neither you, Mum, nor Simon suffer.' She looked again at Enzo. 'There's only one person here who could have passed that on.'

Enzo dragged his eyes away from Kirsty to look at Linda. He saw that her face had flushed pink, with crimson highlights on her cheeks. Simon, too, turned to look at her.

Kirsty said, 'Simon's not my father, is he, Mum? You lied to him.'

'Kirsty—'

'Don't lie to me, too,' Kirsty cut her off. 'Don't you dare. A simple paternity test will prove it.'

The silence was punctuated only by the distant murder of poor Handel. But none of them heard it. Then Linda said, 'When he left –' and her glance at Enzo was so full of mal-evolence he almost recoiled from it – 'I tried everything to keep Simon close. He was all that I had left. I was lonely . . .' It was a plea for understanding that fell on deaf ears.

Kirsty said, 'So you lied to him about being my father.'

Linda turned her gaze down towards the floor and couldn't bring herself to deny it.

Kirsty swung fiery eyes, then, towards Simon. 'And you used that to hurt my dad. A club to beat him with. You *knew* what it would do to him.'

'Kirst . . .'

'Don't call me that!' She almost spat her contempt in his face.

'I only wanted what was best for you. I was concerned for your safety, and all the shit he was dragging you into.' He threw a withering glare at Enzo.

But Kirsty shook her head. 'Seems to me the only person you were concerned about was you. And, of course, for anyone to believe that it might be true, that I really could be your daughter, you would have had to have slept with my mother. Your best friend's wife. You can't deny that, can you?'

And there was a finality in Kirsty's voice that pre-empted further discussion.

'Well,' she said, 'I hope you two enjoy your time together in Paris. But I'd like to make it clear to you now. I don't want to see either of you again. Ever.'

'Kirsty . . .' Pain was etched into every line on Linda's face.

'Ever!' She folded her arms. 'You know where the door is.'

For a long moment no one moved, then Simon turned and walked briskly out into the hall without a backward glance. They heard the door open and slam behind him.

Linda stood, staring at the floor, before slowly lifting her head to turn twenty-five years of resentment on the man who was the father of her child. The man who had left her for another woman. It was a look filled with both hatred and

self-pity. Still a young woman, she had sworn when he left that she would never be with another man. She said now, 'You took the best years of my life.'

Enzo shook his head. 'I gave you the best years of your life, Linda. You squandered the rest yourself.'

Something in her eyes told him she knew that she had sacrificed herself on the altar of her own martyrdom. A sacrifice made, not for love of Enzo, but as a means of punishing him by punishing herself. And he could feel nothing but pity for her. For now he had taken her daughter, too.

She held Kirsty in a long look of pained regret, before turning slowly away and walking out into the hall.

When the outside door closed behind her, Enzo and Kirsty stood listening to the silence. Even the pianist had given up.

Finally, she turned to look at him, eyes brimming, and in two short steps she had thrown her arms around him, burying her face in his chest, sobbing like a baby. He drew her to him and held her close and ran a hand through her soft, long, silky hair, just as he had done when she was a child.

When, eventually, she found her voice she said, 'It never made any difference to me, Dad, thinking that Simon was my blood father. I always knew I was my daddy's girl.'

'And you always will be,' he said, and wondered if he would ever have the strength to let her go.

THE END

# ACKNOWLEDGEMENTS

My grateful thanks for their help in my researches for this book to: **Joël Capucci**, *École Nationale d'administration pénitentiaire*, for his expertise on the French prison system; **Dr Steve Campman**, Medical Examiner, San Diego, California, USA, for his advice on forensics and pathology; and **John** and **Karen Lamb** for allowing me to plagiarise their fabulous château in the Lot et Garonne, France. And a special word for the man without whom my career as a novelist might have well have been still-born – **Dr Richard Ward**, whose connections with the Chinese police enabled my writing of the *China Thrillers*, and whose subsequent contacts and encouragement gave me access to a worldwide network of criminologists. Sadly, Dr Ward passed away in February 2015. RIP.

Peter May
January 2017

COMING SOON

A new Hebrides-set
crime thriller from

# PETER
# MAY

Available 11 January 2018
in hardback, ebook and audio

petermay.co.uk
riverrunbooks.co.uk

# THRILLINGLY GOOD BOOKS
# FROM CRIMINALLY
# GOOD WRITERS

CRIME FILES BRINGS YOU THE LATEST RELEASES FROM TOP CRIME AND THRILLER AUTHORS.

SIGN UP ONLINE FOR OUR MONTHLY NEWSLETTER AND BE THE FIRST TO KNOW ABOUT OUR COMPETITIONS, NEW BOOKS AND MORE.